THE
JORDANS

THE
JORDANS

BY

GEORGE BOWER

ARBOR HOUSE
New York

FOR LAURIE, STEPHANIE AND MICHAEL BOWER,
WHO HAVE ALWAYS HUNG IN THERE WITH ME

AND FOR JAY ACTON, LARRY MOULTER
AND ARNOLD EHRLICH

BOOK
I

1

HE DROVE INTO THE HOT EARLY DECEMBER AFTER-
noon as the sun glided into the Pacific, moved the Chevy past
seventy, breathed and let it drag back under sixty. He was the
enemy now, and he didn't want to get arrested.

B.D. Jordan rubbed the back of his hand across his forehead.
Having your ego snapped is no fun, he thought. None at all. He
swallowed.

He had been in the west for almost fifteen years, and had used
his talent, gained fame and fallen in love and married here, and
only an hour ago he had been traded into the dark Boston winter,
close to the place, perhaps, where his real identity waited patiently.

When Jerry Diamond called him into his office from the gold
and white locker room just before the afternoon's scheduled light
workout, he thought he was going to be named player-coach.
For the past three weeks they'd all thought it was going to happen.
Steph, and Mike Corvino and Chuck Darwin, his close L.A.
teammates. But as soon as he'd seen Diamond, serious, unable
to look at him directly, he knew.

Boston and Los Angeles had finished badly last year, and were
losing again. Attendance was down in both places. The trade
would bring three young players and a draft choice to L.A., and
send B.D. Jordan to Boston. The senator-elect's older brother,
fifth this season in scoring, married to Stephanie Green, co-star
of "Dial California," ABC's top-ranked female detective series.
Boston loved its Irish pols and athletes, he knew, and if their
bikini-clad wives ignited twenty million sexual fantasies once a

week, so much the better. They'd line up in Boston to see him play, some with the hope that Stephanie might cross her legs behind the Boston bench once or twice a half—if he went along with the trade and played out the season in Boston. But he was too sick, too thoroughly pissed now to know what he was going to do.

He breathed. Economics. Boston and Los Angeles had to sell out almost every night to sustain thin margins of profit, and he and all the other aging stars were vulnerable because they were paid so well. If he hadn't been so attractive to Boston, or his playing ability had begun to slip even a bit, he might easily have been waived to Cleveland or Detroit, or deep into the south or southwest.

Stephanie would be home now, freed early from the last of six days of filming near Malibu, and would be on the deck or beach in a white bathing suit and sunglasses. He shifted and snapped the air conditioner on. Most players had trouble focusing on basketball in winter heat. But he liked it. Basketball, since he'd left Lawrence and Tufts in the winter of 1963, and especially since he'd turned pro in 1967, had brought sundeck lovemaking, beach runs, desert breezes whispering that life with the perfect twenty-foot jump shot would go on forever. Anything lied, he knew now, if you let it lie.

He was sure Stephanie wouldn't know. Boston had agreed to keep it quiet for three hours. Diamond would. He'd keep his mouth shut, otherwise he knew there'd be no deal. There might not be one anyway, B.D. had told Diamond, especially if he went home and found out that his wife knew and that there were calls waiting from his mother and brother.

2

SHE WAS DRYING HERSELF ON THE BEACH, HER SKIN black against the pale green and orange sea, the white towel a gentle wind comforting her shoulders and hair. She'd know right away that something was wrong.

They had barely accepted the separation and loneliness of his three eastern swings last year, her week-long publicity tours—the two weeks of on-location filming she faced in Hawaii in early January—he could quit basketball now. She'd want him to.

He moved back from the kitchen windows, took a drink of cold water and walked across the glass and wood living room to the deck. Traded into the frozen east after fifteen years. Christ. The sun and water and the distant beauty of his wife only drove the hurt deeper now and scarred his blood, perhaps forever. How could he leave her and play in Boston? And how could he give up basketball?

He sat on one of the white iron and plastic chairs and watched her walk toward the house, across the copper, wind-combed sand. Wet and dark and young and successful, though another year with vapid scripts would begin to weaken her talent. They knew that.

He stood and she tossed her hair and smiled, looking a bit surprised to see him home earlier than he was supposed to be, back from the workout before games with Seattle and Golden State. She kissed him, her breath and skin as cool and confident as the breeze that stirred their blood.

"You're early," she said.

"It didn't last long."

They went into the living room and sat on the small beige couch.

"How'd today go?" he asked.

"I don't know. It was exhausting." She moved her hair back with both hands. "So, just a quick practice?"

He nodded, touched her shoulder, then kissed it and looked at her as she leaned back and closed her eyes. Boston was in last place in the eastern division of the NBA, their glorious winning tradition in shambles. He'd give them shooting and play-making stability. Maybe with luck they could slip into the playoffs, win a few early games and build momentum.

He was forgetting his anger. Just the thought of playing well did that. He'd been traded, abused. His life had been shredded and tossed from an upper balcony.

"We'll be shooting late into the afternoon and early evening beginning next week," she said, her voice quiet, pleasant, floating in light fatigue. "It's definite for Hawaii in January. That means two weeks without you, darling. Unless you can break away from the team between home games and fly out."

He looked slightly away.

"I don't think on-location filming is going to keep us number one. We'll be in the top five for another year, at least, so what difference does it really make? Our basic audience will be the same even if we fall to fifteenth, which we won't, whether Tina leaves the show at the end of the year or not." She stared at him for a moment then touched his cheek. "It's going to be hard being away from you for that long. We haven't been separated for more than a few days in a long time."

"Not since last winter."

She started to say something, hesitated, brushed at his hair. "Something's bothering you. What is it?"

There'd been no rumors, no speculation in print or on television. He'd scored twenty-eight points on national television last Friday night.

"I've been traded," he said.

She stared at him and said nothing.

Traded. After eleven years. Boston had its needs. And L.A. needed a backup center, a faster power forward and third guard who could shoot. How could he go back to the place that it took so much agony and hurt to leave fifteen years ago, back to Boston, thirty miles south of Lawrence and the distant pull of the mills, the river, his mother's house on Tower Hill? Visiting for a day or two even now was tough enough.

"I'm not sure what you're saying, B.D.?"

He tried hard to mask the sense of dread that moved like a blue corpse through his blood.

"I was traded to Boston this morning. Diamond called me into his office a little over an hour ago and told me. Swift and sure and clean, as if I were an animal in a fucking stainless steel slaughterhouse. If I want to keep playing in the NBA, then I've got to go to Boston. There's very little I can do about it. In fact there's nothing I can do about it. I never wanted a no-trade clause. We've talked about that. I guess I was too arrogant to—"

"Jesus, B.D., they really traded you?"

"Yes."

"This morning, without even consulting you about anything?"

He nodded.

"And to Boston?" She was standing now, her anger showing in the tight smile across her almost perfect mouth.

"To Boston," he said. "I'm sure there's all kinds of irony in that."

"Jerry Diamond told you?"

"Jerry Diamond."

"I thought he liked us. I thought we were friends."

"I thought so, too, but I guess he likes other things more. I told him what a dirty bastard he was. The Reischlers must be putting a lot of pressure on him to turn things around, and he's used me to try to do it."

She walked into the kitchen, ran water into the gleaming red sink, turned the faucet off. He went in and leaned against the table.

"I just don't believe it. There hasn't been a hint, a rumor."

"Nothing," he said.

"You're the only one who's been doing anything for them."

He stared straight ahead and listened to his heart pumping. She was right. Besides being fifth in scoring, he was third in the league in assists. More reason for Boston's hunger for him, despite his age.

She came to the table, took his hand, kissed him gently on the cheek and sat next to him.

"I'm not naïve," she said. "We're certainly not innocent, but I honestly thought you'd be named player-coach by now. That's the kind of news I expected."

"I was wearing a smile when I walked into his office."

"Wait till the people find out," she said.

He leaned toward her.

13

They had met on the beach a year and a half ago, on a cool, hazed, Southern California day after two of warm rain. His brief affair with a divorced Beverly Hills mother of two had ended a month before, and the planned inactivity of the off-season was wearing on him. He did few commercials and had given up searching for a television script he felt comfortable with. She was wearing a dark blue nylon running jacket, and was moving easily toward him as he walked north from his beachfront home. Her legs and face were deeply tanned. She looked familiar and when they got closer he remembered seeing her at a party somewhere along the coast where they'd stared at each other from a short distance but hadn't spoken. He said "hi" when she passed on the beach, and she waved. He'd seen her a week after the party in a made-for-television movie. She had one of the three female private detective leads, and did much of her public investigating around beaches and swimming pools in a blue bikini. Her legs were lean and slightly muscular and her breasts struggled for freedom from a tight bikini bra. The movie had carried its title into the weekly series that had moved quickly to number one in the ratings. Legs and tits and cockteasing, and few stretches of dialogue longer than a ten-year-old could retain.

"I liked your movie," he'd said and didn't think his voice had reached her. But she'd stopped, turned and walked a few steps back.

"Which one?"

"'Dial California.' I don't think I've seen you in anything else. How many others were there?"

"One. Another television movie. I was on screen for five minutes, total."

He laughed. "Were you good?"

She nodded, stared at him for a moment. "B.D. Jordan."

"How many miles you doing?"

"Maybe three."

He watched her stare at him, slip her hands into her pockets, hunch her shoulders slightly. Hardly anyone in America knew her then, though millions had watched her movie. But they'd know her soon enough.

She was a few inches shorter than he was and he felt her breath cruise past his cheekbone.

"Are you married?" he said.

She shook her head slightly. "No."

"Involved with anyone?"

"For Christ's sake, Jordan."

"I know," he said. "A bad question."

He thought she might leave then, simply turn and jog away. But she didn't.

He asked if she lived on the beach.

"I'm staying with a few people from the company till I can find something right. You?"

He told her. "It's got a nice view of the ocean," he said. "Want to come up for some coffee and toast?"

When they made love two nights later, when he pressed himself against her flesh, he knew he was going to fall in love for the second time.

Stephanie Green.

She'd grown up in a small brick house in Mayor Daley's Chicago neighborhood and gone to a Catholic high school where she'd been a cheerleader and studied three hours a night six nights a week and had begun to accept the lips and legs and cheekbones that would permit her to have anyone she wanted whenever she wanted him, at Northwestern and in California. Her father, a high school history teacher and assistant football coach, had delivered two or three precinct blocks for whomever the Daley machine wanted every year. Her mother had stayed home until she and her brother, a senior now in law school, had left; he worked now in one of the swollen departments in city hall. They were delighted by her television success and marriage to B.D. Jordan, an athlete from a political family with an Irish last name.

She had moved in with B.D. two weeks after they'd met. They'd have children, when his vision beyond the NBA became clear, when her acting career broke from its current formula.

Sometimes, especially in the last six months, on long, sun-drifting afternoons when there was nothing to do but calculate the time it would take through August and September to bring himself back to perfect, early-season shape, he did ache to have children. He was thirty-five, and it was time to recreate himself.

"It really throws everything into a mess, doesn't it?" she said. The afternoon had begun to cool now.

"It does."

"And it makes no sense, really. You are L.A. You've meant so much to them."

"I agree. It all comes down to money. L.A. has to win to sell out, and they have to sell out almost every home game to survive. They can't win with me and Chuck Darwin alone. And too many blacks have been showing at Boston's home games. They need white, suburban season ticket holders, with money to spend at all the nearby white restaurants before and after the games, especially in the new Faneuil Hall area. White suburbia simply won't come to the games if there are too many blacks around. I'm white and I'm good and Tom Jordan's my brother. Two of the three guys going to L.A. are black."

She stared at him. "Have you talked to Mike about it? Or Maury Golden?"

"Maury knows. But I haven't talked to him yet. I didn't want to talk to anyone until I told you."

She touched him, then got up and put on water for coffee.

"It must hurt," she said.

"It hurts."

She leaned back against the counter near the sink, sunlight framing her shoulders.

"What are you going to do about it?"

"I'm not sure. I'm as good as I've ever been. Better."

"Fight it," she said.

He said nothing.

"Don't go along with it. Refuse to go to Boston just to make some bastards richer."

"Legally, I can't."

"Just refuse anyway."

He walked halfway toward her, stuffed his hands into his dungaree pockets. Six-foot two. The smallest white guard in the league. The second shortest guard in the west. He'd never been quite as fast as the others, not as quick or strong, and maybe he was a slight liability on defense when a bigger guard took him inside. But he had the kind of peripheral vision Cousy and Bradley had and could hit the open man from anywhere on the court without looking at him, and he could hang forever in the air on a jump shot. And hit. Seventy percent from the floor. Ninety-three from the foul line. L.A. was getting youth and speed. But fucked-up youth and speed. Boston always traded for attitude, and never traded down. And they never released talent, white or black, unless there was a serious attitude problem. Good luck.

"Fighting it would be futile, if I still want to play."

"Diamond is a rotten bastard." She snapped the stove off. "I hope you made that clear to him."

"Among other things I told him I wasn't sure what I was going to do. I'm sure he expected that."

The truth was that basketball was almost over for him. Next year would certainly be his last and he didn't know what he was going to do then, though television, in many forms, beckoned.

In 1963 he'd used his talent and reputation from one season of basketball as a post-grad at Phillips Andover, and transferred from Tufts to Cal, where he'd started as a sophomore, became an all-American, a first-round draft choice, and a success at L.A. far beyond his teenage dreams. The irony was he'd gone to Andover after Lawrence High to better his chances of getting into Harvard or Princeton or Yale, and had played basketball only because everyone had to play a sport. He'd always been good anyway, though he hadn't played at Lawrence High, and then perversely had gone to Tufts because Andover with its smugness, its cold, Ivy facade, had turned him off to anything resembling it. And when his father died just before Christmas of his first semester

17

at Tufts, he'd used the basketball scholarship offer to get out of Lawrence, out of the northeast before it and his mother could trap him into becoming the loyal son staying home.

She breathed, and smiled for the first time. "Things have been going so well—the show, your getting off to a great start, Tom's success. I guess we've both always known how fast it can change."

Her smile faded.

"Christ, B.D."

"I know," he said.

3

THEY SAT ON THE DECK IN THE EVENING DARK now, drinking gin and tonic from thick-bottomed glasses. News of the trade had been released and been the lead story on television at six. Soon he'd answer calls from writers who had his unlisted number. He'd always had excellent press.

After swimming alone, he'd taken a long walk down the beach, and then a hot shower. They had made plans to meet Mike Corvino and his wife at Morgan's at eight, and had agreed when he'd called at six-thirty that they shouldn't change them.

"You'd like to prove something in the east," Stephanie said. "A lot of things." Her voice was light. She was wearing a beige dress and heels and her hair shone black in the dark.

"Maybe."

"You would."

"I left home when I was nineteen, after my father's death, with my mother and Tom devastated. I guess I've wondered every once in a while if I had simply run from responsibility then. That's what a lot of people thought I did."

"Not Tom."

"He did, at first. I think he still does, somewhat. He made it out, got out on his own, without *running* out." He felt himself shrug. "The thought of going back to Boston, living so close to Lawrence—"

Now he had money enough and fame to do, or try to do, what he wanted. Except that quitting now, after he'd been traded, would diminish his value. Images can change fast in sports. How many people would remember his fifteen years of excellence in California if he went to Boston and did badly? How would he be remembered if he quit now? He wasn't sure—he wanted to play, and hoped he'd never do badly.

He listened to the ocean, to the breeze moving across the deck and into the house.

"If I decide not to play anymore, I don't want to just hang around for the winter waiting for something to happen. I've really got nothing substantial lined up. All of our talk's been about two years from now. That's probably the biggest reason why they didn't kick Graham out and hire me. They want a long-term coaching commitment." He thought it sounded hollow. Quinn Harrington, the Boston coach who'd brought home two world championships in five years and played on five world championship teams when he was a Boston forward, was about to be fired. B.D.'s life, which had seemed so stable a few hours ago, was a mess. He had talked to Maury Golden, his agent, briefly after swimming. They'd talk again soon.

4

THE CORVINOS WERE ALREADY AT THE FAMILIAR corner table at Morgan's when they arrived. Danny Morgan, the owner, said how sorry and shocked he and everyone else was, and B.D. assured him that even if he went along with the trade he'd never leave the coast. "We'll always come here," he said.

Corvino, thirty-four, looked exhausted. He'd been playing badly when he played at all. He was losing weight and the trade certainly meant that L.A. would release him in a day or two. Maybe they already had and hadn't told him.

He hugged Stephanie and B.D. took Karen Corvino's hand. Her eyes were filled.

"How're you doing?" Corvino said. On the phone he'd said that everyone at practice, including Graham, had been blown away.

"Still surprised," B.D. said. "And still trying not to get too pissed off."

"Did Darwin call?"

"No."

"He will. He was really ripshit."

"I'm devastated," Karen said. She leaned slightly forward, her blonde hair moving across her cheeks. She'd been a basketball cheerleader at Ohio State, Corvino's school, though he'd never earned a degree from there or anywhere else.

"We all are," Stephanie said. "But these things happen all the time to everyone who plays."

B.D. looked at her for a moment.

"What are you going to do?" Corvino said.

"I'm not sure." No one had died, he thought, and then almost said it, and was glad right away that he hadn't.

"I just don't understand it," Corvino said intensely. "What the fuck does it do for us? Coleman can't shoot to save his ass. And Drucker at forward is too slow and selfish for any part of our offense. The last thing Darwin needs is a backup. He never comes out of a game, for Christ's sake. And you've been our offense, almost all of it."

"Thanks, Mike," he said.

Corvino leaned back and stared at him.

"Go ahead," B.D. said.

"I don't want to sound selfish, B.D., or self-centered, certainly not at a time like this, but—"

"I know," said B.D. "I wish I could tell you right now what I'm going to do."

20

Corvino drank some water and nodded. "They'll drop two of us, and I'm one of the two."

Karen began to cry then and Stephanie told her, pleasantly, that it wasn't the end of anything, their lives were only changing direction, they'd always be friends and always be together. Karen nodded then, and touched Stephanie on the wrist. Over a decade of living in professional sport, with its trades and half-ass writers and self-serving owners and general managers and rude spectators who knew nothing of the poetry and intensity of the game and cared only about winning, had made her brittle, older looking than thirty. And then, by the time they were ready to order, she'd flicked her knuckles across her cheekbones and scattered any traces of bitterness.

Corvino had come to Los Angeles from Chicago two and a half seasons ago and been an immediate power on the offensive boards, a tough seventh and eighth man last year, but an almost-forgotten spot player this season. He and B.D. had gotten along well right away, maybe because Corvino released so well to him after rebounding to begin a fast break. How quickly the seasons with the Corvinos had passed; fame and athletic excellence, quick passengers bound for emptiness, bitterness, regret, middle age, stops on the way to obscurity.

They drove back to the Corvinos' house at ten and sat in the muted light of their vast patio, the baby-sitter released, the Corvinos' three young children asleep, secure, enough money working in banks and corporations and real estate offices to keep them affluent and one breath ahead of screaming nights forever. Maybe.

He and Corvino drank tall glasses of beer, and when Steph and Karen left the patio for a moment, Corvino leaned toward him.

"I'm going to go in and ask for my release tomorrow, before they do it for me. I'm not sure what's next. But I'm only thirty-four. We're young for the world, and the kids won't have to give up any strong attachments. We'll go back to Pittsburgh for a while, through the holidays. There are two local television offers there.

21

One looks like it might work out. Sports reporting, during the week, an anchor spot on weekends. I don't want it to look like I'm taking the job because I can't play anymore."

B.D. thought he should say something then, but he couldn't.

"California threw a lot of money at us and we took it," Corvino said. "It's going to hurt to leave, but it's time to leave and admit it's done."

No one had been playing for free, and they all knew how vulnerable they were. No one in sport was innocent or naïve anymore, at least not for very long. Everyone had a lawyer-agent, and they all knew their market value. Diamond and the owners would love Corvino for quitting, for saving them further embarrassment in the press. They would praise him beyond his worth, leaving the implication that he could have stayed if he'd wanted to, helping him enormously in Pittsburgh. It was the nature of the game.

5

THEY MADE QUICK, ALMOST DESPERATE LOVE AT two o'clock and moved apart without speaking. He accepted her breath. The silence let in the sound of the ocean. He hadn't been aware of it at night for months.

"Come to Boston with me," he said.

She stirred, touched him and waited for several moments. "I'm going to miss the Corvinos. Karen cried so damn hard when we left. I'm sure we'll never see them again."

"We won't," he said and got up, went into the bathroom and splashed cold water onto his face. He avoided the mirror and walked back through the shadow cast by the security lights guarding their driveway and doors. He got back into bed and held her.

"Really," he said, "come to Boston with me."

She breathed more deeply.

"Leave the show. I'll just play out the year and—"

"I'm not going to have the baby now," she said.

He nodded. "I know—"

She turned and kissed him, the gray outlines of her beauty stunning this moment that talent and making money had brought them.

"You really don't want me to hang around an apartment in Boston while you're on the road for two or three days or even longer with the team, after having just violated a contract." She sat up. "I'm sorry, I know you didn't want me to answer, I didn't have to answer."

He said nothing.

"Oh, Christ, Jordan, I love you. I don't want to spend even one more night without you."

"I'm going to talk to Maury tomorrow morning and explore all my options, and then decide what to do." They both knew he was lying. He'd already decided what he was going to do.

"It's still hard to believe," she said.

"It always will be," he said.

She let another moment slip away, then held him.

"I don't want you to go," she said. "I really don't, B.D. I know how much you love the game, but you can change things now. Tell them to go to hell, that they can't manipulate you. Begin something else."

He breathed against her and said nothing.

"I love you," she said. "I know I'll be going on location in January, but it will be so much better, easier, if you're here. I'm just so vulnerable now."

He was going to make this year his last as a player, then coach for a year if Los Angeles named him player-coach, and then he would do something else.

She was going to quit "Dial California" in the spring, become pregnant sometime in the late winter, and use the time of her pregnancy to find the right film script that would challenge her talent and allow her to grow. They'd never fixed a precise late winter or early spring date when all of it would happen, but it

23

was understood, he knew, that it would happen.

"Everything will be all right," he said, "no matter what I have to do now."

"It will," she said softly, and he felt her breath on his neck and shoulder until he fell asleep.

6

DIAMOND CALLED HIM AT ELEVEN, JUST AFTER HE'D finished talking to Maury Golden, who had assured him that whatever B.D. decided to do would bring him, eventually, several hundred thousand in new income. Boston was willing to go beyond his L.A. contract to put white star quality back in the Garden. They'd fly Steph to him whenever she was free, if that's what they both wanted. He could stay at the Ritz Carlton on the edge of the Public Gardens, winter-blue and beautiful in December. He could take his time looking for an apartment. A real estate agent would be awaiting his call. Boston had character. If he wanted to go there, if he wanted to keep playing, fine. But if he wanted to tell them all to go fuck themselves, Golden would set up several other options—in network sports announcing, television series appearances. His only advice was to go to Boston and do it soon. "It'll give you immediate national attention beyond the sports pages," he said, "and I'll put that attention to work."

He had taken early calls from reporters, Tony Fagan from the *Times*, John Slattery from the *Examiner*, others. They were angry at the trade, they said, but sounded high with a good story to tell.

"B.D.," Diamond said now, "you've really got to know how sorry I am about all of this. I know how hurt and angry you are. It wasn't my idea. I don't think I made that clear enough yesterday. I never would have traded you. Christ, we've known each other for a long time."

"I understand the brutality of sport," B.D. said evenly, his eyes glancing through the house. Steph had left at six to film on the streets of Watts.

"B.D.—"

"You called to find out what the hell I'm going to do." He knew Diamond had been blown away by the outcry, the negative press. He'd promised Maury Golden a definite decision by this afternoon. Diamond and the Reischlers would be happy then. "You thought you'd made a shrewd deal, Jerry, but you've made an asshole deal. Coleman's a fucking drug—"

"Who said that?"

"Everyone knows it."

"That's bullshit, I don't know it."

"You will, Jerry, if I go along with everything. It's why Boston dumped him on you. He's a fucking coke machine."

"That's only a dumb rumor."

"Balls it is. And Drucker's going to give you about two decent minutes a game before he starts fucking off. Among other things he's burnt out from the three women chasing his ass for money and god knows what else."

"We need Drucker," Diamond said.

"Good luck."

"B.D., I—"

"Just don't ever come near me again."

"The Reischlers insisted on making the move. I told you that yesterday, and it's true. Boston has always wanted you badly."

"Boston's afraid that Roxbury's moving into the Garden. Will you stop the bullshit."

"B.D., I—"

"Just don't ever try to speak to Stephanie. If I hear of your going near her, or the Reischlers even looking at her at a party or opening or anything else when I'm not there, I'll beat you and them into a fucking wheelchair. I will, honest to god I will."

He slammed the phone down and then took it off the hook. He ran a mile down the beach, walked back and swam for fifteen minutes, sat on the deck in the cool, wet-orange sun, then showered and walked back out onto the deck and stared at the horizon. He felt his blood fill with anger. How could they have done it to him, as if he were a piece of fucking meat? But they'd done it.

He breathed deeply and let several minutes pass. If he waited too long his anger would turn into hurt and he'd get up every morning and sulk his way to lunch. To hell with that—he didn't want to sit on the deck all winter and wait for the phone to ring and his wife to come home from work. His ego cried to get out and get even.

He called Golden.

"B.D.," Golden said. "What's the decision?"

"I'm playing. I've already hung around long enough. I'm going to Boston and lead them to the fucking playoffs."

"When?"

"I'll leave tomorrow and be able to play Thursday night in Boston."

Golden laughed. "I'm sure Sid Anderson will arrange a public signing. As I said, they're going to give you the moon."

"I'll take it."

7

"I KNEW YOU WERE GOING TO GO," STEPHANIE SAID. "It's in your blood and impossible to deny all of a sudden." She hesitated. "Everyone's angry about it."

He'd grilled steak and sliced tomatoes over lettuce for them. She'd showered after getting home, driving up in her red Porsche at six. They had drunk beer and talked of her day's filming in Watts, far from the ashes of the late sixties, but still with its smoldering edge on. He'd told her about his conversation with Diamond, Boston's urgency to sign him, and then that he'd decided to go.

"I've got to do it," he said. "I can't just hang around and let anger burn me out. Guys have done that. I've got to get even right away."

"I know you do," she said and swallowed some beer. "The winter will go fast enough—"

Her eyes filled, and he felt himself choking up.

"We'll have ten days at Christmas," she said.

He said nothing, then held her.

"Oh, shit, B.D., I hate this."

She would stay at the house, or with friends for a few nights if she felt uncomfortable alone. She might even convince her mother to come out for part of February.

He called his mother in Lawrence and explained that he'd be in Boston late tomorrow night, would call her on Thursday and see her sometime Friday. She was pleasant, almost too reassuring, and didn't, thank God, offer him his old bedroom while he searched for a place to stay. He also called Tom, catching him in Washington on his way to a meeting. They'd agreed that L.A. had made a bad mistake, but Tom didn't say B.D. had made the right decision. He'd call again when B.D. arrived in Boston. He sounded cool, even distant.

It hurt too much to make love and he and Stephanie held each other in bed at eleven and stared into the dark.

"We'll bury ourselves in the details of what we do," she said, "and it'll all go quickly."

"It will," he said.

"It's going to be tough," she said, "all of it."

8

HE LANDED IN BOSTON AT ELEVEN. GOLDEN WOULD meet him at the hotel tomorrow at ten and be with him at the noon press conference at the Garden. The American Airlines lounge—a few Christmas decorations on its counters, a two-foot silver tree on a table in a corner—was almost empty. The flight had been fast, smooth, whispering him back across America. He'd been recognized and spoken to ("How are you, B.D. Jordan?" a dark, slightly heavy stewardess had said an hour into the flight, staying a bit too long after he'd said he was doing fine), but no one had bothered him and he was grateful. He found his name in two separate stories in *Sports Illustrated*, and Tom's picture in *Time* and *Newsweek* within stories about the senate's new young liberals.

There had been two decent stories about the trade in the L.A. *Times* and a column by Tony Fagan denouncing it, calling for Diamond's resignation and saying that Jordan was the only reason for anyone going to an L.A. game since the season began. Maybe Fagan was simply being nice to him because B.D.'d always been open and honest with the press and willing to talk more than he had to. It didn't matter. He was gone. A moment later he had fallen into the tight surface sleep he'd always found on long flights east.

He snagged his two suitcases and walked outside. He was surprised, then disappointed, that Boston television wasn't there, though he'd told no one of his arrival time.

The December night drove his loneliness in deep. It wasn't brutally cold yet. Blue, shattering cold would come in January and February, and it was still a long way till April.

His anger was complete now. He despised Diamond and the Reischlers for forcing him to spend his last season here in the winter that he'd tried to avoid since he was nineteen. He'd get even. L.A. was due at the Garden in January. He'd be patient.

He reached for a cab door just as Brian Gallagher of the *Globe* called out his name. He had talked to Gallagher, a good reporter and intelligent columnist who'd played at Providence College ten years ago and had then hung on for two seasons at guard with the Knicks, at the beginning of the season about becoming the L.A. coach if things came apart as quickly as everyone was predicting. Gallagher had told him then of the rumor slipping through the discontented Garden about the all-out move Boston was planning for him. They had both laughed at its absurdity. L.A. would never let him go. Boston needed youth.

Gallagher was wearing a navy blue ski jacket and looked young and in shape. They shook hands. They'd guarded each other for five minutes in a game in L.A. in 1970.

"I can't believe you're here," Gallagher said.

"I think I can."

"Jesus Christ."

B.D. nodded.

"It's not southern California, is it. But it's not fucking Greenland yet, either."

"It's never been Greenland," B.D. said.

"I thought Anderson was calling us all in yesterday to tell us he'd fired Quinn Harrington."

"When's he going to?"

"Soon."

"You think I'm part of that?"

"Yes. Are you?"

"No, not at all. I haven't even talked to Anderson. Maury Golden's handled everything. He didn't tell you my flight time by any chance, did he?"

"I just guessed you'd be in about now. An ex-ballplayer's instinct."

They stepped back from the curb. A few people, in spite of the cold and late hour, slowed, said hello, wished him well. A cab driver called out their names and waved. Another stewardess stared for a moment, then slipped into the back of a slick yellow cab and was gone. At eleven o'clock everything had been promised and paid for.

"Television was here about an hour ago," Gallagher said. "Two of the stations."

"You've been here that long?"

"Just about—where're you staying?"

B.D. told him.

"Let me give you a ride in."

He nodded. "Anything else I say is off the record for now."

"Sure."

"I hate to say it but it has to be that way."

"Why'd they do it?" Gallagher said as they pulled out of the lot and drove into the violent green of the Boston skyline. They'd slip through the Callahan Tunnel, cut through the north end, glide beside the Boston Garden under the ancient MBTA tracks and head along the Charles River on Storrow Drive past Massachusetts General Hospital before cutting off into Back Bay and reaching the hotel.

L. A. was playing tonight without him. All-American, all-pro. Traded, and driving into Boston on a December night, three thousand miles from his wife and home. He could have rolled down his window and yelled into the yellow rush of wind in the middle of the tunnel. Maybe that would have made some fucking sense—

Already he missed Stephanie; and it was insane to be away from her now. He was too old to sleep alone, and it was insane to give up even one night of holding one of the most beautiful women in the world for basketball, for Boston.

He should quit. He hadn't signed the new contract yet. He could still get out of it, let Gallagher drop him at the hotel, then grab a cab back to the airport and fly home.

"L. A. needs a power forward, that's why they did it."

Gallagher nodded.

"Boston needs a guard who can move the ball and shoot. They met almost all of Golden's demands fast enough. I think they were surprised that we didn't give them much of a hard time."

"You didn't?"

"Not at all. I really didn't have to."

"They make you rich?"

"I'm already rich," he said. "And I'm white, I grew up in Lawrence, my brother's the new senator-elect and Boston's drawing badly. They can't wait till next year. They need a white guy to chase all of the blacks away. Whites buy season tickets in Boston. Blacks don't. They figure I'll start building attendance momentum and add a little glamor. They've got a first and second round draft choice for next year from a previous trade with New York, plus their own."

"One of which they gave up for you."

He nodded.

"Holloway's still here," Gallagher said after a moment. "But his ability left two years ago."

"He's no longer a draw, is he."

"You can say that again."

B.D. nodded again and tried hard to contain his loneliness.

"He's unhappy, really unhappy at your coming."

"I don't blame him."

"They wanted to unload Coleman and Drucker, especially Coleman," Gallagher said, "and weren't happy with the kid, Tolman, who's brittle and hasn't played at all, even though he's over seven feet."

"Coleman and Drucker are fast."

"But they've got rotten attitudes, and the whisper of drugs around them. Shit, almost certainly drugs."

"So I've heard."

"And they're not at all nice looking. Boston blacks have to be nice looking, practice hard and kiss the white coach's ass."

"Coleman and Drucker never did that, and never will."

"Attendance will climb for a month, at least," Gallagher said, "but if you don't win for them it'll trail away."

"We'll win, and make the playoffs."

"A prediction?"

"Sure."

"I doubt it," Gallagher said. "No reflection on you, but the team's simply not good enough. They're bringing Clint Remmington off the injured reserve list and activating a rookie from Texas, Danny Price. Neither has any speed. And Harrington just doesn't give a shit anymore. It's too bad."

"Maybe I'll be able to save his job for him."

They approached the entrance to the tunnel, a taxi and a station wagon in front of them.

"Can I get a little personal?" Gallagher said.

31

"Why not?"

"How's Stephanie Green reacting to all of this?"

"She wanted me to quit. But she's an actress, and understands things. Part of her TV series is being filmed in Hawaii in January so we'd be away from each other a lot anyway." He breathed the unfamiliar defroster heat. He knew he was giving too much away. "You know about all of that. The loneliness that goes along with athletic and acting success. It's a true son of a bitch."

"So I gather," Gallagher said.

B.D. looked at him. "When are you selling out to one of the magazines?"

"Never."

"Offers?"

"From *Sports Illustrated*, and *Newsweek*. The serious one from *Newsweek*. And ABC."

"Where with ABC?"

"New York, and everywhere, I guess. We never really got down to that."

"Why not take it?"

"I like it here. I do this and baseball and some road running. And the Wednesday and Saturday columns that you've been in. I've got time and space to write, and a big New England audience. I suppose it would be good to be read in New York and Chicago and San Francisco. But I've got Jennifer and a daughter, and the house on the south shore. Both still aren't sure they like what I do, but they'd hate it if I did it in New York. They wouldn't want to leave the Boston area. And I certainly don't want to go chasing around the world after a bunch of fucking elephant hunters."

They moved from the tunnel and flicked across the edge of the north end, drove past the Garden where the Bruins, Gallagher said, had tied Toronto in the last thirty seconds tonight. They weren't drawing either, and had no white god just in from the coast to bail them out. Hockey players didn't have television stars for wives. Would Stephanie Green have married him if he'd been a high-scoring winger for the Los Angeles Kings?

They drove down Storrow Drive. In a few days he'd rent an

apartment with a view west into the blood-red winter sunsets to remind him that this wasn't going to be forever. Tom had told him that Beacon Hill, thick with fags and dogshit, in spite of its few expensive charming streets, would depress him. Parts of Back Bay, close to the Common and the Public Gardens, were good. The waterfront was noisy and rat infested. He'd need a parking space, and privacy. Boston was paying for whatever he wanted.

"How many years were you with them?" Gallagher said.

"Twelve."

"Some people still think of you as an easterner."

"Because of where I grew up."

"And because of your brother. That was a hell of a primary campaign, wasn't it?"

B.D. nodded.

"What does he think of your being here?"

"We've only talked briefly about it."

Gallagher looked at him, then back at the road, smiled, and said nothing.

"I'll be gone in April, or whenever the season ends. Back to Malibu."

"For good?"

"Yes."

"I can speculate on that in a column."

"I hope you do."

"What will you do then? Act? Coach? Run for office?"

"No, not that. My father was a state senator. Now Tom's the senator. I won't get involved in politics beyond raising money and campaigning for him if I have to, if he wants me to. I think I'd make a lousy actor."

9

B.D. UNPACKED IN THE MEDIUM-SIZED ROOM. EVERY-one in the lobby had been polite, correct, efficient. There were no autograph hounds, no celebrity watchers at the Ritz. Or at least they weren't obvious about it. He'd promised Gallagher an on-the-record interview in a week or two. He was glad Boston had kept its promise not to meet him. No favors. No inside edges. Nothing to be grateful for.

He called Tom at his apartment in Washington. Except for yesterday, they hadn't talked since Tom's victory party at Sullivan's restaurant in downtown Lawrence at the end of November.

A young woman answered. He didn't recognize her voice.

"B.D.?" Tom said a moment later. He sounded slightly distracted. "Where are you?"

"The Ritz. Sitting on top of the fucking world."

"You've arrived in Boston then."

"Yes."

"Things happen fast, don't they?" Tom said. He said it evenly and it sounded right.

"They do," B.D. said and sat on the edge of the bed. It was too quiet here.

"When's the signing?"

"Tomorrow morning."

For a minute he thought Anderson might have asked Tom to come to it, which would have been a big mistake. But Anderson obviously knew better. Tom never wanted to be overshadowed.

"How do you feel now?"

"Tired."

"And still angry."

"Yes."

"Good," Tom said.

He'd been through a brutal campaign for the democratic nomination for the senate in September, had lost on primary night by twelve thousand votes, and then gotten the nomination two days later when the winner, Dante Marino, the state's fifty-year-old attorney general, was killed, his car slamming into a tree in the rain in the late afternoon on Route 2 near Concord. Nothing in sports or politics, or the world of real and imagined power was certain. Except that Tom was a senator, or would be when he was sworn in in a few weeks. And B.D.'d been traded. Not too

34

many people, of course, would feel sorry for B.D. And he certainly didn't feel sorry for himself, or even angry at himself.

"Any new insights into why they did it to you?" Tom asked.

"Still the obvious reasons, and the fact that I'm your brother and—"

"I'm your brother, for Christ's sake. And you're a great player and will be for another two years, at least. It's as simple as that." There was an edge to Tom's voice, something that hadn't been there since they were kids. Death had given him the nomination in September, and even though he'd won easily in November, it would take at least one more big win to put his ego back on track.

He heard Tom say something away from the phone.

"Have you called Ma?" Tom asked a moment later.

"I did yesterday. She takes everything very well these days. She's been conditioned, I guess, for the unexpected. I'll try to see her tomorrow afternoon after the press conference, but probably won't be able to go there until Friday."

"I'm a little worried about her."

"Oh, why?"

"She's lost some weight. She said she had the flu and lost her appetite, but I'm not sure. She used to think of ways to make us feel sorry for her. Now, she's almost too stoic. Maybe that's just another way of her playing the martyr."

B.D. almost agreed. He stared out across the Public Gardens, its trees blackened against the inky Boston sky, and ached for the warm sound of the Pacific, the feel of his wife in his arms. He swallowed. He'd left and he was here. It was as simple as that.

"I talked to her doctor. He said it was nothing. That was a week ago. I haven't been able to see her as much as I should. Kate doesn't seem too worried."

"I'll check it out." B.D. waited for a moment. "How are the boys?"

"Great. Looking forward to coming down here for the swearing in. They want to see where I'm living. It's Georgetown, but it's not that impressive. How's Steph?"

He told him. He almost asked about Kate, Tom's former wife.

If he ever got back with her he would have a better shot at becoming President, if that's what he eventually wanted. Kate was understanding, and had the kind of looks that attracted women's votes for her husband, but that men wanted to hold and kiss. But she'd never let anyone use her again, and they all knew that.

"Are you going to be around Boston this weekend?" B.D. asked.

Tom hesitated for a moment. "In the central part of the state on Sunday. I have a few obligations there."

B.D. waited for him to say something else. He obviously didn't expect Tom to fly to Boston to take him out to dinner. It had been his decision to come east, but B.D. did think they should make definite plans to get together soon.

"Try hard not to become bitter about everything," Tom said.

"I'll simply get even."

"That's the only thing to do, B.D. I'll be in touch soon. Good luck."

"You too," he said.

He needed sleep. There was a game tomorrow night at the Garden, one on Saturday night in Philadelphia, then back at the Garden on Sunday afternoon. Boston was in last place in the eastern division. Nothing had gone right. Quinn Harrington was angry, Gallagher had told him. He hadn't been consulted about the trade and had stopped talking to Anderson and the new owners whose fast-food chain money was supposed to stabilize the team forever. And the coach was thoroughly pissed at local radio talk show hosts for letting momentum build to get rid of him. He might split any day, taking what was left of his ego back to the suburbs of Worcester. B.D. would try to see Harrington alone tomorrow, assure him that he wasn't looking for his job. B.D.'d always been loyal, attentive, positive in practice and games, no matter who the coach, and would never become part of any cruelty toward Harrington. But it would probably be better to stay away. Assuring Harrington of his pure intentions would be an arrogant act, and arrogance kills. His father had told him that often enough.

36

10

MAURY GOLDEN MET B.D. IN THE LOBBY OF THE Ritz at nine. It had turned warm and the sun cast lean black shadows through the bare oaks and the iron fence lining the Public Gardens. They walked to one of the small restaurants on Boylston Street in Copley Square, a time and temperature sign above the sidewalk blinking fifty degrees. Golden was wearing a light gray suit and a red and blue striped tie; he was five ten, lean and dark-haired. He'd graduated cum laude in English lit from Harvard and had been in the top five percent of his class at Columbia Law School. His clients included some of the highest-priced athletes and television personalities in America, but no one now with L.A., and only Daryl Jackson, a forward, with Boston.

A few people nodded to him in the restaurant. Boston was always distant in the morning. At least here. It probably wasn't the same in the neighborhoods, but he doubted if he'd go to South Boston or Roxbury or any part of Dorchester to find out.

"The contract's about ninety-five per cent ready," Golden said as they sat at a corner table. "We'll keep Anderson waiting for fifteen or twenty minutes and then press hard for the final few things. I don't want them to tie you into anything tightly for next year, and I want to make it simple enough for you to get out if you get homesick in a week or two."

This morning, when B.D. had accepted his wakeup call at eight, he'd felt more lonely than he had since the first, long, cruel nights away from Lawrence at Cal.

"It'll take a year or two more to get you guys close to a million,"

37

Golden said, "but it's coming. And six hundred isn't bad at all."

"Not at all."

"You'll fill the Garden. I understand their phones rang off the fucking hook yesterday. I could push once more for an attendance clause if you want."

B.D. shook his head.

"Okay." He leaned back and accepted the toast and coffee and grapefruit from the waitress. "The playing time clause is vital at your age, for commercial value, and for your own sake in dealing with any possibilities for next year. We shouldn't go for anything less than two-thirds of the game, and probably three-quarters unless you're injured. Then, of course, they'd be happy to let you get out of your contract."

"I don't need a playing time clause."

"You do, Jordan, and you know fucking well that you do. Image is vital when you go back to the coast in April. And you also can't put yourself at the mercy of some jealous fucking coach like Harrington who doesn't give a shit if he wins or loses as long as he's tucking it to the great B.D. Jordan, husband of the beautiful Stephanie Green."

Golden was right. B.D. swallowed some of his coffee, chewed some toast and looked at him. They'd been together for five years. The lawyer had tripled B.D.'s salary, doubled his investment income, negotiated the lucrative razor blade and sport clothes commercials for him. Golden had been married twice during that time and had just separated from his second wife.

"We're doing the shaving cream commercial you agreed to do in Manhattan on Monday morning." Good agents anticipated everything.

"Monday?"

"It's outdoors, in Central Park. Why in the winter, I'm not sure. But wait till you see the piece of ass model they've paired you with. Unbelievable, except she's as dumb as this formica top." He stared at B.D. "Miss your wife?"

"Completely."

Golden nodded. "They've put away two tickets just for

38

Stephanie, besides the ones you automatically get, just behind Anderson's row at midcourt, unless you want her near the bench."

"I don't think she'll show up for many games, if any. She doesn't want to be put on display. That's all it would be at this point."

"She likes basketball, and she went to a lot of games in L.A."

"That was different. Friends, people we know, were there. But she didn't go very often last year. And she's pissed off." He watched Golden sip his black coffee. "Do you understand why I went along with the trade, why I'm here?"

"Sure."

B.D. smiled at him.

"Of course I understand, for Christ's sake. Everyone knows the B.D. Jordan story."

"Which is what?"

Golden ripped a piece of toast in half, flipped both pieces back on the plate. "What would you have done if you'd been traded to San Antonio?"

"I wouldn't have been, so I won't answer."

"How about Cleveland?"

He stared at Golden.

"Or any other place except Boston?"

"You're not going to try to sell any athlete going home searching for his past bullshit."

"The *Times* has floated some interest, for the Sunday magazine, and the *Globe* and *Sports Illustrated*," Golden said.

"I talked to Brian Gallagher yesterday. He said nothing about it."

"Gallagher wouldn't be doing the story."

"Who would?"

"A writer for their magazine."

"Then completely forget about it," B.D. said.

"I'm sure they'd go along with Gallagher if you insisted. It'd make a hell of a story."

"It would make a mess."

"Nothing would hurt your mother, or Tom," Golden pleaded.

"Any going home shit would be inaccurate. I'm here to play because I can play, and because, at thirty-five, I don't want to hang around the fucking beach, waiting."

"You wouldn't have to wait very long."

B.D. laughed quickly.

"Okay," Golden said. "You've helped make me a very rich man."

B.D. looked slightly away.

"The owners hate my ass. The more, of course, the better." Golden gave a bitter laugh.

"They want us to be grateful to them for having talent. You've helped a lot of us."

"They give a shit only about money, nothing else. They're like porno kings. They buy and sell flesh. If you had let me push L.A. on a no-trade clause—" Golden put his hands up. "It probably would have made you look insecure, and you would have had to give up other things." He leaned forward. "I've got you protected here. You're in charge. Healthy or crippled, alive or lying fucking dead on Beacon Street. They're bleeding through their noses to get you. It would be nice if Stephanie showed for a game or two, maybe around Christmas. Then sometime in late January or early February to keep the interest alive. The publicity wouldn't hurt her ratings. She could be with the senator and his kids."

"It would certainly make a great picture. If the public knew half the manipulation— I bet they really think she actually says all that crap they put quotes around in the people columns."

"I'll bet they do," Golden said.

11

COPLEY SQUARE WAS QUIETER NOW. B.D. KNEW Golden would have had a limousine waiting if he'd wanted, or a cab double-parked and humming. They walked for a block without talking. What deals, B.D. thought, was Golden plotting miles from here? The agent would be back in Manhattan by early afternoon, was flying to the coast at six. They stopped at an intersection, the sun a graceful moment on the wide sidewalks and the glass and stone of the low buildings.

"Will Boston love me if I don't hit double figures tonight?" B.D. asked.

"It'll love you for coming back and reinforcing its belief that Boston is the best place in America. Every city is hometown America, but especially here. It's something I learned at Harvard."

12

THE PRESS CONFERENCE WAS HOT, LOUD, CROWDED. Young television camera and sound crews and male and female photographers, wearing sweaters and faded dungarees and looking ghastly white, forced the older press to the sides and to the back of the room. Gallagher nodded from a corner.

B.D. sat between Sid Anderson and an assistant general manager. Harrington wasn't there. Golden leaned against the wall behind them, out of camera range. A few minutes earlier in Anderson's office, packed with the trophies and plaques and photos and ancient basketballs and bronzed figures jump-shooting and dribbling and all the daunting symbols of Anderson's thirty years in pro basketball, Golden had threatened that he and Jordan would walk and fly west if Anderson didn't agree to a clause that said Jordan could shed his contract whenever he wanted if he were injured and another clause guaranteeing him at least thirty minutes of playing time per game for the rest of the season. The contract was good for two years. Aging players had to protect themselves and their families, Golden said, and Anderson called him a prick, which was exactly what Golden wanted to hear.

"How does it feel to be back where you belong?" a television sportscaster said after they'd signed again for the cameras and Anderson had introduced B.D.

"I've been cold," he said evenly, and then wished he hadn't said it.

They laughed and waited for him to say more and when he didn't, and didn't laugh along with them, the smiles faded and for just a second quiet slipped into the room. He was thirty-five. He'd played basketball for fifteen years. And this news conference, which Boston had insisted on, was a mistake. He was embarrassed by it now. The senator's older brother. A talk show's sports reporter had called him that last night. It was part of what he was, and what he'd accepted by coming here—where was Stephanie now? It was eight o'clock in California and the Pacific would wait all day for the sun. She was on location, being made up, or sitting outside sipping black coffee, waiting to be called into a scene, thinking of him—thinking of the best way to control her own loneliness, that dark invader.

"Did the trade surprise you?" Chris Swann, of the *Herald*, a good, objective writer asked.

He looked at Anderson, who was staring into the center of the room, his lit cigar a few inches from his lips. Anderson hated losing, and half-empty Boston Garden echoes were obviously haunting his early winter nights.

"I was surprised," B.D. said, looking away and then back to Anderson, trying very hard not to sound angry or careless.

"Did it hurt, being dealt out of L.A. after twelve years?"

"No," he said quickly. "You learn right away not to take anything personal in professional sport."

"Is Stephanie Green still in California?" someone else asked.

He stared the question away.

Another television voice. "Have you talked to your brother since the trade?"

"Come on, fellas, just basketball," Anderson said.

"I've talked to him a few times," B.D. said. "He's happy as hell to see me wearing green." He accepted the slightly delayed laughter. "So am I. I'm honored Sid Anderson wanted me in Boston, and was able to pay so nicely to get me out of the

42

California sun." More laughter. "Boston has an excellent chance of making and advancing in the playoffs. They have balance and promise."

No more lying, baby.

"Are you going to jump right in and start?" someone he'd never seen before asked.

"I'll do whatever Quinn Harrington wants me to do."

"His record this year has been less than sensational. How do you think he's—"

"Gentlemen," Anderson said, "Quinn isn't here."

"Why not, Sid?" Gallagher asked.

"He had personal business to attend to today, planned for a long time. And don't draw any foolish conclusions from that because there's none to be drawn."

Some laughter.

"Coaches seldom attend things like this," Anderson said. "You people should know that."

"Quinn Harrington was on three world championship teams," B.D. said. "I went up against him in an NBA final when he was playing, and lost. He's coached two NBA champions. He was a great player." He shifted. "Before the question comes up—I'm here to play, only to play." They stared at him. Lying about your intentions, in politics and sport, had long ago become a Boston art form.

Anderson answered two rambling questions about the other players who'd been traded, how long the trade had been in the works.

"We've wanted B.D. Jordan right here for a long time," he said.

A young reporter asked if it wasn't true that he'd promised his mother and brother that he would play his last season in Boston, and had been pressing since early September to be traded.

He shook his head and heard mild laughter.

"What about the rumor," the reporter pressed, "that the blacks on the Lakers wouldn't speak to you after your brother beat Ed Brooke so badly in November?"

"He's from one of the crazy weeklies," Anderson said into

43

B.D.'s ear. "He's a fuckhead. Thinks Freud invented the game. You should see what he does with football."

Chuck Darwin had called B.D. yesterday morning to tell him how much he'd miss him and then begun to choke up. "And not just your passing, Jordan. Not just those great blind passes." They'd played together for seven years. Darwin had always thought Senator Ed Brooke was white.

B.D. found Harrington in his office a half-hour after the conference. He was wearing a green nylon warmup suit and had his feet up on his desk, a Coke can in his right hand. He didn't get up when B.D. walked through the open door.

Harrington had put on a lot of weight, and the team's third bad start in a row had slipped its nightmare into his eyes. Sitting there, motionless, he looked hung over, unsure, on the edge of darkness. Maybe B.D. would save his life.

"It's good to see you again, Quinn," B.D. said.

Harrington nodded. "You too," he said and motioned Jordan to the chair in front of his cluttered desk. "I'll bring you off the bench at about the five or six minute mark of the first period tonight and let you play as long as you want. New York sucks. We should kick their ass and then move past them in the standings next week. I hate every fucking thing about them, but mostly that they're in front of us."

"Sounds good," B.D. said after a moment.

"Off guard, to the left. You can move to the point if that's what you want to do after a while."

"Sure."

"Obviously, if we're not setting up you can go where you want, and shoot when you want. Still comfortable this year on the left side of the break?"

"Either side," he said.

"Evans likes to swing to his right, and Jackson's been going back door from the left well. He's been effective."

B.D. nodded.

"Hollowell's had his moments. He's always been a great forward."

44

B.D. said nothing.

"It'll all develop. I've never overstructured anything, in the good times as well as the bad. I just hope we can keep what we've got now together for the rest of the year. We might even make the playoffs." He smiled, let it go. "Wouldn't that be a pisser," he said and took a slug from the Coke can.

"A real pisser."

"I'd love it—I thought you'd tell them to shove it right up their asses and go with one of the networks."

"I thought about it."

"You're not in your twenties, you know."

"I know."

"Neither's Holloway. He's slipped a lot. He really should have retired at the end of last year. He's blaming last year and this one on me, and he's been trying to get rid of me." He looked at B.D. "You must really be pissed."

"I am."

"Take it out on New York."

"Sure."

Harrington stared into his desk.

B.D. stirred. Maybe Harrington wanted him to get up and leave then, or disappear—or score a hundred and ten points tonight and make everyone in Boston look like a genius so they'd leave Quinn Harrington, once one of the best coaches and forwards in the NBA, alone for another season.

"I don't want your job, Quinn. And if I did I'd never come into town like this with you still here. I wouldn't even be here talking to you now. You know that."

Harrington nodded. "I know it."

13

AT FIVE O'CLOCK B.D. SAT ON THE EDGE OF HIS BED and stared at the dead television screen. He'd made an appointment to look for an apartment tomorrow morning. The constant sense of old Boston here had begun to smother and depress him.

He'd eaten nothing since breakfast and wanted nothing now. Hunger made him more aggressive. He'd take a cab to the Garden just before six and shake hands with the other players. He knew some of them well. Evans was a good guard, Jackson a solid forward. They'd score, but their defense would be terrible. Coleman, no matter what else, became a motherfucker on the boards when he got pumped. Boston had little rebounding power now.

The game was at seven-thirty. He breathed and stood and was swept with loneliness again. He felt cold and isolated. He needed Stephanie. He called their house knowing there'd be no answer, then hung up before the answering service clicked on. It was easy enough to comprehend the three-hour difference between them now, as easy as it was to shrug at three thousand miles. Time and distance, after so many years of flying across America, meant little. But in January of 1963, when he had arrived in California for the first time, alone and exhausted and bleeding with guilt at having left his friends and mother and brother, three thousand miles was the distance to infinity, and three hours was the time it would take to get to the day of his death.

He paced the room. He didn't want to get to the Garden early. And if he lay down he was afraid he might sleep till noon tomorrow. A good game, and a long night's sleep following the eleven to midnight radio talk show interview Golden had scheduled, would give him the patience to get through the hours with his mother tomorrow afternoon.

He'd told the hotel to let no calls through until after tonight, and if anyone knocked at his door, which was almost impossible here, he'd simply send away whoever it was. He needed privacy now. He couldn't be distracted.

Enough people had tried to meet him, at airports and restaurants, at baseball games and on the street and in the lobbies of theaters and hotels. Only a few had been nasty. At a restaurant in New York an older man in a blue suit had gotten his and Stephanie's autograph and then had become angry, his face tightening and becoming blood-dark, when they wouldn't let him sit at their table and order. Outside a San Francisco hotel a woman in spiked heels and red dress had begun to cry hysterically when he wouldn't let her touch his shirt, and two well-dressed, middle-aged men had followed him and Stephanie to their seats at Chavez Ravine in late September, insisting that Stephanie had won her part in "Dial California" working on her back, and that Tom Jordan had arranged the death of Dante Marino. Two Dodger security guards had saved him from a fist fight. He'd never touched anyone in public, except to shake an extended hand, and then only with witnesses present.

B.D.'s mail was filled with passion, sickness and absurdity. Marriage and sex proposals, and a threat or two of maiming that he'd handed over to the L.A.P.D. He'd received hundreds of invitations to invest his money in new housing developments, chains of sporting goods stores, major league teams and the careers of young and old politicians. An amazing number of crazies wanted to hold office in California, especially the governorship.

Stephanie's mail, of course, was heavy with loneliness and the wet, outer limits of perversion. Everyone desired her, and sometimes illustrated their wants in red crayon, and about once a week she was scolded by a midwestern lady who was outraged at Steph's willingness to display her body on television.

B.D. put on his jacket and looked in the mirror. His hair was too long. Flecks of gray had invaded the dark brown. Gray looked great on aging baseball stars, pitchers in particular. It symbolized wisdom, valor, the ability to use spit and fingernails with cunning. But not on basketball stars, black or white. How many black basketball stars had gray hair?

He put his hands in his pockets, hunched his shoulders slightly. Every athlete had to live with loneliness, had to contain it, keep it from eating at his soul.

He turned from the mirror. Visiting his mother now, for a few hours, was as close as he could afford to get to his past in Lawrence.

* * *

47

Tom had had his victory party in late November at Sullivan's big, popular restaurant in downtown Lawrence. B.D. and Stephanie had been there and they and Sullivan, a close high school friend who'd graduated from Princeton and had his right knee shattered in his first month in Vietnam, had talked at one of the long, oak-panelled bars and later alone in his office—of the people Sullivan and B.D. had known in high school, especially Arnie Levine.

Levine, Sullivan's roommate in his freshman and sophomore years at Princeton, and B.D.'s best friend in Lawrence—until the night before he'd left for California when Levine had told him in front of Sullivan and several others, all beer-drunk, that he, B.D. Jordan, was a no-good prick to be running out on his mother and brother and friends, and especially the memory of his father and family roots and heritage by going to California.

All of them had laughed at Levine, with his white, blue-veined neck and anger-stricken face, not because of what he'd said, but because of his almost comical, terror-ridden, high-pitched voice. Levine had thrown his beer can in the street then and had taken a roundhouse swing at B.D.'s head, missing because he'd tried so fucking hard to hit him. Levine had stumbled and fallen, and they gathered around him as he gathered his five-foot-eight body in the hard, Lawrence snow. Their breath and silence had shown how much they understood and cared, until a soft female voice from the edge of the group whispered "Come on, Arnie, this is the last good time we'll ever have together." Levine got up then and told her, too, to go fuck herself.

When B.D. called the next day, Levine wouldn't come to the phone, had already left for school, his mother and father said at the door in the afternoon when B.D. went by Levine's house. The Levines had been cold to him then (if B.D. left Lawrence, then Arnie would too, and he knew they hated him for showing their son that freedom was possible), just a month after his father's death, almost as cold and silent and devastated, he thought, as his mother had been the week before, when he'd told her he'd been offered athletic scholarships at Stanford, USC and Cal, that he'd accepted the offer from Cal and was leaving. He'd taken his last final exam two days earlier and had come home late in the afternoon by train and had put off telling her but knew, after sleeping late the second day and spending most of the afternoon with Levine and Sullivan and a few others home for semester break, that he'd have to tell her then, and tell his brother as soon as Tom came home from basketball practice that night. It was four o'clock and she was already beginning supper, trying hard to fill the tough end of another deep-winter afternoon.

He'd sat in the chair near the window and watched her move into the pantry, back to the table, the stove.

"I've got something very important to tell you," he said, sounding almost too matter-of-fact.

"Something about one of your finals?"

It was almost completely dark now. After he told her he'd go for a long walk through several neighborhoods and then come back and hope Tom was home—and then tell him too and get it all over with.

"No," he said.

"You did do well, didn't you?"

"I did well. I don't know yet what I got in English and math, but I'm sure I got A's in the others."

She smiled and nodded. "Good for you," she said, and let her smile fade slightly. "What is it then?"

"I'm not going back to Tufts."

She looked at him.

"After Pa died, just before Christmas, I wrote to Stanford and Cal and USC, schools that were interested in me because of basketball at Andover." He breathed hard, his blood roaring. "Cal, the University of California at Berkeley, has offered me a lot of money to go out and play basketball. It's an excellent school and—"

"You're going to leave Tufts to go to California?" Her voice was labored, still bruised by death and loneliness.

"Yes," he said.

"Why? When?"

"In a week," he said. "I'm flying there next week."

She stared at him, her hands smoothing the front of her pale blue dress. "Next week?"

He nodded and stood and walked a few steps further from her.

"But why? What's the matter with Tufts?"

"I want to get away," he said. "I have to break from some things." He knew he could never explain why to her. "And I really want to start playing basketball again," he said, lying slightly. "I miss not playing more than I thought I would, and now I'll have to play."

"They've given you money to play?"

"Yes."

"Play at Tufts."

He shook his head. "Basketball's not good enough there," he said and knew he sounded absurd.

"You're going to leave both of us here, after your father's just died, and even though you're doing so well at Tufts?"

"I'll come back in June, when the semester's over," he said, and knew he should have said nothing.

She leaned forward, touched her right cheekbone with her fingertips. "How can you do this to me?" she said, almost hissing the words, and left the kitchen.

He was standing in the same place when she came back moments later.

"When did you decide to do this?" she said, staying near the stove. "When did you decide to play basketball in California?"

"In December, early this month when I knew they wanted me. I have to get away from Tufts, from Lawrence, and Cal is a great school."

"How much money did they give you?"

"Enough to cover everything."

"Everything?"

"Almost. I still have some money from working last summer, and some that Pa gave me." He felt himself choking up then.

"How can you, B.D.?"

"I have to."

"How can you hurt me like this? Why do you have to keep hurting me like this?" and she began to cry hard.

Whenever he became tired or ached for the certainties of love and a place to be that first winter in California, he remembered her voice, her frightened eyes, and felt guilt explode inside his heart.

Tom, a junior in high school, and still struggling hard with their father's death, had told him that night he really didn't understand why B.D. was going, that it would hurt like a bastard not having him just thirty miles away at Tufts, and that he'd probably hate him for it, for leaving him alone with their mother and the emptiness of their seven-room house. But Tom had driven him to Logan airport and they'd shaken hands and B.D. promised to write, even if it were just a sentence or two, once a week and to come home for as long as he could in the summer.

"I've got to do this," B.D. said in the bitter wind outside the terminal.

"I know you do."

"Take care of her."

"I will," Tom said. "I'll take care of her."

They'd seen each other in June when he came back to Lawrence for five days before summer basketball in Berkeley.

Levine quit Princeton that March, breaking his mother's and father's hearts. More than anything else Hershel Levine wanted to give his son, his only child, the land he'd bought next to the nearly abandoned railroad station in downtown Lawrence. But Arnie had tricked him, snapped the cord and said no to his father's plans to imprison him, and had gone on, Sullivan had said in November, to the University of Wisconsin after disappearing for the spring and summer in New York. There were rumors of his arrest at anti-war rallies in the midwest, of getting his head opened in Chicago in '68, and of his flight to Canada. "Like a crazy bastard," Sullivan said then in his office, lifting a heavy-bottomed glass filled with ice and Scotch in front of his tight, dark Irish face, "I never ran with him. Both of you got out, as painful as it must have been. The only pain I got locked me here." He laughed quickly, stirred in the chair behind his massive desk. "But I'm doing well. I've never had to marry, and I'm rich. Certainly not as rich as you are, Jordan, but I'm there." He

51

looked into his chest and then up and they stared at each other until, a moment later, people came through the half-open door, looking for them. Tom, senator-elect Tom Jordan of Massachusetts, a credit to his family and the city that nurtured him, in spite of his divorce, was about to speak.

"Your brother's a fucking senator," Sullivan said, standing. "That's amazing. And what a great guy he really is. He'd do anything he could for anybody. If you knew some of the ways he's helped people around here—he's going to be President, and a great one."

He wouldn't see Sullivan this winter. He'd see no one he knew but his mother, and Kate O'Connell and her two sons, Tom's sons.

B.D. waited for the elevator alone in the corridor. He felt lean and hard and superior now. Isolated. Cool. He'd play well for as long as he wanted to play well, and endure whatever loneliness there was. He smiled. He did want to play.

14

HE CAME OFF THE BENCH HALFWAY THROUGH THE first quarter to a standing ovation. The Garden was just over half full. The real test of his pulling power would be next week when people had had a chance to make plans, and he had a chance to score a little. He'd always hit double figures here, and five years ago had hit forty-two in a playoff game.

Because of the empty seats the crowd seemed less immediate than in Los Angeles, or in New York or Philadelphia, and it was easier to concentrate than he thought it would be.

He took a sharp in-bounds pass, drove to the corner and hit a twenty-foot jump shot. The crowd stood and cheered again. He grinned as he backed into Boston's defense, lingered at half-court, stole the ball, drove underneath and hit a reverse lay-up.

Then, fifteen seconds later, a quick jumper from the top of the key, soaring into the hot, shamrock-emblazoned Garden air. Nice. Nine points in the first half, fifteen in the second, five assists playing three-quarters of the game at shooting, then point guard. He felt young and in charge in the second half, in spite of the halftime quiet in the Boston locker room, almost as silent then with the score tied, as it was at the end of the game when they'd lost by eleven. Gallagher and Swann and a few others were waiting when it was over. B.D. gave them several positive sentences before telling three television cameras that he thought Boston would jell soon and that he was happy enough with his own performance, though he hated to lose. He showered and dressed alone. Few players hang around a losing locker room.

No one had asked him to dinner or drinks. He thought Anderson should have, and he was a little disappointed that his brother wasn't there, in spite of what he had said on the phone, and that Golden hadn't sent a beautiful blonde to the locker room door.

He'd never played on a losing team, and the taste of defeat, especially this early in the season, was depressing. Part of a coach's job was to build a positive emotional high early in the season and to sustain it. Or at least instill a quiet, positive sense of confidence that would hold through the winter, no matter what happened. Unless Boston began a winning steak, or fired Harrington soon, the locker room would turn into a danger zone.

Colin Holloway had been cool to B.D. when they'd shaken hands in the locker room before the game though they'd been in seven all-star games together and had spent a month touring Europe with an all-star team three years ago. Holloway was, as Harrington knew, putting pressure on Anderson to change coaches. He was obviously angry at his own failures this year and last, had scored only six points tonight and been beaten badly a few times on defense. On the way into the locker room after the game he asked B.D. why anyone would leave California for a rotten winter in Boston.

"Because I'm not ready to quit yet," he said.

"When they begin treating us, the guys that invented the game and put it on national television, badly, then it's time," Holloway said. "And that's all that Boston's doing now, just trying to get through this season with decent attendance. The team's a fucking disaster, and things are going to get worse."

Stephanie called him at one o'clock.
"I miss you," she said. "It's going to be awful without you."
"I know," he said and held the pillow against his chest.
"But we'll make it."
"We will."
"How did you do?"
He told her.
"You're fantastic," she said.
"The team's awful."
"You'll make them better."
"I'll have to."
"B.D.?" she said after a moment.
"Yes."
"I'm going to spend a few days with the Chandlers. It's hard being alone here now, and their house is closer to where we've been shooting, and the studio."
"All right," he said, though it bothered him, after they again said they loved each other and hung up, to think of her now spending time at night with other people. The Chandlers, Gordon an ophthalmologist and Vicki a writer and producer for daytime television, were Stephanie's friends before they'd met, not his.

15

THE WIND HAD SHIFTED IN THE NIGHT AND December was cold again. Not bitter cold. It rarely got bitter cold in Boston in December, and seldom for more than a few days even in January and February.

He met the real estate dealer Golden had put him in touch with in front of the hotel. It took less than two hours to take a one bedroom furnished apartment on the tenth floor of a new building on Beacon Street. The living room had a picture-window view of the Charles River and MIT and the affluent, balconied apartment houses along Memorial Drive. The bedroom, with a double bed and two bureaus, had the same river view, and the kitchen and dining areas, orange and yellow and white, gleamed with fresh paint.

He rented a car, checked out of the hotel and had unpacked in the apartment by one o'clock. Stephanie, he thought, would find it pleasant enough here. She had liked Boston when she'd been on a "Dial California" publicity tour, and again last September during Tom's senatorial campaign.

The real estate office would arrange to have his phone connected late in the afternoon, and before driving to his mother's house he sat on the living room couch and watched car windshields along Memorial Drive clicking off pieces of the sun. His life had certainly become a distant winter afternoon, he thought, and he knew he'd better decide quickly what he was going to do next year.

16

LAWRENCE WAS THIN GRAY CLOUDS AND LONG, hulking mills the color of dried blood, their windows dark now even though parts were occupied by small manufacturing companies, electronics firms, printing presses. He drove with the radio too loud over the rushing, black Merrimack River and beside the two- and three-family houses that led to his mother's house on Tower Hill. When he turned the corner, he saw Kate walking to her Mercedes in front of the house. She looked up and smiled when she saw him.

Katherine O'Connell, Tom's former wife and the mother of his five- and six-year-old sons. Tall and blonde and slightly athletic looking, almost beautiful, and always good to their mother.

She still lived in the red brick Georgian colonial in Andover that she had shared with Tom. Her father, a prominent Lawrence and Andover pediatrician, hated Tom—for divorcing his only daughter, for becoming successful politically without the O'Connells' help, for the fact that Kate still cared for Tom and his family. But Kate had wanted the divorce. She couldn't stand the loneliness, the neglect that political ambition had forced on her after Tom's first state senate win, especially after she'd learned of his affair with a Boston television newswoman who had eventually screwed her way to New York.

Kate was wearing an open, knee-length fur coat, chocolate brown corduroys, high-heeled boots; her hair, pulled back, emphasized her high cheekbones. Leaning against her car, she seemed as much out of place in Lawrence as Stephanie always did whenever he saw her location scenes in "Dial California." Kate wasn't as good-looking as Stephanie Green. But then, no one was.

He hesitated before getting out of the car. He was in Lawrence and here was Kate. He lived in Malibu. This was his brother's turf, the center of Tom's base of power, the place where his heart beat—and for an instant B.D. went cold. Nothing here was his. He had run from it fifteen years ago to save himself, and now had let himself come back, crowding his brother only a few weeks before Tom was to become the junior senator from Massachusetts. Had he made a terrible mistake? Or was he simply too tired, angry, even guilt-ridden to think straight, to keep all of his emotions stacked in the right piles?

Kate took a step toward him. Watch out, he thought. Watch out. There's always blood on the wind.

They hugged, stepped back. She felt comfortable, and it surprised him. He couldn't remember that they had ever kissed, except at the wedding, or more precisely, the reception in Andover at her father's spreads and lawns. She was better looking now at thirty-three than she'd ever been.

"Nice surprise," he said. "You look great."

"You, too, B.D." Her voice was pleasant.

"Where're the boys?"

"With friends for the afternoon. They'll stay there for dinner

56

tonight and I'll pick them up. Next week it's my turn for dinner. It's how I spend a lot of my afternoons, waiting for the children." She smiled. "They're excited about your being here."

He nodded. "I'm sure I'll see them soon." He and Tom and the boys would get together after a Sunday game, a locker room visit, dinner at a Boston restaurant afterward.

"The last time I saw you, in September, I was just leaving the house," Kate said.

B.D. and Stephanie had come to Lawrence with Tom during the campaign visit to film a commercial along the Merrimack, and Kate had just dropped the boys off at the house in time to see them when they arrived. She'd been embarrassed, though she'd handled it well, and must have hated herself for looking like a nice, devoted servant.

"So how're you taking all of this, the trade, being back here?"

"I'm not sure. It's only for the winter."

"Where're you staying?"

He told her.

"What about Stephanie?"

"She's filming until a few days before Christmas, and then coming here before we go to Chicago for Christmas. She's upset about the trade, and pretty angry."

"You must be, too."

"I am." He watched his breath come apart in the wind. He smiled. "It's good seeing you here, though." He looked toward the house, the brick, three-bedroom ranch on one of Lawrence's few affluent looking streets, though decay had already crept to the houses only a few blocks away. The older women in the neighborhood were terrified that Puerto Rico was coming to Tower Hill.

Kate had never known, of course, what it was to fight against the limits of a place like this, with its polluted river and brooding mills, the dirty starting place in America for his grandfathers who had wound their blood into the promise that their children would never have to work in the darkness of twelve-hour days. Unless fighting against the stifling predictability of her father's home in Andover was the same, or worse because it all seemed so terrific

57

on the surface. Everyone knew that the mills symbolized exploitation, indifference, cruelty—society's mangling hatred of children, the tuberculin rattle of death in winter, the sweat of imprisonment in summer.

"You have a game tonight? No? You played well last night."

"Thanks," he said.

"How long are you staying here?"

"An hour, two." He hesitated. "It'll be hard enough to stay that long. It always is."

"Then back to Boston?"

"Back to Boston."

"I'd like to talk to you for a while," she said and stared at him. "Why don't you come by the house on your way back to Boston?"

"This afternoon?"

"Yes. About four or four-thirty, or whenever you want. I would like to talk."

"All right," he said.

"Nothing else planned?"

"Nothing."

She held her coat collar close to her neck, breathed and then slipped her hands back into her pockets. "I'll see you about four then."

He nodded. But she didn't move and looked slightly troubled, almost sad.

"Your mother doesn't look good, B.D."

"How bad is she?"

"You haven't seen her since last month."

He shook his head slightly.

"We'll talk about it," she said.

He walked quickly down the driveway to the back door. The basketball rim still had a net attached, and the backboard and pole his father had sunk at the end of the driveway when he and Tom were in grammar school looked smooth and sturdy. The pole and the trim on the house got a new coat of paint every three years.

His mother was in the kitchen, near the stove, and smiled

58

when she saw him. At the election-night victory party at Sullivan's, she had been quiet, but looked good. The change was startling. She seemed smaller now, older, and was very thin. He hugged her and she cried, and he knew she was dying.

"Look at me," she said. "I'm down to almost nothing."

"Have you been sick?" His voice was distant, almost absurd.

"No, not sick—"

He sat at the kitchen table when she did. She had tea ready, and cookies in a white dish. He watched her sip her tea.

"I've lost most of it this week, since Sunday, or Saturday. Saturday—"

She looked at her hands, folding and unfolding them on the table.

"I'm not sure what it is," she said and stared at him. "I don't think it's cancer. I've always watched myself so carefully, and felt so good. Until two weeks ago. I began to feel tired in the afternoon. I don't mean just tired, but exhausted. And it's still happening."

"You must have been to the doctor?"

"Yes, twice. For blood tests and X-rays and other things. They've found nothing at all. My weight hasn't changed today from yesterday, and only just slightly from the day before. But I don't feel any better. I'm going to Mass. General next week, on Monday, for more tests." She looked away. "Something's just burned right through me, in such a hurry. I can't quite grasp it."

He didn't know what to say then, or what to do. He leaned forward and touched her hand.

"I'm sure everything's going to be all right." He hesitated. "Are you seeing the right people about it?"

She nodded. "Kate's helped me. She's always been very good." She took a deep breath. "Tom hasn't seen me for a while. He knows I've lost some weight, but not this much." She looked past him through one of the kitchen windows and into the small backyard, the dead grass still partly covered by the pale green sun. "I was frightened. I'm not now." She wiped at her eyes with the heel of her right hand. He swallowed and didn't look at her.

* * *

It was amazing, he thought, that she was so composed now. But religion had helped her. The same Lawrence Catholicism that had spread guilt and terror through his grammar school friends had given her not just a place to go with her neighborhood friends on Sunday morning, but something beyond herself to believe in—a carefully programmed trip to heaven, and a basis, finally, for understanding most of the people she had lived with all of her life.

She had grown up as a Protestant, with church never a very important factor in her life. Her husband didn't go to church, and Tom and B.D. seldom did after grammar school, though she wanted them to because it made her feel better. She had become a Catholic in Tom's sophomore year at Notre Dame, three years after the death of her husband.

Now, whenever she grew lonely or afraid, the Catholic Church was there. It had given her a means to forgive B.D. for going to California, and because she could forgive him, she was free to begin to understand him.

They had never talked about her conversion. Tom had told him about it. She wasn't out to impose her will on either of her sons anymore, and she never asked Tom why he hadn't become Catholic too, though he'd gone to Notre Dame, married Kate in a Catholic ceremony, and run for office in Massachusetts. She only wanted to stabilize her own life, and she'd done it well enough to be able to leave them alone. And now she could face this.

"Are you unhappy with the trade?" she said.

He raised his shoulders lightly.

"Be honest about it."

"Yes, of course I am."

"I don't blame you. But you and Tom have seen tough things through before. I want to tell you something."

He looked at her carefully.

"I realize how selfish I was fifteen years ago," she said, "trying to hold you here with guilt because of my own insecurity, before and after your father's death. I never told you that before, but I want to now. Tom helped me realize what I'd done—he's going to make such a great senator. Both of you have had the strength to become what you wanted to become. Your father almost did. But you two have." She looked away from him again, then back, almost as if she'd forgotten what she had said.

"Can I get you anything?" he said. "Get you anything at all?"

"No—I'm going to sleep in a little while, and then go over to Carrie Mallon's house for dinner. I can't seem to sit for very long in one place. My back, my lower back begins to stiffen and hurt. That's never happened before."

"Are you in a lot of pain?"

"No. It just hurts a little, like now, and then I get tired."

He waited for her to say more. He wanted to tell her then that he knew how much he'd hurt her when he left for California, but that he'd had to go, that it wasn't easy for him to leave, that the loneliness of being away during the first month had almost killed him, but that he had made a life there, was happy with it, and would go back to it.

"Your wife's a very beautiful woman," she said.

"Yes."

"Is she all right alone, after all of the publicity about your leaving?"

"She's with friends for a few days. The house is secure. She'll be here, we'll be with you as we planned a few days before Christmas. And I'm just in Boston. I've rented an apartment, on Beacon Street." He didn't want to say too much, promise too much. He had to protect himself, despite her condition.

She let several moments slip away.

"I'm sorry, B.D., I really am, but I think I've got to lie down for a while."

"Are you sure I can't do anything?"

"No, I'm all right, really. I'm just very tired. But I won't be if I lie down for an hour or a little more. Carrie's going to call. And Kate will. You've got enough to worry about now, and think about. I listened to part of the game last night. You were marvelous, like you always are. But the team isn't very good. It must be hard playing on a team like that."

He watched her get up, hesitate at the stove, stare through

61

one of the windows, then run water at the sink in the pantry and come back to the table. He got up.

"I'm so tired all of a sudden. Don't tell Tom how bad I look. He'll want to do everything all at once for me, and there's nothing that can be done."

She walked to the front door with him, past the mantel and desk with framed pictures of him and Tom and the children, of his father and Kate.

He held her at the door and felt her hands on his back, clinging tightly.

Before going to Andover, B.D. drove across Tower Hill to the cemetery where his father had been buried almost fifteen years ago, and sat in the idling car on the narrow road beside the rise that held his father's stone and hundreds of others. He got out and walked up to it, planted next to smaller ones for his grandfather, grandmother and his father's only brother, who was drowned in one of the city's packed swimming pools when he was five years old.

"David Jordan, 1914–1962." The only markings on his father's stone.

B.D.'s father had been a lawyer, a state senator who, in 1950, lost in his one try for Congress by fifteen hundred votes. In the spring of 1962 he had fallen in love with a twenty-three-year-old woman and would have left B.D.'s mother for her that winter. But he had died of a heart attack while he and B.D. were walking along the Merrimack at the bottom of Tower Hill on a warm Saturday morning just before Christmas. B.D. remembered a few patches of snow melting across the pale yellow grass, the river flowing gently toward the distant downtown mills—the Ayer where his grandfathers had worked, the Wood and Pacific. His father had told B.D. how he had let Lawrence trap him after his only political defeat, how much he hated the city's provincialism, its acceptance of the death and decay in its own blood, and had urged B.D. to make a clean break when he had the chance, if he waited too long he'd never get out and would soon give up the idea of leaving. And then he told B.D. about the young woman. Carol Fisher. B.D. supposed that was the only time he'd hated his father, then—when he learned about the infidelity. But he'd also known that his parents' marriage had been dead for a long time.

He hadn't seen his father fall. They had turned from the river and begun walking across a narrow field where kids were playing football to get to the car. B.D. had moved a few feet ahead, glanced back and had seen him on his knees, both hands at his chest. B.D. had sent the kids for help, but neither he, nor a motorist the kids managed to stop, nor the police who limped across the field with oxygen could pry death from his father's body.

B.D. stood close to the stone. Wind struggled with his hair, snapped at his jacket. "David Jordan." He would have been sixty-three now.

He had met Carol at the funeral parlor after he'd gone off to a corner to be by himself, away from a cluster of desperate aunts and uncles and friends of his mother. Carol had come up to him quietly, brushed back her reddish-brown hair and introduced herself. He was stunned by her warmth, composure, her mature good looks. Her hurt and loneliness were obvious, and he was glad, suddenly, that his father had found her.

They met again in a downtown Lawrence restaurant in the late afternoon after the funeral and were soon comfortably talking about themselves, about his father. On a street filled with lights and Christmas shoppers, they had hugged and said goodbye, and promised to see each other that weekend. They never did. Later she married, and he thought she was living on Long Island.

An orange pickup truck slowed on the drive behind him, went a few yards beyond his car and stopped. Idling pale blue exhaust hung in the air for a few seconds before being torn away by the wind. The two Lawrence city workers in the truck, collars up, hats pulled over their ears, turned and were staring through the cab's side and back windows at him. He waved and they waved back and drove slowly away. Maybe, he thought, he had given them something to talk about.

When they were out of sight, and he was alone with the wind and the dead, he stepped to the grave, knelt in front of it, put his arms around the stone and held it for several moments, remembering how he had held his father's hand in the back of the ambulance that had wailed them through the city.

He got up, backed a few steps away from the grave, walked to his car and drove to Kate's house in Andover.

17

KATE'S CAR WAS PARKED A FEW YARDS DOWN THE long driveway that curved behind the house. Maples and oaks defined its wide front yard. He pulled up behind her car, breathed away any doubt about seeing her now and rang the front doorbell. She had changed into dungarees, loafers and a blue turtleneck; her hair was still pulled back.

"How are you?" she said and led him into the familiar den off the long bright living room, and sat on the couch with him. One wall was lined with books, a few pictures of the kids and her parents. A television set and two leather chairs faced a medium-size red brick fireplace with a drawing of the house over the mantle. A rug covered most of the darkly stained, polished floor. He had drunk Scotch here with Tom at a Christmas party a few years ago, and again in the early autumn after Tom's first state senate primary win. There were no traces of politics now. He watched the pine trees move in the wind on the front lawn of another brick house several yards away.

"I'll put water on for coffee or tea in a minute," she said. "Unless you'd like something to drink."

He shook his head. "She looks terrible."

Kate nodded.

"She said she's had tests, and is going to Boston for more."

"I've talked to the doctors. They've found nothing, but want to see what happens next week."

"What do you think?"

She stared at him. "I don't know, B.D. She did have a bad cold. She worried about Tom's campaign all summer. She didn't show it, but I knew it really hurt her to see him trailing in the polls. Primary night took an awful lot out of her. And she worried, still worries, that people think he had something to do with Marino's death."

"I think she's dying."

Kate looked away, then got up and walked to one of the long, draped windows. Darkness was already there.

"I don't think so. I'd certainly tell you now if I knew. I'm sure she thinks she is—let's go for a walk. I haven't picked up my mail. It'd delivered late in the afternoon." She slipped her fingertips into her pockets. "Then please stay for a while. I can always get the boys later." She waited. "All right?"

"All right," he said.

They walked out the front door and through the cold to the sidewalk and narrow street, their faces visible in pale-white light from a distant street light. He watched her open the mailbox and take several letters from it, glance at them, smile and look up.

"Cold?" she said.

"My blood's still thin." At one-thirty in warm California Stephanie Green was on location—he concentrated on Kate's cheekbones, her white teeth, forcing the need for his wife back beyond the setting sun.

"Want to just walk for a while?" she said. "Just down to the end of the street and back?"

"Sure."

Windows in the big brick homes set back from the street were turning pale orange, light green. It was too quiet here, especially after listening to the ocean at Malibu, cars in the night on Storrow Drive, and he could hear his heart working, the ticking in his breath and blood. New England on the edge of winter. God—

"What's been happening to you?" he said. "How have things been going?"

"All right. There are people, my mother, but especially my father and others, who think I've stayed much too close to the Jordans. I guess they want me to escape."

"What do you mean?"

"They want me to ignore Tom and stay away from your mother, turn my back on all of you and get completely out from underneath your influence. They want me to remarry soon." She smiled. "I don't think that's going to happen."

"I'd heard you were close."

"Did Tom say that?"

"I think so."

"I was seeing a couple of people. And for a while I guess it got serious with one of them. But that's over with now."

"Are you seeing anyone now?" It was none of his business.

She stopped and looked at him.

"I make love when I want to make love," she said.

He felt himself stir. His brother's former wife—

"I'm sorry," he said.

"Don't be." She touched his arm. "Let's go back, it's early." She didn't move.

"Do you want me to leave?"

"That's the last thing I want you to do, B.D."

The phone was ringing when they got inside. She took it in the family room and he walked through the dark, thickly carpeted dining room to the gleaming kitchen and sat at the table. He could hear her voice. She laughed. He got up when she didn't come in right away and filled a red teapot with water. He stared through the kitchen windows, across the bare, lighted patio, the fading yard, a still swing set and massive maples several yards beyond it. When he listened closely now he could hear the traffic on routes 495 and 93, cars speeding into the black-green horizons of the weekend.

The temperature in Los Angeles had been seventy-five degrees at noon today. L.A. would be playing at the Forum in six hours. The offensive flow last night had been slow and uncertain, and it seemed, for a moment or two at least, as if the others were hanging around, waiting for him to star or fall on his ass, willing to let their attention and terrible season slide away.

He lit the stove. Kate came back into the kitchen and sat at the table with him.

"A neighbor. She saw us and wanted to know if it really was B.D. Jordan."

"Did you tell her?"

"I told her. She asked if I knew how well you'd done last night."

He looked away, then back at her smile as she watched him, and he wanted to reach across the few feet that separated them and touch her smooth fingers, steady now on the table, and almost did.

"I told her I knew. I keep up with everything because the boys want to know." She leaned her chin on the back of her hands, her elbows lightly on the table. She was wearing no lipstick, little makeup.

"You miss her a lot, don't you," she said.

"I miss her," he said.

"I won't tell the kids you were here," she said after a moment.

"All right."

"It's been a hard week for you."

She had slipped into the safe repetition of the obvious. Maybe she thought she'd gone too far outside. Maybe not.

"It's been easy," he said. "Everyone does everything for me." He leaned back. "I feel good when I'm playing. It's always been that way."

She answered the whistling kettle and poured the boiling water over tea bags in tall blue mugs and brought milk and sugar back to the table with her.

"I had to keep playing," he said. "There was nothing else for me to do. They caught me unprepared."

"What will you do?"

"After basketball? I'm not sure."

She nodded, watching him. He was certain now as she sipped from the steaming mug that she wanted to make love and for a

67

moment, two, his heart slammed. He'd have to leave soon.

"What do you do during the day, when the kids are at school?" he said and thought it sounded right. The initial uncertainty of his being here was drifting away. She was easy to be with. He didn't feel compelled to talk.

"I teach two sections of freshman English and composition at Merrimack."

"I didn't know that. Good—like it?"

"Sometimes. Most of the kids write badly and resent having to think about anything. And most, maybe all, are taking it because they have to. But a few of them do have sensitivity, and promise."

"How many kids in a section?"

"Twenty-two."

"Not bad."

"It's a little too big," she said.

"What are you going to do when the boys get older?"

"I don't know. Maybe I'll just watch them gain fame on the playing fields of Phillips Andover and Notre Dame, or wherever they decide to go." She looked into her mug. "No, I'm not only going to do that. I'm going to have to change things a little soon. Soon enough."

He didn't want to ask what she meant.

"Want to have dinner here?"

"I can't. I've got to get going. I've got a few things to get done."

They walked through the dining room and into the front hall.

"I'm going to see your mother on Monday night when she gets back from the hospital tests," Kate said. "If you like I'll call and let you know how she's doing."

"All right." He hesitated. "She looks so devastated, burned out."

She nodded slightly. He opened the door.

"I would like to see you again," she said.

"I would, too."

"We could get together on one of your open days next week, here, or I could see you in Boston, if that's all right. Why don't we talk about it on Monday?"

"All right."

Nothing would happen between them, he thought, nothing could. The winter would be swift. December breaking into the new year, January and February quick darts of light. In April, Steph would quit the TV series and he would quit basketball. And in the warm California spring, he would plant the perfect seed and make her pregnant. Time was running out. Kate's loneliness, his mother's terror, his father's cold, aging grave told him that time was running out.

She walked with him halfway across the lawn, stopped, touched his arm, and he held her briefly.

"I'll call," she said. "I promise I will."

18

FRIDAY NIGHT IN BOSTON. HE DIALED THE HOUSE in Malibu at ten o'clock and let it ring until the answering machine clicked on.

"It's me," he said to the tape. "It's just after ten o'clock and I'm watching the Charles river freeze under a strict New England sky. I'm warm in my safe, expensive apartment, and I miss you and love you."

He left his number, and then remembered that Stephanie had said she was going to the Chandlers for a few days, and hung up. He wouldn't call her there.

He watched the local news, including thirty seconds of Sid Anderson saying he thought B.D. Jordan would lift them to a contending position in the east, and a few seconds of a sportscaster saying that Mike Corvino, who'd left Los Angeles the day after the Jordan trade, had been picked up for a five-day tryout with Houston, which needed help at forward. He stared at the television. It was hard to believe Corvino had done that, and then, not hard to believe at all. He'd ask Stephanie to get in touch with

Karen and find out what was going on. Whatever it was Corvino was making a big mistake.

Just as he reached to snap the television off, his brother appeared on the screen, wearing a dark blue pin-striped suit and a red and blue striped tie, moving through applause and smiling faces to the speaker's rostrum. The newscaster's voice-over explained that senator-elect Tom Jordan had been in Boston tonight to address a meeting of the National Federation of Teachers. The story, a filler, lasted for only fifteen seconds and then the news team, three razor cuts and a good-looking woman, smiled its way into the weekend, and B.D. swallowed. Tom had been in Boston tonight without telling him even though, two nights ago, B.D. had asked about his weekend plans. What message was Tom sending him? Was he really crowding Tom here on his own turf? His playing well last night had generated headlines in the *Globe*'s sports section for the second morning in a row....

He shrugged and turned the television off. To hell with it. He couldn't bother with Tom now.

19

GAME TWO. SATURDAY NIGHT AT THE SPECTRUM arena in Philadelphia. A loud, physical, sellout crowd and a torrent of dirty language aimed at him. Basketball crowds in winning cities in the east were less than mellow.

"Boston got white overnight," Tyler Williams said to B.D. at half-court during warmups. "Green and white must look better on television than green and black."

Carl Robinson, tall, rugged and fast, and a few others, laughed.

"Look white, play white," Robinson said.

"It might be an interesting night," Williams said. Holloway smiled and drifted away.

Maury Golden represented both Robinson and Williams, and

had fifteen percent of more than three million a year standing at half-court now.

"Everything working out okay?" Williams asked. "No cut, no trade?"

"Two years," B.D. said.

"You white boys learn late in life," Robinson said. "You should've got your ass to Boston ten years ago. But you know what?"

"What?"

"Your tan's already fading fast."

They laughed.

"A spade fade," Robinson said and they hesitated and then laughed again.

Williams lingered next to him.

"Is this going to be it?"

"I don't know."

"Grab the coaching job if it happens that way. Take it and make them give you three years. There're all kinds of deals going down. Boston's hungry for white meat. You can have it all."

"What about my wife and home in California?"

"I wouldn't know about any of that B.D., but it doesn't mean shit compared to what you can do for yourself with all of this. You're on a rotten team right now because Harrington's burned out his soul. You might even turn these fuckups around."

B.D. said nothing, took a pass, unbuttoned his warmup jacket and spun the ball on his index finger.

"I hear Corvino's connecting with Houston," Williams said.

"I hear."

"He needs a better agent. He needs Maury."

"Maury doesn't want him. Corvino's making a big mistake by taking Houston's bait. I'll tell him, if he ever calls and asks for my advice. He knew L.A. was going to release him. We had dinner with him and his wife the other night and I thought she was going to come apart."

"Corvino's not making a mistake," Williams said. "He's doing the only thing any of us know. I hear he's going to Villanova in a year anyway, or maybe Penn."

"Where'd you hear that?"

"I forget. But college coaching makes you old in a hurry. I wouldn't touch it."

They shook hands again.

"Good luck, B.D. said and Williams dribbled away, shot from thirty feet and dazzled the net.

B.D. started at shooting guard as the game began. He'd try to hit Holloway more, and would easily enough if he only moved a little better, broke a little faster for the basket, he'd thought as they moved toward center court after the introductions, the boos and fuck yous, after the dark, silenced Spectrum arena with the spotlight on the American flag and the organ as a baritone sang the National Anthem, had been broken at the end by cries of "Jordan sucks!"

He was sure Holloway would quit soon although no one had yelled that he sucked too. He and B.D. hadn't talked in the locker room. Hardly anyone had spoken to anyone else on the way down and there was no pre-game tension in the warmups. Harrington had told them to go out and kick ass and then sat on the end of the bench and smiled as if he'd been drinking since dawn.

B.D. scored ten in the first quarter, on a twenty-foot jumper off the key, a reverse lay-up, then steal and another lay-up, and four out of four foul shots in the last minute—eight points in the second quarter. When Robin Jones, a six-eight white forward from Idaho, elbowed him in the ribs for the third time at the beginning of the third quarter while he drove into the middle, with the score tied at sixty, B.D. stopped, grinned and snapped the ball off the right side of Jones' mouth.

B.D. heard Williams say oh shit, and he thought for a moment that Jones was simply going to wipe the blood away, laugh and keep playing. Instead he came at B.D. and B.D. drove a right to his face and felt his fist hit something else and was lost in the chaos of knuckles, bone, sweat and shouting, and the copper taste of masculine bodies.

But no one was really pissed enough to keep it going or turn it into a team effort. The season was too young, Boston too bad,

Philadelphia too good. If B.D.'d been elbowed in Los Angeles he would have smiled at Jones, asked him to please cut the shit because he wanted to get laid tonight, and gone on with the game. It wouldn't have happened in Los Angeles anyway. Corvino and Darwin were around. Boston had no enforcer, and if they began climbing too high in the standings, he'd take a severe beating every time he went underneath. He knew that, and knew he was vulnerable now, but the message would go out that he wasn't going to take anyone's bullshit, and though someone might hurt him, he was more than willing to hurt the bastard back.

He and Jones should have been thrown out, but weren't, and maybe because they felt guilty missed their technical fouls.

Holloway, turned on by the sudden violence, got hot and put Boston ahead by four at the end of the third quarter. Then he threw in six straight long jumpers to silence the crowd and finally, with B.D. and everyone else hitting, leave the Spectrum half-empty with three minutes to go and Boston up by eighteen.

They won by twelve, and minutes later the locker room was alive with handshakes, laughter, reporters and television. *Sports Illustrated* photographers had been shooting the game, he knew, and they caught B.D. leaning back against a locker holding a plastic bag of ice against the right side of his face. Tonight's fight, and probably the picture they'd just taken, would make the next issue.

Gallagher sat next to him.

"You hear about Corvino?" B.D. asked.

"Five-day tryout. It'll become more than that because they really need a power forward."

"I think it's a good story."

"It isn't unless he starts averaging thirty a game, or kills himself—or gets arrested for drug dealing," Gallagher said.

"None of the above."

"He might hit thirty a few times if they let him shoot."

"I guess that's what he must be thinking too," B.D. said.

20

THE FLIGHT HOME WAS ALMOST SILENT. IT WAS
late, and one big upset win wasn't going to cure all of Boston's
problems. But it was a good win and even Harrington had been
grinning like a bastard and shaking hands with everyone at the
end of the game.

"Maybe you'll turn us around," he said to B.D. before getting
on the plane. "You showed balls going after Jones the way you
did."

"We don't have enough speed and rebounding."

"You can shoot, and so can Holloway. He proved it again
tonight."

"That might get us to the playoffs."

But B.D. didn't believe it, he was tired from the game, the
fight, the afternoon with his mother, and the control he had to
put on his ego to keep from getting suspicious that Stephanie
might be having a very good time at a party in Beverly Hills.
The side of his face felt as if it were going to burn away. He
needed sleep, and he needed to make long, caring love.

"We could do a lot better than just make the playoffs,"
Harrington said.

"We need rebounding. Young rebounding, Quinn. And fast-
break speed."

Harrington stared at him. He was searching for a way to survive. This win had bought him at least a week. A convincing
win tomorrow against Atlanta at the Garden on national television
would buy him another. A winning streak snapping the team
into playoff contention would get him through January. But

chances were, he knew, that Harrington would be out with the old on January first.

His apartment was cool and silent. He sat on the couch. Two cars moved across his sliding glass window, bleeding their rear lights into the edge of the river.

He got up and made himself coffee. He was hungry. There were frozen hamburger patties, soup and hot dogs, English muffins he could toast, and frozen pizza he could heat in the electric oven. He wouldn't chance going out to Copley Square now, or Faneuil Hall or Harvard Square. Not on drunken Saturday night.

He heated the pizza and ate it in the kitchen, read *Time* and the capsule movie reviews in the *New Yorker*, then studied the photo of a woman modeling a diamond bracelet. Black hair, green eyes, impassive mouth, no breasts. He'd been with her three times, and he remembered now the second time, the long, sure pressure of her fingertips on his back, his legs. She'd said little that night and nothing in the morning when swimming with him, drinking coffee, making love once more. Then she'd only said goodbye, bursting her pearl-white Ferrari away from his expensively shrubbed driveway. After the third time, in her blue Fifth Avenue apartment, he had tried talking to her, but she was deep into some shit, and he had given up. He didn't remember her name. It was nice to see that she was still working.

The phone awakened him. A sign, at least, that he was alive.

"B.D.?" Maury Golden said.

"It's after one o'clock in the morning and ice is forming on the Charles, Maury. I'm homesick."

"Twenty-eight, Jordan. You can't be that goddamn homesick when you score twenty-eight points on a Saturday night in Philadelphia. I just saw a film clip of the fight."

"Some fucking fight," he said. "I hit him with the ball."

"You looked great."

"Thanks."

"Are you alone?"

"Of course I am, Maury. Where are you?"

"New York. Manhattan."

75

"Alone?"

"No. Some friends are here. How do you feel?"

"Fine."

"Nothing hurts?"

"No. But I'm sure I'm going to really start to hurt in February if we don't pick up some muscle. Maybe they should have picked up Corvino."

"Maybe. How's the apartment?"

"Comfortable."

"Good. I'm going to try hard to get in for tomorrow's game."

"I'll look for you."

"Don't forget the commercial date in Manhattan on Monday morning."

"I won't."

"The car'll be waiting on Beacon Street at eight. We'll give you a wake-up call at seven just in case."

"Good," he said and accepted the fatigue washing over him.

"You're doing damned well," Golden said, his voice a touch lower, more intense.

"Thanks, Maury, that's good of you. I think the season here's going to turn out all right."

In bed a few minutes later, B.D. let the pillow turn into his wife. Perhaps she was just smiling into a corner now at eleven o'clock on the coast, listening to stray voices or talking someone out of trying to make love to her—or making love, her wrist touching his shoulder, her incredible mouth inhaling the first careless laughter of an illicit orgasm.

The ringing phone snapped him away from the second layer of sleep. Her voice was quiet, perhaps too composed.

"I watched the end of the game on local television," she said.

"Kate," he said evenly. He thought it sounded right.

"I know it's late."

"No it isn't," he said. "Where are you?"

"Andover."

"Oh."

"You played very well," she said.

"Thanks."

76

He felt his blood pump. It would be good to have someone to talk to here in Boston, someone to be with and drink coffee with. He smiled.

Kate had been around, had tasted other parts of America. It was December, closing in on Christmas. Her parents were aging, Tom was gone for good and his mother might be dying—and each day raced by more quickly than the one before, and months snapped the way weeks once did. Love all of a sudden was as distant to her as the first kiss at Seabrook Beach in the summer of 1968, the night of the first political victory, the birth of her first son. She was as lonely and vulnerable now as he was.

"I thought you might be back about now," she said.

"Good timing."

"Were you asleep?"

"Not at all," he said. He liked the liquid sound of her voice.

"You are alone, aren't you? I'm not disturbing you or—"

"Of course I am, I'm a married man."

She laughed easily.

"The boys are with my parents tonight. My father's taking them to the Patriots' final home game tomorrow. They'll be treated very well. Fawned over. They always are. Tom wasn't able to get to see them this weekend."

"Are you with anyone?"

"No one's here," she said.

"Come here, then." The words slipped easily off his tongue.

"I'd like to very much. But I can't, not now."

"I know—"

"We'll see each other soon," she said.

"We will."

"I'm going to watch the game tomorrow. Good luck."

"Thanks, Kate, good night," he said, and it was at least a quarter of an hour before he drifted, finally, into a deep sleep.

21

HE GOT TO THE GARDEN EARLY, DRESSED IN HIS white home uniform, green low-cut sneakers and white nylon warmup suit. Two of the locker-room assistants were around, no one else. He spent ten minutes stretching, then two to three focused on who would guard him and how. He figured his strategy, work behind screens, shoot from whatever picks he could set up, take every opening they gave him and shoot. Others drifted in, still hanging onto the threads of the high that an out-of-town victory brings to a losing team.

He nodded to Evans. Holloway hadn't arrived yet. Jackson slapped B.D. on the shoulder and they shook hands and B.D. got up and told one of the ball boys he was ready, and jogged out to the Garden court. A few spectators were already in the upper and lower balconies. Three kids leaned on the railing of the first balcony and yelled out his name and waved, and he waved back, and when he did they cheered.

He did ten stationary lay-ups, five from each side, five short jumpers from the left, five from just off the foul line and five from the right, then moved out past the foul circle, drove in hard and sank the ball, repeating it ten times until he was warm, breathing well, on the verge of breaking more than a thin sweat. He never dunked, though he could from a lay-up drive. His fingers, his fingertips, his touch were too important to fool with. He didn't want to crack his wrist bone or bruise his knuckles or jam his finger on the front of the rim.

He took twenty foul shots, hitting eighteen in a row after the first two rolled out, then began perimeter jump shooting from fifteen and eighteen feet, starting at the base line, moving three steps to his right, completing the semi-circle and shooting again when he missed any. He hit five straight jumpers from the top of the key and five just inside the key after driving from left to right, then practiced more foul shots until he hit ten.

Others were on the court now, lazing through hook shots and lay-ups. He went back to the locker room, drank water, stretched again and then went out and practiced—short jumpers, eighteen-foot baseline jumpers, foul shots. He needed an intense warmup now, at thirty-five, to give himself inner momentum, confidence that he could score from anywhere he wanted. Everyone else in the NBA was sensational, and it took everything he had to keep his sharp edge.

On the bench after the introductions, Harrington, looking as sharp as when he had led Boston to championships, told them they were good enough to beat the piss out of Atlanta today or any day, and they walked out onto the court to a standing ovation. The Garden was sold out for the first time in a year and a half.

He scanned the crowd behind the bench looking for Tom. Not a sign of him, and still not a word from him.

They leaped to a ten-point lead; the Garden roared, and he felt sensational, scoring six of the first ten, feeding Jackson on a perfect fast break for two more. And when they broke to a 35–20 lead in the second minute of the second quarter and came off the court for a television time-out with the crowd ecstatic again (time-outs for television commercials being planned to co-incide with crowd enthusiasm) he thought they really could be good if they wanted to be.

"We've got them by the nuts," Harrington said. "Just keep hitting and playing tough defense against the stiffs and we'll bury the pricks."

"It's Sunday, don't swear so much, Quinn," Holloway said, and they laughed and flicked their hands together and walked easily back onto the court to the increasing roar for victory. Boston did love its basketball, and if they kept winning Quinn could be their coach for life.

He hit a quick, twenty-foot jumper from the left. Atlanta

missed, Jackson got the rebound and B.D., playing point guard now, slowed things a touch and brought the ball up into the middle, then drove to the left and moved right without the ball, took a pass from Holloway, drove to the baseline and hit Jackson with a pass underneath while looking away. He stepped and slam-dunked it. They slapped hands going back on defense.

Playing was fun again. As soon as the game was over he'd call Stephanie and plead with her to meet him in Phoenix on Wednesday night so they could make love before and after the game.

B.D. took Jackson's outlet pass on the run to the left after he'd rebounded a missed jump shot, drove hard to the top of the key, head-faked, moved nicely behind a screen to the right, hit the jumper and got fouled coming down. The contact threw him off balance and he landed heavily on his right leg. The pain was immediate, smacking through his knee and up into his thigh. Jesus.

He almost fell, straightened, inhaled and let his breath whistle out, then limped to the foul line. It hurt underneath and just below his kneecap. He couldn't put any pressure on it, or move sideways. He'd never had knee problems. Pulled hamstrings and bruised hips and elbows and two broken fingers and a badly sprained wrist, three missing teeth and three broken noses—

But knees: he had to have his right knee to drive and leap and wheel and rebound. To take his beautiful fucking jump shot.

He barely made it to the foul line. Evans asked if he was O.K.

"I'm not sure," he said. He breathed and took the ball from Dave Manning, one of the refs.

"Bad?"

He nodded.

"Where?"

"Right knee. I must have pulled or jammed something."

"Want a time-out? You look gray, for Christ's sake."

Harrington was up now, hands on his hips, watching from the end of the bench.

"No."

"Sure?"

"You're right. If I rim it I'll fall down trying to get back on defense, and maybe ruin myself for life. All right. Time out."

He limped to the bench. The pain was fierce. Ligaments, he thought. He was thirty-five and had pushed himself too far and had probably strained some ligaments.

The crowd was up, applauding. A hand-held camera closed in on his face. He hated both for trying to get inside the privacy of his pain. He had always hated it when the crowd applauded the wounded.

He sat at the end of the bench, his leg outstretched. Gordy Jonson, the trainer, touched the edges of his kneecap with his fingertips. There was no swelling yet.

"Does it hurt when I touch it?" Jonson asked.

"Just below and to the side of the knee, the outside, but not badly. I can't put any kind of pressure on it."

Jonson nodded and unwrapped an ice pack.

"There's no immediate swelling," he said. "A good sign for now. Let's pack it anyway and I'll arrange to have it X-rayed. It looks like a pull. I don't think anything's torn."

"Let's hope not," B.D. said.

A wheelchair was waiting for him when he arrived at the emergency room entrance in his warmup pants and street jacket; the rest of his clothes were in a traveling bag on the back seat. A television set in a small waiting room flicked out the beginnings of the third quarter of the game. Boston still led by ten.

A resident and a nurse, with others watching, helped B.D. onto a table in the X-ray room. He could still hear the sounds of the game. The nurse helped him off with the warm-up pants and gently positioned his million dollar legs. He was a basketball player, just a basketball player who'd been wounded, whose team was playing without him, and he was sure Anderson was already making plans to absorb his loss. A knee injury at thirty-five. Oh, baby.

He was also sure his mother and Kate had seen him get hurt. Maybe Stephanie had too. It would feed her anger. Maury Golden was probably in cardiac arrest, he thought, and smiled, except, of course, all of Golden's money was protected. And Boston would have to pay through the nose even if B.D. were dead.

81

His ego had been torn apart in Los Angeles. Now his knee and probably his career were finished in Boston.

Maybe not. A sprain could mean as little as a week, perhaps two. But by then it would be almost January and the team, without him, would have come apart. He supposed he had to believe that.

They took several X-rays. The nurse and the resident left, then came back and told him they were waiting for Roger Goodman, the team physician, to arrive and read the pictures.

He stared at the floor, waited for several minutes, then moved off the table and hopped to a chair and stood next to it on his good leg. The nurse came back in, her eyes widened slightly.

"I'm sorry," she said, "one of the aides is getting you crutches."

"I'm all right," he said, and hopped out to the lounge and sat in one of the easy chairs in front of the television. He smelled badly of sweat. Christ. . . .

Jackson fouled out with two minutes to go and Boston up by five, and then Evans with twenty seconds left and the score tied. But Atlanta missed its free throws and Holloway, who'd scored thirty, drove in from the right, hit a lay-up, got fouled and made the shot, then he stole the in-bounds pass and hit a soft jumper as time ran out. They'd become NBA champions without him.

Thirty minutes later Goodman told him the ligaments around the knee were badly strained. He was certain nothing was torn, broken or fractured. They would examine him again at the Garden on Wednesday. The only thing he could do now was go back to his apartment and stay off his knee for three days.

The apartment was dark and cold. He swung himself on crutches into the kitchen, took a beer from the refrigerator, went back into the living room, and pulled the phone over to the couch and called Stephanie. He listened to the ringing in all the expensive rooms in his California house, then stared at his leg stretched across the couch and touched his knee again, lightly. Sonofabitch. He couldn't quite bring into focus that he'd been hurt, that it might keep him out of action to the point where he'd lose his timing, that quick edge he needed to get off his jump shot.

A thin black and blue mark had spread along the outer ridge of his kneecap.

So he wouldn't go to Phoenix with the team on Wednesday. He'd stay here and rot.

Stephanie. Where was Stephanie? Still at the Chandlers'. She must have watched the game. Maybe she was walking along the beach now, biting her beautiful lower lip, praying that his career wasn't over—or was, so that he'd come back to California and become something else. What else? There was nothing else for him to do—

He'd heal quickly and play in a week, a week and a half at the latest. After Phoenix on Wednesday, Boston had games in Atlanta on Friday night, in New York on Saturday night, then Philadelphia at Boston Garden a few nights later.

He called his mother. There was no answer at her house either. The world was dead. He had the operator dial her number and he let it ring ten times and hung up.

Tom called him.

"How bad is it?"

"It's hard to say."

"They take X-rays?"

"Right away. They think it's just badly strained. They'll be able to tell better in a few days. I've never had knee problems, did you?"

"No, surprisingly. I'm sure you'll be back in a few days."

"Maybe a week," B.D. said. "Where are you?"

"Springfield. I had an obligation left over from the campaign. I'd drive in to see you but I've got to fly out of here soon to keep a commitment at a fundraiser in Manhattan for Robert Wein, the new congressman from the Upper West Side. Part of something I have to do and then he'll owe me. I'll be in Boston in the middle of the week. Wednesday. I've got to see Ma. She must think I've abandoned her by now."

"That's the last thing she thinks."

"Why don't we go up to Lawrence together," Tom said. "After they check your knee out. It'll give us a chance to talk."

"Sounds good."

"I think it's important that we see her together. Does she look terrible?"

"No, not terrible," he said.

"Do you think she's dying?"

"I think she's just lost weight from a bad cold, or the flu, whatever she had."

"That's what the doctors think. Take care of yourself. I'll be in touch."

B.D. said nothing about seeing him on television on Friday night. No matter what, he looked forward to being with his brother. Wasn't Tom the political future of America?

22

B.D. SHOWERED, STANDING WITH HIS WEIGHT ON his left leg. Each slight, right leg move, each touch of pressure, shot pain into his thigh.

He hopped back to the living room, put the phone back on the hook and snapped on the television, dressed while sitting down, watched the second half of a football game from San Francisco and waited. He was certain Stephanie would reach him soon, and when she didn't he called their home again and listened to the phone ring, then called the Chandlers and let their phone ring into the answering service before slamming the receiver down.

And then it was almost seven o'clock and dark in the apartment except for the sharply defined TV colors of San Francisco and Washington in ferocious line play. He drifted and when he woke Mike Wallace was talking to someone with a foreign accent. B.D. stood up, a bit confused, and almost fell.

"Jesus Christ!"

He grabbed his crutches and went into the kitchen and, after swallowing three aspirins and holding his head under cold water, he sat down at the table. He was as hungry as a bastard. Famous and crippled. A deadly combination if you had to go out and eat alone. He'd fry three hot dogs and heat some soup.

Someone buzzed his apartment from the lobby. Friends in from the suburbs, he thought, all young and shot in the ass with an early spirit of Christmas, dressed for a champagne or cigarette commercial. He'd never done either. Perhaps he would this year.

The buzzer went off again. Maybe it was his mother and Carrie Mallon, needing a place to sleep.

"I'm still alive," he said into the intercom speaker.

"I'm glad," Kate said.

When he saw her seconds later in front of his door, her hair spreading across her shoulders, he simply stopped caring about Boston and the distance between here and California and whether or not his brother was really on his way to New York hoping that B.D.'s knee was damaged beyond repair so he'd be off his turf for good.

"Can I come in?" she asked.

"I think so," he said and moved backwards on the crutches.

She walked across the living room, stopped a few feet from the glass doors that led to the balcony overlooking the river, turned and stared at him.

"It's nice," she said. "It's warm and comfortable, and I like the view of the river and Cambridge, even in the winter."

He nodded and said nothing and then moved to her. "I had nothing to do with it. It came furnished. I'm not even sure who's paying for it. It's cleaned three times a week and someone picks up and drops off my laundry. Not that I need a lot. California and basketball taught me to dress like a bum and travel light. You can do both if you're rich."

"I was hoping you'd be alone," she said. "If I'd called and asked how you were I'm sure I would have talked myself out of coming here."

"I'm glad you didn't."

"I am, too." She opened her coat and sat in the middle of the couch. "I saw you get hurt."

She leaned slightly forward. "Are you all right? The crutches make it look bad."

85

"It's just a question of how long I'll be out, and how much being out will affect my game. I'm not going to hang around the bench playing at three-quarter speed."

"Does it hurt?" she said. She stared at him.

"It does, but not badly."

"That's the first thing I should have asked you, but I couldn't."

He nodded.

"It was tough watching you limp to the bench."

He smiled at her. "You're all right, you know that."

"Thanks," she said.

"Take off your coat and stay for a while."

She obeyed, removing it with confidence, as though she knew she looked better without a coat on.

"You're not on your way to somewhere else, are you?" he said and sat next to her.

"I came to see you, and see how you are. My parents came back to the house with the boys. Let me get you something."

"All right."

"Had anything to eat?"

"Not since breakfast."

"That's terrible. What were you going to do?"

"Wait for a beautiful woman to knock at my door and save me."

"Consider yourself saved."

"All right... There are hamburgers and hot dogs in the freezer. And some orange juice and beer and Coke. And a few cans of peas."

"Sounds good. I'll share it all with you."

He watched her get up. She was wearing a dark blue sweater, corduroys and loafers. Her hair picked up the kitchen light, held it. She slipped from sight and he listened to her working near the stove.

Gallagher called and B.D. revealed the details of his pain and promised to get in touch with him right away if his own plans differed in any way from what Boston would tell everyone.

"It's tough," Gallagher said.

"It is."

"Jesus you were looking good. You'd picked everyone up. They actually looked like a team, a solid playoff team today."

"And last night, too—I'll just have to wait and see what happens."

"What if it doesn't come around?"

He let a few seconds slip away watching Kate. "Then I'll just have to go back to the coast. But please don't print that now."

"I won't," Gallagher said.

Kate came back into the room and sat next to him. "I've got everything going, even English muffins," she said. "Did you do the shopping?"

"A few days ago."

"Better watch it or you'll starve to death."

"I'll watch it."

"You played awfully well this weekend." Her eyes and mouth had softened.

He touched her shoulder, her hair, then moved his hand away.

She hesitated, leaned forward and kissed his cheekbone.

"We can't do anything now," she said. "We shouldn't."

"Not yet," he said. "I'm not sure what's going to happen, but not yet." Not unless I recover and make a commitment for the winter, he thought. The injury had given him the chance to say goodbye to Boston before the winter had really begun, and he'd better take it.

They ate in the kitchen and then she brought coffee into the living room and they sat together. He kissed her, quietly, on the lips. They were full and warm and unhurried.

"Oh, God," she said.

"I know," he said, and did nothing more than hold her.

23

THE TELEPHONE JOLTED HIM AWAKE. HE SAT UP, his heart racing, not knowing, again, where he was for five, ten seconds, and then he saw the clock on the desk against the opposite wall and knew. Two in the morning.

He remembered his knee in time and didn't stand up. He removed the blanket she must have put on him before leaving him, asleep, on the couch.

It had to be Steph, he thought; it was.

"I'm sorry," was the first thing she said.

He breathed against all of the beauty and distance of her voice.

"This is absurd, B.D. I didn't even know. I didn't even watch the game. I found out just moments ago listening to the news. Christ, I'm sorry. How is it? How are you?"

"Terrible."

"Oh, shit."

"I agree."

"Does it hurt badly?"

"No, not badly, and I'm not sure yet how serious it is. It's good to hear your voice."

"And yours, B.D. What's going to happen?"

Holding the phone under his chin, he told her. He rubbed his arms against the cold and his body came all the way back from sleep.

"And what happens after Wednesday if it's serious enough to keep you out for weeks?"

"I'll come home and find something else to do."

"That won't be hard, B.D. There'll be offers everywhere."

He waited for a moment. "My mother's been sick and lost a lot of weight. No one seems to know what it is."

"Oh hell."

"I've seen her and she looks bad, and I think she thinks she's dying. Tom and I are going up together on Wednesday. We'll know more then."

"She looked fine in November." She sounded more distant than the three thousand miles, almost careless.

"She did," he said. "She did have a bad cold. It could just be the effects from that."

"I'm sure she'll be fine, B.D., I'll write her a note."

88

He stood, tried putting weight on both feet and fell back onto the couch.

"Why'd you miss the game?"

"I got up too late because I went to bed too late."

"At the Chandlers?"

"Yes."

"Why? What happened?"

"They threw one of their parties and it was fine until about midnight. And then it got crazy. There was fighting. Someone's bodyguard and a newsman the Chandlers know. Other people jumped in and it turned into a goddamn mess. There was blood in the pool, and threats were made. I thought we'd have to call the police. It was about five before we got to bed. We slept past noon today and then the Chandlers wanted to drive up the coast to look at some horses. I took a few scripts along."

Perhaps she'd said too much, too quickly. Though she hadn't said it yet, she hated him for leaving.

"I wish I were with you now," she said. "I hurt for you."

"I love you," he said. "I think I'll recover quickly."

"You will."

He moved deeper into the couch and thought of Kate and tasted her lips on his own. It was absurd, wasn't it, he thought. He was here, alone and cold, and could stare across the dark movement of the Charles to Cambridge while Stephanie Green was in California, using someone else's house, and he'd just kissed another woman, his brother's former wife—

"Where are you?" he said after a moment.

"Still at the Chandlers. I have to be in makeup at six. Staying here makes everything a lot easier."

"Sure it does," he said. And wondered, didn't it?

89

24

THE COMMERCIAL WAS CANCELLED. AT LEAST HIS part in it was.

"They wanted you to spin the broad in the air and catch her against your chest," Maury said. "Then you were supposed to run off together outside the park, hand in hand. What some of these fags think up to sell shaving cream is unfucking-believable. Anyway, some of their people were watching yesterday's game and got in touch with me late last night. They don't want to change the script."

"That's fine with me."

"They move fast. It was for a lot of money."

"Money's not a problem," he said.

"It always is. You should know that. Someone's always willing to come along and take half of what you've got."

"I'll try to remember."

"CBS is hungry for you if the knee is gone."

"It's not gone."

"Just in case it is, B.D. And I'm sure ABC'll be calling today. You're in demand at the networks."

"For now."

"Things are always for now," Golden said. "Has Anderson called?"

"No."

"He can be a cold bastard. He won't talk to you until you get re-examined on Wednesday. He only deals in certainties, and there's nothing personal and no emotion involved. The perfect fucking general manager."

He took a cab to Faneuil Hall and, on crutches, found a small restaurant with several empty tables and with a stern look on his face to keep any assholes away, he read the *Globe,* and ate two orders of English muffins with coffee. A few of the waiters, young men in white shirts, black bow ties and short haircuts, stared at him, and one smiled. But no one tried striking up a conversation then, nor later when he got up and struggled to the door after paying the bill, and no one bothered him when he got a cab on Atlantic Avenue.

Among the messages waiting back at the apartment was one from Kate asking him to call later in the afternoon, and one from Bill Singleton to call when he got in.

Bill Singleton. B.D. had seen him about a year and a half ago after a playoff game in L.A., the first time they'd talked since they'd been starting guards at Andover. Singleton hadn't scored many points there, but had played tough defense, passed well, and was always breezy and interesting to talk to. He'd played at Princeton with Bill Bradley and known Sullivan and Levine, but was friendly with neither. He spent a year in the Marine Corps along the DMZ. His father had played football and basketball at Villanova, and later made a lot of money in housing amd shopping mall development in eastern Connecticut and Massachusetts. But he had put no pressure on his son to come back to the family business. Singleton had used his father's influence to get an assistant coaching job at Villanova, moved on to Notre Dame for a year, to Colgate for two years as head coach and then to Penn for two more as head coach before Charlie Mulhern, the aging head of the athletic department at Cushing University on the western edge of Boston, retired. Mulhern had been at Villanova when Singleton's father was there and through him got his son to take the job, perhaps only for a year or two while they searched around for someone else. And so Bill Singleton—Andover and Princeton, a quiet, rugged, Vietnam war hero, the kind that Cushing could accept and respect and might even love, a winning coach—brought himself and the possibility of his father's serious money to Cushing.

Singleton had told B.D. and Stephanie all of this on the deck at Malibu while they drank cool white wine and a blonde friend of Stephanie's moved her deeply-tanned fingers across Singleton's right shoulder. Singleton doubted he'd stay at Cushing long, and the blonde, a regular on one of the afternoon soaps, asked why he didn't stay in California to swim and make love. They did— for the rest of the night and most of the next few days.

On the flight from California last week B.D. thought he'd hear from Singleton if he were still at Cushing. He knew from reading this morning's *Globe* that Singleton's basketball team had lost its first five games, and had been blown away Saturday by a weak Dartmouth team. He knew no more than that. He hadn't read beyond the first few paragraphs of any story since the trade, except those in news magazines about his brother and the one in the current *People* that quoted Stephanie as saying she supported her husband's decision to play in Boston, just as he supported her decision to stay with her TV series, though both assignments would keep them apart much longer than they wanted to be. The story carried no picture of him, but showed Stephanie dangling her feet in the pale-blue luxury of the Chandlers' pool. God she looked beautiful, and thinking of her now lessened his need to see Kate again.

But then he sat in the kitchen and called her.

"I thought you'd be teaching now, Kate, but I wanted to try anyway."

"Just one section today at nine. How do you feel?"

"Better, I think. Thanks for covering me."

"I was going to wake you and take you to bed, but I didn't want to hurt you."

"You're very good to me."

They said nothing for a moment.

"What are you doing?" he said.

"I've got to make a couple of appointments and then pick up the boys and drop them at separate places. I promised your mother I'd see her this afternoon. Can I call you tonight?"

"I'll be here," he said.

"Then expect my call," she said.

He returned Bill Singleton's call before he had a chance to

keep the promise he'd made not to get involved with people he used to know.

"B.D. Jordan," Singleton answered. "It's been a while."

"It has, how are you?"

"Doing well. How's the knee?"

"I'm not making the trip to Phoenix."

"It's serious then."

B.D. went through the details of his condition again and asked how his teams were doing.

"The fall was a big success. Hockey and track are doing very well. But our glamor's in deep trouble."

"Basketball."

"Zero and five out of the gate."

"I read about it."

"The easiest five games we were supposed to have all year. Thank God we didn't jump into any Christmas tourneys. We might not have been able to put a team on the floor."

"Why not?" He was sitting on the couch again, watching the early afternoon sun soften behind clouds over Cambridge. The river turned dark green as it moved toward the Atlantic, and a southwest wind stiffened flags atop one of the utility company buildings in Cambridge. Sometimes Boston in December felt like San Francisco—sometimes.

"Did you hear what happened today?"

"Tell me," said B.D.

"Paul Simmons, the head coach, quit before I fired him. There's been pressure from everywhere to get rid of him. The gym only holds six thousand. The university wants to pack it every home game to help pay for the new indoor athletics complex. We're competing with demands for a new library and science building. It's hard to make a case with a terrible basketball team drawing only fifteen hundred for the last two home games."

"Whatever happened to the purity of sport?" B.D. asked.

"I wouldn't know. Simmons was on the second year of a five year contract when I got here, and went twelve and ten. Last year he only won five. He had all of the freshmen he'd recruited pissed off because he wasn't playing any of them and had everything over-structured and disciplined. It got out of hand."

"I don't know him," B.D. said after a moment.

"He never played in the NBA. He coached well in the southwest and then had five good years at Vermont. Things can come apart quickly if the mix isn't right. Whatever, we've got talent. It's diverse, lively, real."

B.D. said nothing.

"Simmons' two assistants, both as tightass as he was, went with him. The only one left is the freshman coach, a nice young kid I picked in his first year. He doesn't have the experience to take the team, and I can't possibly devote full time to it."

"I don't see how you could."

"It'd be impossible."

"I can give you a few names if you'd like, guys on the way out who could be talked into a year or two of trying it. Mike Corvino, who's just gotten five days with Houston might—"

"He wouldn't work out, but I'm sure you would."

B.D. sat up a little, blinked and brushed his fingers through his hair.

"You're offering me the job?"

"Yes, if you're hurt. I know my timing's off. I know how you must feel after everything that's happened in the last few weeks. I—"

"You don't have to explain anything to me, Billy."

"I want to. I'm in a bind. The team has real talent. But there just aren't any class coaches walking the street. I could always find someone mediocre—but that would cause a bigger problem than I already have."

B.D. hesitated. "I'm not sure what you want me to say."

"I'd like you to come up here, to Cushing, just a ten minute ride straight up Beacon Street, so we can talk."

"I'd be leading you on if I did that."

"No you wouldn't."

"I think I would."

"How bad is the knee?" Singleton said after a moment. "Really."

"I'm thirty-five. It it doesn't come around soon, it'll mean the season, which means basketball would be over for me. I can't be out for three weeks and come back and expect to have my edge."

"There's a strong rumor that Boston's going to put the heat on you this week to take Harrington's job."

"That's the same kind of rumor I started to believe in L.A. They know I'd turn it down. Maury Golden's made that clear. The owners are looking for a three-to-five year commitment, and I'd never give them that."

"Where are you living these days?" B.D. said when Singleton offered nothing further.

He should never have seen Kate, never have talked to Singleton. He was making attachments, becoming part of the winter. He should simply catch a flight home now, quit basketball and never come east again. Just slip in and out of Chicago for Christmas and let Tom worry about their mother—

"I'm living in Weston," Singleton said.

"Weston?"

"In a big sprawling house with all kinds of trees and shrubs and a huge pool and patio."

"Then you're married again?"

"Back with Barbara and all of her money. We were only separated when I saw you in California. That crazy actress Steph fixed me up with only made me want to screw. Christ, she almost killed me." He paused. "You on the waterfront?"

"Beacon Street," B.D. replied.

"Good for you, the waterfront's filthy. It looks good from the expressway, but the harbor's a sewer and there are a million rats crawling underneath it. I know, I lived there for a year. Now we're in Weston, with a seven-month-old baby."

"I didn't know that. That's great. Congratulations."

"Thanks, it is great. But I still need a coach by next week."

"Next week?"

"By the end of next week latest. I'm going to run today's practice session. They've got tomorrow off, then a Wednesday night game against Maine that I'm coaching, a game we should win. Come up here and we'll talk about it. I'll send one of the athletic department's cars."

"Billy, really, it's not a good idea."

"Just let me show you around and we can shoot the shit about Andover and other things."

He laughed.

"After Christmas, if your knee keeps you in Boston, we'll have you out to the house for dinner. I might even find you a wild co-ed or two, just to return the favor. And they're here, believe me. Cushing attracts good-looking young women."

"I'm an old man," he said.

"So am I."

"All right, I'll be up tomorrow. You can buy me a beer. Just promise you won't offer me the job again."

"Count on it," Singleton said.

B.D. waited to hear from Kate, and at seven dialed her number and hung up.

He took his crutches and stood and fought off the need to feel sorry for himself. He was a millionaire, had just been offered a major college coaching job, and two of the three networks would sign him to a contract tomorrow if he wanted. He was married to Stephanie Green and his brother was a United States senator.

He swung himself around the living room and stood near the door to the balcony. He smelled of sweat, non-athletic, hanging around the apartment sweat that even a perfect shower could never rinse away, and he'd smell the same hanging around the coast, he knew, as he did here.

He got a taxi on Beacon Street and ate at a small table in a quiet corner of the dining room at the Ritz. Back at the apartment he called his mother. He'd taken two steps putting weight on his knee on Beacon Street and it hadn't hurt, then tried turning in place slightly to his right and the pain almost blew his head off. The knee throbbed now. In the kitchen he held a towel packed with ice cubes against it and let the phone ring ten times.

He put the ice into the sink, waited for an hour for Kate to call or appear at the door, then got undressed and into bed. He knew when he was beaten. To hell with it. No one was going to call now. Not Kate. Not his brother. Not his wife. He turned on the clock radio and drifted away. It was eight o'clock in Malibu and the waves were breaking warmly across the beach and he wasn't there.

25

THE NEXT MORNING HE DROVE IN HIS RENTED CAR to Cushing, finding it easy enough to brake with his left foot.

Most of Cushing was set on a hill overlooking Brookline and the western outskirts of Boston, and Boston's downtown office buildings rose blue in the distant noontime haze. December had turned unusually warm again. The campus buildings were a mix of red brick and stone and the neighborhood it crowded and sometimes angered, especially during its roaring college football weekends, was one of the most affluent in America, filled with slate-roofed tudors and enormous center entrance colonials. Mercedes, Volvos and BMWs slipped from wide, glazed driveways bearing distant, green-eyed women who kept their faces tanned, their hair straight and dark or glossy blonde, their thighs semi-heavy and hungry. Occasionally they would seek out a young lad from Cushing—if the odds were right, if they happened to idle at an intersection where a sophomore or junior, sweatered and clean-looking and carrying an engaging smile, happened to walk by.

Cushing wasn't Harvard. Nor was it Brandeis or MIT or Tufts. Nor did it pretend to be. A small, local, Jesuit college from the twenties through the fifties, filled with unfashionable, glum-looking commuting students from the Irish neighborhoods of Boston and its small surrounding cities, Cushing had begun to grow in the sixties, upgrading its academic programs and deepening its commitment to nationally ranked athletic teams. There were eight thousand undergrads now, about six thousand living on campus or in the blocks of apartment houses to the east in the Brighton-Allston section of Boston. The football team, an eastern power, had been ranked among the top twenty in the last two years, and the basketball team, before its slide, had drawn national attention, making it to the eastern regional semi-finals of the NCAA tourney four years ago.

Cushing athletes went to class; there were no all-athlete dorms.

Finals, B.D. knew from talking to Singleton, would begin in a few days, but many of the kids walking past the wide stone steps of the athletic complex seemed friendly and relaxed. A girl wearing an open jacket and dungarees, her red hair flowing, smiled, said hello and asked how his knee was.

"A lot better," he said and rested for a moment on his crutches before climbing the steps and heading for Singleton's office.

Three students had slowed and walked with him for a few yards and asked how he felt and when he thought he'd be playing again, but most simply stared or smiled and said his name or waved at him. No one had done that at Berkeley in the sixties, even when he was averaging thirty-two points a game in the middle of his senior year and had appeared on the cover of *Sports Illustrated*.

It was nice, though, to be recognized and not pressured. Cushing had made a good first impression on him, had chased some of the darkness from his blood.

Singleton, tall and blond and rugged, was waiting for him in his big, cluttered office a few yards down the corridor from the gleaming basketball court, its five tall windows overlooking the main campus.

They shook hands.

"I already like the campus," B.D. said.

"It's nice, especially on a warm day. Maybe one of the best-looking around."

"On a warm day."

Singleton smiled. "Can I sign you up right now?"

They laughed and sat in chairs beside his desk and B.D. felt a quick jab of pain in his knee.

"I thought this was a Catholic college?" B.D. said.

"It is," Singleton said and leaned back. Team pictures, action shots of Cushing players driving for lay-ups and touchdowns and extra bases lined the walls, and trophies, silver and gold and bronze, struggled for recognition on his desk, in cabinets, and on tables. Where, B.D. thought, have all the young athletes gone?

"Where are the priests and nuns?"

"They're walking around, they just don't look like nuns and priests anymore."

B.D. looked at him, then past him and through one of the partly opened windows to the campus that sloped toward a cluster of brick dormitories where a statue lifted its white arms and face skyward. Cushing. New England Catholic. For a moment he forgot why he was here. For basketball talk. Catholic colleges existed to play basketball, B.D. thought.

"How does it feel today?"

B.D. blinked. "What?"

"I know the campus is beautiful," Singleton said and laughed, "and it's easy here to get caught up in the blonde flow of morally certain Catholic girls in camel's hair coats and smiling faces, but I meant your knee."

"It still hurts when I move laterally," B.D. said, "even slightly."

Singleton nodded.

"I'm being X-rayed again at eleven tomorrow at the Garden. Anderson might or might not call a press conference about it. If he does it'll be a sign that I'll be back soon enough." He breathed. "So, I don't know."

"Will you go back to the coast to recover? If playing's still possible?"

"I'll have to, though that would be dangerous, wouldn't it."

"California," Singleton said and put his hands in the pockets of his dark slacks. He was wearing a brown and gray tweed sport coat, blue button-down shirt and a wheat-colored tie. "That blonde Steph fixed me up with—Christ she was good. And nice. Pleasant. She made breakfast for me and told me all about her growing up in Tampa and going to the University of Miami. We swam and fucked the day away. If I never thanked you formally for all of that, thanks." He smiled.

B.D. nodded.

"Now Barbara and I are in Weston." Singleton looked at the

floor. "Why not come up for dinner tonight or tomorrow night? She wanted me to ask you."

"Thanks, Billy, but it's all day-to-day for me now, and I'm distracted. Tom and I have to travel to Lawrence tomorrow afternoon to see my mother—she hasn't been feeling well. Having to leave Stephanie was hard—"

Singleton nodded. "I understand. Lunch?"

"Sure."

They drove to a small restaurant a few blocks from the edge of the campus and ordered meatball subs and beer in a booth with some privacy. He had turned down Singleton's offer to go the faculty club.

Singleton told him his life at Cushing was good, that excellent coaching could quickly overcome a lot of team difficulties, that the winter program had begun smoothly in everything but basketball. Only nine players, including two freshmen, had shown for yesterday's practice. He was pissed and had sent word out that scholarships could be on the line. Losing was hard enough on the kids, but eventually it would begin to diminish Cushing's overall national reputation, make recruiting in every sport and fundraising more difficult and restrict their teams' chances of appearing on local and national television.

"I've looked hard for someone," he said, folding his hands on the table, "and come up empty. A couple of good high school coaches are around, and a few older former college coaches, Tommy D'Angelo, Barry Workman. Remember them?"

He nodded.

"The schedule gets tough in January, and without someone decent, we'll be lucky to win a game and hold the team together." He swallowed some of his beer. "I'm not supposed to be talking to you about any of this. Sorry."

"It's all right," B.D. said. "It's interesting. Why only nine at practice?"

"Simmons really turned a few of them off, but I think, I'm sure, two of them'll come back. Danny Collins, a junior forward with all kinds of power and shooting ability, was there but didn't look happy. He hates losing more than anyone I know. He's a

100

good kid. He's also six-six and was a hell of a football player at Waltham High. The football people here have always been after him. I'm sure he would have quit if Simmons had stayed." He hesitated. "Some of the others are excellent. Bobby Smith's a talented guard. He was mentioned in *Sports Illustrated*'s fall preview. Heard of him?"

B.D. nodded and drank, and the beer smoothed his blood.

"There's enough talent here to have a winning team. I thought we had enough last year. I should've fired Simmons before the end of the season. It's my fault and I've taken some heat for it, especially in the last few weeks. It's okay to lose for a while if you have the support of the kids on the team, but not if two high school all-Americans threaten to quit and you get your ass kicked by teams you should be whipping."

"What else have you got on the team, besides Collins and Smith?"

"I thought you didn't want to get involved in this?" Singleton said and brightened.

B.D. leaned back and smiled at him. "I'm not involved in anything. You are."

Singleton nodded. "About Smith. He's six-three, a junior, is fast and quick, and has a deadly jump shot. He could become an excellent point guard. Simmons had him moving all over the place, dissipating his strength. But he's a point guard, and was a good one, basically, for Hillhouse in New Haven for three years. He's tough, quiet, bright, and has savvy. Danny Collins is rock solid and unafraid. I'm going to move him to a low post tomorrow night. Chet Davis is six-four, the quickest kid on the team, and maybe the best pure shooter. He could become one hell of an off guard. He played at Cambridge Ringe and Latin where they take basketball very seriously, and he was a *Globe* first team all star."

Their subs came and he watched Singleton bite into his sandwich and wipe at his mouth. Maybe it was unfair to let him go on.

"Donny Cunningham's the other big man at six-eight, maybe six-nine. But he's obviously not *that* big, which, to be honest

101

and obvious, is one of our problems. He's from Elizabeth, New Jersey. A senior. He doesn't score but can rebound and move on the break, and could learn, I think, to shoot decently. He hurries a little, or has been hurrying his shots for the last two weeks, and did last year. He's got a decent left-handed jump shot and I'd let him, will let him take it a little more often from the corner to loosen things underneath for Collins. But he's our only real height and his strength is the boards. Last year Simmons sat him down for two games for fighting with a senior in practice. He's a lot quieter this year, and very bright. He took a post-graduate year at a prep school in New Jersey and was suspended in the spring for being caught in bed with two women, both over thirty. His coach told me that."

They smiled.

"Cunningham wants to go to law school. In fact I think Georgetown's already accepted him."

Singleton told him then about Clayton Toner, a six-seven sophomore forward from Providence with a soft, developing shooting touch, and Luther Sizemore. Sizemore, a six-five junior guard from Philadelphia, had scored twenty-two in the season's opener, and had dropped his shorts a week ago in front of Simmons and his assistants after a grueling three-hour practice, grabbed his enormous joint and told them to suck the defeat out of it, which they could do in a second, he'd said, because they looked like they'd had a lot of practice. Sizemore had been suspended from the last game, but had been at yesterday's practice, and looked terrific.

"Sounds like they've got the potential to be very good," B.D. said.

"The key is really Danny Collins. He could become great, and if he made a new commitment to the team it would have all kinds of symbolic value."

He looked up and saw her then, her light smile and full lips and blonde hair drifting below the shoulders of her camel's hair coat. As she stood before them, her fingers touched the edge of the table. The beer had re-established a California mellowness in the wintered places of his brain, and he watched the freckles

102

scattered on the bridge of her nose and across her cheekbones, and he knew he was making her better looking than she could ever be.

"What's the athletic director of Cushing University doing drinking his lunch?" she said. She put her hands in her pockets and hunched her shoulders slightly. A lot of care, and training, he thought, had gone into the way she stood now, and he thought he knew her from somewhere.

"Still trying to cling to my youth," Singleton said. "Sit down and join us."

"Just for a second." She sat beside him, facing B.D. "I'm with two other girls. We're trying to decide whether to start studying for finals tonight or simply get stoned for a week and a half." She nodded to B.D. "Hi," she said.

"Hi."

Singleton introduced them. "Janet and my wife are first cousins, unfortunately."

She smiled gently and he liked her for it.

"We've met," she said.

He nodded.

"You don't remember."

"I should."

She shook her head slightly. "No, you shouldn't. It was in September, in Boston. I worked for your brother in the Boston campaign office. You came through with your wife. We were all amazed at how beautiful she really is."

"Thanks. It was a great campaign, wasn't it."

"Primary night was hard. But election night wasn't."

"I guess it worked out all right for him," B.D. said.

"I enjoyed the whole experience, and learned a lot. Politics can be tough, can't it."

"It can be," he said.

They looked away from each other, then at Singleton.

"Jordan and I played basketball together at Andover," he said. "We're reliving old prep school days."

"Oh—how's your ankle?" she said.

"Knee," Singleton said.

103

"It's all right. It's getting better."

"Do you like being with Boston?"

He nodded.

"Stephanie Green's not with you, is she?"

"Not now. She's filming the TV series every day."

She hesitated, then smiled and asked Singleton something about his wife, a trip to New York, a car they were buying, and looked back at B.D. and said she had to get back to her friends.

"I wanted to say hello," she said.

"I'm glad you did," B.D. said.

"I was a little surprised to see you here," she said to B.D. "Please say hello to your brother for me when you see him, and wish him good luck."

"I will."

"He won't remember who I am."

"He'll remember who you are," Singleton said.

She told Singleton she'd see him, tossed her hair and left.

"It wasn't my idea," Singleton said and laughed. "I'm not trying to lure you to Cushing with anything."

"Nice looking girl. And pleasant."

"She's always been like that. Maybe just enough of a bitchy edge when she has to have one to keep some people slightly off balance. But nice. Open, and beautiful."

"She treated us with deference," B.D. said. "We must be getting older."

"We must be," Singleton said. "She does have manners—Her father's one of the most successful divorce lawyers in the country."

"I don't need one yet," he said after a moment.

Afternoon was slipping in. Midafternoon, with shadows and responsibilities and things to be accomplished. What would he do? Go back to the apartment and unlock the voice of his answering machine. He'd return the calls from the right people. He might even call Kate again and ask why she hadn't gotten back to him yesterday. She didn't have to play some kind of suburban game with him. If she was afraid, then let her tell him straight. Maybe she was simply a cockteaser and that was the reason why his

104

brother had divorced her, or neglected her to the point where she had to divorce him.

He breathed hard. He might never sink another basket again. Tragedy. All of the world's backboards would come tumbling down. Maybe he and his crutches would slip under a car on Beacon Street and become a neat little obit in tomorrow's papers. Maybe that's what he was going to become anyway.

Singleton got the check.

They waved to Janet and the other girls at her table on the way out.

"Want to go over and say hello to her friends?" Singleton said.

"Some other time."

It was almost cold out of the sun now on Beacon Street.

"I'm not quite sure why Janet decided to come to school here," Singleton said as they stopped and breathed and Jordan leaned against his crutches, nodding back at the few students and others who nodded to him. "She could have gone just about anywhere she wanted," Singleton continued.

"Is she Catholic?"

"Yes."

"And she's blonde and rich."

"It's not Wellesley," he said, then shrugged. "There're a lot of drugs and drinking on campus, and there's very little Catholic about Catholic colleges now. Twenty percent of the student body's Jewish."

"Drugs on the team?" B.D. said.

"None. I'd never ask you to come near the place if there were. There were some problems on the football team, but not with my guys."

They drove back to the campus, stopped in the parking lot next to B.D.'s car and got out.

"Thanks for lunch," B.D. said. "Good seeing you again. It's a beautiful campus. You going to spend your life here?"

"No way."

"What's next?"

"I'm not sure. Be my guest here at a game after the holidays."

"I will."

105

They shook hands.

Singleton gave him a long look. "Good luck, Jordan," he said.

"You, too," B.D. said. "And tell your cousin I think she's beautiful."

He was sure he'd never see either of them again.

26

B.D. HOBBLED AROUND THE KITCHEN, HEATING soup, making toast, drinking cold milk. It was six o'clock and he tried to picture her young face again and couldn't, and he smiled thinking of Singleton's offer. A challenge, a way of testing himself.

Kate called.

"I'm sorry I haven't gotten back to you," she said.

"Don't be." His voice sounded more cold than he intended.

"I called earlier."

"I was at a job interview," he said.

"Oh—" She laughed, then hesitated when he said nothing. "Really?"

"Want to hear about it?"

"All right."

"I can't tell you over the phone."

"Then we'll have to get together," she said.

"Okay." He felt himself stir, his blood thicken.

"I'll be there at eight, maybe eight-thirty," she said.

"You want to."

"I want to," she said.

It was almost nine before she arrived, her hair loose, her breasts firm beneath her beige sweater. As she stood near the couch, he kissed her, her cheeks and fingertips still cool from the night, her breath warm against his.

"It's stupid not to keep seeing each other," she said.

"I agree."

"We're going to feel guilty if we do this."

"What?"

"Make love."

He nodded and moved his hands across her body, kissed her neck, felt the shadow and movement of her hair.

"Is your blood pounding as much as mine is?" she said.

"I think so."

"Are we—"

"Don't," he said and kissed her lips again and explored her mouth.

She moved her head slightly back and smiled at him. "How are you going to get to the bedroom?"

"I'll figure out a way."

"Want me to help you?"

"No, I'll follow you."

He watched her slip from her sweater, lay it across the chair next to the bureau, unbutton her blouse and take it off. Her stomach was firm and he went to her and kissed it. She moved a step from him and watched him almost impassively as she took off the rest of her clothes and got into bed and watched him kiss her shoulders, her hard, still-tanned thighs. She whispered no and urged him up on top of her and accepted him, and he moved into her, banishing the dark, uncaring winter. He couldn't believe how good and comfortable it was, she was, his brother's former wife, the mother of Tom's sons, and when she came, pressing hard, then trembling back away from him, he came too, giving all of himself to her. He rested and waited for guilt to destroy him, but she kissed his cheeks, whispered something and guilt stayed away.

She took his hand, worked her hands against his, moved on top of him on her knees and came again just before he did.

"God," she said against him. "I never thought it would be this good, B.D."

He swallowed and felt her bite gently into his left shoulder.

"I don't feel guilty," she said.

"There's no reason to."

"There is," she said, "but there's no reason for me to feel guilty. I just don't want *you* to."

107

He smiled at her and kissed her. "I don't want any New England guilt. I've spent my life avoiding it."

She stirred. "I know," she said. Her skin was hot against him. "I know all about it."

"What was the job offer?" Kate said.

"It wasn't a serious one, not really."

They were at a table against a wall at his breakfast place at Faneuil Hall. He had his back to most of the tables, his leg extended and it was almost comfortable. He was sure anyone seeing him would wonder who he was with, and then someone would know and word would spread around for the next few days and might even appear in print, and Tom and Stephanie would find out.

In the taxi B.D. had asked Kate what they'd tell Tom if he heard that they'd been together. "That's easy," she had said, "I have friends in Boston. I was seeing them and called you to ask how you were feeling and we went to dinner. If Tom was in California, he'd certainly ask Stephanie to dinner, or at least drop by to see her. Besides—"

"What?"

"I was going to say that what we do is really none of Tom's business. But that doesn't sound right." She took his hand then. A mist was drifting across Beacon Street and the cab's wipers pushed it gently away from the windshield.

"Tell me about the job offer," she said again in the restaurant.

"I played basketball at Andover in 1963 with Bill Singleton—he's the athletic director now at Cushing. We talked today."

She watched him. Her lips, her mouth, had been so warm and positive. Enormous amounts of care and work, he thought, had gone into maintaining her hard stomach, her toned thighs. She'd come strong both times, gliding down the white light of her orgasm into his breath.

"I think I might have seen Singleton at an athletic banquet at Notre Dame," she said.

108

"He was an assistant coach there for a while. Once in Malibu Stephanie fixed him up with a beautiful blonde whose name escapes me but whose breasts and thighs adorn daytime television and the pages of *Playboy*. They spent two days together."

"Good for them," she said.

He stared at her. "I'm sorry."

"Don't be, go on."

"Cushing's basketball team was supposed to be good, but now they're zero and five. The coach and his two assistants quit two days ago to avoid being fired. Singleton offered me the head coaching job, effective immediately."

"Wow." She said it softly.

"If, of course, I can't play in the NBA anymore. If I'm so badly injured that I'll be out for the rest of the year. Knee injuries are tough to figure. I've never had one. If I were a six-ten center it wouldn't matter as much. But I've got to have completely healthy knees to play guard. The betting is, I guess, that I'm done."

She waited for a minute, smiled, and then let the smile disappear. "What was your reaction to the offer?"

"I said no."

"Would you like to coach?"

"Maybe for a while, if the situation was right. It would be a way of easing myself back into the world."

"It could be interesting."

"It could be," he said. "I asked you the other day what your plans are."

She shrugged and leaned back. "My plans, simply, are to make breakfast for the boys tomorrow morning, comfort your mother if I can, teach my two sections at school well enough, and be home for the boys in the afternoon. I'll always be home for them in the afternoon through grammar school, but I'm never going to indulge them, or smother them. I'm thirty-two and eligible, but I'm certainly not hungry, or desperate to get married. The boys are good. They're awfully good. It would take a lot for me to put them in another family."

109

She looked slightly away. He knew she didn't want to say the last sentence.

"I thought I was falling in love with Tom again during the primary campaign. But it wasn't love. It was a lot of other things. Physical desire, loneliness, the need to help him. I made the boys available to him whenever he needed them. I was pleasant, and cooperative, and I made damn sure I told anyone who asked what a good person he was. I hurt for him when he lost the election. God did I ever, but mostly I hurt for the boys when he came by and told them. We all cried. Then when Marino died and Tom had the nomination and it became obvious that he was going to win in November and become a senator, I didn't have to fall in love with him again. Tom didn't see the boys as much as he had during the summer and early September. Maybe it was his way of easing them into our separation and his moving to Washington."

"Maybe," B.D. said.

"He could be President. He's deep enough, and he's lived. And he's brutal enough, too. He scared my father and his friends to death when he had to. You must know about that."

B.D. said nothing.

"Andover is a beautiful place," she said after a moment. "I like it in the winter. Skiing isn't far away, and the boys and I love Seabrook Beach in the summer."

"They have a lot of friends?"

"A lot. They're lucky."

"What about you?"

She shook her head and stirred sugar into her coffee that had come after small steaks and salad. "Not many," she said. He watched her put the spoon in the saucer, lift the cup to her mouth. There wasn't the slightest tremble in her hands. "I've really only liked one other place."

"Which one?"

"Colorado. Boulder, especially. I know it's become almost trite to say that. I do have friends there. People I went to college with—have you ever missed New England?"

110

"I missed it a lot the first year I was away. And then I really began to like California. I like southern California."

"Are you close to anyone there, besides Stephanie?"

"No," he said. "Not close. But I know a lot of people."

B.D. thought of Corvino then. He'd scored nine in Houston last night. He'd hang on this year; but where would he be next year?

"If the medical reports are bad on Wednesday, when would you go back?"

"I don't know."

"It could be this week though?"

"Yes."

"I've got to see you again," she said. "More than once."

They taxied back to her car on Beacon Street. He stood beside her, under the bare trees and soft blue street lights.

"I have to get back," she said. "I ache to stay with you, but I'm already late."

He kissed her.

"Thursday night," she said. "Let's see each other then. I've made plans to attend a PTA meeting. My mother's going to be with the boys. I'll be able to stay with you until eleven, later. B.D.—"

"What?"

"Don't feel guilty tomorrow morning. Please don't."

"I won't. I promise I won't."

"You might, but don't let it get in the way of what we had tonight, and don't let it change our plans for Thursday."

"Count on me. And if I feel bad I'll just concentrate on you."

She laughed easily against him.

27

THEY X-RAYED HIS KNEE AGAIN AT THE GARDEN AT two. Roger Goodman, the team doctor, was there along with Golden and Anderson and two assistant general managers.

B.D. sat on a table and Goodman touched the edges of his kneecap, moved his leg below the knee gently to the left and right until he winced, then re-examined the X-rays. Golden was grim and silent. He knew when the value of a ballplayer had slipped and how far before anyone else knew. He and B.D. stared at each other and said nothing.

In an hour B.D. was due to drive to Lawrence to visit his mother with Tom, who told him on the phone this morning what the doctors at Mass General had diagnosed on Monday. Cancer had eaten its way into her spine. No one understood how it had gone undetected, why all the previous tests had failed to reveal it. She was in pain, and would be going into Lawrence General for treatments tomorrow, or Friday. She didn't want to go back to Boston. Death, B.D. knew, had already docked again somewhere along the Merrimack, waiting for the right winter night to slip through its silence and get her. Kate, he thought, must have known last night.

He stood and walked carefully across the room, but the slightest movement right or left drove a sword into his knee and thigh, and his balls wouldn't even permit the thought of taking a jump shot. So, he could drive a car and screw, but he couldn't drive and stop and hit in a basketball game.

"A series of bad ligament pulls," Goodman said after telling Anderson that it was a bad idea to have him walk across the goddamn floor. His voice implied that both Jordan and his agent were assholes for doing what Anderson had asked. "The same thing we knew on Sunday. Want the medical name?"

"No," B.D. said.

"What does it all mean?" Golden said.

Anderson was staring at the floor.

"Weeks, I think," Goodman said, "before he can even begin to play hard."

"Who's he?" B.D. said, almost snapping it.

Goodman looked at him. "You. It's your knee, and your career."

"No shit."

"How many weeks?" Golden said.

Goodman shrugged. He looked pissed. "B.D.'s in sensational shape, but that can only help him when the knee's good enough to practice on."

"And how long from now will that be?" Anderson asked, impatiently.

"I just don't know that."

"Then it could be forever," B.D. said.

"What's that supposed to mean?" Anderson said.

"You know what it means, Sid," Golden said.

Anderson said nothing for a moment, then touched Golden on the shoulder. "Why don't the three of us go up to my office and talk about this. We'll tell the press that today's exam confirmed what we all knew on Sunday, and nobody knows how long Jordan's going to be out. Okay?"

"Sure," B.D. said after Golden nodded.

B.D. used his crutches to reach the elevator and then to walk from it to Anderson's office. He sat on the arm of a chair near the door. Anderson sat behind his desk.

"I've only got two minutes," Golden said, looking at his watch, his voice laced with irritation. He was standing in the middle of the room, his hands on his hips.

Anderson picked up his phone. "No calls for ten minutes," he said, listened for a moment and then gave other instructions and put the phone down.

He stared at Golden, then at B.D. "Where are we?"

"I wish the Christ I knew," B.D. said.

"You ever had a knee before?"

"You know I never have."

"So you really have no idea whatsoever how long it's going to take."

"None."

"Can you dress and sit with the team, at least at home?"

"Of course not, Sid, for Christ sake," Golden said.

Anderson said, "I'm not sure what to do. I need another shooting guard, but obviously I'm not going to find one like you, Jordan. You've ignited us. Holloway couldn't miss on Sunday. I think Harrington might even go on the fucking wagon." He hesitated, leaned back. "But we all know it won't last. We need you back for it to last. Otherwise we're through till next year. You've also been selling tickets. If I put you on the injured reserve list that means there'll be no game day ticket sales and the season ticket sales will stop. They already stopped when you limped off on Sunday. Every corporation wants to take its clients to see B.D. Jordan play ball. Now they might not be able to. Life gets complicated, doesn't it."

"I'll be honest, Sid. If I can recover fast, within a week, then I'll be back and be as good as ever. After that I'm just not sure, and I'm really pissed off about it. This isn't exactly the way I wanted to go out. It's not what I had in mind last fall."

"Don't make it sound as if it's my fault," Anderson said.

"It's partly your fault, Sid. You brought me here, got me fatigued and pissed off enough so I had to really press to be sensational and—"

"You didn't have to come. You could have said fuck you to everyone and everything. You wanted to play, it's as simple as that. And L.A., the assholes, were willing to trade you. The dumb bastards. I'd never trade you, anymore than I'd trade Holloway. I think we could make it deep into the playoffs this year because your playing well pisses him off enough to play well. It's not only attendance, you know. Everyone thought it was just attendance. Dump the wiseass black studs—and they're great

114

ballplayers, too, believe me—get the aging white god, B.D. Jordan, and bring the white, upper-middle class season ticket holders back. Sounds good, but you don't get anything unless you win, and start feeling good about yourself and let the good feeling spread out through the crowd. Coleman and Drucker spread shit throughout the crowds, when we got two or three. They wouldn't go for a fucking loose ball if their week's supply depended on it."

They stared at him.

"I know what you're waiting for me to ask. The next logical thing."

"What are we waiting for you to ask, Sid?" Golden said evenly.

"You want me to ask B.D. to stay on, effective immediately, as the head coach, becoming player-coach when the knee mends, if the knee mends."

Golden smiled. B.D. said nothing.

"I can't offer it. I told the owners I wanted to and they said no. You know why?"

"Why?" Golden said.

"They're afraid you'd say no, and they don't like being turned down."

"Don't try to start playing games with me, Sid," Golden said.

"I'm not playing any fucking games Maury. What I say is the truth. They also think it would be bad to fire Harrington. They say they've got their business to think about and they don't want to start screwing around with New England traditions. Harrington is, in his own way, a tradition. He was great at Holy Cross, and certainly was great here. They want to let him go at the end of the season and then sign someone to at least three years. They're going to produce a winner people will come to see." Anderson looked at his hands, then back up at the group. "But I'm sure I could talk them into something."

Golden smiled.

"If you committed for even two years, I'm sure I could get them to listen."

Golden turned away and winked at B.D., who smiled at the floor. So much for tradition, he thought.

"We can walk any time we want," Golden said.

"I know what's in the contract, Maury," Anderson said. He didn't get up even though it was obvious they were about to leave. He watched them. "Where are we?"

B.D. stood and shrugged. "I'll let you know how my knee is in a week."

"What do you think?" Golden said in the back seat of his chauffeur-driven car.

"I won't be able to play beyond eighty percent of what I've been this year for at least four weeks. And eighty percent won't be good enough. And, Maury, I don't want to coach Boston, not even for just the rest of this year. I don't like most of the guys on the team, especially Holloway. He's always been a moody, backstabbing sonofabitch. I really thought he'd quit when I arrived. The team's death right now. Everything Anderson said about going deep into the playoffs with me is bullshit. We both know it. He knows it."

"What are you going to do for the next several days?"

"I don't know."

"The networks'll take you right now."

"Let me just wait," he said. "Tom's meeting me at the apartment in a little while. We have to spend time with my mother in Lawrence."

"How is she?"

"Fine," B.D. said, quietly. "She's doing all right."

They waited for a light change on Beacon Street, then rode in silence for a block. Two men were stringing Christmas lights around the entrance to his apartment building. Christmas—Chicago. He thought of Stephanie and his defenses broke down and his blood sank into its own agony.

He had called home late last night, no answer, then had called at nine this morning, knowing she should have been up for fifteen minutes, at least, sipping black coffee, going over what she had to do and say on the set. There was no answer then, and when the answering machine had finally clicked on he almost whispered that he was still alive and loved her, but he hadn't spoken.

He opened the car door part way and remembered.

"I've been offered the head coaching job at Cushing."

Golden hesitated, then smiled.

"It's true," he said.

"Singleton make it?"

"He's the only one who could."

"He's got their program streamlined and moving."

"He was one of the few good guys I met at Andover. And he was a good guard."

"Not good enough," Golden said.

"He was good enough for Princeton."

"I know, but nothing beyond that. There's a lot of money in his family. Real estate development, some construction money."

"Don't hold it against him. Some of it went into the Jordan campaign."

"So did some of mine."

"Sometimes you have to sink money into certain places in order to raise a hell of a lot more."

"You should run for governor of California, Jordan."

"I'm too busy hiding from guys who are."

They let several moments drift away.

"Is it a serious offer?"

"Yes. The head coach and his two assistants quit over the weekend, before they were run off campus."

"So I heard."

"And Singleton can't find anyone. When he saw me get hurt on Sunday, he decided to make the offer. We got together yesterday. Cushing's a beautiful place."

"And I hear the women are blonde and great looking, but dumb and unfuckable. The worst kind."

"They're zero and five," B.D. said.

They listened to the motor hum, the traffic swish by on Beacon Street.

"Are you interested?"

B.D. shrugged. "It'd be till March, through March if they made a tourney. Singleton says they have talent."

"They do. I've been tracking some of it."

117

"Smith and Collins?"

"And Luther Sizemore. Maybe even Donny Cunningham."

"I've read about Smith," B.D. said. "He must be awfully frustrated."

"They all are."

"Singleton certainly is, with the basketball team. But everything else is going very well for him. What would it mean? What would it look like?"

"You taking the job?"

"Yes."

"It would surprise the hell out of everyone."

"And what would it do to my value in the marketplace?"

"You're not supposed to care about things like that."

"I sold my ass to Cal in 1963 to get out of Lawrence. I've known the price of things. I want to know the price, the consequences, of this. It doesn't mean I'm going to do it. I'm certainly not going to do anything I don't want to do."

"If you lead them to the NCAA final four, or even come close after their start, you could probably get a high exposure slot with one of the networks for a lot of money, certainly a solid pro or major college coaching job on the coast, for a lot of money. Right now CBS will hire you for NBA commentary, and other things could be worked out. ABC will take you for general assignment work; Cushing's the only coaching job around."

B.D. stared through the window at Beacon Street.

"If you go to Cushing and win, you'll be the center of media attention. Singleton's no jerk. He'll make a big deal out of your being there. So will the Boston press. If you lose, it won't hurt too much because they've already established themselves as a losing team. But it could be a very long winter for you personally if you don't win, or only go five hundred. Win and it'll fly like a bastard. It'd be like going back to college. Except that it's not Cal. Cushing will never be Cal."

B.D. nodded.

"How much did he offer you?"

"He didn't. I never told him I was interested. If I am he'll have to negotiate with you over the salary."

"He might not like that."

"I don't think he'll mind at all."

"You seem close to signing."

"I'm not. My knee's going to heal. I'll be back in uniform next week."

They both knew he was lying. He felt his blood freeze. Fifteen years in the game, and he was never going to play again.

"You going to be in New York for the next few days?"

"For the rest of the week," Golden said.

"I'll be in touch."

28

TOM CAME TO HIS APARTMENT AT THREE. THEY shook hands, then hugged briefly.

"How the hell are you?" Tom said.

"Great. You look great, senator." Tom did, indeed, look successful. He was two inches taller than B.D., and heavier now than he had been in November, away from the insanity of the autumn campaigns.

"You, too, Jordan. What did they say?"

"Same diagnosis as Sunday."

Tom stared at the floor for a moment. He'd been an all-American split end at Notre Dame, one of the best ever to play the position in college in the sixties and not have to carry his brains in a plastic bag at graduation; he had been a first round draft choice of the New York Giants. Then, in a highly publicized move, he'd announced that he was turning down pro football for Harvard Law School, his first calculated move in building a political career. He was giving up all of that bread and stardom for stability and substance. Grandmothers and suburban liberals would remember and vote for him a few years later. Tom's second calculated move toward the White House, B.D. knew, was marrying Kate. He married her for all the right reasons—financial, political—but he'd never counted on a divorce. He had needed to have her around him all the time—though he had never really loved her. Kate hinted as much. But he certainly loved his two sons, and was driving north again to Lawrence now as much to see them again as to see his mother.

"I'm sure you'll recover fast," he said now to B.D. and walked across the living room. His hair was dark, a little too long, and he was wearing a black topcoat and a blue pin-striped suit, a blue television-effective shirt and a maroon and blue striped tie. Pretty conservative for a thirty-three-year-old liberal senator from Massachusetts with a lot of luck and glamor, though the luck had come through Dante Marino's death and couldn't be called luck in public. The glamor, perhaps, had been tarnished slightly by B.D.'s trade, and now by his injury.

Tom walked past him into the kitchen, checked himself in the bathroom mirror and looked into the bedroom.

"What's this costing you, about a million and a half a week?"

"I never see a bill."

"Who does it go to, that crazy agent of yours?"

"I think the team picks it up. Maury figures they've already gotten it back in ticket sales." He looked at Tom and waited for guilt to attack. It didn't. It lay quietly in his blood for a while, cooling.

"I thought we could stay with her till about five or five-thirty, when Kate promised to drop the kids off, unless she's too sick to see them today. She doesn't want to go in for treatments. I don't blame her. Chemotherapy will kick the shit out of her, and there's very little chance that it'll help."

B.D. stood glumly.

"Kate's going to try to talk her into taking them. Radiation first, and then chemotherapy. What do you think?"

"I don't know," he said.

"I don't either."

They looked at each other, helplessly.

They drove north on route 93 out of Boston. Forty-five minutes at sixty-five miles an hour. In a few minutes they were slipping

120

through Medford, and he could see the chapel bell tower atop the Tufts University campus. Tufts—where he'd spent the first semester of his freshman year before leaving for California. Tufts, where he'd fallen in love with a junior from Greenwich, Connecticut, a blonde with heavy thighs and an easy laugh. They'd made love on the warm September campus, in his dorm room, in a small cabin north of Seabrook Beach in October where she'd taught him how to make her come, in a hotel room in Cambridge at the start of Christmas vacation just before she broke up with him. She was another reason, he supposed, that he went to California. She was still a part of him now, he thought, her perfect tennis-tan, her perfect white teeth. She'd told him coldly, while he stood beside her train for Connecticut in South Station, that she wasn't going to spend New Year's Eve with him in Lawrence, nor invite him to her parents' annual party in Greenwich. Yet in the evening of the day of his father's funeral she'd called from Andover. She was staying at a former roommate's house for the night and asked to see him there, as if the train station scene had never happened, as if she'd had no idea that she'd wiped him out. She hadn't heard of his father's death and was genuinely sorry when he told her, and maybe because she was so sorry about it, and certainly because he was still in love with her, he drove to Andover that night to see her. It could have turned into a disaster, but he'd been strong enough to leave after she told him she liked him very much, was attracted to him but could never fall in love with him and never intended to get involved. And so he left her then in the Christmas warmth of an enormous house in Andover not far from where Kate lived, and, ironically, it had helped him leave his mother's house in January.

"What are your immediate plans?" Tom said.
"With the knee, and Boston?"
"Yes."
"I've got to get a few things in order here, then I'm going back to the coast." He stared through the windshield. The sun had already gone from the highway and shadow was quickly dissolving

121

the woods and small hills. "We'll be in for a few days before Christmas. If the knee responds I'll come right back, or even stay and meet Stephanie here. We're going to be in Chicago for Christmas."

Tom looked at him quickly, seemed about to say something, but didn't. They moved past a gray lake, small homes with their bedrooms pressed close to the breakdown lane, a spread of bleakness.

"I'll have to make a final decision, certainly, by Christmas. If I can't play on my knee by then I'm done. I'll have lost everything, or at least the edge on my passing and jump shot—which is everything."

He waited for Tom to tell him again that everything would work out; instead he let several moments pass and then ground his palms into the steering wheel.

"It's going to be tough for me to see her."

"I know," B.D. said.

"I'm glad you're with me."

By spring both their father and mother would be gone, he thought, and how insignificant his injury was now compared to that. Then they'd sell the house and there'd be nothing left to draw him there, except the city itself. He stirred. She wasn't going to die now. Not this winter.

He watched Tom's eyes fill. They drove in silence for several miles, past the distant edges of small cities and towns, the sun catching the top of a church steeple a few yards from a supermarket parking lot. The sight brought back the wooden Methodist church where he and Tom had attended Sunday school classes through grammar school with a handful of other Protestant kids from Tower Hill. But unlike the thousands of Catholic kids from Lawrence who suffered their masturbation guilt, their guilt at missing mass or confession, he and Tom grew up free from religious guilt. There were no sins to commit, and no one would punish them if they missed church on Sunday. The elder Jordans didn't care, didn't push in that direction. Stephanie had talked about the guilt she sometimes felt after lovemaking, especially when he made her come with his tongue, and the dread she

122

often felt in Chicago after her dark, moist, adolescent fingertips had worked too well beneath the pictures of Gregory Peck.

But while Stephanie, all Catholics, suffered religious guilt, they could free themselves of the guilt of having cheated on a test, dragged on a joint, told a lie or having been cruel to their parents simply by going to confession, spilling it all out to the invisible priest and cleansing their hearts and souls. Sexual guilt lasted forever. Social guilt seldom did.

B.D. had never suffered guilt of any kind until he'd gone to California and thought, in his vulnerable moments, of Tom and his mother locked into their winter grief. And when guilt came it stayed for days until he willed it, forced it, finally, into the dark place of his blood while he studied and played and grew. It would have been nice then to have a place to wheel his guilt and dump it free of charge. But he wasn't Catholic, and nothing was free.

Perhaps, in a way, he and Tom had always suffered from envy of Catholics, yet they couldn't stand the righteous expressions on their faces when they came out of mass or confession; and they had refused to learn the names of saints, popes and the holy days of obligation. Once stupidly he had let it slip in grammar school that he didn't know why Fridays were meatless, and later he'd been beaten up by a tough fifth-grader for saying that Catholics were all potato heads. Their parents had never said an unkind word against the Catholics. Maybe Tom, the politician, had gotten even by going to Notre Dame, marrying a rich girl from Andover, getting elected to the state senate from overwhelmingly Catholic Lawrence and Andover, to the U.S. Senate from Catholic Massachusetts. He'd always been able to manipulate his environment to suit his ambition.

It would be nice, B.D. thought now on the highway, to be able to get a prayer just right, get it perfectly on his tongue and lips and teeth, and whisper it through a crack in the window so this darkening New England December afternoon—its bruised sky and freezing lakes and ponds and rivers and barren woods, its history and its god—would forgive him for leaving Lawrence and becoming a man, for leaving his wife in California so he

123

could play out the last days of the only thing he knew how to do well enough to make money, for getting hurt, for making love—Jesus—to his brother's former wife.

"You've talked about acting," Tom said after flicking the radio on and off.

"It would be a major commitment. I'd never be good enough."

"You might be."

"Guys have done it for a lifetime, and become actors from the inside out. I just couldn't walk into any kind of complex role. None would be offered anyway. I'd be playing stereotypes. Besides, everyone would look at me and see my jump shot. I'd never become the character I was playing."

"I disagree."

B.D. looked away.

"How about broadcasting, network television?"

"That's a definite possibility."

"Offers?"

"Some," he said.

"ABC?"

"And CBS if I want to do commentary on weekend telecasts, and an occasional week night from the coast, and the all-star game."

Tom glanced at him. "Would that be tough?"

"I think so."

"I understand."

B.D. lowered his window and breathed in the afternoon. "Have you gotten what you wanted in Washington?" he said.

"Not a bad office. But getting the right committee assignments is tricky. A lot of it depends on promise. Sometimes you can get things because of what you might become, and sometimes you don't because no one wants to help you on your way to becoming it. There's a lot of jealousy and suspicion, but a lot of intelligence and substance, too. I'm going to be friendly enough, as senatorial as a bastard and work hard and learn how it all works and where all of the real power lies and why, just like I did in my first term in the state house. I heard Pa telling someone once that if you know the mechanics cold, know the process perfectly, you can

124

free yourself and stay on top of almost anything you want, and at the same time concentrate on the substantial things you want to accomplish and stake your reputation on. I'm getting along, and not giving anything away. I gave my plans away to Marino last spring and he hung me with them, almost."

"Never give anything away."

"I won't. I'll never screw another senator's wife or daughter, or mother or first cousin or niece."

B.D. stared at him.

"Christ did I make a mistake with Marino. He never wanted to be a senator. And when he let word get around that I was running and he was going to support me, what he was really doing was keeping the field uncluttered, letting me become arrogant enough to think I didn't need much of an organization to win while he kept things open for a last minute one-on-one fight with me. You just never know. He'd built so much power in the attorney general's office that people were really scared shitless of him all during the primary. I still can't figure out why he ran. He wouldn't have liked Washington. He would have had no promise of power there, and would have lost most of the immediate power he had here. Not that you don't have influence as a senator. Obviously you do. But Dante had real power here, and liked state government and at one time was a very good attorney general." He nodded. "A lot of people think he was killed, that there was a contract out on him for whatever the reason. But he was always a crazy driver and the rain was heavy that afternoon. Route 2 can be treacherous. The car really did go out of control. I know some people think I had something to do with it, and a lot more people are afraid of me because of it."

"So I've heard."

"You have?"

"Here and there."

Tom laughed briefly.

"It sounds as if you're really going to like it," said B.D.

"I'll like it."

"Good."

"There's already talk about the vice-presidency."

"Don't listen to it."

"Of course I won't. I'm just very glad I had my education in Massachusetts politics, and this kind of a senate race, before I got there, and that I had to deal with national fame in college. There's so much ass-kissing, so many chances to fall in love with yourself, so many chances to blow the whole deal early."

"There'll always be people who'll delight in flattering you, then fucking you over," B.D. said.

"I've just got to keep remembering where the real power lies."

"Where's that?"

"With the voters. It's as clean and as simple as that. Six years'll fly by. That's what all of the veterans say. It'll go in a flash, so I've got to take care of the people, do a few very positive things, and then get re-elected overwhelmingly."

Tom glanced at him.

"If I marry Diane Collier that might be a little hard to do." Diane Collier was a black woman, beautiful and smart, a definite political handicap for a white senator.

"What are the chances?"

"Zero. How's Steph?"

They were getting close to Andover now, their familiar winter territory.

"She's bitter about everything that's happened, and she's angry."

"I don't blame her."

"Neither do I," B.D. said.

29

THEY CROSSED THE MERRIMACK, AVOIDED THE downtown mill district and climbed to Tower Hill. She was in the kitchen, waiting, when they came through the back door. She looked the same as she had last week, and when Tom hugged her gently, her tall body as fragile as the shadows made by a small

126

table in the corner, she cried hard. He didn't cry, but Tom, looking shocked and then almost baffled, wiped at his eyes with the heel of his right hand.

They went into the living room and Tom sat beside her on the couch. B.D. eased into the wooden rocking chair next to the fireplace.

"Kate's bringing the boys in a little while," she said. She sounded exhausted. Her eyes were distant and seemed amused, as if she were trying to figure out why her two sons were there at the end of a weekday afternoon. She looked at them, then at her hands. "I had a lot of tests done on Monday." She swallowed. "It's everywhere, even into my spine."

They watched her eyes fill; her fingers were twisted around in her lap.

"Your father was lucky. He went quickly. I wasn't with him when it happened. B.D., you were. Wasn't it fast?"

"It was fast," he said.

"Are you in a lot of pain?" Tom asked.

"Some of the time in the last few days. Not now. I have some things to take—You two look fine," she said and smiled.

B.D. said nothing and listened for a minute as they talked quietly together. Then he got up and left and took a long cold drink of water in the pantry, listening to the sounds in the house knit death into the afternoon. He cupped water into his face and dried himself with paper toweling. His home, he thought, until he was nineteen. It was as if he'd never left, and never lived there, and then, for a moment, he could almost hear his father pulling into the driveway after another gray day in his law office, facing another terrible night. Until Carol Fisher. She was his health, his youth, and finally his death. Don't laugh now, B.D. thought. Don't laugh in the half-dark at absurdity. It'll always get even.

Tom came into the kitchen.

"I'm going to call Andover," he said. "I don't think the boys should be here today. We'll go there, if it's all right with you."

He felt his stomach chill. "All right."

127

"We can take them to dinner at Sullivan's, unless you don't want to."

"How about Casey's?" he said.

Tom nodded. B.D. walked out through the back door and stood near their mother's car. He was cold now even though it was still close to fifty degrees. He'd been cold since the first night he got off the plane at Logan. Playing in L.A., he hadn't been cold for more than a few days in a row. Maybe that's why his knee went.

He leaned against the car. For a minute he thought of taking one of the basketballs his mother kept inflated around the house and testing his knee with a hard reverse lay-up. If he made it he'd fly back to California tonight, make Stephanie pregnant, heal completely, then come back to Boston and lead the team to the NBA championship.

He limped toward the back door. Reverse lay-up. Bullshit. He'd run every morning at Malibu when L.A. was home. It had been seventy yesterday in Los Angeles. It might have been higher in the sun along the coast. He needed to go home, to hold his beautiful, dark wife.

Tom was standing alone in the kitchen.

"Is she sleeping now?"

"Just lying down, I think."

"We're going to have to hire someone to watch her, to take care of the house, maybe even cook for her."

"She won't hear of it. Her friend, Carrie Mallon, comes over all the time. She'll be here at five-thirty today—I got Kate just before she left. She's going out, but her mother'll be at the house when we pick up the boys. She might be back when we drop them off. The boys are excited about going to dinner. I don't know why I thought meeting them here would be a good idea. I guess I just didn't think she'd be this bad—and going by the house isn't easy for them." He shrugged. "I phoned ahead for a good table at Casey's. The boys like it. Basic french fries and hamburgers."

B.D. nodded. "When's she going into the hospital?"

"Tomorrow, or Friday. Kate's taking her."

They said nothing for several moments.

"I'm going to fly back to the coast tomorrow," B.D. said. "I've got to see Stephanie, and discuss everything with her."

"I think it's a good idea." He leaned against the table. "I never thought anything like this would happen to her."

"Neither did I," B.D. said.

30

KATE'S MOTHER, TALL, WHITE-HAIRED AND HAND-some and giving the appearance that she really cared about everyone, was in the living room with David and Michael. They cheered when he and Tom walked in and hugged and kissed their father, and hugged B.D.

"We going to Casey's?" David said in the front hall, zipping up his jacket. Michael was pulling on a red ski hat while he stared at B.D.

"Casey's," Tom said.

"It's our favorite place," David said. He and Michael smiled at each other.

"One of mine, too," Tom said.

Kate's mother, arms folded across a blue sweater, smiled up at B.D. "How do you feel?" She hadn't asked about their mother. Maybe she didn't know, or want to bring it up in front of the boys.

"Getting better," he said. "I think I'll be able to play again soon enough."

"We saw you on television," David said.

Michael nodded.

"Some kids say you're never going to play again," he said.

Nice east coast innocence, B.D. thought. He longed like a bastard just then for the dirty, decadent slickness of southern California.

"I'll play."

The boys smiled at each other again, and then the adults did.

"We ready then?" Tom said.

The boys kissed their grandmother goodbye and went out through the front door.

"Good to see you again," Tom said to Kate's mother.

She stared at him. "Things must be very busy for you now."

He shrugged slightly. "They are, but they're interesting."

"Kate told me your mother hasn't been feeling well."

"She hasn't," Tom said.

"How is she today?"

"Better."

"Sometimes Kate tries too god damn hard not to worry people," Tom said on the way to the car.

They ate french fries and hamburgers and cole slaw at a big corner table, and B.D. told the boys about the playing styles and pregame habits of all of the Boston players, making everything up, and then relived great playoff and all-star games, making nothing up.

"You're the best basketball player in America, Uncle B.D.," David said.

"Thanks, David," he said.

"Mike gave a poster of you to a girl in his class."

"You guys are all right."

"And one of my father's bumper stickers."

"No wonder I won," Tom said.

"Martha Gedman," Michael said.

David looked at him and they both laughed hard.

Your mother's beautiful, B.D. thought, and your father's rich with promise.

Kate's car was in the driveway when they got back to the house.

"I'll come in just to say hello," B.D. said, and Tom nodded, the boys running ahead again through the dark, silent night.

Kate came into the hall wearing a dark blue dress, had her hair pulled back and looked slightly flushed.

"How are you?" she said to B.D., taking a step toward him, her eyes and smile without the slightest hint of desire or regret, or love. Maybe he liked her a touch less because of it.

130

"I'm fine," he said.

"We were watching when you got hurt and were worried about you."

"I'm going to recover," he said.

"I hope so."

There was little traffic on the highway and they reached his apartment in forty minutes.

"Do you think there's a chance for her?" B.D. said.

Tom shook his head.

"How long will it be?"

"All of the doctors say the same thing. The winter. No longer than that. Maybe until March."

"When she dies there'll be nothing left in Lawrence," Tom said after a moment, "will there?"

"For me, no—It's still your home base."

"Something I'll always have to remember," he said. "Always."

He got in touch with Golden. "I'll take care of everything," Golden said. "It'll be good for you to get perspective." There was no answer at his house in Malibu and he left a message with the answering service that he'd be home late tomorrow afternoon.

He made himself tea and turned on the Cushing game and settled gently into the couch. It was half-time and Cushing, with Singleton coaching now, was down by ten. He leaned forward and turned the sound down and called Kate.

"Did it bother you seeing us together?" he said.

"No. How have you been today?"

"I felt a little guilty this morning," he said. "Just a little."

"What happened with your knee?"

He told her.

"What are you going to do?"

"That's one of the reasons I'm calling," he said.

"Oh?"

"I'm going to fly back to California tomorrow. I've got to make a few basic decisions. I won't be able to see you tomorrow night."

"All right."

131

"I do want to come back and play."

"I want you to—What about Cushing?"

"It's still open, I think. Singleton's coaching them tonight. They're on television, and down by ten at the half."

Cushing was back on the silent court now, warming up. They looked tall enough, smooth enough. But they were down by ten to another team they should have been blowing out, and with Billy Singleton on the bench.

"When will you be back?" she said.

"I don't know."

"Come here later tonight," she said. "I really want you to."

"What time?"

"Whenever you want. The boys'll be asleep."

"All right," he said.

He showered and then watched several moments of the second half. They'd moved to within two points, and it looked, for a moment, as if Singleton would give them a win before Christmas. Bobby Smith, whom Singleton had praised yesterday, easily broke through double teams and full-court press variations, dribbling quickly and well with either hand, and hit jump shots from the right and top of the key. Luther Sizemore, playing an off-guard, and Danny Collins, at one of the double low post positions, looked tough, quick, promising. But the team wasn't quite aggressive enough, and wasn't boxing out and breaking with the ball. They did have talent, that was obvious, and probably could be taught the right pacing and flow, some of the inner techniques of rebounding well. Whether they won or not this year would depend on how well they shot and kept everyone else off balance, and on whether Collins and Cunningham could be ignited for a whole game inside. They should have been undefeated with their light early schedule, and could be winning tonight, he thought, if either Collins or Cunningham had dropped Maine's six-eleven center three rows behind the cheerleaders once or twice.

He left with the score tied, and picked the game up on the car radio, Cushing behind by nine with two minutes to go. Smith scored five in the last minute, but they still lost by four. Zero and six.

She was at the back door a few seconds after he knocked gently. He held her against him and tasted her shampooed hair and warming skin and felt her heart pump.

"Let's not even talk about whether you're coming back again," she said. "Let's not even talk about it."

31

HE DROVE A RED FORD TO MALIBU IN THE LATE afternoon. It was just under sixty degrees, not much warmer than it had been in Boston when he'd left, and the sun on the beach was flat, pale, distant. There was no surf.

The house was cold.

She'd called at two last night and said she couldn't wait to see him. She'd be home before six.

He went into the bedroom and put his suitcase on the bed and sat next to it. Too goddamned cold. He got up and put on a sweater and made himself coffee, brought it out to the deck and smoothed away a film of salt from one of the chairs and sat back. His house and deck. His piece of sand and chair. He stared at the green ocean. A wind moved through his sweater and hair. He swallowed the coffee and huddled within himself for several minutes and then went back into the house and made two pieces of toast and more coffee. It was eight-thirty and dark now in Boston, he thought. His apartment was dark and Kate was saying goodnight to her children, Tom's sons, and his mother was slipping another pill into her blood to deny the ancient night. He stood and told himself out loud to cut the shit.

He watched the six o'clock news alone. There was no mention in the sports segment of his injury or of his coming back to the coast. Maury would tell anyone who asked now that B.D. had

133

left Boston for two or three days to rest his knee. Singleton hadn't called. Neither had Anderson. Why would he?

He called the studio at seven and got no answer, the Chandlers at seven-thirty and got their answering service and hung up.

He waited in their living room, reading the *Times*, walked out to the cold deck and down to the beach and back until her Porsche rumbled into the driveway, revved and died.

She was wearing faded dungarees and a dark sweater, and though she looked tired and too lean and too pale in the kitchen light, she was still startlingly beautiful.

She hugged him too hard, then stepped back.

"Christ I missed you," she said.

"I missed you," he said and kissed her.

"I'm sorry it's so late."

He stared at her. It was as if they'd been away from each other for a long time.

"Have you had dinner?" he said. It was after nine o'clock.

She shook her head.

"I was here at five-thirty. I thought you couldn't wait to—"

"Don't be angry," she said. "I know you're hurt, and tired— We were on location again, and everything kept getting messed up. It was supposed to be over at four. But nothing's ever over with the damn series. Shooting ran until six and then Stegman insisted on everyone having drinks. There was no chance to call. I didn't think it would get this late. I didn't drink. I hate drinking with them."

He held her again and let several moments drift away.

"I need you," she said.

"I need you, too."

"Let me see your knee."

"There's nothing to see. Just a fading bruise and—"

She put her fingertips to his lips.

"I'm going to kiss it, and then everything else on you, and then let you come deeply into me. I hurt for you, Jordan. I hate everything that's happened to you."

32

HE STARED AT THE CEILING NOW, LISTENED TO HER breathing beside him, watched her prop herself on her right elbow and lean gently against his chest.

"I almost walked off the set last week and came to Boston. I can't stand it without you sometimes."

"I know," he said.

"Do you hurt now?"

"Not now, lying here, but most of the time."

She nodded against him.

"It's not going to get better for a long time," he said.

They got up and dressed and cooked steaks and he watched her as they ate and drank red wine; he thought of Kate and regretted nothing.

"Remember Bill Singleton?" he said.

"I fixed him up with Susan Randall."

"I think he's still recovering from her."

They laughed.

"She's acting, or working in soaps in New York."

"Singleton said he caught her holding her breath in a recent *Playboy*."

"We shared a beach house for a while with two other people. She was crazy then. She never slept, and was deeply into every chemical anyone had to sell or offer. I don't understand how she's still alive, never mind working. Singleton in love with her?"

"He's married into a lot of money."

"Where'd you see him?" she said after a moment.

"In Boston, Tuesday."

"What's he doing?"

"He's still the athletic director of Cushing. He's living in Weston, one of Boston's rich suburbs."

She'd grown up in Chicago, but he wondered if she could begin to understand New England's winters, the hollow loneliness they implanted in the soul, the brutal glare of foot-deep snow at noon, the way the woods and hills turned blue in February against blood-red sunsets that promised spring would never come back, that the snow would never melt, that it would forever be five o'clock with wind gnawing at the empty oaks and maples and whistling high-pitched death songs in the pines. And through it all, through his heart still ran the black Merrimack carrying the dreams of children long dead from the mills out to the ocean that had lured them with its promises of cool summer nights and love. He closed his eyes against his knuckles and thought of Kate and was sure he was going to have to pay a price for her, knew he was going to have to see her again.

"Cushing," she said, just in time. "The only east coast school with good-looking women."

"Where'd you hear that?"

"I'm not sure. From a script Jonathan showed me once."

He watched her finish her steak. Her eyes were half-closed with sleep.

"Did he offer you a job?" she said.

He smiled. "How'd you know that?"

"It wasn't hard to figure out."

"The head coach and his two assistants quit a few days ago. They should never have been allowed to start the season. In any case Singleton's been left hanging. His freshman coach is too young and inexperienced to take over."

"When did he offer it?"

He told her.

"He was the only person at Andover you felt comfortable with, wasn't he."

"I guess so."

He waited for her to get angry. To stand and breathe sharply, laugh and tell him it was over—to walk out of the house and blow her Porsche down the coast to another house already rented and waiting. But he hadn't taken the job; he'd only brought it up.

"If Diamond had offered to make you player-coach would you have taken it?"

"Yes."

"And what if you'd hurt yourself in the next game, would you have stayed on as coach?"

"For the rest of the season, no more than that, and spent the winter lining up other things, solid options."

She nodded. "The Cushing job, now, could be a way of doing the same thing."

"Except that it's college basketball and I'd be in the east for the winter, and the team hasn't won a game. It could turn into a disaster."

"B.D.?"

"What?"

"You wouldn't even be talking about it if it didn't look good to you."

"I guess not. They've got talent—I thought you'd laugh at the idea, or get very angry."

"They're talking about three weeks in Hawaii now."

"That much?"

"And you know what'll happen with that. It's bound to turn into three and a half."

"Or four," he said.

"And they're also planning a week in Dallas, or Phoenix, in February."

He said nothing.

"I know how much you'd hate hanging around, especially in a season when you've never hung around."

They looked at each other.

"I haven't quit basketball yet," he said. "We've been talking as if I had."

She moved her plate a few inches from her, stared at it.

"All right," he said. "The simple fact is that I'm never going to be well enough to play again." He shrugged. "So, it's over, just like that, and I've got to realize it."

She leaned slightly forward.

"No sympathy," he said.

"I'm not giving you sympathy."

He told her then about the CBS offer, and ABC's.

"ABC's leaves me with little control over what I'd be doing, CBS's with a lot of time. And it might be tough just watching."

"I think it would be hard for you," she said. "Almost impossible."

He got up and walked into the living room and lay back on the couch. "The goddamn thing is it's beginning to heal already," he said. She followed him in and was standing beside him, hands in her pockets, her shoulders hunched. "It doesn't hurt badly when I walk now. It did yesterday."

She sat next to him, and he stared out past the deck to the moon cruising at the edge of the cold, velvet horizon. Oh, baby—

"Dangerous talk," he said. "Self-deceptive, aging athlete talk. In my first few years with L.A. I watched guys trying to squeeze one more year out of their battered thighs. Miles and miles of tape on shattered ankles and brutalized hamstrings. I finally learned to ignore them. And now here I am, lying to myself, telling myself that I'm really feeling better." He sat up. "Except that I wasn't fading, or hanging on. I was great. As fast and sharp as I ever was."

She nodded.

"That hurts a lot."

"I'm sure it does."

"But it doesn't matter, does it. Once it's gone, it's gone. Suddenly or not. And I can't burn out thinking about it."

"No," she said. "You can't."

He laughed. "And there's Mike Corvino, driving himself insane for one more rebound in Texas."

"Karen called and told me about it," she said.

"She can't be happy."

"She isn't. She's thinking of leaving him."

"Really?"

"Really," she said evenly.

"Christ—"

She moved her hands across his thighs.

"He's been scoring. He'll hang on for the year. But the price he's paying."

She held him.

"If you take the job at Cushing it'll generate all kinds of publicity," she said.

"Maury thinks so, too."

"Do they really have talent?"

"Yes."

"When does Singleton have to know?"

"Right now. He might even have found someone else, but I think he'd call and ask my opinion on his choice as a way of offering it again."

"Accept it," she said.

He waited for a moment. "You really think so?"

"Do it just for the season and I'll go to Hawaii, and travel to Phoenix or Dallas, and we'll be together again in the spring with new plans that'll keep us together. The winter's been shattered, and we've just got to blow through it. It'll go fast enough. Location filming takes me away from you, but it certainly makes the days and nights hurry, partly because it's so exhausting. There's only time to act and sleep."

She stood. "I can't afford any more anger and pain, any more being fucked over by greedy people, B.D. We'll have the end of the month together, all through the holidays, and I'm sure there'll be time for us to get together in January and February. I know there will." She moved her hands back through her hair. "I've got to get up at six. I'm wiped out now, I really am."

He pressed against her in bed and she stirred.

"I'm sorry, B.D. I really am."

"Why?" he whispered. "What's the matter?"

"I haven't even asked about your mother."

"That's all right."

"How is she?"

He told her.

"That's terrible," she said. "God, I'm sorry."

"It happened awfully fast."

"Can they do anything at all?"

"Just try to make her comfortable," he said. "No one expects her to make it through the winter."

33

SHE WOKE HIM AT SIX-THIRTY, DRESSED IN LAST night's clothes.

"I've got to go," she said.

He walked into the kitchen with her and held and kissed her.

"Take the job this morning," she said.

"I will—I probably won't be here when you get back tonight."

"That's all right. I love you."

"I love you too," he said.

"We'll meet in Boston just before Christmas."

She stared at him for a long moment, then kissed him on the mouth softly and held him for several seconds and kissed him again.

He called Singleton. It was almost ten o'clock in Boston.

"B.D. Where the hell are you? I called your apartment and got no answer."

"I'm in Malibu."

"Shit."

"What's the matter?"

"I haven't found anyone. I thought you might have one or two more names to—"

"I'm interested."

"You are?" His voice rose slightly.

"I am. I'd like to talk seriously about it. Can we get together tonight?"

"Sure. You mean you really are?"

"I'm not certain of the flight times. Maury set me up with all kinds of options."

"There's a hockey game here tonight. I'll either be there or in my office. I'll wait for you."

"Are the kids still hanging in?"

"They were all at practice yesterday. They're going to stay. Most of them have no choice. They came here to play basketball."

"What about Collins?"

"He showed, but he wasn't happy."

"As long as he showed—just so I'll be able to tell Maury, how much will it be?"

"Forty thousand."

He said nothing for a moment. "You're going to have to deal with him over that."

"I know. No sweat. I'll see you tonight."

Golden was at his office when he called.

"The knee's never going to respond in time," he said. He felt his throat tighten. He smoothed his fingertips across the counter next to the kitchen sink, turned slightly to his right and caught the pain again.

"What would you like me to do?"

"Break things off with Boston."

"You're sure—"

"I'm sure," he said and waited for his blood to die and when it didn't he leaned forward and swallowed and rubbed his hand across his forehead. "I don't want to go out scoring three fucking points a game."

"You were one of the greats, Jordan," Golden said after a moment.

"Thanks, Maury."

"Boston's gotten blown away in its last two."

"I know."

"Chicago really kicked their ass last night."

"I'm not surprised."

"There were inside rumors around that they were going to offer you the coaching job."

"Never. It'd be a horror show."

141

"I agree."

"And I don't even want to talk to Anderson. He's a cold bastard."

"He is. Maybe that's one of the reasons he's been so successful—what are you going to do?"

"I've made plans to meet Singleton tonight at Cushing. Stephanie and I talked things through. I'm going to take his offer."

"CBS is willing to get very serious, B.D."

He gave a long sigh. "I just want to get through the winter, Maury, from now till the end of March. Cushing's a way of doing it, the only way right now."

"You're sure?"

"Yes. They play tomorrow night, and I want to coach them."

"Don't even hint that you might consider more than one season, and don't even talk money."

"He already told me the salary."

"What?"

"Forty thousand."

"You didn't agree to it, did you?"

"Of course not."

"I'll get him up a lot higher. He's got a maximum and I'll force him and the school beyond it. This is the best fucking thing to happen to Cushing since it was founded, and they know it."

BOOK
II

1

SINGLETON HAD CALLED A TWO-THIRTY PRACTICE. The game with Fairfield was at seven-thirty. The press was delighted to have pictures and film of the noon signing in Singleton's office with the Reverend David McCormack, President of Cushing University, smiling beside B.D. Jordan to neutralize any crap Anderson might throw out about his abandoning the team.

At just before two, B.D. and Singleton stood under one of the baskets in the silent gym just off the main corridor of the indoor athletic complex. No one else was on the floor or in any of the six thousand seats that threw back the sound of the ball that Singleton bounced once, twice. He was dressed in a gold nylon warmup suit with maroon trim. B.D. had on dungarees and a red sweatshirt. He'd never liked wearing school or team colors at practice.

Singleton sank a ten-foot push shot and B.D. snagged the ball and held it. He'd felt light and in charge and good about what he'd done and was doing all morning. He'd called Malibu late last night, Andover early this morning. No answers. His mother was in the hospital. He'd thought of calling Tom and decided against it. Tom wouldn't be happy with B.D.'s decision. He'd resent this new encampment on his turf, the publicity that would rival his taking power in Washington.

B.D. wrist-flicked a pass to Singleton at the top of the key and watched him leap and hit again.

B.D. held the ball. He'd need only one assistant. They had two student managers and a trainer, and a doctor who sat somewhere near the end of the bench during most home games. He'd talk to the press again after tonight's game. It would be interesting, Singleton had said, to see how many people showed tonight. Only eight hundred tickets had been sold before the announcement.

They looked toward the locker room door and watched Chet Davis and Donny Cunningham move slowly onto the court, each carrying two basketballs, wearing ragged gold shorts and tee shirts. They stopped at the top of the key, nodded and smiled at Singleton, said hi coach, then stared at Jordan who looked away. Maybe they didn't know yet. It was two-twenty. They walked to the bench and watched the others—Sizemore, who nodded to Singleton, smiled at Jordan and dunked the ball the first three times he touched it before moving to the foul line—and Smith and Toner.

Sizemore said wow when Smith, silent and shooting only the fifteen-foot jumpers B.D.'d watched him hit on television Wednesday night, hit five in a row.

At two-forty Danny Collins was the only player not there. He'd have to find him today if he didn't show, and convince him to play, though B.D. certainly wasn't going to spend his first day at Cushing begging.

Singleton clapped his hands and signalled them over to the bench and they sat and eased back.

"Jordan going to put on a passing clinic for us?" Davis said.

"No one believes the rumor I passed on in the locker room," Sizemore said.

"What's the rumor, Luther?" Singleton said, squeezing a ball in front of his chest.

"That Jordan's our new head coach."

They stared at him. Cunningham smiled lightly.

Singleton hesitated, held the ball at his side.

"As you know," he said easily, "B.D. Jordan was suddenly traded to Boston two weeks ago, and then last Sunday hurt his right knee. Yesterday he formally retired from professional basketball, and at noon today signed on to coach you guys for the rest of the season, effective immediately."

146

They looked slightly stunned, unsure. Smith leaned forward and tightened one of his laces.

"So, I give you your new head coach, B.D. Jordan."

They hesitated, looked at one another, then back at him.

"It's not a dream, for Christ's sake," Singleton said. "Jordan and I have known each other for a long time. We played together during his post-grad year at Andover. He's here and you're going to win tonight and go on to win a hell of a lot more."

They applauded, quickly and well.

"My knee hurts," B.D. said after a moment.

They laughed.

"So why don't we go back into the locker room for a few minutes. I'll tell you how I got here, and I'd like to go over a few offensive and defensive changes for tonight's game. I want to keep everything as simple as possible, but keep the passing crisp, the shooting positive and the blocking out very physical. Maybe that's the most important thing of all. We've got to hit inside."

Singleton had walked to the end of the bench while he was talking, nodded and disappeared.

B.D. sat on a table with a blackboard behind him, and they sat on the locker room floor and benches facing him. He asked if there were any questions.

"We're zero and six," Chet Davis said, his voice a bit too quick. "You were an NBA all-star. Why us? Why now? I find it all a little hard to understand."

"The rest of you agree?"

Smith and Sizemore nodded.

"Singleton and I have been friends for a long time. We were guards in sixty-three at Phillips Andover. We've stayed in touch. When Simmons quit and I got hurt he called and asked if I was interested. I was. He couldn't tell you that he and I had been talking. It would have made things impossible. I know you're zero and six. But I watched part of Wednesday night's game and know you shouldn't be. You've got a lot of talent, and can win."

"Danny's missing," Sizemore said.

"We'll talk about that." He let a few seconds slip away. "I want you to understand that nobody's doing anybody any favors here. I'm being paid. My agent, Maury Golden, doesn't think it's nearly enough, but I'm being paid."

They laughed again.

"I had options. I wanted to do this. So, let's just play basketball. The press and television'll be around for a while, out of curiosity, and if we start winning they'll stick around. But that's fine. It'll only make us better."

"We're going to need Collins to win," Cunningham said. "I'll get killed inside without him."

Toner agreed. "He can be a mean bastard on the floor. The arms on the guy. He could club someone back to the stone age."

"Where you still hunt for pussy, Doc," Sizemore said and they laughed at each other.

B.D. smiled. He couldn't get too close to them. Jesus—

"Where is he?"

No one answered.

"We can't rely on only him. If he doesn't show tonight we'll have to adjust and win without him. I agree that he's good, and could become great, and for this one time I'll see if I can find him and talk to him after practice. All right?"

"All right," Cunningham said.

"I want to simplify the offense. I know all of you move well enough, and can shoot. So I want to set the offense where everyone's a threat, though obviously some of you are going to shoot and score more than others. But whatever evolves, promise me that you'll shoot if you have the shot. Take it, unless someone's closer with a better one. No gunning. No bad shots, but if you're free for something you know you can hit, don't be afraid to put it up."

He'd build on what Singleton had begun on Wednesday night. Bobby Smith at point guard; Collins, if he were still on the team, at a moving low post with Cunningham on the other side; Davis and Sizemore on the wings with Davis on the left; Toner a frequent sub at one of the wings and for Cunningham. Collins

148

and Smith would have to play most of the game, and B.D.'d have to find at least two more players.

"We don't have Fairfield scouted that well," he said, "so we'll have to match our defense to what they throw at us, and to what the situation is. We'll start, in any case, with a two-three and then a three-two zone, and maybe a two-one-two, just to throw them off balance, and an occasional zone trap and man-to-man press. We'll go full court man to man if we fall behind, too far behind. But pacing is important, and I don't want to blow all of our energy in the first half."

"Fairfield hasn't played anyone," someone said.

"Neither have we," Davis said.

"We will soon enough," B.D. said with just enough edge on it. He waited. "All right. Let's go out and move through the point guard offense Singleton had you in, with Toner in Collins' place for now. And then we'll flow through some defensive patterns. Remember we have a game tonight, so we won't make this very long or too intense. No one has to prove anything to me—And one last vital thing here."

They stood and looked at him.

"Have a good time. Basketball has to be a good time."

They applauded him again.

He walked, then ran them through basic point guard, double low post offensive patterns, with Cunningham moving outside to take his jump shot every once in a while to keep the defense loose, and Davis freeing himself on the left for his jump shot, setting screens and picks for Smith before moving to his left again.

He walked them through defensive patterns and then studied their moves in a short four-on-five scrimmage, and ended practice at ten of four with a brief shooting and rebounding drill and quick exercise on boxing out on any kind of shot.

"Dress at about six forty-five," he said at midcourt. "Play hard. Don't be afraid of making mistakes, of missing shots or fouling out."

They put their hands together for a quick, sharp "Yes!" It surprised him.

Smith and Davis stayed on the court with him when the others jogged to the locker room.

Davis went to the foul line.

"You're really going to be here for the season then?" Smith said. He was lean and hard and sweat poured across his face.

"Bet on it."

"No matter what?"

"No matter what."

"And then what?" Smith said.

"I don't know."

"I'm a junior. It would be nice to look forward to some stability. We're all embarrassed by this season, what's happened to us."

"I understand."

"Did you ever play on a losing team?"

"Never."

"Neither did I till this one." He took a few steps toward Davis, sinking fouls, getting his own rebounds, dribbling back and putting the ball up again from the foul line. "Who's going to help you?"

"Who's going to be the assistant coach, you mean?"

He nodded.

"I don't know. Singleton's looking around. Tony Gordon's going to stay with the freshmen."

Smith smiled slightly.

"What do you want to ask?" He knew what Smith wanted to ask.

"Never mind," he said, but said it a bit too carelessly and started walking toward the foul line again.

"Wait a minute, Bobby," he said and Smith turned to face him. "No bullshit now. I'll pick who I think is good and who'll be able to work with me, black or white."

Smith didn't move.

"You're the point guard," he said and walked up to him.

"I know that."

"You've got to know it, and got to know how important and good you are. Everyone is. You don't need a black coach or a white coach, all you need is room to play well and win so when you get out of here next year you'll be flooded with options." He was beginning to sound like a television commercial, and he promised himself it was the last time he ever would. "I don't have time to look for quality and color."

"I only wanted to ask about it," Smith said, sounding neutral. "Don't be angry."

"I'm not angry. I'm being honest with you." He'd already said too much and knew it.

They reached Davis at the foul line.

"What's your foul shooting percentage?"

"Sixty-five, I think," Davis said.

Smith laughed, thank God. "It's more like forty."

"Up yours, Bobby. What's yours, eighteen?"

"Eighteen in a row without looking," he said and hit a quick jumper.

"Can I tell you something?" B.D. asked.

"Sure," Davis said.

"You're releasing too high. Drop the ball about two inches and move it an inch or two to the right. You'll be able to follow through better." He smiled. "Try it for a while. If it doesn't work or feel comfortable, go back to what you've been doing."

Davis missed two in a row, hit the next three with Smith under the basket feeding him.

"Nice," B.D. said. "But use whatever you feel good with. See you guys about six-thirty."

"How's the knee?" Smith said. He'd caught up to B.D. at the locker room door.

"It hurts."

"Badly?"

"Sometimes," he said and then told Smith what had been pulled and how long it would take to heal.

"I'm sorry about just now, coach."

"Don't be."

He nodded slightly.

"It's just that we all expected a lot better than what's happened, and our response to just about everything is to be pissed off or wiseass. Having a black assistant really isn't an issue, at least not an important one with me."

"Is it with Davis?"

"No. We both just want to win badly."

"You will. We're going to win a lot of games."

Singleton was in his office, talking to someone on the phone about him. B.D. sat in front of the desk and watched darkness move across the campus, dissolving the colors of the buildings and defining the lighted windows in the distant dorms. The sky above Boston had already turned black-green.

As soon as Singleton had hung up the phone lit again. He left that call and the next for his secretaries.

"I know you're big, Jordan, but I didn't think it would be this big. All of the papers and magazines and television, local and national, want a piece of the action. We might even sell out, which is incredible."

"I guess we'll have to win then."

"Psyched?"

"Yes."

Singleton studied him. "How'd they look?"

"Good. They can shoot and move and they're bright. And there's a lot of talent. But we need Collins. It's just going to be impossible otherwise."

"He didn't show at all?"

B.D. shook his head.

"They're supposed to call if they can't make practice. It's a rule I've reinforced this week."

"Why don't we find him and talk to him?"

"Now?"

"I'd like to."

"I can't. I'm really up to my neck here."

"I'll look then."

Singleton told him how to get to Collins' dorm and room.

"If he's not there, and he might not be at this time on a Saturday afternoon after having missed practice, then he might be at his girlfriend's apartment at B.U., Linda Murphy."

"I'll look around."

They stood.

"It would make everything a hell of a lot easier if we won tonight, wouldn't it, and ignite belief and enthusiasm."

"It would," Singleton said and looked then as if he hoped he hadn't made an enormous mistake. Jordan had brought instant promise and attention, and he'd set himself up to take a wicked beating if things didn't go right.

Collins lived in a corner suite on the second floor. Rock music and female laughter drifted from some of the other rooms and sections of the floor. Only light and silence slipped from underneath Collins' door. B.D. knocked and waited, then knocked again and heard stirring and a male voice, neither deep nor particularly threatening, told him to wait a second. He should have called first. What if Collins' girl were with him now, and they'd been making love?

Collins swung open his door. He was big, bigger and more rugged than he'd looked on television, dressed in a gray tee shirt, dungarees and sneakers. B.D. sensed, as Collins stepped a half step back into his room, registering surprise at seeing B.D. Jordan at his door, that he moved well and would be hard to drive on. He looked as if he could block down, get up and catch anything thrown over the middle. In the spring he'd done the hundred in nine-nine.

B.D. introduced himself and they shook hands.

"Congratulations," Collins said. "I just heard."

"On the radio?"

"Just a little while ago. I'd been studying and flicked it on for a break. It's been quiet here this afternoon."

B.D. waited. "What are you studying?"

"Economics."

"Your major?"

"I think so."

He waited, then said, "Are you still on the team?"

153

"I don't know—" Collins walked back into his room and sat at his desk beside a window with a sweeping view of the lower campus. Two books and a notebook were open on the desk. "Come in," he said.

B.D. sat on the arm of a chair. There were two other desks in the room, and two smaller rooms off this one.

"It's true then," Collins said. "You really are here."

"Till the end of the season, for however long it goes."

"Why? Can you tell me why?"

"That's what everyone else wanted to know," he said and told him what he'd told the others.

"It's a little hard to grasp."

"I know, but you'll get over that right away."

"I've got three exams next week," Collins said. "Economics, Comparative Government and American Lit."

"That's what I majored in at Cal."

"What?"

"American Lit." He folded his arms and looked at the floor. It was hard not to like Collins. He breathed an immediate sense of quiet self-confidence, probably because of his size and good looks and easy smile. And yet he seemed vulnerable, unhappy. "A long time ago."

Collins looked at him, and then away. "I fouled out Wednesday night. I scored twenty-two but I should have had forty. No one was on me tight. I kept missing the jumper. We should have won."

"Maybe you were taking it too far out, or not taking it inside enough."

"That's what Singleton said. But the way we've run the offense for the last year and a half always frees me at twelve to fifteen feet, and then tires me out. Singleton had me underneath more, and insisted that I move less. It helped." He flipped a pencil onto the desk. "I was ready for a good year. I really was. But Simmons and his two coaches—talk about negative shit and overcoaching."

"They're gone."

"I know they're gone," Collins said and got up and slipped his fingertips into his pockets. "I made a decision yesterday to quit. I was going to walk over and tell Singleton about now."

"Are you?"

He said nothing.

B.D. got up.

"I want you to play, Danny. Obviously, that's why I'm here. You'll stay at one of the two low posts, most of the time, but with all kinds of chance to maneuver inside. Cunningham'll be out a little higher, and move to the right corner once in a while to give you room. Smith's going to be at the point, all the time, with Sizemore and Davis at the wings and Toner subbing. We're not going to run right away. I don't think the team's deep enough or in good enough shape, but we'll break when it's a good idea. And we'll take it to the basket and hit the boards more. I want you to shoot inside, it's part of your strength. If they're collapsing or double-teaming you, you can always go behind a screen, or move outside and then go backdoor. But your primary thought has to be to take it to the basket, and to hell with anyone dumb enough to be in your way. We'll use fewer man-to-man defenses, and stay mostly in a two-three or two-one-two zone tonight, unless we have to go full-court man-to-man to pressure them, or catch them. Ever play the two-one-two?"

"All the time in high school."

"Be there tonight at six-thirty."

Collins looked at the desk.

"Okay?"

"Okay," he said. "I'll play tonight. But there are other things I'd like to talk about, later."

"Any time you want," he said. "We'll win tonight. I know we will. I need it as much as you guys do."

155

2

HE GOT TO HIS APARTMENT AT FIVE-THIRTY. THERE were no messages from Kate, or Stephanie, or his brother or Maury Golden.

He sat in the living room and stared at a gentle mist blowing across the top of the Charles. The windows in the expensive apartment houses along Memorial Drive flickered with indifference. He made himself soup and toast and drank a glass of milk, then showered and shaved and dressed in a blue shirt and tie, sport coat, slacks and loafers. He hadn't dressed for anything since the night he and Stephanie had gone to dinner with the Corvinos and Karen had choked up and cried on the patio of their home, which was probably still for sale.

He avoided watching or listening to the news and drove back to Cushing, getting there at six. Smith, Cunningham, Davis, Sizemore and Toner were already there, dressing, silent and staring at the floor. Casey Swift, Frank Shaughnessey and Jamie Watkins—none of whom, except Swift, would see any playing time unless it became a blowout—were talking quietly a few lockers away. Only Orlando Carter, the tenth man, and Collins were missing.

Out on the gym floor the freshmen were losing by ten with three minutes to go. He'd take two freshmen next week and carry twelve players. He walked to the edge of the stands where Singleton was waiting and watched Tyler Young, one of the guys he'd move up, hit a twenty-foot jumper. The stands, half full and filling, responded with too much noise. He felt his blood pump. It was, he thought, a good night to begin.

"I'm nervous," Singleton said.

"See Collins?" B.D. asked.

"We talked in his room and he said he'd play."

"Good."

"He's not here yet."

"He will be if he said he's going to be," Singleton said.

"I'll ask Tony if he wants to sit with me on the bench."

"It'll be good for him."

"I just hope Smith responds well at the point, and keeps Collins underneath as much as he can. He can't foul out. Smith, I mean. Davis'll take the point if he has to, but both he and Toner are a little too slow for it. I'm going to use Sizemore on the wing to the right, Collins underneath on the left. Toner can come off the bench for Cunningham, and then spell Collins for a minute or two." His voice was just a touch too high and quick. "I'm going in with the guys," he said.

Singleton smiled and they shook hands.

"Good luck, Jordan," he said.

Collins was in the locker room getting dressed. He nodded to B.D. and B.D. nodded back.

He got their attention and went over their basic offensive and defensive patterns again. They'd open in a two-one-two zone. They might, he said, have to adjust quickly depending on the early flow.

"Any questions?"

There were none. He felt the tension waft off their bodies, and when someone opened the locker room door he could taste the force of the crowd.

"Warm up easy," he said. "Two lanes of easy lay-ups, right, left and then a little harder down the middle. Dunk if you want, but don't slam or strain it. Stay within yourselves after that and practice what you're going to take in the game. The crowd'll be screaming. It's Saturday night and everyone's here." He looked them over. "I'll try not to talk as much next time."

They got up and clapped their hands. All except Collins, who hung back a little. Sizemore, so loose and breezy in practice,

157

looked stunned for a second, then took a deep breath and whispered obscenely what they should do to Fairfield.

Their appearance ignited the crowd. Big-time college basketball, local television and a sold-out gym. He remembered other, intense, deafening entrances, at home and on the road with Cal. There'd been nothing like this since. Cheerleaders, college voices, and a good brassy band roaring.

Christ he was high now and he breathed deeply and leaned slightly forward as his team went into its lay-ups, doing them much too fast, photographers snapping away, someone's hand-held camera tight on the right side of his face.

B.D. waved to the crowded press table. Some of them waved back. He had talked to Gallagher, who didn't cover college sports, last night. He didn't see him now.

He put his hands in his pockets and walked onto the court, the crowd calming.

"Slow it down," he said to Bobby Smith. "Ease back. Let's not leave it all in the warmup."

Smith obeyed and then the introductions were being made and there was a roar when his name was announced.

Fairfield got the opening tap. Their low pivot man hit a soft banking hook shot to his right while Collins fouled him. Fairfield sank the foul and Sizemore threw the in-bounds pass into the hands of the man guarding Bobby Smith in their surprising man-to-man full-court press, and he stuffed the ball. Five to nothing with less than thirty seconds gone, and the full-court press again forced Davis to lose his dribble out of bounds near mid-court. Fairfield worked the ball for a minute before their point guard hit a jump shot from the top of the key.

7–0.

Time out.

The crowd was almost silent. He thought he heard laughter. They sat on the bench and leaned forward as he kneeled on his good knee in front of them. The band had begun the Cushing fight song.

"Smith'll pass the ball into Davis or Sizemore if we get full-court pressure again. Danny, stop at mid-court, then come back into the back court for the lob pass from Bobby. Donny goes to the corner to take a man out of the initial action. Don't be afraid to throw the ball the length of the court if you have to. This is just the beginning of the game. They're not going to run seven straight against us like that again."

They put their hands together.

"Let's score," he said, maybe too sharply, and they came up with a shout and walked back.

He felt sick. How'd he ever get himself into this? What madness had trapped him? It was Saturday afternoon in California and his beautiful wife was there, making love to someone else, and would soon have her lawyer draw up a quick divorce settlement.

He stared at Singleton seated next to Father Joe Flaherty, who'd been to every Cushing home game for the past twenty-seven years. Singleton shrugged and raised an eyebrow and he knew Singleton was in as much agony now as he was. If they got blown out tonight—they wouldn't get blown out. They wouldn't lose. They were too good to lose again.

Smith got the ball back from Davis and easily beat the press over half-court, lobbed a pass to Cunningham in the corner who whipped it back to Smith at the key. He drove right, hit Davis open on the left and Davis, alone, sank a fifteen-foot jumper. The crowd exploded. He stood and applauded. They'd looked sensational and moved back into a tight two-one-two zone. Fairfield missed a jump shot and Collins cleared the boards with his elbows smacking the air and the crowd erupted again. Smith hurried over half-court, slowed until Collins worked himself free underneath and stuffed the lob pass.

7–4.

Smith stole the in-bounds pass, darting in on his own to do it, and hit a ten-foot jumper, and five seconds later Fairfield threw the ball out of bounds. Smith hit another jump shot for the lead. The crowd was almost overwhelming now, an enormous physical pressure that sustained itself.

They traded baskets, foul shouts, and with seven minutes left

159

in the half, the score hung at twenty-eight all. Collins had picked up two fouls and B.D. moved him to the corner of the zone where Fairfield seldom shot. He needed Collins in the game. He'd already scored twelve, had thrown Fairfield's six-ten center across the floor in a ball possession struggle, and had pointed his finger warning one of their forwards after being fouled on a breakaway lead from Davis.

Cunningham tipped in a Davis miss.

30–28.

B.D. sent them into a quick, man-to-man full-court press with Cunningham guarding the in-bounds pass, forcing Fairfield to throw the ball out of bounds again.

Collins hit a jumper from the corner. Toner, in briefly for Davis, sneaked behind Fairfield's point guard at half-court, stole the ball from his dribble, drove and slam-dunked it. They were breaking away, and with luck, B.D. thought, they could sustain it into a big win. But Smith got called for his third foul and Sizemore and Davis their second each. B.D. slowed things down, fell back into a tight two-three zone and they led 42–38 at the half.

They were alive and composed in the locker room. He let them lie back and suck on oranges, then stood and told them how well they were playing, that Collins, Smith and Davis should keep playing tight, tough defense and let him worry about their fouling out.

"If we get the second-half tap, we'll run a little off the clock, if they're in a zone. If not we'll take it to the basket right away. I want them to have to think a little bit about what we're going to do next."

He stepped back and waited.

"Anyone want to ask or say anything? You really are doing fine. And nothing's going to take this one away from us. We're going to win it."

They got the tap. Fairfield fell into a tight zone, and Smith and Sizemore and Davis ran two minutes off the clock before Collins slipped free for a quick lay-up. They were up by ten at the five minute mark, by nine at the ten. But Smith and Sizemore had picked up their fourth fouls, and Collins and Cunningham had three. And then Collins, with Cushing visibly tired and leading by eight with seven minutes to go in the game, stepped in front of a driving guard and got called for a blocking foul. Collins fell backwards and came up angry and Sizemore and Cunningham held him back from getting a technical—with Jordan shouting that it was an asshole call.

"Don't swear at me," the referee said from ten, then five yards away. "I'll let you get away with that, but consider yourself warned."

"It was an obvious charge."

"Sit down. This isn't the NBA."

"Don't tell me what this is or isn't." He was shouting now to be heard above the crowd.

"I just told you."

"Fuck you!"

"Technical foul! And one more sound out of you and you're gone!"

B.D. turned sideways and walked a few feet down the bench and put Toner in for Sizemore and Swift for Smith, moving Davis to point guard. Cushing had committed more than five fouls in the half, and every time one of the Fairfield players got fouled now while he wasn't shooting he'd have one foul shot plus a second if he made the first—the one-and-one penalty.

The guard made the first and second foul shots, then the technical foul.

65–60.

Fairfield had the ball and the same guard threw one in from the top of the key.

Collins missed a ten-foot jumper, Cunningham missed the tip in, but Fairfield, with just over five minutes left, knocked the ball out of bounds, then, partly because two of their starters were in foul trouble too, sat back in a two-three zone and let Cushing run the clock.

B.D. called time with two-fifty left and put Smith and Sizemore back in, and the guard who'd scored Fairfield's last five

161

points stole the ball at half-court, drove, made the lay-up and got fouled by Sizemore, his fifth.

He made the foul shot, tying the game.

Smith moved the ball over half-court with two minutes left, hit Davis on the left; he missed an open fifteen-foot jumper. Fairfield cleared the boards, worked forty-five seconds off the clock and, with fifty seconds left, called time when B.D. ordered a tight, man-to-man press.

He bent toward them, his knee hurting like a bastard. If they lost he'd say screw it, go back to the coast, sell everything, buy an orange grove and mellow out alone.

"Reach back for everything now," he said. "Play it as if it's the end of the world. Go for the steal on the in-bounds pass. I don't care if you foul. I don't want to wait around to die. Make them beat us. Take it from them and then to them."

Smith dived and deflected the in-bounds pass and Collins grabbed it out of the air, tore it out of the air, snapped a pass back to Smith who hit Cunningham with a bullet that led him in for a lay-up.

67–65.

Fairfield rushed the ball up the half-court and travelled with it to the right. Smith took the in-bounds pass after a Fairfield time-out, was fouled with twenty seconds left and hit both of the one-and-one penalty shots.

69–65.

Davis stole a hurried pass, dribbled alone into the corner—the crowd was ecstatic—flipped it out to Smith who fed it back to Davis, who hit a long jumper as the clock ran out.

71–65. A win. The first of many.

There were hands and faces and hugs and voices while the band pumped and the cheerleaders spun, but no one grabbed his hair or tried to take his suitcoat off and he and the others made it to the locker room intact. Singleton had agreed to keep the press out for three minutes.

"You looked great," he said. "We're a very good team and we're going to win a lot more. I liked the way you hung in, and

162

I'm sure you did too. Practice on Monday at three."

They cheered and the doors opened and television and newspaper and magazine men and women crowded in and everything blurred. After tonight, he thought, the locker rooms would become much quieter, at times silent. But maybe not.

She was in the lobby an hour later, after almost everyone else had gone, after he'd politely declined Singleton's invitation to a late dinner in Weston where his wife and two other couples were waiting now, and most of the team had headed for the restaurant where he'd first met her. She was wearing the same camel's hair coat, was alone and smiled and said hello when he walked up to her, heading for the door.

"Congratulations," she said.

"Thanks—" He stopped a few feet from her.

"It was an exciting game." She brushed her hair from the edge of her shoulder, put her hands back in her pockets. Her coat was open and her breasts smoothed out against a gold and maroon "Go Cushing" sweatshirt. God, he knew, would approve if he only admired, but wouldn't if he asked her to go somewhere with him, which he might have considered if her coat had been buttoned.

"I was looking for my cousin," she said and laughed easily. "To congratulate him. But I couldn't find him."

He didn't have to say anything.

She hesitated. "I saw you coming out and did want to tell you how great it was."

"I'm glad you did."

They moved to the glass doors that opened out in the cool night, and the sharp view of Boston from the wide stone steps leading away from the athletic complex. He watched his breath climb against the skyline and knew all he had to do was ask her to go for coffee, offer to walk her back to her room, and he'd be back in college again.

"Where are you going now?" she said.

"Back to my apartment in Boston on Beacon Street."

163

"Is Stephanie Green there?

"She's in California."

"I've never gone to California," she said.

"You will."

She hunched her shoulders slightly and he fought now to stay in control. They'd reached the bottom of the steps.

"I've got to get going," she said.

"Where?"

"The dorm."

"How many roommates do you have?" Why didn't he just say goodbye?

"Two. We've got four rooms. They're really nice. Maybe life's too pleasant here."

He tried not to stare at her breasts.

"You going with anyone?" he said. Why not?

She nodded. "He's at Princeton, struggling with finals, I think. Me too. I've got four next week. You and your team provided a neat escape tonight."

"We did," he said.

"I'll see you again then," she said after a moment.

"I'll be here through the winter."

He watched her walk onto a path lined with globed, muted-orange lights. Nice, he thought, except, of course, it was 1978 and pot and coke and everything else clicked and wheeled and maneuvered and laughed through the blood and darkening dreams of a generation with few goals other than going back to the affluent suburban bedrooms and kitchens of their childhood. It was hard to forge any character, he thought.

He was being unfair. His team had showed some character tonight, and he could easily be accused, now, of running home again. Except that he wasn't. He wasn't even close to home.

She passed two people coming toward her, turned and waved to him. He waved back. If they'd lost the game tonight, he knew, there wouldn't have been much waving.

3

HE HELD KATE AGAINST HIM, KISSED HER SHOUL-
der, its warmth, the smoothness of it against his lips, then kissed
her lips and ran his tongue across her teeth.

She moved slightly away from him, brushed her fingertips
across his face, his chest, then moved against him as he lay on
his side after coming hard and deep into her for the second time
and bringing her into her second orgasm with his tongue, trying
to release all of the imprisonment she had known in Andover.

She sat up.

"I can't believe all of this." Her voice was quiet.

"I know—"

"You're going to be here for the winter."

"All of the winter," he said. "Whenever it ends, in March."

She had called just after he returned from Cushing. She and
the boys had left the mountains in the afternoon. Skiing, because
of the warm weather, was terrible. She'd heard about his signing
with Cushing in the car on the way back, and had watched
tonight's game on television. The boys were spending the rest of
the weekend with her mother and father.

She stirred and kissed him again. "Are you really doing what
you want to do?"

"Yes."

"I mean by coaching a college team."

"I am," he said. He began to drift. Sleep was just a pale blue
breath away. He sat up and watched her begin to dress.

"Do you want to come back to Andover with me?" she said.

"I'd like to."

She pulled on her sweater and let her hair fall into place. "My mother might, for some reason, come home early tomorrow morning with the boys. It would be a scandal if she found us in bed. But I've got to go. If I stay I'll never get up and leave."

No calls from California or Washington, no answer when he called both places.

4

HE GOT UP EARLY ON SUNDAY, DROVE TO COPLEY Square and got the *Globe* and *Times* and read about his taking the job, the victory. The *Times* was factual. Two *Globe* columnists ran through all the possible reasons for his taking the job. Neither mentioned his mother's illness, his guilt at having left Lawrence fifteen years ago, and neither paper quoted his brother or his wife.

He called his mother at the hospital. She was going home tomorrow morning, she said. The treatment had been devastating. Tom had come by yesterday. Kate would today, or tonight.

"It's hard for them to see me like this," she said. "I don't want you to now. Just stay in touch. Let me know where you are. Your life's changing. Changes always happen all of a sudden."

5

PRACTICE WAS FAST, AGGRESSIVE AND POSITIVE ON Monday. They had a game on Wednesday night against St. Michael's at Cushing and then didn't play again until the first week in January. Not being in a Christmas tourney close to Boston was a definite mistake. It would be tough to recover timing and momentum, he thought, after not playing together for twelve days.

He stayed in the lobby for a moment after practice and looked at pictures of former Cushing teams, including the 1958 NIT champions and 1975 NCAA regional semi-finalists. Good days, he supposed. Good teams. But this team was much better than either. Faster, bigger—

"Trying to take in a little Cushing tradition?" Collins said beside him.

"I guess so."

"Cushing's never won anything nationally," he said. "They've been close, and the football team's gotten to a minor bowl or two, and looked good. But no national championships."

B.D. nodded.

"It felt good to win," Collins said.

"It always does."

"But we should have blown them away early."

"If it had been late January we would have. The first win after an initial losing streak is always tough."

"I've got to study," Collins said after a moment. "If you flunk here you're really screwed."

"So I've heard."

"But I'm doing all right," Collins said. He didn't leave.

B.D. looked at him.

"We've got a twelve-day layoff after Wednesday night."

"I wish we were in a tourney," B.D. said. "Just to keep us sharp. You got a place to work out?"

"The Waltham High gym. Three or four friends of mine and I'll work out every afternoon. One's playing at Colby, another at Wesleyan. Not exactly competition. And I guess I could come over here, just to stay used to it. But it's a little too far."

"Don't hurt anything."

"I won't."

"Concentrate on foul shooting, and moving with the ball underneath. And have fun."

6

TOM CALLED AT SIX. HIS VOICE WAS NEUTRAL.

"I haven't been able to get back to you. I've been tied up and overscheduled and fighting like a bastard all of a sudden for the right committee assignments. Ma's been in the hospital. I got to see her Saturday. She decided to let them do whatever they wanted to do to her."

"I talked to her yesterday," he said. "She's being brave about it. Where are you?"

"Andover, with the boys and Kate. They're holding Ma for at least one more day. I think it'll be longer."

"She's really bad?"

"Yes—I'm going by to see her in a while. Kate's coming later."

"I'll drive up."

"Good," Tom said. "Oh, congratulations." It sounded genuine enough.

"Thanks, Tommy."

"Why didn't you tell me about it?"

"It all happened quickly. I did call. You're just too damn hard to reach on weekends."

He got to the hospital just after seven. His mother was in a private room filled with flowers and get-well messages. The senator's mother. She'd always turned her back on publicity, and stayed out of sight during the campaigns, mostly because of the agony her husband's politics had brought her, and the media had stopped trying to interview her. She was, however, with Tom on the stage of the Sheraton Boston on election night, and had been at the victory party at Sullivan's.

168

She was propped on two pillows and turned and smiled when she saw him. He hugged her gently and kissed her. He was grateful that she didn't start to cry.

"Tom said you were staying another day. I wanted to see you. Things have fallen into place well at Cushing."

"Do you believe all of the flowers," she said. Her voice came thinly from the loneliness of the white sheets and pillow cases. "And the get-well cards and telegrams. From just about every politician in the state. At least those with ambition." She laughed quietly. "It's hard to believe, isn't it. Until I look at you two, and then I know."

He tried not to stare at her. She understood that there was no safer route to the newly elected senator's heart than through the vanity of his ailing mother. Dying mother. They didn't know she was dying. Or few did.

"Tom's in the lounge down the hall. Kate promised she'd be here. It's hard to get away at this time of night, in this season." She looked at him for a minute, and then looked away and closed her eyes.

"Are you comfortable now?" he said.

She looked back at him and nodded.

"They giving you everything you need?"

"More than enough," she said.

He smiled at her.

"They've got me drugged, B.D. They have to kill the pain. And they've been talking about an operation—but it's just talk. They'll have to remove all of me if they're going to remove anything."

A few seconds later Carrie Mallon and her husband came in, trailed by two other neighbors he hadn't seen in several years, and after shaking hands and accepting their aging breath and lips on his cheek, he left and walked to the lounge down the hall, nodding at nurses and interns, and a priest in a raincoat who said, "Hi, Jordan, nice first game."

He thought the lounge would be crowded, but Tom was alone, standing with his back to the entrance, staring down into a filling parking lot.

He turned quickly when B.D. came in and they shook hands and sat in hard chairs near the window.

"I just talked to two of the doctors here," Tom said. "Benson and Halpern. And John Shaffer in Boston."

B.D. waited. "And there's no hope at all?"

"None."

"What I expected."

"So we'll just have to go through it with her. Christ—" Then, "How'd Cushing happen?"

He told him, quickly, about Singleton's offer, his decision with Stephanie.

"Their whole basketball program's in trouble."

"Who told you that?"

"That's the word around everywhere."

"Where? Washington?"

"Everywhere."

"We won last night."

"You almost didn't, against a team that'll wind up well under five hundred."

"They were four and two going in—it doesn't matter anyway. I'm there for the season."

"You are?"

"Why?"

"Have people asked you why?"

"Of course they have." His voice was calm, too calm and pleasant.

"What have they said?"

"They haven't said anything. They've simply asked."

B.D. didn't want to look at him.

"I thought you might have talked to me about it first, since it's here."

"Tom—I called you this weekend, I told you that."

"After you'd accepted."

"After I'd accepted."

"I might have been able to find things out about the place that you'd want to know."

170

"Like what?"

Tom didn't answer.

"I know and trust Singleton. I watched the kids on television and they looked good, and they did tonight. A few already have national reputations. And Maury knew."

"Maury?"

"My agent."

"I know who he is." He almost snapped it.

"You never cleared your decision to run for the senate through me."

"But I didn't go into Los Angeles to raise money without talking to you about it first."

B.D. stood. "I'm the only one who could have got you serious money on the coast."

"All right," Tom said and walked across the room. "All right."

Two priests smiled at them and kept walking by.

"They all think we're Catholic," Tom said.

"And my taking the job at Cushing won't give any secrets away."

"I guess not."

B.D. walked into the corridor, then back.

"You really think you can win with them?"

"I know I can."

"You've got a tough schedule. Almost an impossible one. Cushing's always done that, overscheduled so their teams get blown away at the end of the year, especially in football and basketball."

"I think we'll endure. I know how to pace things."

Tom stared at the floor, then at B.D. "I still don't understand why you took it."

"Because, with my knee gone, there was simply nothing else to do. I just told you that. I don't want to do weekend NBA color for CBS and rot on the beach for the week waiting for the perfect commercial, or interview cliffdivers in Mexico for 'Wide World of Sports.' And I like Bill Singleton. He was a friend at Andover. My only one."

A few other people drifted into the lounge and Tom quickly looked pleasant.

"Ever have regrets about not playing pro football?"

"Never."

"Never miss the game?"

"I've missed the game, a lot, you know that. But I made a decision early, and have regretted nothing."

They searched each other and B.D. knew they had no more real words.

"I think we should go back and see Ma now."

"You've signed a contract then."

"Maury put it together and I signed it, Saturday, before anything else. I never would have—"

"For how long?"

"Just this season. Nothing more than that. I'll be done in March."

Perhaps it was a good thing that Kate appeared then. His blood stirred when he saw her. She looked very good.

"Some neighbors and a few relatives are with her," she said, "The nurses won't let them stay much longer."

"I hope not," Tom said.

"Congratulations on your team's performance Saturday night," she said.

"Thanks."

"Are you enjoying it?"

"I think we're going to do all right," he said and smiled. Don't be a stupid jerk, he thought. Don't say or do anything stupid.

They walked back to the room. Only the Mallons and a cousin he rarely saw when he lived in Lawrence were there. They kissed Tom and pumped his hand, and looked genuinely happy to see him. He did make people feel at ease.

The Mallons buttoned their coats. They told B.D. again they were glad to see him, wished him well at Cushing and then hugged and kissed his mother. Carrie Mallon cried softly for a moment. Her husband, flushed from bending over the bed, brushed at his eyes. The world was cruel and brief. The cousin,

172

a woman in her fifties, kissed Tom, smiled at him, kissed Kate and left. Several of his mother's people hated him. The Mallons left behind her.

Tom and Kate sat next to the bed and B.D. sat in a chair and drifted. In an hour a segment of "Dial California" would flick across millions of television sets, his wife's thighs and lips slipping into the fantasies of the lonely and frustrated.

They kissed her goodbye at eight-thirty. He left first, telling her that he'd be in touch soon and went into the corridor. Kate, wiping at her eyes, joined him a few seconds later.

"It's hard to believe, isn't it," she said. "I don't think she's ever going to go home."

They moved a few steps down the corridor, careful not to get too close, not to touch.

"You're beautiful, you really are," he said.

"I wish I could see you tonight. But my parents are there and they'll stay late. We'll be together tomorrow." She said it quietly, close to him.

"Do you think he knows?"

"No," she said. "But I don't care."

"Yes you do."

She stared at the floor.

"I want it all to go smoothly."

"It will," he said and almost said he loved her.

Tom came out of the room and they walked to the elevator bank.

"You haven't changed your plans for Christmas, have you?" Tom said on the way to the lobby.

"No. We'll be here on the twenty-third, and then we're flying to Chicago early the next morning."

He was uncomfortable under Tom's hard scrutiny.

"It's got to be that way, Tom. Stephanie hasn't seen her family for six months. I'd like to be with her for Christmas, especially if she has to be here. But I'm not going to change anything."

"All right," Tom said, and they looked at Kate, standing a few feet away.

173

"I'm sure we'll see each other soon," she said to him outside the hospital entrance.

"I'm sure we will."

"Have a good Christmas anyway."

"You too, and the boys. We're having presents for them sent to the house."

"They'd love to see a game some time at Cushing."

Tom glared at her.

"Sounds like a great idea. We'll talk about it when I see you," B.D. said.

He hugged her briefly, shook Tom's hand and left them in the cool December darkness.

7

HE DROVE ACROSS THE EDGE OF PROSPECT HILL, Lawrence's darkened mills hulking beside the river, their dead smokestacks and the Ayer Mill clock tower rising against the black sky where a jet sailed west under the hard white stars, and he wasn't sure how he was going to handle all of the winter nights Lawrence would bring before his mother died.

8

SIZEMORE HIT A TEN-FOOT JUMPER WITH EIGHT minutes to go in the first half to put Cushing ahead of St. Michael's 22–20, the gym not quite filled now since most of the students had fled the campus for Christmas vacation. But the crowd stood and cheered and helped ignite a ten-point surge in the next minute. They were ahead at the half 45–30, midway through the second half by twenty-two, 65–43. With nine minutes to go in the game Collins took the ball inside from the left and was hammered across the mouth and cheekbone by one of the St. Michael's forwards for the third time since the game had been tied. He staggered, watched his shot rim and fall in, then straightened, stepped back under the basket and hit the forward with a clean, whistling left to the face.

Blood flew. The forward froze, then fell, and Collins hit him in his right eye on the way down. Someone swung at Collins then and he blocked it and dropped whoever'd thrown it with a snapping left hook. Then someone else had him around the neck before Cunningham began swinging at everyone in sight. The benches cleared and some of the crowd ran onto the court.

B.D. went to Collins' aid too quickly and knew his knee would never recover.

It took Newton, Boston and Cushing security police fifteen minutes to clear the court, and another five to restrain Collins and Cunningham from clubbing at every angry St. Michael's uniform being restrained by coaches and police.

Collins' right eye and mouth were bleeding heavily and swelling when they finally got him beyond the bench and through the entrance to the locker room. Sizemore's knuckles were scraped. Bobby Smith, his lip split and bleeding off his chin, managed eight foul shots in a row in the last two and a half minutes as B.D., while subbing, let them pour it on, 97–55. Collins had knocked one of the forwards cold, and broken the center's nose.

Word would spread, B.D. knew as he limped off the court, ignoring the St. Michael's coach whom he'd threatened to tear apart if he didn't get his bloody hands off Chet Davis. No one was going to fuck with them again.

Two and six into the Christmas break. Not bad. When they came back they'd find out how really good they were. He suspected that they were very good and felt, with a pleasant ache in his stomach that offset the fire in his knee, that they had a decent chance of going a long way. It would be fun to find out.

"You're one mean fucking man, Danny," Sizemore said after

the game. "I mean I'm really glad you hammered those two fuckers, even though they were brothers."

Collins nodded but said nothing and Sizemore moved away, noise and laughter engulfing them, and after talking to several reporters and giving thirty seconds of tape to the three local television stations, B.D. was able to sit between Collins and Davis. Davis was half-dressed and smiling. Collins, his bleeding stopped, still wasn't smiling.

"What's the matter, beyond the obvious?"

"Nothing."

"You had every right to hit both of them."

"I know."

"I'm serious, you did. I would have done the same thing. Anyone in the NBA would have. You have to establish turf once you start winning and become very good, and you established it.

"I don't feel good about it."

"You will."

Collins shook his head.

"You all right?"

"Yes." Collins looked at him. "No, not really." He leaned back against a locker and breathed. "I'm being recruited, in the beginning of basketball season, to play football next year. Tight end. Some lineman and a back I played with and against in high school, and two assistant coaches. I like football. I love the game. But I love this, too, and I've made a commitment to it, especially after talking to you and after Saturday's game. I think we're going to be good. We already are."

"We are. Want me to do anything?"

"I'll make things clear, finally. I don't enjoy hitting guys like that, even when they ask for it. I don't mind banging under the boards and being fouled cleanly."

"No one's going to cheap shot you again," he said and smiled and waved to Singleton who was shaking hands all around, making his way toward them.

He and Collins stood.

"You know what Simmons would have done?" Collins said.

176

"What?"

"Suspended me for two games."

"Incredible. No wonder he failed."

"He was a Division Two coach. No fighting, no violence. No balls. I think he's queer." He smiled fully then for the first time.

9

HE MET STEPHANIE AT LOGAN ON THE NIGHT OF the twenty-second. He saw her, walking with the others from the coast, before she saw him. She was wearing high heels and loose-fitting dungarees, and her hair swung gently at the shoulders of her waist-length jacket. She was tanned. She took off her sunglasses, looked around and recognized him.

They hugged and said nothing. Her breath and lips were cool; she searched his face for a moment, kissed it gently and accepted his lips on her cheekbone. He could feel himself growing.

"Hi, coach," she said and her eyes filled. "Merry Christmas."

"Merry Christmas."

"Oh, Christ."

"I know."

She had surprised him by calling last night, after having called the night before to go over their holiday plans; to tell him how much she missed and loved him, how sick she'd grown of the show and the Chandlers even though they were happy to let her share their house whenever she didn't want to be alone at the beach. Kate had left his apartment just before the second call, with promises of seeing each other again in January, her love imprinted across his bed.

"You look great," he said now to Stephanie. "You always do."

"You, too," she said and hooked her arm in his and slipped her glasses back on. No autographs, no pressing crowds.

"Easy flight?" he said.

"Smooth."

"Did you sleep?"

"I read. Part of a novel Alan sent me that's being developed into a screenplay. He said I'd be just right as one of its women."

"What do you think?"

"I'm not sure. She's in her mid-twenties and was devastated by love, and falls now for an older man."

"What's it called?"

"*The Quiet Connection.* It's very moving in places, and has been selling well and getting good reviews. I'll let you read it this week if you want. And I looked through a script for a made-for-television movie."

"Any good?"

"I don't know. They're both possibilities. But everything changes so quickly. By the first week in January everyone might be on something else, no matter how much money they've spent on options."

He took her three suitcases and they moved across the parking area to his car.

"It's dirty," she said.

"What is?"

"The car." She said it lightly.

"So's Boston."

"I know, I can taste it, and it's cold."

"It's warm," he said and put the suitcases in the back seat. "For this time of the year, anyway."

She watched him for a moment, smiled slightly, and got in and locked her door. He went around and got in beside her and hesitated.

"Everything all right?" he said.

"I'm tired. But, no, everything's fine."

He started the car.

"It's crazy, isn't it," he said.

"It's crazy," she said.

He watched her move back her hair, ruffle it slightly.

"I think you'll like the apartment."

178

"Wasn't Boston paying for it?"

"They still are."

"You've got a good agent," she said and he backed out of the space and connected with the road to the tunnel that would take him to the North End, Storrow Drive, Back Bay. Boston. Old Boston at Christmastime.

"Did you win last night?" she asked. They hadn't talked about basketball on the phone.

He told her by how much and what had happened.

"Sounds exciting. You're two and six now."

"On our way," he said. "But there are no vacation games. Nothing until the first week in January, which is good for us, but the team should have played at least one next week."

"It's going to work out then."

"I think so. Yes."

She shifted, hugged herself. "I was able to get some shopping done."

He stopped for a light before the tunnel. "Great."

"We'll have to do more tomorrow, before going to Lawrence."

"All right."

"How is she?"

They'd talked about his mother last night, and what they'd do if she died when Stephanie was in Hawaii, and had come to no conclusion. They both knew it would be impossible for her to leave the filming there.

She brought his hand to her mouth. "I want to make love so badly," she said.

10

SHE CAME OUT OF THE BEDROOM AFTER HER shower wearing a white robe and high heels. She opened the robe and took it off slowly in front of the glass doors and they

179

stood together in the living room, pressing against each other before moving back into the bedroom, beckoning smooth, distant orgasms from their blood.

"Christ I've needed you," she said. "I can't stand the house without you."

It was one-thirty. They were sitting in the kitchen eating cereal with milk and strawberries and toast with jelly and sipping coffee. She ran her fingertips across the rim of the cup, looked at him and then down at her plate.

"I hope you believe that," she said.

"Of course I believe it."

She touched his knuckles, then leaned back and looked past him to the living room. "It's really nice," she said.

"I like the view, especially now with the lights in the windows in Cambridge." Her absence in January and February would only make his rooms more empty, he thought. But he'd be too busy, too involved with basketball to care about it for very long.

"We have no decorations at the house," she said.

He shrugged slightly.

"Don't you find Boston awfully dark and old, remote, even now?"

"Sometimes it can be."

"Do you feel as if you're a part of it now?"

"Part of what?"

"Boston, Cushing—"

"No. I never will."

"You felt part of L.A."

He agreed.

"This year?"

"More this year because I knew it was my last as a player, even though we were losing." He stared into his hands on the table. He was going to tell her then that he missed playing more than anything he could remember now, more than he ever imagined he would, that he couldn't believe how much he hurt being away from it, that he had no idea, still, what he was going to do when this was over in March.

"I've never felt part of the TV series," she said. "How can you feel a part of something that no one takes seriously, that'll go into reruns for ten years, but never be watched by anyone who thinks? I've never been involved with the character I've played. She's never become substantial enough to be involved with. How could 'Alicia Sterling' ever have any substance? I've got more time now on screen, and bigger parts of the script are being written for me, much to the unhappiness of Tina and Suzanne and their agents. But I'm saying less, and acting less. I mean I know what I look like, and how I sound. I turn people on. I ignite fantasies in thousands of bedrooms, or dirty lonely rooms. And that doesn't really bother me at all because I know I'm beautiful and that's why so many people watch. They hunger for flesh. For my thighs, for Suzanne's shoulders and hair and Tina's ass and my tits." She stared away from him for several seconds. "I think there's potential for a very good movie in what I'm reading now. And if not the novel then the movie-for-television script. I'm going to break away from the show in April, when the contract's up. We've certainly got enough money for me to do what I want. I'm just not going on with the series. I can always model to keep my name and face alive, all of my possibilities alive—"

He wanted to mention children then. It was Christmas. It was time for them. But he didn't.

"I'm so tired now," she said and rinsed their cups and dishes in the sink. "How late are you going to sleep?"

"I don't know. Till late morning if you want. We can see her in the early afternoon."

"She's really suffering, isn't she?"

He looked away from her.

"I think our seeing her together will be good for her."

"I know it will," he said.

Moments later on the edge of sleep she put her arms around him and said his name.

"What?"

"I've got a lot of anger left."

"I know."

181

"I'm so glad to be with you now."

"I love you," he said and kissed her shoulder. "I'll always love you."

"Have you been lonely here?" she said.

"Yes."

"Very lonely?"

"Very lonely," he said.

"How do you deal with it?"

"I played basketball, and now I bury myself in the details of coaching it." He was sure she knew he was lying, or at least not telling her everything. "Stephanie?"

"What?"

"I've got to say something."

"Go ahead, darling."

"The knee would have slowed me just enough, if I'd tried to make it back, to make me mediocre. I would have gotten eaten alive. I didn't want that to happen. It's one thing for Corvino to go out the way he is, but not for guys like me."

"I understand," she said. "Go to sleep, darling."

11

LAWRENCE WAS YARD AND ROOFTOP COVERED with two inches of sullen gray snow from a brief, early morning storm whose trailing clouds still blocked out the sun. It was one o'clock. They climbed Prospect Hill, the streets wet and narrow, and parked in the hospital's crowded lot. A silver tree blinked in one corner of the lobby and Christmas music drifted faintly toward the ceiling.

His mother was awake and smiled when she saw Stephanie. Steph had been too quiet at breakfast, during the ride, and B.D. knew she'd probably be this way for the rest of the time in Boston.

In Chicago she could use laughter and banter with her family instead of quiet to protect herself.

"You look wonderful," Stephanie said after kissing his mother and they sat on chairs beside the bed. No one else was in the room now. They had brought two shopping bags full of presents.

A nurse came in, looked at a sheet of paper and stared at Stephanie before she left. No one in the crowded lobby had tried talking to them or taking a punch at him for leaving Boston for Cushing. A *Globe* columnist and two in the *Herald American* had called his move typically west coast and slick and dishonest, spurred on, B.D. thought, by the promise of free tickets from Sid Anderson, who had been savaged in a column by Brian Gallagher for not offering Jordan the coaching job. If he did well with Cushing, Anderson and L.A. would look stupid, another reason for his driving toward the NCAA final four.

"Christmas is in two days," his mother said. "I haven't had a chance to get you anything. You understand that."

They didn't have to say anything.

"And the last weeks have gone by so fast. I would have thought the opposite—that they'd crawl by. But they haven't. It's amazing." She stared away for a moment. "The doctors think they can help me if they keep me here for another week."

"I'm sure they can," Stephanie said.

"Help me to stay alive a little longer," she said evenly.

He'd already explained their holiday plans. They were flying to Chicago tomorrow, back to California on the morning of the twenty-sixth.

"I'm going to have another treatment after Christmas," she said. "Just one more."

"Are you comfortable now?" B.D. said.

She stared at him for a moment. "You've won two in a row now, haven't you."

"Yes. I think I've got a good team."

"Good," she said. "Good for you. You've got the winning touch. Not many people have it. And luck. I'm sure you don't think so after being traded and then hurting your knee, but it'll work out, and force other things. Tom has it. Sometimes it seems to come in the form of bad news." He watched her swallow. "Luck, I mean."

Stephanie was staring past her then, through the window with its glimpse of a bend in the Merrimack, the tops of the row houses in one of the decayed parts of lower Prospect Hill where the nineteenth century still limped. Nothing moved on the river now except clouds on a changing winter sky. It wasn't Malibu. It wasn't Boston or Chicago. Just part of a small city far enough from sophistication to die without anyone caring. It was just a half-stagnant, half-decayed, half-dead place where Americans lived.

"Was I making sense just then?" his mother said.

"Very much so," Stephanie said and took her hand.

"Stephanie and I have to make a long-distance call in the lobby," he said. "And then we'll be right back. All right?"

She nodded.

"I'm sure she wanted to fall asleep," B.D. said in the elevator. "She wouldn't let herself, with both of us there." He waited for a moment. "She looked terrible, didn't she."

Stephanie didn't answer. She took his arm and leaned against him.

They sat at a table away from the door in the small cafeteria after picking up coffee. Two of the gray-haired women working behind the cafeteria counter had stared at her, asked how his mother was feeling, told Stephanie how much they liked her show. Their hands trembled slightly when they handed them the coffee. Stephanie told them they were sweet and gracious, and wrote her name and the date and a brief phrase on the pieces of paper they gave her and wished them Merry Christmas.

"I didn't want to cry," she said now at the table and leaned forward. "I guess I'm tired, and vulnerable because I'm so tired." Her eyes reddened. "I'm not going to cry here, don't worry about that."

"Go right ahead if you want to."

"No." She shook her head.

"We'll go back in a minute. She'll be asleep. We'll stay for a while longer and then go back to Boston. We can have an early dinner out and then get some rest. I'm looking forward to seeing everyone in Chicago again."

"They're looking forward too."

"Tom'll be with her tomorrow. She'll have people around through the holidays."

"Do you have to talk to the doctors?"

"No. I don't want to and they don't want me to. I'm the athlete, the son from the coast. Tom takes care of the details. He's the senator."

He watched her and knew she felt uncomfortable now. Word had obviously moved through the lobby that they were there, and too many people were walking by, stopping to talk to each other, glancing at them, looking away and glancing back.

"Want to go back?" he said. "I think we'd better."

She was asleep when they got back to the room. They put the presents on one side of the bureau, arranged flowers at the window and sat and said nothing. A few minutes later Kate appeared at the door. His blood rushed and he stood. Jesus—

She was wearing a dark dress, her coat open, and looked as if she hadn't expected them to be there. Perhaps she'd even dropped by early, thinking they'd visit in the late afternoon, the time for celebrity visits. They'd been together two nights ago and hadn't talked about this, and Stephanie, staring at her now, must have known they'd seen each other. Kate looked composed enough to do whatever she wanted to do—to make love to B.D. Jordan, comfort him through the dark winter, help him find his soul and lock it, finally, in place and return with it to the sun.

"I didn't think anyone would be here," she said, quietly, hugged him and Stephanie, then broke into a smile almost as good as Stephanie's.

"Good to see you again," Stephanie said, and sat down.

"You, too."

They glanced at each other, then at the bed.

"How is she?" Kate said.

"Not good at all. Exhausted," B.D. said.

185

"I guess it's a normal reaction. It's been so sudden."

"How've you been?" he said."

"Fine. Haven't seen you for a while."

Don't, he thought. Please fucking don't.

Stephanie watched her, the former sister-in-law.

"The boys still in school?" he said.

"Till two, then out for the holidays."

"They're very handsome," Stephanie said.

"They like watching you, just like they enjoy watching their uncle."

In a moment they walked to the lounge and talked quietly about their going to Chicago, about movie making, California, the skiing in Colorado where Kate had gone to school and Stephanie had spent part of a winter, and then drifted back. His mother was awake. She was being examined at one-thirty and they'd leave in a few minutes.

"It's not worth it," she said to them. "Being here just isn't worth it at all."

Stephanie hugged her and stepped back, wiping at her cheekbones, then B.D. hugged her but didn't cry. His mother was crying.

"I might never see you again," she said.

"You will, Ma."

"Did I change after you left for California?" she asked, touching his forearm, almost whispering it so the women, glancing away now, slipping away from the bed, wouldn't hear.

"Did I?" she repeated too intensely. "It's important for me to know that, B.D.; I know I made it impossible for you to stay here after your father died. I understand that. Tom helped me to understand it."

"You changed," he said. "You changed a lot. We all did."

"I did. I tried and I did."

"You did," he said and kissed her cold ancient cheek and almost said that it didn't matter.

"I love you, B.D.," she said. "Be good. Do the right things. And be kind to her. She loves you and needs you."

He hesitated. She pleaded silently at him and he couldn't say it, damn it. He simply couldn't say the words back to her because he thought that if he did the dam would burst and everything would come rushing out. He'd lose control, and he had to have control now.

"I will," he said and kissed her cheek again, her fingers clinging to his forearm.

They promised Kate at the door that they'd all see each other again, and she avoided looking directly at him.

"Have you seen very much of her?" Stephanie said in the car on the way back.

"Kate or my mother?"

"Kate."

"No—once briefly in front of my mother's house the first day I went there. And then for a few minutes when Tom and I took his sons to dinner." Don't say any more, he thought. He took her hand then and she moved closer to him. "Why?" he asked.

"I'm just curious about her. She's very good-looking; she seems substantial."

"She is. Both."

"Why'd your brother leave her, then?"

"I don't think he ever loved her, and she was at home with the boys while he was on the political make. A young state senator with promise, a former all-American. All kinds of women wanted him, and he started sleeping with a Boston anchorwoman who went on to L.A. and is in New York now, I think. Self-centered, vapid, and Kate found out. She wouldn't let herself be destroyed. It really hurt her, deeply. She divorced him."

"Did she tell you that?"

"Tom did. She and I have never really talked, except about my mother."

"Why does she give her so much time?"

"I don't know, but I think it's partly because the boys like my mother, and like being around her house. I know how they feel. I used to like it when I was their age. Just hanging around the yard or driveway or kitchen, watching my mother and father

187

doing whatever they were doing. And I spent hours, from fourth grade through high school, shooting baskets in the driveway. My father had the area floodlit and one night in my senior year in high school I wouldn't let myself go into the house until I'd hit twenty-five fifteen-foot jumpers in a row. It took me from nine to ten-thirty to do it. My mother was worried sick about what the neighbors would think because I'd been shooting and playing one-on-one with Tom since six-thirty. She worried all through high school about what the neighbors would think, especially since I spent all that time playing in the driveway and never bothered going out for the high school team."

"You never played in high school?"

"Not at Lawrence High, no."

She laughed. "That's great. I didn't know that. Why not?"

"I didn't like the coach or his philosophy. He had everything restricted and patterned, and sometimes froze the ball for five minutes at a time, just for the hell of it."

"Why?"

He shrugged. "Some guys are like that. They're very arbitrary. They think the kids are on the team to let them play out their own coaching fantasies, rather than to simply develop as students and kids and to play. Tom was an excellent basketball player, but didn't play in his senior year. He ran indoor track, which was a lot better for him anyway as long as he was going to play split end for Notre Dame."

"How good were you at Andover? Really."

"Singleton told you—I was the best anyone could be."

She smiled at him and then looked away.

"My mother did change a lot," he said. "My father's death at forty-eight, my leaving, Tom's going to Notre Dame, forced her into reality. She decided sometime in his freshman year that she wasn't going to just hang around and decay. And she finally realized that the only way not to lose Tom forever was to let him go, let him play at the top and stop trying to direct his life. She left him alone and he married Kate O'Connell from Andover, made Lawrence the heart of his political future. It's always been

188

painful for me to come back here because she tried to direct me, decide everything for me." He breathed hard. "That's not the only reason it's painful."

"Is it now?"

"Yes."

"You were awfully uneasy here in September."

"I was."

"And this afternoon."

"I guess so—it's not that hard being in Boston, though, not as long as I know I'm going to leave in two and a half months."

12

CHICAGO WAS COLD, THE AIRPORT CROWDED AND they moved slowly through the midafternoon traffic to her family's brick, three-bedroom home.

Steph's mother, tall and gray and handsome, almost as tall and more gray than his mother, said at the door, oh my god you're beautiful, and hugged and kissed them and cried. Her father, heavy, an inch taller than B.D. and flushed with whiskey and cigar smoke, hugged his daughter and laughed and pumped B.D.'s hand and said it was damn good to see him. Stephanie's brother, in his last year of law school at Northwestern, was there with his fiancée, a third-year med student. She was tall and athletic looking and hung back a little, stunned, perhaps, at suddenly seeing celebrities in the foyer of a middle-class neighborhood in Chicago. They'd never met her. Her voice and breath and lips were warm.

B.D. and her brother and father drank whiskey and water in the living room with a fire going and a Christmas tree blazing against the midwestern dusk. Christmas music played softly from another room while Steph and her mother and Ann, the fiancée, sat at the kitchen table and sent out shafts of laughter.

After they'd talked about Chicago's cold weather, and briefly about the regime of Mayor Daley, Connie Green, her father, asked, "How's the knee?"

Steph's brother had mentioned B.D.'s two wins at Cushing, the hectic life of a senior in law school looking for a job, and the possibilities of his going to Washington soon. B.D. suggested that he talk about the future with Tom Jordan. The whiskey had rushed to B.D's head. He seldom drank more than a beer, half a glass of wine, and he really didn't give a damn about anything now.

"It hurts. There was a fight in the game the other night and in the middle of all of the violence I pulled it badly again." He smiled. "I think I limp a little, just a little."

"I read about the game," Steph's brother said and swallowed from his drink. "There was a piece about it in the *News*. Who's the tough kid playing for you?"

He told him.

"Pro prospect?"

"I'm not sure. He might not be quick enough, or tall enough for the speed he has, or doesn't have."

He was waiting for his father-in-law to ask why he was coaching. After all, it separated Jordan from his daughter for most of the winter. The neighborhoods of Chicago and Lawrence were a hell of a long way from Malibu.

"Will you ever play again?" Connie Green said.

"No. I think I've already lost it." He felt the words sink back into his blood. He drank and watched the balls on the tree pick fire and faces from the room. But he hadn't already lost it. If his knee healed tomorrow it would only take a few days to get back into playing shape.

But he was out. It was over. He'd quit Boston. He was Cushing University's head basketball coach. He'd won two in a row and would win a lot more in a row. Winning was almost everything now. It had to be.

"How do you like coaching?" Connie Green said and seemed relieved that he'd finally asked it.

"I like it. Just two games and a few practices, but I like it a lot so far." He'd slurred the first few words and felt dumb.

"Not better than playing, though?"

"No."

They looked at him and he smiled back.

"I played for sixteen years. Fifteen and a half. All of my youth."

"Your early youth," Connie Green said. "You've got a hell of a lot of youth left."

They laughed and B.D. bent slightly forward and felt more in control.

"Steph told her mother over the phone that it's just for the season."

"What?"

"Your coaching."

"Just for the season," he said. He shifted. "You've coached football."

"Line coach at the high school Steph went to—not the one I teach at—for fifteen years. I liked it well enough, but gave it up last year. I thought I'd miss it this fall. I didn't miss it as much as I thought I would."

They pondered this for a moment. Steph and her mother and future sister-in-law came into the room and they talked about the promise of another bitter cold, snowstruck winter and the chaos it would cause at city hall, and her mother's plans to spend a week in Malibu.

"Will you be there at all?" she said to B.D.

"No," he said and stared at Steph, who returned his stare until her father asked his son something about law school. Then Ann was talking about the rigors of being a third-year medical student and then the attention was back on Stephanie who explained why they were shooting in Hawaii next month—to generate new publicity, to give the writers an excuse to expose more legs against more pools and seasides, to keep their ratings firmly in the top five through March and April, and to provide a backdrop for advertising a movie their network was showing in early March with, naturally enough, a Hawaiian setting.

191

"It doesn't have much to do with art, does it," she said and they laughed.

"A lot of the guys watch the show every week," her brother said.

"Thanks, Chris," she said, "but it's not quite *Macbeth*."

"Maybe it is. Shakespeare's plays were the most popular form of entertainment in Elizabethan London."

"Nice try," she said, pleasantly. "I hope we're not going to be taught in high schools."

"You probably already are," B.D. said.

"Where?"

"Everywhere between classes, where all of the real learning takes place."

They laughed easily.

"How much more time are you going to spend with it?" her brother said.

"I don't know." Stephanie moved across the room from a rocking chair and sat next to B.D. on the couch.

"Any movie offers?"

"Some," she said. "But nothing's definite yet."

"Nothing's ever definite out there," her mother said.

"Or here," her father said and they laughed again.

They ate roast beef with gravy and mashed potatoes and peas and green beans and drank red wine, and when the talk moved to politics again, to how Carter had no chance at all of being re-elected and would lose by a lot in Illinois, her father asked how the senator-elect was finding things in Washington.

"He's been busy," B.D. said. "We've only seen each other a few times since the trade."

"You won't see him over the holidays then," Stephanie's mother said.

"I seldom have since my sophomore year at Berkeley."

"That's unusual?"

"Basketball. There's always been a game around Christmas-time. Cushing's not in a Christmas tourney. We should be to keep the momentum we started this week." He drifted. "Basketball has kept me out of the east, and now it's brought me back." He gave the table a wide smile. Steph drank some of her wine.

"How's your mother?" Mrs. Green asked after a moment. "We've talked to her a few times this fall."

"She told me." He looked at Stephanie, who shook her head slightly. "She has a lot of friends and family, still, around the area. And Tom'll be with her tonight and on Christmas day."

"We'll have to get together some day soon."

"In California, this spring," B.D. said. "I think we should all plan on that."

"I've read that your brother wants to be President some day," Ann said.

"All politicians do," Connie Green said. "Every alderman I know's waiting for the call, the great draft. The only draft they'll ever get is up their backsides."

"That's one of the things my father always said," B.D. said after laughing. "They all really believe they can be it. I guess he dreamed it, too."

"What was he?" Ann said.

"A lawyer. A state senator. And almost a Congressman."

"How old was he when he died?" Connie said.

"Forty-eight," he said and fought off the need to cry.

Stephanie asked Ann about her family. They lived in Dallas. She and Chris were flying there on the twenty-seventh. Her father was a heart surgeon, her mother taught second grade in a private school. She had two brothers, both younger, one at the University of Texas at Austin, the other at Rice. "They don't play football or basketball," she said and smiled, and B.D. watched her blush slightly against her red sweater and he laughed to relieve her embarrassment. How tough would it be—being married to Stephanie Green's brother, B.D. Jordan's brother-in-law, defined by the deeds and reputations of others? Tough, he thought, especially if you were from Dallas and were bright and ambitious. Maybe they'd break up in Texas on New Year's Eve.

They had warm apple pie and coffee for desert while Stephanie talked about the two other women on the show, Connie about discipline problems in overcrowded high school classrooms, and B.D. about his brief stay with Boston, the ice that formed on Anderson's lungs every night, the silence in their locker rooms, the impending complete disaster of their season. They'd lost five in a row. He never would have accepted their coaching offer. There was no life, no innocence on the team.

By late January, without Cushing, he thought, he'd be starring with thin, vapid women in shaving cream commercials—as long as he didn't have to spin them in the air—and talking through time outs for CBS. . . .

After dinner and before midnight mass and the exchange of presents he and Stephanie went for a short walk. Christmas lights and cars and cold and safety. There was no wind and their voices sounded almost hollow in the pure night air. Christmas Eve, and he was half drunk and thirty-five and he'd never play basketball again. He tried to hold it all in his breath now—including the fact that he was walking next to Stephanie Green and his brother was a United States senator and he was making love and would again to Kate O'Connell—but he couldn't. Of course he couldn't.

The last time he and Steph were in Chicago they had walked, on a warm night, to a park at the edge of her neighborhood and had gone a few yards into the half-dark when she turned and kissed him hotly and told him to make love to her there, in the shadow of a tree, standing up. She'd pulled her dress to her waist and he'd moved her pants down and watched her step through her shadow from them. He couldn't come, but she did, quickly, hanging on, laughing almost too loudly as voices passed and cars swung through blind Chicago intersections.

"Ever done this before?" he had asked and she hadn't answered. Who was she making love to in California?

"Feel at home?" he said now.

"I guess so."

"Want to have a baby?"

"Yes, very much."

"Tonight?"

She inhaled and didn't answer and a few yards later said yes.

"We can make love and try, but I know the time isn't right."

They slowed and walked another block.

"Remember the last time?" he said.

"I remember," she said and smiled.

"Want to try again?"

"It's too cold," she said.

"Want to do it in church?"

"Sure," she said.

They went to midnight mass at a huge, packed, cold church near the house and during one of the silent moments of praying, he thought of Kate and her hungry mouth and warm, amazing thighs, and then of his mother waiting for death to sprint across her hospital room floor, and guilt raced into his heart and almost got him.

He coughed quietly and leaned forward, pressed by Steph and her brother on either side. He wished for a moment that he could pluck a Catholic prayer from the lips of one of the priests moving across the altar now, say it right and free himself, save himself—but he wasn't Catholic, and he'd never be able to externalize anything that he did and have it dissolve in the taste of a magical phrase. Never. It would have to slowly, quietly, turn to dust in his blood. He wasn't Catholic, and the guilt that he felt now—for having left Lawrence fifteen years ago, for having made love to his brother's former wife, for not telling L.A. to go fuck itself, for playing with Boston, for letting Boston and himself down by ruining his knee, for taking the Cushing job and for leaving his wife alone in California, for searching the dirty streets and roof-tops of Lawrence for what he was, for not telling his mother that he loved her, for crowding his brother's turf only days before he became the junior senator from Massachusetts—would attack him whenever it got the chance. And Catholic Lawrence and Boston, and now Chicago, would sin and pray and confess and mock him.

Stephanie touched his knee, smiled and winked at him.

"Never promise more than you can deliver," he whispered.

"Part of the enduring wisdom of Boston and Chicago politics."

"I can deliver," she said.

"Here?"

"Sure. No one would believe it was happening, so they'd deny its existence."

"Chicago's making you deep," he said.

"Church turns me on."

The house was crowded with cousins, aunts and uncles and neighborhood friends, city hall workers and ward healers and three or four aldermen, and whiskey and wine and laughter ran and tumbled. People hugged Stephanie and a few women cried at seeing her for the first time in a few years and several congratulated him on the two Cushing wins. He answered several times that his career in basketball was over, that when the season was done he was flying back to the coast and buying a football team or baseball team. No one was paying any attention. And then it was almost three o'clock and all of the visitors were gone and they hugged and kissed and wished each other Merry Christmas again and exchanged presents—gloves and scarves and books and necklaces and rings and earrings. "Oh, god, B.D., it's gorgeous," she said when she opened the box holding the diamond bracelet he had bought in Boston a week ago.

He stayed up late with her father and brother listening to a neighbor—who'd come by loaded at three-thirty—spin out tales of precinct counting maneuvers in the Kennedy election in 1960 ("So Brian says how many more fucking votes do you need and Davey Malloy says three more fucking hundred to make it look good, so Brian says I'll get back. Got back all right. He comes up with a drawerful of four hundred and twenty dead bodies and gives Davey three-twenty-three to make it look good."), the Nixon election of 1968 when they couldn't quite—for a lot of reasons, none of which included a concern for illegalities—give Hubert Humphrey enough, and a day-to-day account of Daley's anger and frustration that summer. "Daley did want to be vice-president, you know, and he would have made the difference for Hubert in the long run. He just should have given all the fucking hippies a tent and a place to piss and yell and some dirty girls and some weed. That's all they ever wanted."

He got into bed at four-thirty and was surprised that Steph was still awake.

"Hello," she said.

"Hi."

She pressed against him.

"It's all over so quickly," he said.

"What is?"

"Everything."

She stirred and said nothing. Her former bedroom, turned now into a guest room, was cool and silent. When he asked, a year ago, if she felt strange making love in it, she'd laughed the way she laughed after coming in the park. He'd never made love in his bedroom on Tower Hill.

"I don't think I can," she said when he touched her.

"I understand," he said. "I'm sure I'd never come."

"I might by February."

He simply held her.

"How much do you love me now?" she said. Her voice was a remote stare, a flick of wind at one of the lean branches above the small front lawn, a lost moment in the familiar sound of an occasional car here on Christmas morning. It was Christmas day, Mr. Scrooge. Where were people going at four-thirty in the morning on Christmas day?

"More than I can ever explain." It was poetic, he thought, and he felt satisfied for a moment, and then tired, oh so fucking tired, darling. Exhausted, and thirsty for the warmth of southern California, his home. At least now, in the truth of this midwestern moment, he knew where his blood belonged. Not here. Not in Boston or Lawrence.

"What are we going to do?" she said.

"Sleep," he said.

"That's not what I meant."

"I know that's not what you meant," he said.

197

13

THE GREENS DROVE THEM TO THE AIRPORT FOR their flight home, and mother, father and daughter cried when they hugged and kissed and had to say goodbye. Airports and bus stations and train stations were built for terror and loneliness and sorrow, grim winter scenes.

She said little in the plane, and when he took her hand about an hour from Chicago she held his too tightly.

She swam at Malibu even thought it was dark and cold, and they ate chicken and salad and drank cold beer and sat on the deck with sweaters on and avoided everything until they went back into the house, into the bedroom and had to make love.

They walked the beach twice in the next few days, even though his knee pained, went to a party infested with glazed eyes and nervous fingers and hands, had dinner out and slept late.

She disappeared for two full afternoons. Once, she said, to go shopping in Beverly Hills, the other to see three women she shared a beach house with four years ago, before she had all the money she needed. Maybe they should have planned to go somewhere after Chicago, but there'd been no time for plans. And he wanted to try to reach Mike Corvino and study scouting reports for his first game back in January, against Villanova in Philadelphia. Villanova had lost once and were ranked fifteenth in the country, and it would be a very good test of Cushing's own excellence. A win against Villanova would bring deserved national attention. No one expected them to win. He, they, Cushing, could afford to lose few, if any, more games.

When he saw her at six o'clock after the second afternoon he was almost certain she'd made love. And he thought, when he stared at her in the kitchen and she stared back, she was going to tell him that it was all over. Then, of course, he'd tell her about Kate, and what a terrific scene that would be.

He'd heard from none of his former L.A. teammates and tried getting in touch with none, other than Corvino, though he would have enjoyed talking to Darwin again. B.D.'d been wounded and had quit the action, and no one still playing really wanted to see him. He gave only one, brief, off-the-record interview over the phone to Tony Fagan about Boston's chances and how far Cushing might go. Boston, he said, would finish last in the east with the worst record in the NBA and his team would advance to the NCAA final four. Fagan didn't believe him.

They went to a crowded New Year's Eve party in Malibu given by the real-estate-tycoon husband of one of the other female detective leads in the TV series. In his early sixties, he stayed young by turning over twenty-five-year-old wives every two years.

Clyde McKenzie, a flanker for the Rams, was there, and just after B.D. and McKenzie had discussed the agony of knee injuries, he walked beyond the drinking and music and laughter through sliding glass doors to the edge of a blue patio. It was too cool to be outside now, but a couple was making love on a reclining chair, she on the top with her dress up over great, tanned thighs, he with a dinner jacket still in place. He had even taken off his shoes and socks. And beyond them, in the shadow thrown by an unlit room, was B.D's wife standing close to one of the blond young writers from her show. He hesitated, then watched her put her arms around his neck. It was a good kiss, he thought, and lasted long enough to tear a hole in his stomach.

He broke them apart with a tap on her shoulder. They looked startled, and he wondered for a second where they thought they were.

"I could break your hands," he said, evenly, to the writer. "But I won't. You're an asshole." He left without looking at her. She said nothing.

He didn't say goodbye to anyone and waited in the car for her. It took her three minutes; he was going to wait five.

"Is he the guy you've been fucking for this week?" he said on the way back to their house.

She glared through the windshield and said nothing.

"He's going to Hawaii, isn't he?"

"Yes."

"Lucky you. What's his name, Alice what?"

"Cut it out, B.D."

"You cut it out, you're the one who was making out with him. Really, Stephanie, the guy's a fucking fag."

"He's not and there's nothing going on. He's a friend, nothing more."

He let his breath out.

"It was just a kiss, B.D. Only one kiss."

"Why didn't you kiss him in front of everyone then, everyone else was kissing anything that moved, for Christ's sake."

"I've made love to no one else but you since we met, and I shouldn't even have to tell you that much."

"What about Kate O'Connell?" she said a moment later.

"What about her?"

"Tell me you haven't been seeing her."

"I haven't."

"I saw the way she looked at you at the hospital."

"She's my brother's ex-wife."

"That only makes it better," she said. "She's just the kind of woman to get you through the winter."

He could have said more, but didn't, and neither did she.

14

HE WALKED A HALF MILE DOWN THE BEACH, THEN tried running, couldn't accept the pain and stopped and rested for several minutes before walking back. What was the point of testing it every day? Christ, he'd prepared himself badly for the negative consequences of a trade, and for an injury this year. But he'd never thought he'd be hurt badly enough to have to quit, and here he was.

He limped back toward the house. It was eleven o'clock, and he couldn't quite shake last night's patio scene from his head, and the uncertainty of what was to come now hung in his blood.

She was up and had made coffee and toast. He sat at the table with her and sipped orange juice.

"Happy New Year," he said quietly.

She looked at him and nodded and then looked away.

After a moment she sat back. "It's our last day together for a long time."

"I know."

"I'm sorry about last night," she said. "I'm really not sorry about what I did because it was nothing. But I am sorry because it's all out of proportion now and it's ruined everything else."

"I'm sorry, too. I blew it out of proportion."

"The winter'll go fast enough," she said. "Being on location, for both of us, will make it rush by."

"I'm sure it will," he said and got up and flipped on the first half of the Cotton Bowl. It was nineteen seventy-nine and he hadn't kissed her yet. Fuck it. He wouldn't. He couldn't now, anymore than she could kiss him.

Mike Corvino called at the end of the first half of the Rose Bowl. Stephanie was out on the beach and B.D.'d been designing a move for Collins off the post to keep one of the Villanova big men off balance underneath and make him vulnerable for a beating. Preparations. Basketball involved him more now as a coach than it had as a player. He couldn't simply go on instinct and familiarity, though instinct counted when he encouraged and criticized and subbed. Most important, he had to cover all of the negatives, to anticipate the bad things that could happen with everything they did. That was the hardest part, and the most vital. He was going to ask Corvino to be his assistant coach. Corvino, because he wasn't a star, had to know everything bad that could happen, and he knew and understood defense better than Jordan, better than anyone else. Cushing would need a tougher defense.

"Watching the Rose Bowl?" Corvino said.

"Yeah."

"What's the score?"

"I don't know. I like some of the cheerleaders. Maybe I'll write one or two a fan letter."

"You sound positive," Corvino said.

"I am and I'm not. How are you? Where are you?"

"Right now I'm in Houston. Karen and the kids are in Pittsburgh, and it's a lonely life."

"I've been trying to reach you."

"I know. I'd just signed a ten-day contract and didn't want to get distracted. I can be now."

"You've made it then," B.D. said.

"A one-year contract. Their chances of going a long way are excellent. They needed a power forward with experience."

"Congratulations."

"Thanks, B.D.," Corvino said after a moment.

"I was going to offer you the assistant's job at Cushing."

"I thought so."

"Not as much as you're getting now, but an almost certain chance of taking the team next year."

Corvino said nothing. He'd said nothing about Jordan's coaching.

"I think you'd make an excellent coach," B.D. said.

He listened to Corvino breathe. "What's it like?"

"The basketball's good. Sometimes it's very good. A few of the kids are talented. The two games I've coached have been against weaker teams. We get into the jungle next week. There's enthusiasm. I think we forget how much there really is, all of the time, all day at a place like Cushing, more so than at Cal in the sixties. Break your contract and come up and help me win the national championship."

"I'd like to, B.D., but I just can't. The kids miss me and I miss them like a bastard. And Karen. We managed to get together at Christmas. Things will never be as good as they were in Los Angeles."

"Never," he said.

"I was surprised as hell you did it, became a college coach."

"Everyone was."

"How'd it happen?"

He told him.

"Sounds logical enough," Corvino said.

"It was."

Stephanie walked across the deck. A breeze worked its way through her hair. In three years she'd be an important American actress. A respected beauty. What was it like living with B.D. Jordan? We had some very good times. We talk occasionally. I like him very much.

"I'll be in Boston with the team in two weeks," Corvino said.

"We'll get together." He gave Corvino his address and phone number, the number at Cushing, and knew they never would get together.

"I wish it had been my fucking knee," Corvino said. "Not just because you're my friend, but because it would have made me quit. I would have had to do something else."

"I understand."

"I'll call," Corvino said.

"I'll look forward to it."

"Is Stephanie with you?"

"She's here."

"She's great, you know."

"I know."

15

SHE DROVE HIM TO THE AIRPORT AT NINE. THE "Dial California" cast were flying west later in the afternoon.

They held each other briefly inside the terminal.

"We've been awfully cruel."

"We have."

"I love you," she said.

"I love you very much," he said and his eyes filled and she kissed him on the mouth while she was crying, the first time they'd kissed since before the New Year's Eve party.

"I'll call you from the hotel tomorrow," she said.

"Late at night," he said.

"It will be late. I'll never make love to anyone else."

"Neither will I," he lied.

"It'll all go by very fast."

"I know. It will."

"We'll have time in April," she said against the airport noise. "We'll have the time we need then." She sounded as though she really meant it.

16

HIS APARTMENT WAS COLD AND DARK AT FIVE o'clock. He put his suitcases in the foyer and sat in the living room and stared across at Cambridge and felt terrible. Practice was at three tomorrow. He'd get there by one. Classes didn't begin at Cushing until mid-January, yet the next home game, on Saturday night, was sold out, and probably Wednesday night's game in Philadelphia. Some things to look forward to.

He turned up the heat, took a hot shower and cooked three hamburgers and made toast and heated peas. He drank one can of beer and listened to the apartment hum around him, and there was nothing he could do now, nothing that he wanted to do but make the winter work for him.

17

COLLINS, SIZEMORE AND SMITH STAYED AFTER practice and rotated through twenty foul shots each until they each had taken a hundred. Singleton joined him at half-court in time to watch Sizemore snap in ten in a row. Singleton had spent much of the vacation searching for a black assistant coach, with no luck. Corvino had scored eighteen last night in Houston to lead them to a ten-point win over New York. It was comforting, in a way, to note in the *Globe* this morning that both Boston and L.A. were rotting in last place. Quinn Harrington was still hanging on. Drucker had missed the L.A. flight to San Francisco and been suspended for a week.

"There's Jack Phillips, an assistant now at Assumption," Singleton said. "One of their assistants and they don't really need two. He and Billy Williams, the head coach, like each other but never had agreed that much, especially about defense. He played at Holy Cross. He's six-three and powerful. Know of him?"

"I don't think so."

"I think he'd work out well. He's quiet, but tough, and a decent head coach prospect. Want to talk to him?"

"He's white?"

"He's white. Few blacks play for the Cross."

B.D. shrugged.

"I know what some of the kids want. I don't blame them. But everything's going well. They like you and respect you and already know they can win. And the alumni are ecstatic. I keep telling everyone what a long way we've got to go. It's amazing what a little positive publicity will do."

"I'll talk to him."

"How about tomorrow morning, before we fly down to Philadelphia?"

"Sure."

"Ten in my office?"

"Sounds good."

He sat next to Smith in the locker room and told him how much they needed an assistant coach right away, especially someone who could work with defenses and keep track of offensive and defensive trends, and that there were few people available.

"I want to keep winning," Smith said. "That's the most important thing right now. I can't think of anything else."

"Neither can I."

Smith looked at him and nodded. "Villanova's going to be tough. But I know them, I know what they've got. They can't shoot the way we can, and Collins is as tough inside as any of them."

"I agree." He stood. "I wanted to let you know what's happened since we talked the first day. Your jump shot's been working so well I didn't want to spring some cool Irish dude on you and screw things up."

He thought Smith would laugh. Instead he smiled and looked away. "Nothing's going to fuck things up," he said.

B.D. called Kate at six and got no answer, then drove to Lawrence at seven. Tomorrow night there was a party at Tom's apartment in Washington to celebrate his becoming a senator. He'd always liked the mix of people who gathered around his brother during his campaigns and victory parties. It would be hard not being there with Steph.

At the hospital, his mother was lying on her side, reading, when he walked into the room.

"I've been feeling better all of a sudden," she said. "Everything's in clearer focus. You just missed Kate. The boys are in Washington for a few days." She breathed hard. "I'm so disappointed I can't be there."

She folded the book closed and put it on the table beside the bed. She closed her eyes for several seconds then turned and propped herself and listened while he told her about Christmas in Chicago, his game in Philadelphia tomorrow night, which would keep him away from Washington.

"There'll be a lot of good people there," his mother said. "A lot of close friends."

"I won't be missed," he said with a smile.

"I'm getting my strength back," she said.

"You look a lot better," he said.

"I'm going to talk to them tomorrow about going home. There's no reason why I shouldn't go home now."

He called Kate from the hospital lobby.

"Are you alone?"

"No, my mother's here." Her voice was pleasant. "The boys are with Tom."

"I know—"

"I called you twice today, and thought I'd see you at the hospital. You really are back."

"I had a long practice session, and we're still searching for an assistant coach. How've you been?"

"All right—I missed you very much." She lowered her voice to say it.

"I did, too," he said.

"Has Stephanie left for Hawaii?"

"Yes."

"When will you see her?"

"I have no idea. I really don't know."

He stared into the lobby. A few people were watching him talk.

"I want to see you," he said.

"I can't tonight. My mother's going to be here with me. My father's out of town until tomorrow afternoon."

"I have a game in Philadelphia tomorrow night."

"I know. I can meet you at the apartment if you're flying back right after it. The boys'll be away till Thursday."

"I'll be late."

"I have the key you gave me. I'll be there when you get back. Just ask me to spend the night."

"Please spend the night with me," he said.

"Only if you win," she said. "B.D.?"

"Yes?"

"Good luck."

18

THEY WERE DOWN BY TEN AT THE TEN-MINUTE mark of the first half. Villanova's press and speed, their outside shooting talent and inside strength, their passing and the roaring crowd had put them in control, and when one of their guards hit a twenty-foot shot over Bobby Smith, B.D. called time.

"They're not that fucking good," Sizemore said and squeezed

a thin line of water from a plastic bottle into the back of his mouth, over his face and shoulders.

"We're not hitting," Cunningham said. "Christ, we've only got sixteen points."

"Okay," B.D. said and they leaned forward from the bench. "Cunningham at mid-court to break the immediate press, then a quick pass to Collins into the key. We'll just have to keep doing that to free Bobby to move one-on-one with the ball. And once we start hitting from the corner they'll give a little more underneath. Tight two-three zone. It's early. Let's kick ass."

They stood and put their hands together.

"Kill the bastards," Toner said and Collins blessed himself on the way back to the floor.

They double-teamed Smith again. Davis lobbed the ball up to Cunningham who turned and fired to Collins angling toward the basket. He hit the lay-up and drove the Villanova forward guarding him over a press table. The basket counted. Collins was called for a charging foul and the crowd focused its anger on him.

Collins watched the forward, blood on his face, being led to the bench. Then, when play began, he pulled down a rebound and led Smith into a fast break out of which Davis hit a reverse lay-up, got fouled, sank it, darted in to steal the in-bounds pass, sank that and got fouled again. And sank the foul shot. The lead was down to four, then climbed to eight again with just under a minute to play in the half, but Cunningham moved it down to six, with two cool, swishing foul shots.

46–40.

Villanova, after killing the clock for the last shot, threw the ball out of bounds.

Their locker room was silent. Cunningham and Sizemore had three fouls each, Collins two, and B.D. could almost smell defeat at the door.

"Six points is nothing," he said after watching them stretch and suck on oranges. "You know that. It can be erased in ten seconds."

They nodded.

"To win we're going to have to keep taking it to them inside, and blocking out on rebounds—and making them pay the price they've been paying whenever they take it in, despite the number of fouls we have. Otherwise they'll kill us." He looked them over. "I think they'll probably start shifting defenses to try and throw us off balance, half-court traps and shifting man-to-mans. So we'll just take our time and take it to them."

"Where're they ranked?" Toner said.

"Fifteenth," Cunningham said.

"They're shit," Toner said. "How'd they ever take the D.C. Christmas tourney?"

"No one boxed out Johnson and Cristoldi," Collins said, surprising them a little. "I read it in *Sports Illustrated*." He smiled.

They hesitated. Toner and Sizemore stood with surprised looks on their faces and pointed at him.

"The first of the season," Toner said. "Your first fucking banter, man. Your first contribution to locker room camaraderie."

He slapped Collins on the shoulder and a few minutes later, after B.D. had re-emphasized that they were only six down and to play hard each moment as it came, they whipped through the locker room door.

Smith cut the lead to two in the first minute and a half with two jumpers from the right, but picked up his third foul three minutes later and the Villanova lead moved back up to five.

"He's out for my ass," Smith said near the bench after getting a warning from both refs when he protested the foul, a holding call at the top of the zone.

"Watch it or they'll hit us with a technical," B.D. said.

"I want them to."

"I'll take care of it," B.D. said and took two steps onto the court and yelled, "How can you blow the whistle when you're pissing in your pants, both of you?" He drew an immediate technical, his second in three games. If he got another soon, Golden could con an agency into working it into a beer commercial.

Despite Villanova hitting the two technicals and then a long jump shot to increase the lead to nine, he thought they could win. Optimism. College ball was filled with it.

B.D. replaced Smith with Tyler Young, the freshman, who took charge right away. He wasn't quite as fast as Smith and didn't have Smith's shooting range and court savvy, but was quicker and dribbled well and he moved through Villanova's predictable, full-court, double-team defense. When they backed off into a zone, he hit a twenty-foot jump shot from the key. Seconds later Collins sneaked inside with a Sizemore pass, scored and hit a foul shot, bringing the lead back down to four. It hung there on traded baskets and foul shots for the next several minutes, with Smith back in for Young, and then Young in for Davis when he picked up his fourth foul.

Toner fouled out with three minutes left. Sizemore, Cunningham and Collins had four each. They were on the verge of being wiped out.

They were down by six with two-fifteen left. Collins spun into the middle for a short jumper. Four down. Villanova stalled and with a minute and twenty seconds left, Young, going for the steal, fouled one of the guards. B.D. put Davis back in for him, and the bench and Cushing fans behind it stood and applauded when he jogged off. B.D. shook his hand.

The Villanova guard missed the first of the one-and-one shots and with a minute five to go, after Cunningham had ripped down the rebound, Sizemore hit a long jumper from the corner.

78–76.

They could win. B.D. sent them into the tight, half-court, man-to-man press they'd worked on for an hour yesterday, a half-hour before leaving for the airport. Villanova, seeing it for the first time, lost the ball out-of-bounds.

He called time with forty-five seconds left and told Collins to free himself to the left for a quick jump shot off a Smith pass.

He missed it with thirty-two seconds to go, but got fouled and sank both shots.

Tie game.

They went into a full-court, man-to-man press. Smith stole the ball at mid-court and hit Davis underneath for a lay-up and the lead.

80-78.

Villanova, its bench and fans stunned, called time with twelve seconds left.

B.D. kneeled in front of them on the bench. They were roaring now.

"I can't fucking believe this," Sizemore said.

The Villanova band pumped.

"We'll drop back into the two-three zone," B.D. shouted. "Smith and Davis up a little higher than usual. No harassment on the take-in. Just fall into the zone. I think they'll expect some harassment and might lose a second or two. Collins in the middle underneath. I don't know what they're going to do, but hands up and don't let them drive. No driving at all. We've got to get whatever rebound there is. Be aggressive going for it and then protect the ball. They'll have to foul to stay alive. If there's a breakaway take it if you think you can make the pass. But only if you're certain. They'll have to sink one from the outside to tie. If they do we'll call time and set something up. We've got them beaten because we didn't play dead with four fouls on everyone."

One of the Villanova guards hesitated at the top of the key, moved to the left, tried passing inside when Davis guarded him tightly, and Collins snagged it and hit Smith at half-court.

He drove and slammed it home at the buzzer.

An 82–78 win.

They jumped and yelled and hugged each other, and when B.D. stood on the bench in the locker room and told them they were an excellent team and could only get better they cheered.

"We do have things to work on," he said. "Three o'clock practice tomorrow. Sleep late."

They shouted again. They were young enough, their scholarships secure enough now, to act, for a few minutes at least, as if they were extras in a 1930's football movie. He'd used ten of the twelve players, and all twelve had played for some time in his three games. Eight had scored tonight. No one was going to be exiled to the end of the bench. Last year three sophomores hadn't played at all and had transferred, one to Georgetown, two to Division II. He'd never force anyone into doing that.

Collins had hung back a little from the cheering and was dressing alone.

"Everything all right?" B.D. said.

"I'll say."

"You played a hell of a game. Nineteen points. Two free throws and the key steal at the end of the game. I don't know how many rebounds."

"Thanks," Collins said and smiled.

"Tell me if anything is wrong."

"I will."

"No one's pressing you about football again, are they?"

"No, not at all."

"About anything else?"

He looked at B.D. and shook his head slowly.

Singleton and a few students and parents met them at the airport. A Cushing bus would take most of the team back to the campus.

"Great game," Singleton said. "I listened to the whole thing. You guys were amazing. Want a ride back?"

"Yes." He glanced around for Kate. He doubted that she'd be in the apartment. She'd thought hard about it without the boys to distract her, he was sure, and decided not to see him. It would be over. Victory would be enough companionship for the winter.

Whenever he stepped into an airport terminal in the last year, and knew he wouldn't see his wife for two or three days, he'd felt empty. Now he wouldn't see her for several weeks, and he felt nothing at all.

"You're creating all kinds of excitement," Singleton said; the Cushing bus was behind them coming out of the airport. He'd shake everyone's hand again in the parking lot. "People have been calling the campus and my house tonight."

213

"Great," B.D. said.

"Tonight proved how good you really are. Tyler Young was a nice surprise."

"He was—Collins is still a puzzle."

"Oh?"

"He's playing like a bastard, but doesn't seem to be enjoying any of it. Maybe it's the violence underneath, I don't know."

Singleton said nothing. He'd sent out word through the head football coach for everyone to stay away from Collins or he'd fucking clean house.

"He wiped a guy out tonight," B.D. said. "I think it was the deciding factor in the game, even though it happened in the first half. It gave us immediate credibility underneath, and we gradually took charge of the boards."

"Pete Castoldi," Singleton said. "He scored only four after that. Ten for the game. He's been averaging twenty-three. Denny Clements, the athletic director, called me right after the game to tell me he'd got a fractured cheekbone. I asked him what the hell his point was and he didn't have any. He was just pissed that we beat him."

"The kid certainly bled enough."

"You're building a quick reputation."

"Me or the kids?"

"Both. Two technicals in three games." He smiled.

"Is that bothering you?"

"Jesus Christ no."

"Good. I think there might be something else with Collins."

"What's the worst it could be?"

B.D. hesitated, then shrugged. "Maybe it's nothing."

"I'll listen, and look around a little," Singleton said. "I hired Jack Phillips."

"Good," B.D. said, "he'll work out fine."

19

SHE OPENED THE APARTMENT DOOR JUST AS HE PUT his keys in the lock. She smiled well, then let it fade a touch.

"You coming in?" she said.

She was wearing a sweater, dungarees, and was barefoot.

"You're here," he said easily.

"I'm here."

She kissed him on the cheek and they moved into the living room and sat on the couch.

"Nice game," she said and looked pleased.

"Thanks," he said and felt their two weeks apart dissolve.

"I listened to part of it."

He took off his jacket, then took her hand, let it go, leaned across the couch and kissed her shoulder, her lips.

"How are you?" he said.

"I'm fine."

It was warm in the apartment now, and the bed, he hoped, would be warm and comfortable. He thought of Stephanie, of her kissing the writer, her arms around his neck, not on his shoulder as if she'd been taken by surprise, or on his chest urging him mildly away, but signalling that she liked him and was glad they'd be in Hawaii together.

"Was the game as exciting as they made it sound?"

"Probably more."

"People are going to take you seriously now."

"We're still only three and six."

"They were ranked in the top fifteen in the country."

215

"Too high," he said and moved closer to her and then she put her hand on his shoulder and kissed him.

"I missed you," she said.

"I know."

"I didn't want to miss you like that. It would have been easier not to see you again."

He nodded slightly.

"We went skiing again for a few days," she said. "All of those great-looking guys around. All of the turn-ons, and none of them as good-looking as you."

She stood, hesitated, and then carefully moved her sweater up and over her head, held it against her, against her breasts and stomach and wide shoulders. She put it on a chair and moved her dungarees down past her bare feet and came back to him. He held her again, kissed her mouth and shoulders and moved his tongue firmly across her nipples, kissed them, kissed her stomach and eased her back on the couch and helped her take off her pants. He kneeled beside her and brought his tongue across her swelling clitoris until she shuddered up against him and whispered "Jesus" into the early January dark.

He came quickly into her, in the bedroom upon the immaculate, expensive sheets and finally gave way to exhaustion, lying next to her, staring at the outline of her body, a white-blue hint of magic now against the diminished breath of Storrow Drive and the silent black run of the river. His wife was too far away for it to matter. Because all of the clocks were still ticking, the sun boiling and the stars still freezing. He had no guilt. Steph might as well have been walking on another planet now, bloodless and speechless, and young forever. The phone didn't ring with news or congratulations from Washington, or death from Lawrence, and he couldn't remember if he'd sent his brother the telegram he'd planned to send, and then he didn't care.

"Are you going to sleep now?" she said.

"No."

"Don't sleep."

"I can't."

216

She put her arm across his chest. "Do you know what I'm tired of?"

"What?" he said, surprised that she'd even begin to mention anything negative now, even though she'd said it pleasantly.

"Nothing," she said after a moment.

But she'd already said it, of course. Tired of being alone, sleeping alone, of letting herself be left alone by the Jordans. Why did she need them so much?

"Make love to me again, B.D.," she said. "Please do that."

She came, rolling gently, and when she did he did, as quietly as rain without wind.

"I really need you now," she said later, when he was almost asleep.

"I do, too."

"I know I'm falling in love with you."

He nodded in the dark, took her hand. "I already love you," he said and they both gave their minor lies time to slip from the room.

"Why the Christ did you have to be traded here?" she said.

"Because I'm old. And age is death in California, no matter what form it takes."

"Oh," she said and soon fell asleep across him.

20

SHE WAS UP AND DRESSED WHEN HE WOKE INTO bright sunlight at eight, standing in the bedroom doorway, wearing the sweater and dungarees she'd removed so quickly only hours before. She looked tired, and older now, and he didn't need or want her as much, and then did at the same time.

"You don't have much here for breakfast," she said.

She walked across the room and sat on the edge of the bed.

"What do you have planned?" he said. "Why are you up so early?"

She pushed her fingers back through his dark hair. It was too long. Maybe Singleton knew someone near the campus who could cut it without drawing a crowd.

"The boys'll be back at noon. They'll be excited and want to talk about everything that happened."

"We'll go out somewhere," he said.

He showered and shaved and stared at himself briefly in the mirror. There was defensive work to do in the afternoon, and he'd have to complicate the offense more. Anyone who'd seen last night's game, or studied the films, would press full-court and trap, and then stall if they started coming on. He'd have to use the whole court more, let Collins and Cunningham handle the ball in the back-court and not depend as much on Smith's ball handling; use Young and the others to keep Davis and Smith and Sizemore out of foul trouble and moving a hundred miles an hour when they were in. He felt good thinking about it. He, they, had a team, and he was in charge of it. In charge, of something for the first time in his life.

They drove to Copley Square and he was barely recognized now in the morning hustle of the restaurant where he and Maury had breakfast before he signed with Boston. It was too noisy and busy for them to talk. They drank coffee and orange juice and ate toast and minutes later were in her car in front of his apartment building.

She brushed her fingertips across his knuckles. "I told you last night that I loved you."

"That you were falling in love with me. I said I already love you."

She simply smiled at him.

She pulled her collar close to her neck in the hard sun. There was little wind on Beacon Street, no traces of snow. Boston just after the Christmas holidays was a bleak and cruel city. But it was neither right now. He held her and kissed her.

She cupped his face. "Let's plan on Saturday night, here," she said, "after your game."

"All right," he said, and swallowed and held her and watched his breath move over her shoulder.

21

THEY GOT BEHIND 6–0 IN THE FIRST MINUTE against Seton Hall on Saturday night at Cushing, then tied them in the next and blew them away, leading by eighteen at the half and winning by thirty-eight. They smacked Rhode Island the following Tuesday night by twenty-three, Sizemore hitting thirty-one and Collins twenty-eight. The St. John's game at Cushing on the fifteenth in front of a loud, hungry, packed crowd was tight, hard, physical, wearing and almost too intense. But Collins hit three free throws in the last thirty seconds to give them a five-point victory.

Six and six.

Mid-January and they were growing like a bastard.

They blew Syracuse away two nights later and after the game, after all the cheering and the television cameras and photographers and local and national reporters had gone, B.D. sat in the Cushing locker room and was left with an empty, January Monday night feeling in his stomach, set off, he guessed, by the sudden drift of warm, southwest wind that had thawed Boston again over the weekend. He'd seen Kate on Sunday, his second short night with her since their long night of early January love. His mother had gone back to the hospital, the restricting pain making her home an impossible, mocking place. She couldn't lie down. Sitting, even with the drugs she was taking, was agony, and now, as Kate had told him yesterday, she was drifting through a cool, timeless, hospital world waiting for death. He hadn't seen her in almost two weeks, though he had talked to her on the phone when she returned home. There was little to say; he'd been swamped with the endless, detailed work of preparing his team to win.

Stephanie had called from Hawaii five days after they'd said goodbye at the airport. It was hot, she'd said, and the location scenes were more difficult, taking a lot longer to put together than they'd thought. She hated the show now, felt confined by it more than ever. She missed him, she said, ached for him, and was lonely and homesick.

He talked to Tom a few days after he officially became a senator. Tom was relieved to finally have all of the power, real and potential. They both knew it was only a question of days with their mother. She would be gone. The house would be empty. There'd be no reason to return to Lawrence. Except to see Kate, in Andover. Kate—

Phillips had immediatley strengthened the defense, making it quicker, more alert, more sure in its movements away from the ball.

He went to Singleton's office after all of the winning voices had left the corridors outside the gym floor. They shook hands and sat and drank from cold cans of Budweiser. One beer and then a long night of sleep and a morning of studying tapes of Connecticut's last three games. If they beat Connecticut, and they should whale them, he thought, they'd be eight and six and close to a top twenty ranking.

"Another great win," Singleton said.

He nodded. "Jack's working out fine."

"We were lucky to get him. He leave already?"

"He doesn't like the long ride back to Worcester every night."

Phillips said little on the bench and tried to impress no one during practice. He showed and encouraged and hadn't come close to trying to put anyone down, and the kids listened to him and liked him.

"I think he'll make an excellent head coach," Singleton said and they turned to the knock at the open door.

Second semester classes had begun. Only Davis was close to academic trouble. Cunningham and Smith had had academic tutors for two years. Collins, who'd been recruited by Dartmouth and Brown as well as by Cushing and Holy Cross, and several schools including Notre Dame and Penn State to play football, had got an A in economics, a B plus in American Lit.

B.D. had seen her in the stands, sitting with other girls, staring at something on the court, aware, he was sure, that he was looking at her then, stirred by her open coat.

"Janet," Singleton said and waved. "How are you? Come in."

"I'm fine," she said and moved into the room and sat next to the desk.

"Want a beer?"

She shook her head.

"We're briefly celebrating seven in a row. See it?"

She nodded. "You're going to become national champions."

"Not yet," B.D. said. "But thanks anyway. I saw you in the stands."

"I waved once, but you didn't see me."

He looked directly at her. She was only twenty-one.

"Begin classes today?" Singleton said.

"I went to one," she said and B.D. wondered if he should leave.

"How's Doug been?"

"He's fine, but I think he's working too hard." She glanced at B.D. for a moment, then got up and walked a few steps toward the door.

"Going back to your dorm?"

She nodded. "I just wanted to say hello and congratulations. Say hello to Barbara and tell her I'll come by the house soon, before I get mired in work."

They stared at the door for a moment after she'd left.

Singleton hadn't asked him to dinner again; he'd talked to his wife briefly last week. She was pleasant looking, but wouldn't be asked to star on daytime television.

"She's beautiful," Singleton said. "And young," he said after B.D. agreed.

"Young," he said.

"She didn't come by to say hello to me," Singleton said and drank his beer.

B.D. hoped she'd be in the lobby later when he left, or on the steps, toying with the idea of wickedness in the warm night. Or in the parking lot where they'd talked before Christmas, and he was disappointed when she wasn't. He swallowed away an urge to call her and drove quickly back to the apartment.

22

"WANT TO TALK ABOUT IT NOW?" HE SAID TO COLlins at the end of practice the next day.

Phillips was running Sizemore, Smith, Young and Davis through zone-press moves against the freshmen. Cunningham and Toner and others had begun the first of a hundred foul shots each. So many games were won on the foul line, especially near the end of the season and in tourneys. No one could really duplicate tight-game pressure in practice, obviously, but they could talk about it, think about it with each shot.

"I think I should," Collins said.

"Here?"

"No, not here."

"We'll go to Singleton's office then."

"Okay," Collins said.

Collins had told him during a brief break in practice that he finally had to get something out before the afternoon was over.

Singleton was on the road with the hockey team until the end of the week. They sat in front of his desk and said nothing for several seconds. The spires and towers of Cushing accepted the red dusk of four o'clock and the world looked important yet peaceful from here.

"We have a chance to go a long way, don't we," B.D. said.

"I think so." Collins was sweating heavily and wiped his chest and arms with a towel.

"Villanova hasn't lost since we beat them."

He nodded.

"You like Phillips?"

"Very much. He doesn't talk down to anyone."

"He was a good guard at Holy Cross. He knows what he's doing."

Collins breathed through his mouth. "Are you staying here next year?"

"I don't know." He said it quickly. He knew exactly what he was going to do.

Collins held the towel around the back of his massive neck. "That's not what I wanted to talk about."

"I didn't think so. The football team screwing around again?"

He smiled. "Since we've been winning some of the guys have come around, been apologetic. That's never really bothered me anyway. Not really. I guess I just used it to hide something else."

"Tell me about it?"

"It happened in late October," Collins said. "Two guys, in their mid-to-late twenties, it was hard to tell, they could easily have passed for students, came up to me on campus on my way to a morning class and said hi and how are things in Waltham. Like a jerk I said not bad and we started shooting the breeze about nothing at all. Then, just like that, they said goodbye and headed off in another direction. I saw one of them about a week later in my economics lecture class. I didn't think I'd ever seen him there before, but it's a big class. He gave me a wave, and then caught up with me and walked me to my next class. He started talking about money right away, how tough it was to make it financially in college and how hard it must be for an athlete, even with a full scholarship, if his parents had no money because NCAA rules were so tough and Cushing followed them strictly, and with training time and practice time there was no chance to get a part-time job. It was obvious what he was doing. A lot of guys playing ball are dead broke and vulnerable. I'm neither, and most of the guys on the team have enough money."

B.D. sat back and listened.

"I eat lunch at Wilson's a lot. They came in one afternoon

223

when I was having a hamburger at the counter and asked if they could talk to me out on Beacon Street when I finished. They were over-friendly, almost too polite. I was smart enough to tell them they could talk about anything they wanted right there. There was an empty stool on my left and plenty of space for three of us." He smiled. "They were just so fucking dumb. They told me right there, standing and sitting next to me at the counter that they could guarantee me serious extra money and other things every week if I'd just do two or three simple things for them."

B.D. nodded for him to go on, praying that he'd done nothing wrong, hadn't even come close to doing anything wrong. Collins wouldn't. He wouldn't throw his life away. None of his players would.

"I asked them if it involved basketball. They said yes."

"What did you tell them?"

"That I didn't want to hear another fucking thing. That I didn't know who they were or what they wanted, but that they had the wrong fucking guy and that I was suddenly very pissed off." He wiped at his face with the towel and looked angry. "They left. They just looked at me and each other and got up and were gone. Three days later I got a phone call in the dorm from a voice that sounded a lot like one of them. He asked if I'd thought the offer over and would like more information. I said what offer; no offer had been made to me. All I knew was that if two fucking creeps tried talking to me again I was calling the police because there were laws against greasers walking the Cushing campus."

How ironic it was, B.D. thought, that he, the non-Catholic coach, had listened to Collins' confession. But Collins had committed no crime, no sin, and he wasn't confessing a thing. He was only talking, confiding in someone he trusted.

"Good. And then?"

"I haven't seen either of them since."

"Did you tell anyone about it?"

"No."

"Why not?"

224

"There was no one to talk to. The team was working out but not really together then. Simmons was a total asshole. I wouldn't tell him anything about anything. For all I know he sent them to talk to me. And his two assistants were creeps. I mean dumb bastards who might have taken the thing on their own to the newspapers. I understand they can't get work." He leaned back and seemed more relaxed now. Collins' knees and shoulders glistened in the fluorescent light. "I'm not close to any of the priests. My girl's worried enough about school, and my mother." He smiled and shook his head. "I bet they knew I have no father." He stared toward the windows, straightened.

"What about the police?"

"One more phone call and I would have."

"Why not Singleton?"

"I would have but none of us realized what a good guy he is until he got rid of Simmons. I thought about everything after the terrible start and just didn't want any part of it anymore. It just wasn't worth it. If you hadn't come by the dorm I would have quit, transfered to a division II or III school and played next year just for the sake of playing. I'm glad now I didn't."

"You did the right thing," B.D. said. "I'm sure they're far from Cushing now, whoever they are. They go where there's no resistance, obvious discontent. That's probably why they showed here in the first place. They look for guys with girl friends, or who are known gamblers, or are pissed about the way things are going. If someone gets angry, the way you did, they disappear."

He gave Collins a tap on the arm.

"Tell Singleton," B.D. said.

"I will, this afternoon."

"I'm glad you told me."

"I'm glad I did," Collins said. "It just got to be absurd. I was here to learn something, and give something back and even had a good time playing ball. I decided against football, but the football team bugged the shit out of me even though they knew they were supposed to stay the hell out of my way and respect my decision. And then I got approached by two front men, or whatever the hell they were, to point shave. At least I assume that's what the hell they wanted. Maybe they wanted me to deal coke."

"It'll never happen again to you."

"Did it ever to you?"

"Never."

"What kind of person would do something like that, throwing a game? What kind of slime would sell himself, his soul for a few dollars?"

"Guys have done it, a lot of guys, and for very little."

Collins stared at the floor for a minute, then stood and shook B.D.'s hand.

"You still worried about hurting people underneath?"

"Not after the shots I've taken in the last two games. Nothing cheap, but they still hurt like a bastard."

They walked to the door.

"Sizemore and Toner are hot shits, aren't they?"

B.D. nodded.

"I never thought so, really, until half-time at the Villanova game. I began really liking them. None of that would have happened with Simmons. We had a whole different edge on then. They hated him and showed it. Singleton got rid of him just in time. One more week and everyone would have gone."

23

THEY PLAYED CONNECTICUT IN HARTFORD ON SATurday night, the game more difficult than it should have been. They were tired from the two and a half hour bus ride down, and Connecticut scored six points in the last minute of the first half to tie them. He watched Phillips re-emphasize offensive and defensive patterns and strategy, and then, just before they went back out onto the court, stood and told them simply to stop screwing around and play basketball.

They fell five points behind in the first two minutes.
He called time.

"Half-court press," he said. "Double-team the ball as soon as they bring it over. Also move the ball to the right more, right into where they're overplaying. It'll free Davis on the left. And play tough. They're getting to the point where they think they can beat us. Don't let them. Take it to them."

Davis hit a fifteen-footer. Collins stole the ball a few seconds later, igniting a fast-break that ended with Smith going in for a lay-up and being fouled. He made the shot to tie the game. Connecticut travelled and Collins tapped in the rebound of Davis' second wide-open jumper. Off and galloping with a sudden two point lead. They won by twenty-two and were hungry for the next game, against Pitt at home on Tuesday night. A win and they'd make the top twenty in every poll, probably the top fifteen in a few, and would be featured in stories around the country.

He was back at his apartment at two o'clock, the sub-freezing morning a nightmare of loneliness at his windows. He wouldn't see Kate till Monday or Tuesday. He called Hawaii. It was still Saturday night there, and she wasn't in. He'd take a long hot shower and search for sleep. He was to meet Tom at the hospital tomorrow afternoon.

He woke startled, anxious, at three o'clock. He sat holding onto his breath, his knee ablaze. It was silent everywhere now except inside his racing body. The moon had brushed its frozen breath across Storrow and Memorial Drive. Where would he be now if he hadn't won all of his games?

He got up and dressed and drove out to the edge of the Cushing campus where he knew there was an all-night diner. In the blue-lit haze of cigarette smoke and liquored breaths he bought three hamburgers and a pile of french fries to go, avoiding the stares of a short order cook, a waitress in her fifties and two men in a booth. He wished them all well and they waved goodbye and he brought the food back to the apartment after buying the Sunday *Globe,* and stayed up reading it and *Sports Illustrated* and *Time* until six o'clock. He hadn't read a novel, a complete book of any

227

kind, since early summer. Basketball had turned him into a literary lout.

24

THE HOSPITAL WAS CROWDED AT ONE O'CLOCK, A Sunday visiting place. His mother was alone, asleep, or drugged into something that resembled sleep, the doctors conditioning her for death. He hardly recognized her.

He went to the bed and touched her arm. It was warm, and he thought for a moment of kissing it, but didn't. He walked away from the bed and stared out the window, across the parking lot where people hurried away from the cold. The mills along the river had turned purple against the wind. Nothing would ever blow them away.

A nurse appeared at the door.

"She's been resting nicely for the last few hours, Mr. Jordan," she said. She smiled at him and moved to the side of the bed. "The senator is in the private waiting room a few doors down from the elevator."

He thanked her and left. The waiting room door was open. Tom was with Dick Miller, his campaign manager and current administrative aide. Miller, whom he hadn't seen since November, got up and they shook hands and told each other they looked great. Miller had been close friends with Tom since high school, had played football and baseball at Lawrence High and, after college, had spent two years trying to move to his left more quickly at short, to his right in the outfield, to stay with the curve and lay off the slider. After a season and a half of triple-A with the Dodgers and a trip down to double-A in May of the following year, he'd said fuck it and got a job the following September teaching history and coaching baseball at Andover High. Tom's

228

victory had saved him from the obscurity of both jobs, though both were honest enough, and vital.

B.D. shook Tom's hand. "A senator," he said. "Amazing."

"Hard to believe sometimes," Tom said and they sat down.

"You're in the *Globe* more than we are these days," Miller said and glanced at Tom who looked, B.D. thought, very much the promising national politician. It would be easier for Tom now, of course, if his mother were well so he could continue to show how devoted he was to her in public. And if he were still married to Kate every appearance with the boys wouldn't remind the midwest of divorce and the black woman from Boston he was seen with too often.

"Blame it all on Maury Golden," B.D. said, "and the fact that the team's playing so well. Boston's always hungry for a winner, you guys know that. And besides, I'm a hell of a lot more liberal than my brother."

They laughed, and then said nothing for a moment, trying, he supposed, to continue to avoid the painful reality here in Lawrence.

"You have them moving," Miller said.

"Thanks."

"I caught part of the second half of the St. John's game on television. You looked crisp. It's always nice when a young team looks that way through the second half."

"It's part of the strategy. Not too fast, but no delays. No one's afraid to shoot. We play a tight zone, or zones, when it's right to, if the other team rebounds or penetrates well. But we don't tolerate stalls. We go after anyone who delays, fouling a lot if we have to get the ball back."

Miller nodded, exchanged brief comments about Boston and L.A., then got up and said he had a few calls to make and would be back.

"You still like it then," Tom said when he was gone.

He nodded. "How's Washington?"

"Interesting. People are in a hurry to get to me and tell me everything. It happened as soon as I was sworn in and had the

229

office. I just have to remain distant enough and keep perspective, and be patient. The senate is six years. Things evolve. After this year, when all of this is over, and you're back in California, try it."

"Try what?"

"This. Politics."

He shook his head. "I'm an athlete. That's all I'm going to be. Politics is your turf." He'd almost said too much. Almost. "She was sleeping when I saw her just now."

Tom stared into the rug. "She won't be able to go home anymore." His voice rasped when he said it.

"Have you talked to the doctors in the last few days?"

"They're trying to keep as much pain away as they can." He swallowed. "She might appear to get better for a day, two, and then it'll be terrible again."

They got up and moved to one of the windows that overlooked a concrete park, flat rooftops, a narrow street with cars parked with their wheels up on the sidewalk. Big American cars. Working class Lawrence would never buy foreign or compact.

"How far do you think you'll take them?" Tom said.

"I don't know. We've got four tough games in a row. It's impossible to say."

"They going to rank you in the top twenty tomorrow?"

"I don't think so."

"I've got to fly back to Washington in a little while. I've got a million commitments. I've got to watch that, too, over-committing myself. Kate said she'd be coming by, and I'll stay in close touch this week." He faced B.D. "It's hard to accept that you're here, after all these years. I've wanted to tell you that since you took the Cushing job."

"I know."

"It really is. And Ma thinks you took the job, partly at least, because she's dying."

"I didn't." He should have lied and said he did.

Tom looked away. He obviously couldn't let it all out here, start a fight now.

"A lot of people in Boston still don't understand why you did it, even though you're winning."

He waited for a moment. "I'll be gone in March," he said. "One day after the season ends."

"Just like that," Tom said.

"Just like fucking magic," he said, too quickly, making it necessary for Tom to answer him, if not now, then soon.

They went back to their mother's room, stared at her for a moment, then went into the corridor where Miller was waiting. They shook hands and said goodbye and nothing else.

He stayed for another half-hour and when Kate didn't arrive took his time driving back to his apartment. He'd watch a basketball game on television, and then prepare for Tuesday night's game against Pittsburgh at Cushing.

She called him at five.

"Did you see her today?" Her voice was light and positive.

"She was asleep. Tom and Dick Miller were there. It's simply a question of days now."

"I feel so badly for her, so helpless."

"I know," he said.

"Come here tonight."

"All right." He needed her kindness, the comfort in her legs and mouth. The smooth beat of her pulse against his chest. Her goodness.

"The boys will be going to bed early."

"I'll be there at nine-thirty," he said.

"I want you," Kate whispered.

25

THEY SURPRISED HIM BY BEATING PITT WITH EASE, the crowd at Cushing delirious with victory, especially when he was able to clear his bench in the last three minutes. On Monday a story about him and the team appeared in *Sports Illustrated*, with pictures of him and Collins and Smith and Singleton, and action shots that included everyone else. The story was titled "Sudden New Power in the East," and Sizemore yelled the words whenever he hit a jump shot.

The article quoted Stephanie Green. She said she missed him, but that they both understood the distances their work imposed. Which one of her agents' writers, he wondered, had given her or *Sports Illustrated* that? And who had released the picture he saw that morning in the *Globe* of her walking arm-in-arm with Gary Prince, the blond writer? It hurt too much to see it, blackening, damaging his blood again. It would make things harder, or maybe easier, in April.

They flew to Washington on Saturday and blew past Georgetown in the final three minutes, winning by twelve, and were ranked fourteenth by AP on Monday, fifteenth by UPI. Stephanie had come back to Malibu on Sunday and called, warning him that a foolish picture of her lying on the beach in a bikini with most of her ass and breasts exposed, Gary Prince lying too close to her, might appear in *People*. It did. At least she was wearing sunglasses. The few sentences under the picture noted that they'd become good friends during the on-location filming of "Dial California" and that she was about to sign a contract for the lead role in *Sweet Thunder*, a made-for-television movie scripted by Prince.

He got up early on Tuesday and walked out onto Beacon Street, accepting February. It was cold but windless and clear and he breathed the light, inch-deep snow that had fallen across the sidewalks the night before. He felt good and walked to Copley Square for the *Globe*, a container of coffee and two plain doughnuts. He brought his purchases back and went over notes and stats Phillips had compiled from scouting reports of Providence College, their opponent tomorrow night at the Civic Center. He'd drive to Cushing at eleven for an hour's meeting with Phillips and Tony Gordon, the freshman coach, on the best way to force Providence into early mistakes. It should, he knew, be an easy win, and it was always best to prepare hard for easy wins.

February. A story would appear soon about his coaching in *Newsweek*, and would certainly stick in his brother's throat. Maybe his rented car would hit a patch of ice and slam into an oak tree. Careful, Jordan.

There were still six weeks left in the season. More, because now they were certain to make the NCAA tourney. Singleton said he was sure that if they buried Providence, and then beat Villanova, still undefeated since the loss to Cushing and ranked eighth now, they'd make the top ten, maybe sail as high as fifth. Nice thoughts.

Golden called just as he was leaving.

"There's been a lot of book interest," he said.

"How much?"

"Five houses. I wouldn't have called unless there were at least five. But there'll be a lot more because you're a hot item now, Jordan. You're perceived as being in control of your life. You had the courage to quit and then take a coaching job with a team that had opened in chaos. You're not limping around waiting to get off a disabled list for two minutes of playing time every three games like some assholes are."

"And I'm winning."

"You are."

"That's the key."

"I doubt if there'd be interest in anything if you hadn't won a fucking game, B.D."

He laughed.

"We can either let them ghost you, do a straight story on you, or do a first person with your name and the writer's on the cover. Whatever you're most comfortable with."

"It's too early for a book on me."

"No it isn't."

"I'm too young."

"You're just right. It's got nothing go do with age anyway. You've won ten in a row after they opened with zero."

233

"We're going to win a hell of a lot more." He was surprised he'd said it, especially to Maury, now.

"That's what I mean, you're just catching fire now. And the ad possibilities. They don't give a shit if you've got a bad knee anymore."

"I think we'll make the final four."

"You do that, Jordan, and I'll have the world at your feet in April. Are you interested, in a book?"

"I'm interested. I just can't be distracted right now. Not at all."

"I've got your go-ahead then."

"To explore things for later, yes."

"I'm glad you said no to one five years ago, and last year. This will have a much wider appeal."

"I'll have to have complete approval of everything in it."

"Absolutely," Golden said. "It'll have to be done right."

26

PRACTICE WAS ALERT AND LIVELY. DAVIS WAS MOVing well to his right now as well as his left, and hitting behind Smith and Cunningham screens. It would force pressure away from Sizemore and give Collins a bit more breathing room on the left side.

He was watching Phillips maneuver them through a slight variation of the two-one-two zone when Singleton's secretary tapped him on the shoulder.

"A phone call for you in the office," she said. "It's the senator."

At four o'clock the sun still lived in the top floors of some of the campus buildings and he stood beside Singleton's desk and picked up the receiver. Singleton was away at a meeting in Boston.

"Tom," he said.

"B.D. The hospital just got in touch with me, one of her

doctors. She died this afternoon." His voice was distant, hollow, as if he'd been crying, or were about to.

"God—" he said softly and felt himself choking up. "Are you all right?"

"I'm all right. I'm leaving for the airport in a few minutes. Christ it hurts, even though I knew—"

"I know," he said.

"It must have torn you apart when Pa died," Tom said.

"It still hurts, and this does, very much." He wiped at his cheekbones. Sonofabitch. "Should I pick you up at the airport?"

"Miller's going to. He's in Boston. I just talked to Kate."

"How is she?"

"She's taking it calmly. She always stays calm. We can meet at Ma's house at eight, if you want, and then go down to the funeral parlor to make all of the arrangements, decide what we want to do."

"All right."

"I've got to go. It's going to be hard."

B.D. stood for a minute and pressed his fingertips into the desk, then walked out past Singleton's secretary, who was on another line and smiled at him as he left. He'd function simply, mechanically, until it was over. Tom and his staff and Kate would take care of all of the details that grief required. He'd simply go along, informing the people who ought to know. Everyone in Massachusetts would know soon enough anyway. The story would be in all of the local newscasts, all of the local papers.

The team had drifted into the locker room for a strategy talk. Phillips stood outside the door.

"Christ, they learn fast," he said. "How'd they get to be as smart as they are and all be here at the same time?"

B.D. looked at him.

"Everything all right?"

"I think I've told you about my mother being sick."

He nodded.

"She died this afternoon."

"I'm really sorry, B.D. I really am." He touched his shoulder briefly. "What can I do?"

"You'll have to take the team tomorrow night."

"Of course. Everything'll be fine. We're well prepared."

"I'm going to tell the kids, then I've got to get back to my apartment and be in Lawrence."

He nodded. "How old was she?"

He told him and watched him shake his head slowly.

"I'll be back for the Villanova game."

"Fine."

He walked into the locker room and got their attention and told them. They looked blank and said nothing.

"Jack Phillips will coach you tomorrow night in Providence, and keep the regular practice and pre-game schedules. I'll be back for Saturday, and Saturday night's game against Villanova." He hesitated, then nodded slightly. "She was very sick all winter. She went down to almost nothing, and is out of the terrible pain she suffered. We're all going to miss her very much."

They came up to him and shook his hand. Sizemore held his arm and Collins said, "I'm really very sorry."

He drove back to his apartment and tried to call Stephanie at the house in Malibu. They'd agreed last week that it wouldn't be a good idea, with his schedule and her fatigue, for her to come to Boston for a few days. She'd said she wouldn't be filming again until Monday and would just hang around the house for the week, recovering from Hawaii. Now she had no choice. She had to come. But there was no answer, and she hadn't reactivated the answering service.

He called the Chandlers. They hadn't seen her or heard from her since December. Neither had the Needhams, nor the Sachs, people they saw occasionally on the beach.

He sat and studied the kitchen table.

Kate called and started to cry and he told her that it was all right, that the suffering was finally over.

"It's better for her now," Kate said.

"Did you see her today, or last night?"

"Last night."

"Were you able to talk to her?"

"I was with her and held her hand." She said. "That's all."

He said nothing.

"It's going to be difficult," she said.

"It is."

She said she'd be at the house in Lawrence at eight, that she'd promised his mother she'd help take care of the details, and then she told him that she loved him.

"I really do, B.D."

"I love you, too," he said.

He called Malibu again and got no answer. Stephanie's agent was out of town and no one at his office or at the studio knew where she was. He left messages for her to call, and included the numbers at the funeral parlor and his mother's house and then sent a telegram with the same information to be left at the Malibu house, emphasizing that it was urgent. But he knew enough now to know that she was gone for the week, or most of it, and that he'd probably have to go through the wake and funeral without her.

He dressed in a sport coat and dark slacks and pulled a tie up under a button-down collar. Tomorrow and Thursday he'd wear a dark blue suit and dark tie and look like everyone else.

So he drove north again, into the dark. But the nights were shrinking now, in less than four weeks it would be March, and there'd be light enough to overcome this final, blood-scarring break with what he once was.

They hugged and shook hands and cried in the living room. Tom and Miller had picked Kate up and they all went to the funeral home together. He listened and agreed to everything, including the expensive casket and the decision to have some people back to the house after the funeral. The wake, it had already been decided, would be tomorrow afternoon and evening, the funeral on Thursday.

"Is Steph going to have trouble getting a flight in?" Tom had asked at the house.

"She was filming on location in L.A. when I called," he said. "I haven't talked to her yet."

Tom and Miller were staying at the senator's apartment in Andover. There was no chance to talk to Kate alone. B.D. drove back to Boston and called Malibu again with the same result, then fell asleep waiting for Stephanie's voice.

27

AT TWO O'CLOCK THE FUNERAL PARLOR WAS SUDdenly crowded with sobbing neighbors, aging relatives. Some shook his hand, hugged him. Others didn't know who he was, or pretended not to, this cowardly betrayer of family love when his mother needed him the most. His return to Boston had probably helped kill her.

Flowers overflowed the enormous room that held the casket into a lounge where he went at two-thirty. He watched Tom and the city's overweight, red-faced mayor grin and listen to a local ward heeler, his head tilted slightly to the right, a slight smile on his face, deliver a tale of greed or woe or political insanity, its punch line spinning Tom and his honor away with laughter.

Kate, in a dark gray dress, hair pulled back, stood in another corner talking to a group of older women. Her mother and father sat on a couch against a wall with someone he didn't recognize. Then he and Tom moved to the closed casket again and shook hands as more people crowded in, lined up to kneel in front of the casket, then maneuvered for a place to sit or stand and shake other hands and talk about the Jordans.

Only a few people had asked where Stephanie Green was. He told them she was on her way in from the coast.

"Did you get in touch with her?" Tom had asked earlier.

B.D. shrugged no.

"Where do you think she is?"

238

"I have no idea."

"We can't delay anything."

"I don't want you to."

The team, along with Phillips, Gordon and Singleton, arrived, to his surprise, at three, and when he choked up Sizemore hugged him and told him he was great, and that he was personally going to kick ass in Providence for him tonight, which made both of them smile. B.D. introduced them all to Tom and Kate and Miller. Singleton talked to Tom and Miller about Cushing and Notre Dame football for the ten minutes they'd allowed themselves before the bus ride south.

He drifted through a smoking area when they had gone, looking young and vulnerable in their coats and ties, which he never required on trips. Only Collins and Cunningham, and then Gordon and Phillips and Singleton, had kneeled and blessed themselves. He took a drink at a water cooler near the funeral director's door. One of the three brother-owners said it was the biggest crowd they'd ever had, and he hoped it wouldn't be too cold tonight because people would be waiting on the street to get in.

"It's quite a tribute to your mother," he said. "Quite a tribute."

Kate had to leave before four to get the boys. They were upset, she'd said last night, but would be all right. Tom had agreed, and at four-thirty he and Tom and Miller sat in the lounge and stared at the thick, dark-blue rug. He'd called Malibu an hour before. Still no answer. Then he had asked Maury Golden, who'd called early in the morning to say how sorry he was and that he wouldn't be able to make the funeral, to help him locate Stephanie, tell her what had happened and when the funeral was. "I'll put people on it right away," Maury said, and told B.D. to try to take it easy.

"Heard from her yet?" Tom said.

"Not yet. She's not filming this week. The whole cast got back from Hawaii on Sunday. I have no idea where she is, but have sent word out for her."

He tapped his fingers against the pockets of his blue suitcoat and stood.

"She really resents my having gone along with the trade, my being in Boston now." He smiled. "She's masked it well, but resents it. I guess she's not the only one."

Tom stood, stepped back. "Let's go over to Sullivan's now," he said. "He's going to join us in his private dining room. I didn't want to ask Kate. Maybe I should have." He looked sharply at B.D. "No, it would have been a bad idea."

Sullivan hugged them at the door, then led them to a three-table dining room just off his office where they sipped red wine from thin glasses and were served roast beef and peas and salad by two waiters in white jackets.

"I loved your mother," Sullivan said. "She and your father were always good and kind and understanding to us growing up, whenever we came over, any time day or night in high school. But she didn't like our parties very much," he said after wiping at his eyes.

They laughed easily. She had been almost hysterical one night during Christmas vacation of his senior year in high school, when she and their father had come home from a late movie to find B.D. and Sullivan and Levine and eight or ten others, all with dates and drunk or half-drunk, rock 'n roll blaring, couples dancing in the dining room and living room and making out in the kitchen and pantry and B.D.'s bedroom; and Tom, a high school sophomore, sleeping in his father's chair in the den with a beer can in his hand and barf on his shirt. The party had begun at Sullivan's house, but had been forced out by one of his older sisters and her friends, and had moved two miles to the Jordans, gotten noisy and crowded until B.D. finally didn't care, even though he knew his mother would piss her pants when she got home.

"They listened to all of our bullshit," Sullivan said. "All of the nonsense I had to say about everything. Did you know your ma came to see me in the hospital in Boston when I came back from the war and couldn't get the damn leg right?"

"I didn't know that," B.D. said.

240

"Neither did I," Tom said.

"I'm going to miss her. I got to the hospital to see her only twice, once just two days ago. The day before yesterday—I don't think she recognized me, Tommy, I really don't. I didn't know it was that bad, and I feel awful that I didn't go more."

Sullivan's eyes had filled again. Tom told him that no one knew, that he was beautiful and that his mother always loved him, got up and walked to the edge of the room, his back turned to the table.

He came back to the silence of the table and they ate for a while without talking.

"She understood you, B.D.," Sullivan said.

"I know she did, finally."

"She knew how good you had to become and could only do it in another place. She finally understood that."

"We talked about it this winter," he said.

"And she knew why you had to come back. She told me at the hospital."

"Why?" Tom said, surprising them.

"She didn't explain why, Tom. She just said she knew why."

"Why don't you tell us why now, B.D.," Tom said. Maybe it was the taste of crying that made his words sound bitter.

"Tom—" Miller warned. So, obviously, they talked about it, his being around and grabbing the spotlight just when Tom Jordan deserved and wanted it the most. He was certain they knew about his affair with Kate. They knew everything. He leaned back, and then he didn't give a shit if they knew or didn't know. It didn't matter. His mother was dead and his winning season would be over in March. Everything was almost over, including his marriage.

"We all know that B.D. had to play out this year," Sullivan said.

"That's not what I meant," Tom said. He was looking into the middle of the table, and B.D. knew that all of the anger, imprisoned fifteen years ago, unlocked now by wine and fatigue and death, was rising in his throat.

He hesitated, waited, then looked at Sullivan who was pushing back his chair, his eyes widening as he looked toward the door.

"Will you look at who just appeared," he said.

They turned. The figure in the back doorway was short, lean and pale, his thick dark hair receding. He was wearing a dark blue suit, white shirt and conservative blue tie, and he put out his hand when Sullivan went to him at the door.

"Levine," Sullivan said. "Jesus Christ, Arnie Levine."

Arnie shook Sullivan's hand, then came to the table where B.D., Tom and Miller were standing now. They hesitated, then quietly shook hands and hugged and smiled and laughed.

"B.D. Jordan," Levine said. "And Tom Jordan and Dick Miller."

"Arnie," B.D. said. "No one knows where you've been."

"Here and there. Around, in the world. On the run, but not exactly on the run anymore."

They sat down. One of the waiters looked at Sullivan and then put plates and silverware in front of Levine.

"I heard about your mother's death," he said evenly. "I read about it in today's New York *Times*. I'm very sorry." He looked at B.D., then Tom. "I liked your mother very much." His voice was almost secretive.

Levine, B.D. thought, his old, close friend. Levine had broken his mother's and father's heart by dropping out of Princeton, and then out of America. B.D. hadn't seen Levine since the long, lonely winter night when youth really ended for them all and they had to start blaming themselves if they fucked up their lives, the night before the day when he took his real first step toward freedom. Tomorrow, B.D. thought, after the funeral, when he drove from Lawrence to Boston, he'd take his last.

"I wasn't able to see my mother and father buried," Levine said with a tight smile. "Not that I really care now. Not really. They wrote me off as soon as I left. Wasn't that nice of them. One of the hallmarks of their generation. They insisted their kids live out their fantasies of what kids should do. I guess that's why we both took off, finally, wasn't it, B.D." He leaned back, not

242

wanting a response. "This yours, totally?" he said to Sullivan.

Sullivan nodded.

"It's a fine place," he said and stared at him for several moments. "I heard the war fucked you over. It fucked me over."

"It fucked me over," Sullivan said.

B.D., like so many athletes, had been guided into the reserves, and had played out his off-season obligations on military bases across America and Europe. Tom had gone to law school, had had children.

"And look at the Jordans," Levine said and smiled. "I loved your father, and admired him. We all did. Your mother worried a lot about you guys, like my mother did about me. But Christ, your mother worried about you."

"As soon as I left for Notre Dame she began to understand about us," Tom said. "She grew."

Levine nodded. "She was a strong lady."

"Where've you been?" Sullivan said. "It's been such a long time."

"I know, it's been an awfully long time. I've been everywhere. Canada, Europe, America."

"Where?"

"Several places, but mainly two. That's all I can tell you. I could tell you a lot more, but that's all I can tell you." He looked at Tom. "I didn't want to come by the funeral parlor today or tonight because I didn't want you to be linked with me in any way. You just never know who's around looking for things."

"Thanks, Arnie," Tom said.

Levine nodded and watched a waiter put roast beef on his plate, pour him some red wine.

"I don't understand," Sullivan said.

"It just wouldn't be good for a young, ambitious, United States senator or the coach of a major college basketball team suddenly ranked in the top twenty in the country to be seen in public with me. This is fine. No one knows I'm here. There are people of mine eating in your front dining room."

"What are you involved with?" B.D. asked.

243

"A lot of things."

"The spread of college games?"

Levine said nothing.

"The pros?"

"I'll tell you this, and you know it anyway. Anything's possible. Where there's a spread there's someone trying to influence it."

They stirred in their chairs.

"Get to Miami much anymore?" Tom said.

"Don't investigate me, senator."

"I'm not going to investigate you. I don't know what you do. You haven't told me and I don't want to know. This dinner is being held, however, and we're all here."

"It's being held, and we are all here, but no one knows about it and no one ever will."

"As far as I'm concerned you can walk through the front door of my place any time you want," Sullivan said. "I don't care what you do. We're good friends. We were roommates at Princeton for almost two years."

"And had some good times," Levine said.

"Some crazy fucking times," Sullivan said.

"We did."

Levine shrugged and smiled slightly. "I've been hurt a lot. People have abandoned me. My parents did, and my country. How's that for a double play combination." He leaned forward, looking old and tired then, and very pale. He'd always looked pale, even when he was angry. "I hear my parents had a bad death; first the collision, then crashing into the abutment, then the fire—So, here I am. Levine the ghost. The spirit of Lawrence past. We did have some good times in high school and college, the first year and a half of college, didn't we. Christ, remember some of the dogs we hung around with? Not you, B.D. Never you, you fucking jock. Whatever happened to that blond bitch from Connecticut you were in love with in your freshman year?"

They laughed.

"I don't know."

"Anything we talk about is going to sound absurd here, you

244

know," Levine said. "We've traveled a hell of a long distance from what we were, and here we are."

"I haven't traveled very far," Sullivan said.

They looked at him, then looked at their plates.

"Don't be an asshole, Sullivan," Levine said and Sullivan said nothing.

"Just look at us," Levine said after another moment. "We don't know what the hell to say next. It's like a high school reunion party. How the hell are you and how the hell are you and what the hell are you doing and you look like your fucking grand-fathers."

They laughed easily.

"Miller, you haven't said a word."

"I just can't believe you're really here, Arnie."

"I'm here. Did you really mastermind Jordan's senate win?"

"Not all of it," said Miller.

He and Tom looked at each other as if they understood some-thing then, or nothing at all.

"Were you in Chicago in sixty-eight, Arnie?" Sullivan asked. "We heard that you were."

"I bashed a cop's face in." He laughed. "It's a lot safer to buy them. Much safer. Not all of them, of course. Just most of them."

"And you lived in Canada?"

"In Europe, too. And six months in jail in Pennsylvania when I came back. Nice time."

"And then what?"

"I met certain people, and used others I'd met before, and learned how to make a lot of money."

"How much?" Sullivan said.

Levine shrugged and pushed back his chair. "Just look at the Jordans," he said. "You'll be President, you know, Tommy, if you don't let that black woman trap you."

Tom smiled. What else was he going to do?

"I'm going too far, so I'm only going to ask one more uncom-fortable thing. Where's your wife, Jordan?"

"I don't know."

"On the coast?"

"Yes."

"And you don't know where?"

"No—she's not filming this week." He'd said enough. Jesus.

Levine nodded. "I watched a lot of your games. You were great."

"That's nice of you, Arnie, thanks."

"In person a few times."

"Where?"

"Los Angeles, Chicago, New York, Phoenix. San Francisco once."

"Why didn't you come down to the bench and say hello?"

"You wouldn't have wanted the possible consequences of that. You were the best guard in the country. Really, I mean it."

"Thanks."

"You were always a tough jock."

"And you were always a good friend."

"I know—" Levine brushed at the side of his face. "Lawrence screwed us, it really did. When you left I had to leave. I just couldn't come home to it anymore. But I didn't have anything to leave to. You escaped to basketball. There was nothing like that for me to hang onto." He breathed slowly and folded his hands. "I've missed you. I'll admit that. You and Sullivan. And you, Tom Jordan, the junior senator from Massachusetts, always handsome, one hell of a basketball player, though never as good as your brother. But you could play football. You were smart to get out. The pros are all a bunch of fucking junkies."

"And you help them out."

"If the madness of the sport demands drugs to keep it going, don't blame me."

He pushed his plate a few inches away.

"I can't stay," he said.

Sullivan started to say something and Levine put up his hand.

"Really, no, I've got to leave," he said. He stood.

"We'll come out with you."

Levine shook his head. "Just me and B.D."

246

"Through my office and out the back way," Sullivan said.

"All right. Wait a minute." Levine went to the door, disappeared for a few seconds, came back. "All right," he said again.

Levine shook hands with Miller, then Tom, and smiled.

"I'm very sorry."

Tom nodded.

"I'll never see you again, Tommy. Stay upright, get married, be good."

Tom said nothing.

Levine hugged Sullivan in the frozen dark behind the restaurant.

"Come back again," Sullivan said.

"I'll try," Levine said and touched his arm.

"I've got to get back to Miller and the senator," Sullivan said after a moment. "Take care of yourself."

"You, too," Levine said.

"Jesus, Arnie—" Sullivan started.

"Take care."

B.D. and Levine moved quickly from the alley, walked a block and were picked up by a black Cadillac. Two men, dressed in dark suits and ties, were in the front seat. It was silent and warm inside, and for a moment, just on the verge of telling Levine to cut the shit, fear crossed B.D.'s blood. In all of the time he'd played, no gambler, no dealer, no criminal had ever approached him. But Collins had told him about a contact and now here he was with Arnie Levine, who, for all he knew, had probably helped turn on a whole generation. Mr. Electricity. If he hadn't grown up and gone to school with Levine, he certainly would hate him. The car idled beside the curb and they got in.

"I'm really sorry about your mother."

"I know."

It was almost dark in the back seat and the absence of light made Levine's face seem even whiter.

"What do you do? What are you into?" B.D. asked.

"Everything."

"Everything?"

247

"Everything there is."

B.D. frowned at him.

"You've been around, Jordan. You know how many people use things and each other. You've seen enough guys suddenly go cold in a game."

"How'd you get into it?"

"I just did. It just built. A lot of people are willing to do anything to make any kind of money at all. Hop into an election they can't possibly win to screw someone else by taking some of his votes away, drop out of one to give someone else an edge, if the price is right, of course. Throw a game, a fight, a race, alter the spread, poison a dog or horse, suck a cock, lead someone into a compromising position. And everyone wants to kill himself with drugs. With cocaine. It's absolutely incredible. You know how many guys use it?"

Levine looked out his window, back at B.D.

"Hollywood's a whole different fucking planet," he said, "though never quite as crazy as everyone thinks it is."

"It's crazy, and stoned," B.D. said.

"But you've kept yourself clean?"

"Absolutely."

Levine nodded. "Your brother, Miller, and all of the people around him are straight. As clean as a fucking whistle, and everyone knows it. And everyone also knows that you are. But your brother's not a jerk, either. He understands certain things. He's a liberal, but he understands that government can't clean up people's souls, and he's not going to shove it down their throats or up their asses."

"What happened to Sullivan in Vietnam is a national disgrace," Levine said after B.D. said nothing. "There are so many like him—he never married, did he."

"No—Tom's been good to him."

"Your brother's the kind of guy who could become President. The election, the primary, taught him a lot. He knows how to get even. He's already got even with a few people, so people are a little afraid of him already, which is good. He knows how to win, and wants to win. Some guys don't know how and don't want to, but he does."

"Was Dante Marino an accident?"

Levine didn't answer. He seemed to shrink further into the corner of the expensive seat.

"Then it was planned?"

"I don't know. I looked into it. There was no word around about it."

"Then it wasn't planned."

"It was probably just an accident. Sometimes accidents, especially like that, are hard to believe, so you're never sure."

B.D. stared straight ahead for a moment.

"He certainly did it to Brooke, didn't he."

"He did," B.D. said.

"Which gets to another point. His black girl friend, no matter how smart and beautiful she is, and she's both—he can't have her and get anywhere. He needs a new young blond wife to go with his sons, or he's got to get back with his former wife, which would be even better for him."

"He won't go back to Kate."

He watched Levine smile. "What do I detect in your voice, Jordan?"

"What?" he asked.

"Inside knowledge."

"You detect that?"

"Are you fucking your brother's former wife?"

"Would I do something like that?"

"Yes, you would, but you'd mask it behind something else, something phony, you hot shit, like it's all part of the journey back to the heart of Lawrence."

They laughed.

"Just don't make her pregnant."

"I won't."

"Jesus, that would be a mess for you, wouldn't it. Catholic women, especially the ones that live around here, have an impossible time with abortion."

249

"It won't happen."

Levine stirred and leaned toward him. B.D. knew it was time to go.

"Where's the beautiful Stephanie Green?" Levine asked.

"I told you."

"I know you did."

"Everyone's been kind enough not to bring up the pictures in the *Globe* and *People*, wherever else they appeared."

"Several other places. The guy's a zero."

"She's probably with him right now," B.D. said.

Levine shrugged. "I don't know. I do know he's about to do well with a script for a television movie, which she's about to sign for a lead in, and also with the adaption of a new novel Columbia's making into a major motion picture. She's being seriously considered for a lead in that, too."

"She told me."

"Has a nice sound to it, doesn't it," Levine said. "Major motion picture."

"Is he a heavy user?" B.D. asked.

Levine shrugged.

"Does he deal?"

"The writer?"

"Yes."

"I don't know."

"Steph's never used anything, would never destroy herself with anything."

"There'd be no reason for her to. She's beautiful and talented, and she married into political and athletic fame, though that could get heavy for some people."

"Not for her," B.D. said. "She's in charge of herself."

"I'm sure she is, and I'm sure she's going to become very famous."

"But the writer's a jerk."

Levine nodded.

"Then why's she seeing him?"

"Maybe simply to piss you off, maybe for all of the other reasons you can think of. I don't know."

Levine watched him for a moment, and B.D., perhaps to break from thinking of his wife, told Levine about Danny Collins.

"Sounds like a good kid. I don't know a thing about it, but if he's telling the truth, then they'll never come around Cushing again while he's there. And certainly not while you're there. They don't want problems. There are easy enough makes around."

"That's what I told him."

Levine looked out the rear window, then nodded to the front seat.

"Don't get nervous," he said. "Nothing's happening. We're just going for a little ride. I want to keep you protected."

They sped from the curb, took a series of downtown lefts and rights and in a few minutes were heading north on route 110, an older, two-lane highway near 495, then cut onto 495, moving fast.

"Don't say a thing," Levine said. "Don't even ask anything. We're fine."

They swung onto the breakdown lane.

"Out, fast," Levine said, and they were into the hissing night, Levine's car was already disappearing ahead of them.

"Follow me," he said, and they moved across a grassy rise, through an evergreen-studded grove to an exit ramp and down to the other side of the highway.

Levine stopped. He was breathing heavily. Pain shot through B.D.'s knee.

"You're slow," Levine said, calming.

"My fucking knee hurts."

"Sorry about that. I forgot how bad it is. How bad is it?"

"Bad. What the fuck is going on?"

"Nothing."

A car pulled slowly off the highway and stopped a few yards from them. B.D. watched it. It wasn't the same Cadillac.

"It's a different car," he said. "It's all right, they'll take you back. Just walk to them. I'm being picked up in three minutes."

"I don't believe this."

"You can't afford to be seen with me."

Levine shook his hand.

251

"Get going," he said. "Don't make Kate pregnant, and kick your wife's ass when you see her. Encourage her to do the movie, but keep her away from the writer. She's beautiful and talented, and she's going to make it big."

"You're full of shit, Levine, you really are."

"Sure I am."

B.D. stuffed his hands in his pockets.

"Your world's always been clean, Jordan, and always will be, no matter what you do, because that's the way you are. I don't count cheating on your wife."

"Not everything's fixed, Arnie," he said.

"Not everything can be."

B.D. took a step toward the car.

"Wait a minute."

He turned around.

"I loved your mother, and your father. I still miss him very much."

"So do I, Arnie, and I loved and miss your parents."

He nodded. "I know," he said and shrugged. "Look at us now. Have we grown up?"

"We have. An awful lot."

"I love you, Jordan," Levine said. "Go through the winter, and then get off your brother's turf."

B.D. got into the dark back seat. Two men, looking like the others, in suits, middle-aged, a bit too heavy, were in the front. They headed back to Lawrence.

Levine hadn't asked any questions about his team. Maybe he knew everything about them already. Maybe not. Maybe he'd spent his last nickel planning this, trying to make them think he was something he wasn't. But Levine had never lied or exaggerated. He said he was involved with everything, and that meant he was.

They stopped a block from the funeral home; the driver acted as if he knew the city and its streets, but B.D. knew he'd never seen either of them before. He got out and the car drove slowly away. No one had spoken.

B.D. walked toward the funeral parlor. He wondered how many games, college and pro, how many elections and fights and races—animal and human—Levine had actually influenced, and what part of the drug traffic he controlled. Maybe he should have asked him for some names of athletes and judges, police and mayors and governors and DAs and senators he controlled. But Levine, of course, would never have given him anything specific. If B.D. knew nothing, then he'd never have to reveal anything under oath. How much did his brother know about Levine? Tom had mentioned Miami. Maybe he knew a lot. He wouldn't ask. He walked the last few yards quickly.

The funeral parlor stayed packed after seven. The governor arrived just after eight and shook everyone's hand and for a moment B.D. thought he was going to tell his mother it was nice to see her. Kennedy was in another part of the country, but two of his Massachusetts aides came by, and congressmen, including Brendan Smith, whose beautiful, thirty-eight-year-old wife had committed suicide in their Washington apartment in September, and Clark Doerr from the first congressional district, and Maurice O'Donahue from the sixth, none of whom had dared to run for the Senate. There were floods of state senators and reps and ward heelers, some of whom had been there in the afternoon, and lawyers and union reps, all wearing blue suits and shirts and muted ties in case of television, all saying what a shame it was that this should happen to such a young woman. A few even told Tom and B.D. that it was time America found a cure for cancer. "If we can get to the top of the sky, then we can get to the bottom of this dreaded disease," Grady O'Rourke, a state rep from Lawrence, told them, his eyes glistening, his breath smelling like the Merrimack.

The President and Vice-President sent letters of condolence.

Sheila Manning, the state senator from Haverhill and a close friend of Tom's since he'd been in politics, hugged B.D., her eyes red from crying, and asked him where Stephanie was. She had flown back from Europe when she heard of the death. She was tall, efficient looking, and would get re-elected once, perhaps twice more, and then run for governor with Tom's backing. B.D. told her he didn't know, but thought Steph would be in tonight. He had called the house again when he returned from being with Levine. There were no messages from her or from Maury Golden's office.

At eight-fifteen he stepped into one of the smaller lounges. Kate followed him. But there was no room to talk and they slipped off to a narrow corridor.

"I won't be able to get away to see you tonight," she said. "It's just going to be too late."

"All right," he said.

"It's hit me harder than I thought it would, B.D." She began to cry. He hesitated, then held her, and she sobbed against him while outside the door in the lounge the priest from St. Mary's, where Tom had attended services when he had to in Lawrence, began a story involving the mayor and one of the aldermen, in a low voice that would help send his mother to heaven tomorrow morning.

"We'll be together after this," he said.

She turned away from him. "I'll be all right."

Others were looking at them now, and some might even have heard what he said.

They moved back through the crowd and she slipped away to talk to some people she knew from Andover, including Bobby Wilson, the new state senator representing Tom's district, and his tall, dark-haired, attractive wife who looked—when he'd seen her briefly in the campaign, later at the victory party at Sullivan's, and even now—one half-step, half-smile from boredom. She and Kate had become friends since the divorce, and perhaps Kate had given her good advice on how not to allow her husband's political ambition to screw up the rest of her life. But there was no such thing as good advice. The wives, and husbands, of professional athletes and politicians were automatic victims of loneliness, often became only neglected moments in a crowded schedule, and especially political wives if they were good-looking

254

enough, were used as props on the road through ambition. Brenda Wilson was good-looking, and she was here. Maybe she knew about B.D. and Kate.

He listened to Miller and Vic Carillo, a political consultant who'd had a string of congressional winners across the country in November, discuss mid-Massachusetts voting patterns for a few minutes, then scanned the crowd and saw Diane Collier. She was standing at the entrance, and he watched Tom go quickly to her and take her hand. They didn't kiss. She was with a white woman B.D. had never seen before. Miller kissed both of them on the cheek, and from across the room Kate O'Connell watched, making it obvious that she was still very much in love with Tom Jordan.

B.D. hugged and kissed Diane a few mintes later, after she had stepped ahead of Tom and kneeled beside their mother, with everyone watching. In heels she was slightly taller than B.D.

"How've you been?" he said. She hadn't been at Sullivan's in November, but had been with Tom in Washington in early January, he knew, and their impending marriage would be rumored for the next two years, and would at least keep vice-presidential speculation away from his door. "How about Tom Jordan?" "What if he marries her?" "Better not chance it." Was Tom really using Diane Collier too? And for what?

"I'm fine, B.D., the coach." She smiled, then let it fade. "I'm very sorry about your mother."

"Thank you." Here she was, he thought, the only black around.

"Is Steph here?"

"She will be for the funeral," he heard himself say. A few minutes later Tom had moved Diane to other introductions and he drifted and found Kate.

"I feel stupid," she said.

"Don't."

"I do."

"You shouldn't."

"I know I shouldn't. She's very beautiful."

"So are you."

"Thanks," she said and touched his arm. "But not like that. I didn't realize you knew her."

"She was with him in California last winter, when Stephanie and I raised money for him."

"Is he in love with her?"

"No—I don't know. Come on, Kate."

"I'm just hanging around. It's stupid for me to do that, just hang around. All of the arrangements have been made. Everything's in the hands of the people here. They know what they're doing."

"Kate—"

"No, really, B.D., I'm in the way. I'm not his wife. No one's here to see me. It was all right for me to be here this afternoon for a few hours. But I've fulfilled my promises and obligations to your mother. All of the neighbors and close relatives have come and gone. I'll be at the church tomorrow, but I'm going home now. All right?"

He stared at her. "All right," he said. "Let me go with you." He disliked himself for saying it and she didn't bother to answer him. She hadn't met Diane Collier and wasn't about to. She left without B.D.

He left Lawrence at ten o'clock after turning down Tom's invitation to join him and Miller and Diane and her friend for about an hour at Sullivan's. They hadn't talked about Levine. Tom had acted, he thought, as if he'd seen Levine before, recently. He didn't ask if he had. He wouldn't get trapped by the ghosts of Lawrence. He'd coach his team and then get out, go back to the west where he belonged.

On the highway back to Boston he caught the final score of the Cushing-Providence game, 88–70. Smith had scored twenty-eight and he felt his ego pump. Another win. He hoped Phillips had cleared the bench early. They had come through for him, and it would make tomorrow easier.

Tomorrow would be his last day in Lawrence. He'd leave and be out forever. There would be people at the funeral he didn't know, friends of his mother who'd been in tonight's crowd, introduced to him by name only, not by what they'd done or meant to her; and young people who had helped Tom and Kate during the first state senate campaign, the most important one of all—helped them with the small, vital details of politics: the mailings and schedules and poll watching and telephoning and driving the aged to polls, making sure those who couldn't get to the polls voted in all the district's nursing homes. Some had small-talked with B.D. when they were introduced, others had stared when they thought he wasn't looking. Most were searching for Stephanie Green. And so was he, all of the time, expecting her to appear at a doorway, drift through a crowd, her beautiful face alive with sympathy and lust, darkly tanned from Hawaii, her legs and thighs soothing against whatever expensive dress she was wearing, only to take it off for him later. Stephanie Green, his love, his wife; his much photographed, celebrated wife. Unaccounted for.

28

THE CHURCH WAS FILLED. SINGLETON AND HIS WIFE were there, and Phillips and Gordon, but none of the kids, and he was glad. He didn't see Diane Collier.

He listened to the priest pray; he was kind and generous. He had visited B.D.'s mother at the hospital and had an audience now of all of the prominent people of Lawrence and Andover and three congressmen, the lieutenant governor and every state senator, DA, rep, alderman and mayor within fifty miles. After the service B.D. stood with Tom and Kate at the top of the wide, gray steps of St. Mary's and looked at the crowd that had gathered across the street, waiting, perhaps, to catch a glimpse of his wife, Stephanie.

He and Tom rode in the back of a limousine alone. Kate rode

with her parents several cars behind them. Their mother's relatives and close friends, and Tom's friends—Sullivan, Sheila Manning, Miller, Bobby Wilson and his wife, a state rep from Lawrence and one from Andover, some people from his Boston and Washington offices, others who'd been close to him and worked on his campaigns, Singleton and his wife and Phillips and Gordon—would be at the graveside and at her home for an hour or so afterwards.

Sullivan, Miller and Wilson, and three of his mother's relatives, were pallbearers.

The procession to the cemetery was long and slow. He and Tom said little to each other. Once, just after they'd slipped past the iron gates a few yards behind a car filled with flowers, with the cruel cold orange sun stunning the enormous empty oaks and maples into windless silence around them, he choked up and almost cried.

They walked up the hill he had walked up in December, stood beside each other and stared at the coffin suspended above the grave dug beside his father's, listening to the quiet, freezing voice of the priest and the sound of Carrie Mallon and others, including Kate, and an ancient great aunt, crying behind them. Then he and Tom stepped forward and placed a flower on the coffin. B.D. stayed close to it for a moment, then stepped back and felt his eyes fill and listened to more crying, coughing, the sounds of traffic on one of the superhighways on the outskirts of Lawrence, a siren wailing from the other side of Tower Hill.

Tom dropped to one knee, his head bent, his right hand against his forehead, and when he did B.D. felt his throat tighten and he cried hard within himself for several seconds, stopping finally and wiping his eyes with the heel of his right hand. And when Tom got up and turned and faced him, his eyes red and slightly swollen, B.D. cried again until he didn't have to anymore.

"It was all well done, understated and brief enough," B.D. said on the way back to the house.

Tom nodded. "It was all carefully planned. A lot of things can be, can't they."

B.D. didn't answer. He shifted as they turned through several narrow streets and moved across the hill.

"Stephanie never called me back."

"You still don't know where she is?"

"No, no one's been able to locate her. Maybe I should have asked for Levine's help," he added sarcastically.

"Is it over between you?"

"I don't know."

Tom nodded.

"She knew Ma was dying, and she usually tells me where she's going."

"It's hard to be alone, especially when you're angry, or hurt," Tom said and B.D. said nothing.

The house accepted the sun and laughter and voices released, briefly, from grief. Some of the older relatives and neighbors drank whiskey and warm water, but most just stood around, talking about what they were and what they were going to do, drinking coffee, eating pastry, accepting hugs; every now and then, the soft sound of crying drifted from one of the bedrooms, the pantry, a corner of his father's den where several family pictures smiled back from immaculate shelves. Singleton and Barbara and Phillips and Gordon left early. Barbara kissed him and B.D. promised he'd come out to their house soon.

And then when everyone else was gone—including Sullivan, who told B.D. sadly that they might never see each other again; and Carrie Mallon, who hugged Kate and cried hard and said she just didn't know what she was going to do now; and all of the relatives who had repeated their goodbyes several times in case they died tonight—then he and Kate and Tom and Miller sat in the living room sipping coffee, talking about the ages of the relatives, the loneliness in the neighbors, the decay in the neighborhood, until Miller said he had people to see in Lawrence and Andover and would be back for Tom at four. It was almost three o'clock; darkness gathered at five.

Kate stood. Why had she stayed so long?

"I told your mother, I promised her, I'd pack all of her personal

259

valuables and keep them at my house, till you decide what you want to do with them. The police will watch everything for the next several days, and nights."

"You can have whatever you want from the house, you know," Tom said, knowing, of course, that she'd say no.

She shook her head. "Thank God it didn't snow," she said.

Tom turned to B.D. "Do you want any of the things here?"

"No."

"Anything of Pa's?"

He shook his head.

"I'm sure there are no surprises in the will. Whatever the house brings we'll—"

"You can have everything," B.D. said.

He kept expecting to see his wife, even here at the house. Kate looked terrible now, even though she was beautiful, and all of the other women who had floated through the funeral parlor, past the grave, through the house, with big legs and firm legs and amazing asses, all had looked grotesque. Only his wife counted now and he hated her because she'd done—he was certain she'd done and was doing—what he had done for the first two months of the winter. But at least he hadn't made out with another woman at a New Year's Eve party or been photographed on the beach with the woman he was fucking.

"I don't want to leave the house unsold for long," Tom said. "I'd like to put it on the market right away."

"Sounds good," B.D. said.

Kate moved out and disappeared beyond the dining room.

B.D. watched the afternoon darken against the windows. He felt enclosed now and, despite all of the pictures of Tom and himself and his father and mother and Kate and Stephanie, felt again as if he'd never lived here, and never belonged.

"I'm sure it'll bring a decent price."

"Use it for future campaigns. Pa would have liked that. Are you still in debt from the fall?"

"No. When Marino died all of the money in the world came rushing in. And a late November fundraiser in Boston brought

260

in thousands. There's a campaign fund surplus. It would make me feel better if you took half of whatever it brings."

"Why?"

"Because it's your house too."

"I left."

"You left," Tom said, "and then you came back, and here we are now."

"And I'm leaving again."

"When?"

"Once I drive away from here today I'll never be back."

"Oh, is that a fact?"

B.D. let his eyes widen. "Yes."

"But you'll still be in Boston, and at Cushing."

"Until the season ends."

"What if your marriage is really all over?" Tom said. His voice was scraping along the bottom of fatigue and hurt and bitterness.

"What if it is?"

"What are you going to do then?"

"I'm going back to my house in Malibu. It was mine before we even met. She moved in with me. I've lived in California for fifteen years. I'm not going to stay here—so relax."

Kate came back into the room then and said she had to get going, that the boys were waiting for her, and needed her now.

Tom said he'd come by with Miller later.

She looked at B.D. Tom had turned away. B.D. wouldn't call her again, and doubted if she'd call him. It was obvious, had been obvious last night, just how deeply in love she still was with his brother, and B.D. was sure she didn't want him anymore.

"I'll see you later this afternoon then," she said to Tom, still half looking at B.D.

He thanked her for everything. She put out her hand to B.D. with Tom watching, then hugged him and he felt her warm, damp cheek against him.

"Promise to come by and see us before your season's over," she said.

"I will," he said.

She cried for a moment. He neither touched her nor said anything. A few moments later she left, whispering a single good-bye. Tom walked into their father's den, came back.

"She left her pocketbook," he said. "Or someone did."

Her car moved away from the front of the house. Tom moved into the kitchen and stood near the table and B.D. followed him. The phone rang and Tom got it and told whoever it was that he'd be there by seven.

"Would you like me to do anything at all?" B.D. said when he'd hung up. It was time to go.

Tom shook his head.

"Are you going back to Washington tonight?" He knew he wasn't. "Staying in town? Want to stay at—"

"No." Tom snapped it across the room. "And don't worry, I'm not sleeping at my former house in Andover, either."

"Meaning what?"

"You know damn well what."

B.D. took a few steps toward the door. "You're being an asshole," he said. "A senator should never be an asshole, even to his brother."

"Bullshit! Just fucking bullshit! I know you've been seeing her." He was glaring at B.D. now, his chin tucked slightly in, his arms straight at his sides. "She didn't tell me, but I know. People have seen you together. You're a celebrity, for Christ's sake. We all are. People see us and talk about us. Didn't you know that?"

B.D. sighed within himself and waited.

"You never lose, do you, B.D. I mean, never. Pa died and in the middle of everyone's suffering and wondering what they were going to do, in the middle of Ma's absolute terror and loneliness, you took off for the coast, you got out clean."

"It wasn't as simple as that. Come on, Tom, we've talked about it. You know why I left."

"I knew why you left," he said. "And then later I really understood and respected it. But now you've come back. You got traded and went along with the trade instead of telling them to go fuck themselves."

262

"You know why I did that, too."

"Of course I do. Even though your coming back after all these years, just before I was to become senator, really got under my skin and pissed me off. I understand how tough it is to back away from a fight, how much you wanted to get back at L.A., and how really tough it is to stop doing what you do very well and get paid for."

He swallowed. B.D. hoped he'd simply laugh then, wave his hand and tell him to get out.

"And then you got hurt," Tom said. "Why the hell didn't you just go home, just quit with your fucking damaged knee and go back to California where you belong? Why'd you have to hang around my turf, become a college coach, for Christ's sake, and start making love to my former wife?"

Tom took a step toward him. B.D. tensed. Shit—

"Why don't you answer me?"

"There's nothing to answer."

"Of course there is."

B.D. moved toward the door.

"Don't leave now. You're not going to leave now."

B.D. stopped and waited. He'd never admit any involvement with Kate.

"Pa taught us enough about politics for you to know that guys have their own areas, and you're supposed to ask permission before you come in and start fucking around on them. I could handle your being with Boston. That had logic. And any ex-athlete could understand and appreciate that. So could the people, especially since you'd been playing so well. In fact, you were the best guard, certainly the best white guard in the league. You were getting about three quarters of a million, and your being here and playing well probably even made me look good, or better, even though it was crowding me, even though you never called and asked for my opinion. You called to tell me what you were going to do. I never would have gone to California to raise money without talking to you about it first. Never. Not even to San Francisco. And I could have, you know. I didn't have to go to you and Stephanie. I'm a former Notre Dame all-American and Harvard lawyer and I was and am in demand on the coast."

"You are," B.D. said. When was this going to end?

"But I'd never just go, never even accept a speaking engagement without calling you first, to be sure it wouldn't embarrass you or your wife or crowd you on your own turf in any way."

He was flushed, breathing hard.

"I suppose that Cushing did have its logic. You'd played with Bill Singleton. He needed a coach and you're proving to be a good one. It's the winter, your wife was away and there was nothing else to do and it was a good way of breaking from fifteen years of playing. God knows I missed football after Notre Dame. Sometimes, especially in October when I was around Harvard, I missed it so much I ached. So even though it looked like a dumb backward move when you took it, and was almost embarrassing, you're winning now, and it's making you look like a shrewd judge of talent and Boston and L.A. look like fools for not giving you their coaching jobs. And you're in commercial demand again. Just like that." His voice, still intense, had lowered. He coughed, looked up. "But why did you have to come around and start fucking Kate?"

"You've said enough," B.D. said.

"Oh have I—"

"Yes, enough."

"Why'd you do it? Why'd you start fucking her?"

"I'm not going to answer that shit."

"You thought you could kill off the winter's loneliness with her in bed and get away with it. Why did you have to do it?"

He turned away, ready. Ready for what?

"How would you like it if I—"

"Enough!" He snapped it. "You've said enough."

Tom took a step around the table. "Why did you have to get involved with her?"

"I didn't."

"I know you did, damn it."

B.D. watched him.

264

"You really never lose. Clean as a whistle, out you'll go after leading Cushing University to the NCAA final four, pulling off a minor miracle to get there, maybe even a big one by winning it all. And then, of course, in two days the country will have forgotten who won the championship but they won't forget you, even though you will have left Cushing and gone back to California—because you and your agent won't let them forget."

Tom laughed quickly.

"What a good guy you are, B.D. Jordan. Bill Singleton calls for help and you come running. Nice guy. Tell me, when did you first start fucking Kate? Before or after you—"

B.D. threw one of the kitchen chairs across the room and off the wall near the refrigerator, its leg cracking. "You know, you're a fucking jerk. You're the user and manipulator, you're the one riddled with guilt, especially about the way you've used and treated Kate, the way you hurt her last night. Did you have to bring that black—"

Tom flinched and his fists tightened. They were close enough now to hit each other.

"You used her all year, in fact since you've known her, and that's the truth and you know it. You used her father's name and her good looks and popularity in Andover to help you get to the state Senate. And she took care of the kids and made them available to you, whenever you wanted them all through the last campaign. And I helped you. I raised a hundred thousand dollars for you on the coast and Stephanie and I came in and helped you in September."

"Helped me to do what? Helped me how?"

B.D. said nothing. He felt his heart slam and regret build in his lungs. He knew Tom was going to explode, and they'd both get hurt.

"Go ahead, helped me how? I lost the fucking primary. Don't you remember, I lost it."

B.D. stood still.

"I had no place to go when I lost, no place to run to. I woke up the next morning to the fucking darkness. I mean fucking darkness. I knew how Pa felt when he lost. I knew then what a long way down it is. I lived with it and I'm still living with it. Dante Marino got killed. It's never been clear why his car slammed into the tree. A lot of people think I was in on it. On what? Who the fuck knows. But his family must think something because they even stayed away from the funeral. I mean not even a fucking flower or card or note. And I was so good to them, so good to his wife and mother. They could have called, sent a message—" He stared at the table. "Dante Marino. He must have had a terrible moment when it was about to happen, when the windshield and the tree came together—he'd beaten me. I kicked Brooke's ass, but I've got to live with my loss, and Dante's death. It'll take me another election, another primary and election, and then maybe something much bigger to clean my ego out." He looked up. "And you haven't helped things at all."

B.D. took a half-step back. "I've never taken the spotlight from you. Never. You've always had the news. You're right. My success has only made you look better. Maybe you simply can't handle that; you've become much more important than I am, and you hate me now for showing you how good and important you are."

"You don't know what the fuck you're talking about."

"I know what I've had to do. There's always been room enough here for me this winter." He felt anger build in his chest and throat.

"Why Kate?" Tom said. "Of all the women around, with your own amazing wife in California just a plane ride away, why'd you have to let her fall in love with you?"

"She's not in love with me. She'd never let that happen. She's in love with you, she's always been, and you know it. You know it enough to use her, and you've used her all the time. But Ma's gone now, and watch out, senator, because—"

"You still don't understand, do you?"

"I understand that she's going to take your two beautiful sons and—"

"Leave them out of all of this, you sonofabitch," Tom said

and grabbed B.D.'s shoulder and coat and flung him against the wall near the door. He felt his knee scream when he hit, his skull crack one of the shelves over a small desk in back of the table. A china teacup and saucer and framed picture of a tranquil seacoast town flew across the floor where the chair lay broken. Tom was on him, with a left into his stomach, a right across his mouth. He felt his lip split and bleed and he blocked another left and right. He crouched, caught two more hard punches on his back, lowered his left shoulder and drove off the wall with his left leg, carrying Tom under his right ribs back hard into the oven door, knocking over the table, snapping the air from his brother's body. And then, while Tom was stunned, clamped a hard, brutal headlock on him, tightened it, his blood falling across the floor and into his brother's hair. He shouted for Tom to cut it out, for Christ's sake, that they could kill each other, and there was another voice, Kate's, a high-pitched screaming voice that sounded so like his mother's telling them to stop or they were going to kill her that he felt his stomach freeze and he threw Tom away, slamming him against the refrigerator door. He bent over, struggled for breath and threw up, violently, into the china cup and shattered saucer and the milk and pastry and silverware that had splattered from the table.

B.D. hobbled into the rocking chair by the window, holding the blood back and watched Kate watch Tom, her hands still tearing at her hair, her face terrified, her voice still screaming for them to stop until she finally dropped her hands, sobbed, wiped at her face and trembled.

B.D. watched blood swell in the heel of his right hand and he pressed it against his shirt.

"Tom thinks he can take me," he said. "He could never take me. He's shit. Second rate shit. He's a fucking loser. He lost to Dante Marino."

Tom stood now, walked into the pantry and brought cold water up to his face, came back into the kitchen without drying himself and looked at Kate.

"Why are you here?" he said.

267

"Because I knew it was all going to come out. I knew what was going to happen."

"Does it make you happy?"

B.D. got up, brushed past Tom and took a towel from the bathroom and came back into the kitchen, pressing the towel to his mouth. The pain in his leg was enormous.

"It's your home now, Tommy," he said. "You can sell it, or rent it out to Puerto Ricans and scare the shit out of Carrie Mallon, or burn it to the fucking ground." His voice was metallic, blood-distorted, foolish. He threw the towel on the floor and walked past Kate without looking at her or touching her, out into the darkening February day.

She was behind him in the driveway.

"Are you all right?" she said.

"Of course." He stopped and looked at her. "He knows about us."

She nodded. Tom came up behind them.

"She offers a lot of comfort, doesn't she," he said.

"Please," Kate said, "no more of this. We all know everything now. Your mother just died, Tom. No more."

"And she's beautiful," Tom said as if she hadn't spoken. "You are beautiful, Kate. Not Stephanie Green beautiful. After all, who is. But beautiful. And good. Christ, you're good. Except that you're something else B.D. doesn't understand. I think he might have understood it, and recognized it, once, but he's been away for fifteen years."

"I know what you're going to say," B.D. said.

"No you don't. You have no idea what I'm going to say."

"Don't be very stupid," B.D. said.

Tom laughed. There was a welt on the right side of his face and B.D., his anger slipping away, felt guilt begin to fill his stomach. No, not guilt. Not guilt at all. Only sorrow and regret. Maybe even shame. No, not shame, either. He wasn't ashamed of anything. He never would be. But he felt tired now and he was overcome, almost—almost—with sadness.

Tom stayed a yard, two, from them. "He's going to go back

to California when his season's over, despite you," he said.

"What do you mean, despite me?" Kate said, her voice laced with her own anger now. "Why don't you just stop talking before everything's destroyed, senator. Before everything's torn apart."

"You haven't trapped him—you haven't pulled him in quite far enough. You might have if she'd died maybe just a few weeks later. But maybe not even then. If Lawrence couldn't do it, then I guess you couldn't."

"What the hell are you talking about?"

"You're a beautiful woman, Kate. You really are. You're a fine woman and a good mother. A great mother."

"Damn it, Tom." She pulled her coat tighter and her eyes filled and she turned half away.

"But you're almost more Lawrence than Lawrence. Today, just now, your sudden appearance and reaction to our violence, our old, competetive, dumb jock violence proves it. Your kindness to our mother proves it. You're really her. You're our mother in a Mercedes and fur. You're the voice in the land, the goddamn death voice in—"

"Cut it out," B.D. said, taking a step toward her. "Just cut the goddamn crap."

"Don't you know that's why you went to her? Why she made herself available to you, gave you her warmth, all of her motherly warmth? She appeared for you, got in touch with you, made the first contact, didn't she?"

Tom was half-smiling at him.

"Of course she did," Tom said. "She's very comforting, very understanding, sympathetic, nice. And local. Stay too long with the locals and you become local yourself. Did Pa ever tell you that? Of course he did. We've talked about it enough. It's so easy to stay, or to come back and die here. Just ask Lawrence's own Robert Frost. The woods really are lovely. And they're dark and deep. He got out—I pulled the greatest move of all. I got out and stayed at the same time." His breath hesitated, darted away. It was silent and cold now. "The death is still in my blood. But you, B.D., you got out soon enough, and you're strong enough, and lucky enough, so she'll never get you. Unless of course your house falls into the Pacific and your wife dumps you for the screenwriter everyone has her in bed with, and you become unstuck with loneliness and are suddenly too vulnerable. Or Cushing University becomes NCAA champs and you get trapped by Katherine O'Connell, mother of my two sensational sons, the quiet martyr of Andover, the real black soul of Lawrence."

Kate glared at him, then breathed deeply and put her hands in her pockets. B.D. moved a few steps away.

"Whatever else, you've become a good politician, Kate," Tom said. "You've learned the bottom line in politics well. You got even with me. You certainly did get even."

"I left my purse in the house," she said, and walked in through the back door.

They said nothing. Tom looked as sad now, as unhappy, as he felt. Kate came out of the house, her face neutral, her eyes dry, and got into the car without saying anything and drove away.

"Nice winter," Tom said. "You know, she's always wanted me back."

"I know."

"She especially wanted me back after my defeat in the primary."

"You're wrong about her. She's substantial, and decent."

"I never said she wasn't. She's an excellent person. But I'm not wrong. She'll always be here. In two years she'll marry a doctor and I'll have very defined visiting rights. Especially after all of this. Actually I might be lucky if I get to see the kids at all."

"She'd never do that to them. She'd never do anything like that."

"We hurt her pretty badly today," Tom said after a moment. "I did. And we hurt each other, didn't we."

"We did," B.D. said.

He drove across the Merrimack and gripped the wheel, fighting away the need to take the Andover exit to her house. He couldn't see her again. Of course he couldn't. Any more than he could see Sullivan again, or Levine, and he could never campaign around Boston again for his brother. He'd help him on the coast, if he ran for President, because he was his brother. And, as he held the accelerator down and hustled away from Andover and into all of the other towns and small cities before Boston, he almost cried again. But he swallowed that away, too. He had a team. They were winning. They'd continue to win, and in six weeks it would be over.

29

HE ATE AT SIX IN HIS APARTMENT. HE FELT COM-pletely alone, and horrible. God—

Why hadn't he left before Kate left? He could have avoided everything. Tom might have been right about her, and he might not have been right about her. It didn't matter now.

Stephanie called him at eight.

"I've been out of reach for a few days," she said, almost too matter of factly. "I just got back and found an urgent message at the door to call."

"Where are you?"

"Home. At home in Malibu."

The death wasn't an important story on the coast, and prob-ably, since he wasn't there anymore, wasn't a story at all. Maury had called him at seven, saying he thought she'd be back in Malibu soon.

"Where were you?" B.D. asked.

"Some of us went up the coast for a few days to rest and get a little perspective."

"Who?"

She named a co-producer of the show and his wife, one of

the male co-stars and his girl friend, two people he didn't know, and Gary Prince.

He said nothing.

"We stayed with the Browns near Carmel. Just doing nothing. Just contemplating the world."

"Sounds good."

"It was for me."

I'll bet it was, he thought. "Was he with you all the time?"

"Gary?" she said, too casually.

"Gary."

"Mostly he was just off by himself, working. You're not paying any attention to the pictures or any of the other stuff the publicity people have been releasing, are you? You know what they do to make it look—"

"What do you see in him anyway?"

"B.D.—please, darling. What's the matter? What's the urgency?"

"What are your plans for the weekend?"

"I've invited them all out here. We're going over a few scripts." Her voice was floating, distant. It was all over with her, too, and he knew it. His lip had begun bleeding again. "The weather's been great, and there isn't that much time left to take advantage of it. But you didn't just—"

"No, I didn't."

"What's the matter?" she said. "Is your mother—"

"She died Tuesday."

"Oh, God, B.D. I didn't think to—"

"The wake was yesterday and last night. We buried her this morning. I've been trying hard to reach you."

"B.D.—"

"Why didn't you leave a number with someone, a message about where you were going? Why didn't you call and tell me where you were going?"

"I'm sorry."

"I tried the studio, Alan Dart's office. I even asked Maury to help me find you."

"I'll get the next flight in."

"Don't bother. I don't want to screw up your weekend."

"I'm going to fly in as soon as I can. We'll have at least two days together."

"Don't. I don't want you to. I have an out-of-town game on Saturday," he said, lying. "I won't be here." He hung up and felt the blood burn through his stomach.

She called back.

"Look, damn it. I'm sorry about your mother. I really am, and it was careless of me not to tell you where I was going. I'm flying into Boston as soon as I can be with you. I love you."

"Bring Gary Prince. You make a lovely couple. Maybe you can pose together nude on the Common."

"For Christ's sake—"

"You'll need him for company, because you're not getting near me."

He took a hot shower and went to bed. His mouth burned and his leg was gone. He knew he'd need an operation in the spring.

BOOK
III

BOOK
II

1

THEY BEAT VILLANOVA AT HOME BY TEN. THE
locker room after the game was filled with life and youth and
victory, and the constant, positive beat of a winning team.

They were eleven and six now and on Monday were ranked
ninth in the country. B.D. got to Cushing early and stayed late
after practice. He had turned down all speaking requests, all
except after-the-game interviews and the ads Maury wanted him
to work into his schedule. He would focus on basketball, only
Cushing basketball. The book would be done in April, or May.

They blew by Seton Hall and Holy Cross during the week,
took St. John's into three overtimes and finally beat them by five
with Collins scoring thirty-two, and then ran away from Syracuse
on the last Saturday in February. They were ranked sixth with
four more regular season games to go, were certain to be invited
to the NCAA tourney and would, he knew, be seeded high in
the eastern regionals if they could win all four, or even three.
But loss, defeat, was always out there, crouched, waiting to leap
and break your heart.

Stephanie hadn't come to him, nor tried calling again. Neither
had Kate. And since he read only the sports sections of the *Globe*
and the *Times* now and watched only basketball on television,
he knew nothing of what his wife or his brother was up to.

Cushing played Connecticut again on the Monday night following the Syracuse game. They were still growing, picking up
speed on both offense and defense, becoming more sure of themselves. Collins and Smith had each been named player of the

week in the east in *Sports Illustrated* and by the AP; Cunningham, a recognized rebounding force, had an excellent chance of being drafted in the first two rounds.

But they were down by eight to Connecticut with six minutes to go in the first half; mostly, B.D. knew, because they'd been overconfident in spite of his warnings, and had started pressing when everything they shot rimmed away or fell short in the first ten minutes. They were down by twelve when he called time out three minutes later.

"You're trying too hard now, you know that."

"We're pressing," Toner said.

"It doesn't matter how far behind we are," B.D. said. "There are three minutes here and a whole second half to go. They'll drop for you. You're doing everything else right, and they're making some lucky shots. Just focus on the moment. Forget our ranking and record and what might happen if we lose, because we're not going to lose. Just play sound and we'll catch and pass them soon enough."

He wondered if he sounded simple-minded, or too basic, revealing a hidden fear that the season was about to come apart and they were going to lose the rest of their games.

Collins took a Davis pass inside and hit the shot and got fouled. He made the free throw cleanly and they were nine down, but Connecticut kept hitting from the outside and though they were playing well, they trailed by seven at the half.

He said the same things in the locker room. Seven points were nothing, it could be erased in less than a minute, but they wouldn't try to erase it in less than a minute unless Connecticut handed them the ball and begged them to. They simply had to keep doing everything they knew how to do well and would, B.D. was certain, take the lead by the five- or six-minute mark.

They tied the game with twelve minutes left, went ahead with eleven and a half left and were up by three with nine. But Connecticut wouldn't die and tied the score on a breakaway and three foul shots with two and a half minutes to go.

Character testing popped up in the most unexpected places.

With a minute left and the score tied at 65, Collins fouled out on a charging call, blood spilling from his mouth after being hit with a blizzard of elbows. He held onto his temper and watched Sizemore hack a Connecticut guard across the arms while he was hitting a twenty-foot jumper to put them, with forty-five seconds left, ahead by two. The guard hit the foul shot.

68–65. B.D. called time.

"Look inside for Cunningham first. But I'm sure they're going to collapse their zone, and hound at the top of the key. So swing the ball right if he's not open, then left for Chet." He looked them over. "Take the jumper if it's there. If it isn't, screen for Toner coming around from underneath. Don't rush it. Man-to-man full court after we score. Don't let them breathe. Cunningham on the ball out of bounds. If we miss, foul right away. They're in the one-and-one. Don't let them run the clock. Make them beat us, or try to beat us."

Davis was covered and Toner came out for the jump shot. He missed it. Connecticut rebounded and Cunningham fouled the rebounder, fouling out, with thirty-eight seconds left.

Connecticut, with the Cushing crowd stunned and quiet for most of the game, but now shouting, made the first foul shot, putting them ahead. 69–65.

B.D. called time again.

"Stay cool, but hurry the ball down court no matter whether he makes it or not, and then foul right away on the in-bounds pass."

They stood and slapped their hands together. It had slipped away. He couldn't quite believe it. Connecticut hit the second free throw.

70–65.

They came up the court quickly and Smith hit a fifteen-foot jumper from the top of the key, then fouled right after the in-bounds pass.

70–67 with thirty seconds left.

The crowd, standing now and hanging in with them, helped the band pump its optimism.

They missed the first foul shot. Toner grabbed the rebound and Smith drove to the right, watched the zone collapse on Toner and hit another fifteen-footer.

70–69. B.D. called time with twelve seconds left.

"Foul immediately," he said. "Don't try for the steal unless they throw the ball right to you, and don't let them run anything off the clock. We've got one more time out."

Smith fingertipped the in-bounds pass to Tyler Young, who just lost it out of bounds, sending the crowd out and back down its throat. Ten seconds left. Connecticut got it in on a lob pass to half-court where Toner fouled their center right away. Nine seconds left. He hit the first shot.

71–69. B.D. held on to his time out.

The second shot rimmed, hung and rolled off to Toner. He fired it out to Smith, who drove to mid-court with six seconds left, fired a pass to the left and watched Young snag it and hit a long jumper to tie the score. Connecticut called time with two seconds left.

"Guard the in-bounds pass tight," he said to Toner. "Everyone else a tight man-to-man, but don't foul. If they get it in, drop off right away. Don't touch anyone. They won't score with two seconds left. Great comeback. Let's hope they fuck up."

The press was tight, dangerous, but nothing close enough to be whistled, and Connecticut, with no time outs left and the five-second limit to get the ball in running out, threw the ball, untouched, out of bounds. No time clicked away.

B.D. used his last time out.

"We've got it under their basket," he said, the Cushing band brassy at their backs, the crowd alive and clapping. "Smith takes it out of bounds. Stack it underneath. Toner breaks left. Davis to the foul line. Sizemore on the one second delay. Hit whoever you want, Bobby, and step in fast for the return pass. Remember, we have no time outs and only two seconds." He looked at them and grinned. "Win it. Put it in."

Toner broke free. Smith hit him cleanly and his shot snapped through at the buzzer.

73–71.

2

KATE CALLED HIM THE NEXT MORNING.

"I tried hard not to do this," she said, "but I do think we should see each other once more."

He felt bad then for not having called her.

"I still care very much for you," she said.

"I care for you," he said.

"I have to be in town today. Can I see you?"

"Yes."

He had to be at Cushing at one. It was vital to win the rest of their games to secure a strong eastern regional playoff position, maintain physical and psychological momentum through the two regional weekends, first in Philadelphia, and then, if they won, in Syracuse. Winning the rest of their regular season games would be tough. They played in Pittsburgh on Saturday night, then faced Georgetown and Providence at home.

She was there before noon, dressed the way she had been when he saw her outside his mother's house in December, in a fur coat and corduroys and a sweater, her hair pulled back emphasizing her cheekbones. It would have been easier, he thought, if she'd looked drawn and tired and older, devastated by the fight, the death, her absence from his bed. But she looked great, and in a second he was glad that his brother, guilt-ridden at having treated her so badly, at having taken advantage of her goodness to his sons and their mother, was so wrong about her. She liked herself. Lawrence women, no matter where they lived, seldom liked themselves.

They didn't touch.

"Want some coffee?" he said.

"No," she said, and put her hands in her coat pockets and sat on the coach and smiled at him.

"It was a terrific scene, wasn't it."

He nodded.

"Your lip all right?"

"It's fine."

"No teeth missing?"

"None," he said.

She got up. "I haven't heard from him."

"Neither have I."

"He's seen the boys. Two of his people from the Boston office picked them up and dropped them off. And he's called and spoken to them when my mother's been with them. It's almost as if he knows exactly where I am, when I'll be home and when I'll be out. So I haven't talked to him, and I really don't care if I ever do."

She looked at the floor, up at him. Her eyes were clear.

"He didn't have to say some of the things he said. I'm not Lawrence, nor Andover, either. I broke from it long before he ever thought it was necessary to break from it. If anyone is the heart and soul of Lawrence, he is. He came after me, and made love to me, and almost trapped me here."

She turned slightly away, and he almost touched her.

"You think I'm still in love with him, in spite of what I've just said, don't you."

"I don't know," he said.

"I divorced him," she said. "He didn't divorce me."

B.D. nodded.

"I care much more for you than I thought I would. It surprised me."

She walked away from him and across the room, looked through his window and came back.

"The boys and I were in Boulder over February vacation," she said. "They loved it. I went to school there for a while, and have friends there. You know that. I'm going to sell the house and go back to Boulder in the spring. There's no mortgage. There was a small one when I took it after the divorce. But I paid it off out of money I inherited from my mother's father, and money my mother gave me. It's going to hurt her to see me go. But she'll have to understand, and she will. My father won't, and I don't care. He's always been narrow-minded and confining. Local, as you and Tom would say. And he's always cheated on my mother. Tom must have found that out—I certainly never told him— and used it to shut him up the weekend before the primary. My father and the people who own the newspaper were planning to embarrass Tom with a poll showing him losing support in Lawrence, and a negative editorial. Tom, I know, had a meeting with him at Sullivan's and must have threatened to expose everything he'd ever done if he didn't back off. He's been involved with a few prominent wives."

"What are you going to do there, in Colorado?" B.D. said after a moment.

"I don't know. I'm not going to worry about that right away. I have enough money not to."

"He's going to object strongly to your taking the boys."

"I'm sure he will. They love him a lot. But I love them, too, and they love me, and I'm at least as important to them as he is."

She smiled. "They are my sons, even if his political commercials identified them as his sons. He never asked my permission to do that, to use them like that."

She touched the doorknob, let it go.

"Your team's doing amazingly well."

"They are. Some of the kids are very talented."

"I'm sorry I never got to see them play at Cushing."

"I am, too, Kate."

"How far are you going to go?"

"I don't know."

"A national championship?"

"They think so."

"What do you think?"

"I just hope they don't get their hearts broken too badly. They're young and resilient, but awfully vulnerable, too."

"Have you talked to Stephanie?" she said a moment later.

"No—yes, briefly, the night after the funeral. She wanted to fly in and I told her I wouldn't be around and hung up and that's been that."

"When are you going back?"

"The day after the season ends."

"That'll be a good time to leave," she said.

They held each other for several moments then.

"I love you, Kate," he said.

"I love you, too, B.D.," she said, and kissed him softly on the mouth.

3

THEY FLEW TO PITTSBURGH ON FRIDAY MORNING, practiced well in the Pitt gym late Friday afternoon, slept in a motel ten miles from the campus on Friday night, then blew away the Panthers, ranked eighteenth in the country, early on Saturday night. Smith and Sizemore had nineteen each at the half, and they probably could have hit a hundred for the first time if B.D. hadn't started clearing the bench early in the second half. They won by twenty-six, the gym half-empty at the end, and only the Cushing band played. They got back to their hotel at midnight and ate spaghetti and watched "Saturday Night Live" and flew back to Boston early Sunday morning. A small gathering of parents and friends was waiting at eleven, and among them, her hands in the pockets of her camel's hair coat, her hair long and blonde, her shoulders slightly hunched, was Janet. Because of the overnight stay in Pennsylvania, he had taken a cab to

Cushing on Friday and the bus with the team to the airport, and he planned to take a cab back to his apartment.

He shook several hands, spoke briefly to parents and a few of the players' girl friends, including Smith's, a tall redhead who drove a gray Jaguar, and then, when he was sure she was waiting for him, went up to Janet.

"Congratulations," she said. He thought there was a trace of nervousness in her voice.

"Thanks," he said and watched her smile up at him.

"Spend the weekend at Princeton and just fly in from New York?" He had to ask it.

She shook her head slightly. "I came to see you," she said, "unless you have someone waiting for you or have other plans."

"No one's waiting."

"Can I give you a ride?"

"Sure."

"Plans when you get to your apartment?"

"Not yet," he said and felt himself smiling.

"I'm parked just outside the entrance," she said. "The red Mustang."

He said hello to a few more people, took his suitcase, told Phillips and Gordon he had a ride back to his apartment and would see them at practice tomorrow. Then he went to her car, the motor running, the front seat filled with warmth against the bright cold Sunday morning.

"Had breakfast?" she said and moved into the traffic heading for the tunnel and downtown Boston.

"Just coffee."

"Flying make you nervous?"

"Sometimes on coast-to-coast flights if I think about it too much."

"You must have planned something for today," she said.

"Nothing much, really. I was going to watch a college game on television, read the *Globe*'s account of ours, study a few scouting reports and think about the games next week against Georgetown and Providence. The car yours?"

"I got it last year." She smiled calmly again and he felt himself stir.

"Bill Singleton give it to you?"

"No," she said and laughed.

"Want to have breakfast together?" he said.

"All right." He watched her thin, dark-brown gloves on the steering wheel.

"I'd rather not go out anywhere. How about my apartment?"

"Sure." She shook her hair out slightly. "That sounds great."

She was twenty-one, he thought, or maybe already twenty-two, and her small gold earrings glinted youth and life everlasting in the Boston sun. He wondered if Singleton knew she was going to put the make on him. Of course he knew, or at least knew as soon as she came up to them in the restaurant the first day they talked.

"I'll drop you off and go for blueberry muffins and anything else you want in Copley Square," she said. "That'll give you a chance to clean up your living room."

"Okay," he said.

They drove beside the light-blue, half-frozen Charles, moved onto Beacon Street and idled in front of his apartment house.

"Get the newspapers, too," he said. "The *Times* and the *Globe*." He reached for some money.

"I've got it," she said. "It's been my idea." She looked at him and for a moment he thought she was going to lean over and kiss him. "I'll be right back."

They toasted the muffins and ate them with jam and drank coffee and orange juice, then walked briefly along the Charles until she took his arm, moved closer, breathed against his cheek.

"Do you like it here?" she said.

"I miss the beaches in California."

"A lot?"

"A lot," he said.

"It won't be long before you can go back to them."

"Not too long," he said.

"Isn't this bad for your knee?" she said a moment later.

"Yes."

286

"Does it hurt?"

"Not much just walking, but it does."

"It won't hurt if we go back," she said and laughed and moved a step away. They stopped and looked at each other.

He kissed her first. They were sitting on the couch, the television following skiers down a fast, flag-studded course in Switzerland, the announcers, he thought, sounding delighted to be there though it was snowing and their voices were a few degrees above freezing.

"Do you ski?" he said.

"Yes," she said and turned to him.

"Oh," he said and kissed her.

She came first, in the bedroom, her young thighs, heavier than he'd thought they'd be, driving with her stomach up against him, her mouth hungry, her teeth gently biting his lower lip until he came hard, cleansing the sky, purifying the earth, feeling no guilt, none at all.

They held onto each other and she moved her fingertips across his mouth, down his neck and chest, held his hand and moved on top of him, bending to kiss him on the mouth, throwing her hair and moving on him until she came again. She slid to her side, her head against his chest, and whispered something with him still in her, her voice hoarse, and he came again when she smoothed her hands across his stomach and thighs. They said nothing then and watched the midafternoon darkness gather in quick shadows away from the sun, a jet disappearing beyond his window, their breathing as quiet as the few cars on Storrow Drive.

At five she said she had to go. There was already too much reading to do for her classes and she'd done little of it. She was supposed to call her parents at seven. She was still a college student.

She met him after practice on Monday, and they drove to the small restaurant where they had met. They drew the immediate attention of students, a teacher or two, scattered across the darkened room, and he supposed he could feel younger than he was if he tried now.

"I applied to five law schools," she said as they ate hamburgers and french fries and swallowed cold beer. "I haven't heard from any of them yet."

"Sounds good. What are your chances of getting in?"

"Probably none at Harvard and Columbia, maybe very good here. I guess in a lot of ways I'm very practical. Not predictable, but practical." She looked at him for a moment, then leaned forward and took his hand, held it, let it go, leaned back and smiled.

"Can I ask you something?" she said.

"Sure."

"Something personal?"

"Go ahead."

"I guess I shouldn't," she said.

"Want to ask about my marriage?"

She nodded.

"It's not going well."

"Are you going back to her when the season's over?"

"I'm going back to my home in Malibu. I'm sure she'll still be living there."

"What if she isn't?"

"She will be."

"Good," she said and her face seemed to relax.

"You are going to marry the guy from Princeton, aren't you?"

"Yes."

He drank some of his beer. "Love him?"

She nodded. "Do you love Stephanie Green?"

"Yes," he said after a moment and they laughed.

"I hope you go all the way with the team," she said, her voice lighter.

"So do I." He leaned on his right elbow.

She looked serious. "But you won't, will you?"

"I don't know. We don't quite have enough speed and height, and I don't know enough about coaching."

"Of course you do. You're undefeated."

"Thanks, but really, I don't. I try to prepare for everything. I consult with Bill and Jack Phillips all the time, but I might very well get out-coached at a crucial moment."

"Everyone's ecstatic about what's happened."

"I know."

"B. D.?"

"What?"

"Can I stay with you for a few nights?"

"I'd like that very much," he said.

"I'll use my own car, and be at your apartment in an hour or two. I've got to do a few things. Unless you're going somewhere tonight—"

"I'll be there."

"I'll have to study part of the time."

"I will too," he said.

4

THEY BEAT GEORGETOWN AT CUSHING ON WEDnesday night by fifteen. Providence on Saturday night by seventeen. They were ranked sixth in the country the following Monday by both wire services, fifth by *Sports Illustrated*, and began practicing on Tuesday for the eastern regionals. They would play the winner of the Holy Cross–Penn game in Philadelphia on Friday night, and then either Duke or Ohio State, placed in the eastern regionals even though they were southern and midwestern schools because their records were less good than others, on Sunday. A victory on Sunday would move them to the regional semi-finals and then the finals in Syracuse the next weekend.

They were seeded first in the east. Rutgers, ranked ninth in the country, was seeded second. They were fast, tough inside, and B.D. was almost certain they'd meet.

Janet had stayed with him until Thursday night. People around school, she said, were beginning to ask questions about where she was spending her time, and it was impossible to watch him in the apartment, make love, stare at the distant traffic on Memorial Drive and do all of the work in her comparative economic theory seminar at the same time. His preparation for the George-town game hadn't been as thorough as it should have been; luckily, it didn't have to be. Enough guilt, and maybe even boredom had set in, he knew, and it was clear that she was in love with the young stud from Princeton and wanted to marry him, maybe more now than ever.

"Another night with you would make it very difficult for me," she said and kissed his cheek. They were in the parking area behind his apartment house, the early March night freezing, though, if he really wanted to and listened closely enough, he could hear spring bubbling from the western edges of the Charles. "That's the truth, B.D. I can't afford to get in too deeply with you, and tonight would make it very deep. But we can see each other again, a few more times, can't we?"

"We can," he said.

"I'll see you on the campus then. I'll come by the gym."

"You going to be at Saturday night's game?"

"New York," she said. "I've got to meet his parents in New York."

She sighed and they held each other, and it took several minutes after he watched her taillights move behind several apartment buildings and join the traffic on Storrow Drive to kill the need to call Malibu.

5

PHILADELPHIA. THEY WERE MOSTLY SILENT, IN-tense, but confident, he knew, in the locker room before the game, then went out to their pinwheeling cheerleaders, the sound of the band and a few thousand Cushing supporters, and beat Penn easily, 93–71. They shot well early on Sunday against Ohio State and cruised in the second half, never letting go of the medium-fast pace they set, and won, 78–63. They would play St. Joseph's on Friday night, and if they won, the winner of the Rutgers–St. John's game. Nothing would be easy.

They moved through a light shooting drill on Monday, then watched tapes of St. Joseph's last three games, ran through hard, complete practices on Tuesday and Wednesday emphasizing defensive patterns. They'd have to be tough on defense to win.

There was a pep rally on Thursday at noon before their bus ride to Logan and the charter flight to Syracuse. The Reverend David McCormack spoke; so did the student council president and Bill Singleton; and then he did, telling the packed gym that even though he hadn't gone to a Catholic college and seldom attended mass, he was still glad to be part of the miracle. They roared.

Janet was there. They hadn't seen each other in almost a week.

"Good luck," she said in the crowd on their way out.

"Thanks. How are you?"

"I'm fine. Can I see you when you get back?"

"I'd like to," he said.

"I'll be watching on television."

He stopped and she kissed his cheek and then hugged him, and Sizemore, watching, winked and grinned. "Cushing's been a good provider, coach," he said.

6

THERE WERE SIXTEEN TEAMS LEFT ACROSS THE country in the four weekend regional playoffs, and he felt the hard pressure to win now for the first time since the NBA playoffs two years ago. It wasn't fun anymore at playoffs time when you were expected to win, and Cushing was one of the favorites now to make it to the final four.

They worked out at the vast Syracuse gym on Thursday night,

freeing themselves of surface tension, re-emphasizing the fundamentals—tight, shifting defenses, tough positioning and rebounding, offensive pacing, crisp passing, deadly shooting.

There was little talk or banter on the bus back to the motel, and through their brief meeting after a late dinner he was afraid that they were too quiet, would tighten and begin to wonder if they were really as good as their record, especially if they fell behind early or, more to the point, fell behind by six or eight late in the second half, that someone would pull a muscle or ligament and send them into mediocrity.

Nothing went wrong.

Cunningham got the opening tap to Smith who drove to the key, hit Sizemore with a quick pass to the right and he swished it through from twenty feet. The Cushing band, several rows in back of them, and the cheerleaders and students and alumni who had come in buses and planes and cars for the weekend, went berserk and stayed on their feet to watch Smith, with Cushing in a full-court, man-to-man press, steal the in-bounds pass and hit Collins for a lay-up.

They had a ten-point lead with three minutes to go in the first half, St. Joseph's back on its heels where they had put them in the first thirty seconds and had kept them, with tight full-court pressure.

Only Collins wasn't scoring. St. Joseph's double-teamed and held and hit him underneath. With two minutes left in the half and the lead down to eight after two foul shots, B.D. called time and insisted that Collins leave the mess underneath and go outside to shoot. It wouldn't look as if he were backing down from a physical challenge; they were going to bury these guys in the second half anyway.

"I want you in perfect shape for St. John's or Rutgers," B.D. said before Collins stepped back onto the court.

He hit three long jump shots in a row from the corner, and Cushing led by fifteen at the half, twenty with ten minutes to go, and won the game by nineteen.

Sizemore, standing with B.D., Smith and Collins off the court for a post-game television interview, said that he'd won it for all the beautiful black Catholic women in America and they'd win by thirty on Sunday. It was quite possible, B.D. thought, that Sizemore was already being represented by Maury Golden—or supplied by Arnie Levine.

"Simmons would have sent me to prison for saying that," Sizemore told B.D. in the jammed, hectic locker room.

"Keep scoring in double figures, Luther, and you'll be able to go anywhere and say anything you want."

There were tens of messages for B.D. at the motel.

He took them all to his room where Singleton, Phillips and Gordon would join him in a few minutes. The team would eat dinner together, sleep late, watch the mid-western semi-finals on television, study films of tonight's Rutgers win over St. John's after an hour-and-a-half practice session tomorrow night at seven, then get up early on Sunday morning and be ready for the one o'clock final. His stomach tightened thinking about it.

He lay back on the bed. He had spent so many winter nights, warm and frozen, on hard, synthetic hotel and motel room beds. And now this one. For Cushing University. They really had come this far, out of the snow and dark and cold. Incredible. He had made them a winner. He was good and he liked it. But he knew the limits of coaching, its deceptions, and the last thing he wanted to do was spend the next decade chasing high school kids through the ghettos and heartlands of America to convince them to shoot baskets for him.

Messages—

Good luck from Maury Golden. He would be sitting behind the Cushing bench with CBS executives. Tom and Miller were coming. They'd try to drop by the motel and wish the team well. He laughed. Tom Jordan, the politician, his brother. His fucking brother. The senator. He had children. Sons. The Jordan name would continue. David and Michael were good little guys. He wondered if Tom was bringing them. They'd be hurt if they were watching the game and the camera picked out their father and Dick Miller with a beautiful black woman between them. But

293

maybe not. Maybe they'd met her in Washington and loved her.

He and Tom would never be close. But they would see each other, and B.D. would see the boys whenever Tom brought them to California, or when they all ever happened to be together in Washington. There would be days when they would be together in Washington. But not for a while.

The other messages were from newspapermen, television reporters, names he recognized and didn't recognize, male and female. He wouldn't return their calls. Cushing had its press information people here and Singleton was protecting the team well. Gallagher's name wasn't among the callers. He knew better.

Dinner was loud, filled with hard laughter and dirty jokes, and made him almost as nervous as last night's silence, but he accepted it and listened and laughed along with them.

Stephanie called at one.

"I'm surprised they let me through," she said.

"Why?" he said, trying to neutralize the sound of his voice. No messages of any kind would get through tomorrow night.

"That's right, it's all right to wake the coach, but not the players. What are you doing in Syracuse on a Friday night?" She said it easily, and sounded relaxed, pleasant. She hadn't sounded as good, as positive, he thought, since Christmas in Chicago, but he hadn't talked to her since the day his mother was buried, and he hadn't seen her since early January.

"Waiting," he said. "It's what big-time college basketball is all about, especially this time of the year."

"Is it as big as it was at Cal?"

"A lot bigger. We never got this far, never had this much attention, even with the great B.D. Jordan's jump shot." He swallowed. "If we win I'll be spending next weekend in Kansas City."

"Nice place to be in mid-March," she said.

"From Lawrence to Kansas City, except I'm not there yet and—"

"I miss you," she said.

He hesitated.

"We haven't seen each other in two months."

"Longer," he said.

"It's just gone by."

He said nothing.

"I wanted to wish you well."

"I'm glad you did."

"Some people are predicting that you're going to win it all," she said. "I'm sure more will after tonight's score."

"It really doesn't mean anything. Rutgers will be tough. They won big tonight too, and against a team we had a lot of trouble with during the season."

"I'll be watching," she said.

"Good."

"At ten o'clock in the morning."

"Where are you now?"

"On the deck."

"Is it warm?" he said.

"It's cool."

She waited for him to speak.

"It's been a tough winter," she said. "But a good one too, in some ways, for both of us."

"It's over," he said. "Or almost over."

"When are you coming back?"

He told her. "Are you going to be there?"

"I'll be here," she said.

7

NO ONE SPOKE IN THE LOCKER ROOM AT TWELVE-thirty. Smith and Collins stared at the floor. Sizemore, leaning back on his elbows on the floor, kept telling himself in a whisper to go to his left. Collins paced the rear of the room. He was still quiet, distant, but he had helped make them a tough defensive team. They would need defense tonight. Rutgers had scored ninety and eighty-five in their last two tourney wins.

Anticipation glistened on their arms and legs. Cunningham started stretching exercises, Davis stood and took a series of deep breaths.

B.D. got up, swallowed against his dry throat and they looked attentive.

"We've come a long way," he said. "You can win, you know that. You can win everything. You're better than they are. You know it and I know it. Play tough, don't be afraid to shoot, and don't be afraid to beat the piss out of them once we get them down."

Getting them down was going to be tough. Rutgers scored off the opening tap on a drive and a quick top-of-the-key jump shot, then went into a tight full-court press—the toughest, B.D. knew right away, that they'd faced all year. They were able to get the ball in bounds and move, with Smith and Davis ball handling, into the forecourt. But the press had thrown their timing off, they couldn't be immediately aggressive, and in the first five minutes fell behind 14–7. Then 16–7 as one of their agile strong forewards hit a reverse lay-up off a screen that left Collins alone.

B.D. called time out.

"We're not being tough enough and quick enough every-where," he said. "But you will, we will. Hang in. Stay alive. It's just the beginning and it's close."

He looked up at the bank of Cushing supporters, among them Tom and Miller and Sheila Manning, and Maury Golden with several men and women who looked expensive and sleek. To Maury's right were two sensational-looking blondes in their mid-thirties. The one beside him whispered something to Maury as she crossed her legs, letting her glance meet B.D.'s. Later, in April, B.D. would remember the move, and the slow movement of her thighs disappearing into darkness, when he made love to her for the first time in her New York apartment, before she left to interview two writers and smile her familiar smile as America woke up.

296

"We'll get the bastards," Collins said as they leaned and put their hands together.

"Just keep taking it to the basket," B.D. said. "They're going to foul."

"We're awfully tight," Phillips said when they headed back onto the court. "Tighter than we've ever been."

Rutgers double-teamed Collins inside now, and had one of their talented forwards playing him man-to-man when he went outside. They'd have to keep Collins outside more, let Cunningham clear out for Smith, with Davis and Sizemore and Young taking it to the basket.

Smith moved the ball from the half-court in-bounds pass to the right; Collins sprang outside and Cunningham faked a hook shot and dropped the ball off to Davis underneath. He missed the lay-up, Collins and Cunningham missed the tip-ins, then Rutgers broke fast and hit their other forward who sailed in for a slam dunk.

18–7.

Collins got bottled up inside again, lost the ball out of bounds, and B.D. called another time out. It probably looked as if he were hitting the panic button, but he didn't care.

"Collins on the outside, Cunningham to the low post right. Slow it down a little. Stay alive and stay cool, it's only the first half."

Give them more of a chance to find themselves, he thought. Don't press them so hard.

Collins missed a fifteen-footer, and Cunningham picked up his second foul crashing in for the rebound.

B.D. took a deep breath and sat next to Phillips. They stared at each other and his blood froze. They'd been down before, but against teams with less talent. They had never looked this bad.

Rutgers missed a ten-foot jumper but banked home the rebound and Cunningham picked up his third foul, and then a technical because, he told B.D. a few seconds later on the bench, he'd told the referee to kiss his ass.

At the fifteen minute mark Rutgers led 38–19. But Smith had

begun to hit, and Collins, whose jump shots had rimmed out, scored on two head-down, muscle-driving moves to the basket off sensational Smith feeds from the top of the key. They were getting their edge back.

Sizemore batted a rebound to Smith who drove the length of the court, put the ball in, got fouled, made the foul shot and almost stole the in-bounds pass.

Rutgers slowed their offense, held back, took almost two minutes off the clock and hit a twenty-foot jumper from the corner, making it 40–22 with a minute thirty to go in the half.

Davis travelled. Collins lost a half step on his man underneath and fouled trying to recover and stop another slam-dunk, and after the foul shot it was 43–22. Twenty-one down.

Collins hit from the corner, then missed another jump shot, and Rutgers' successful fast break off the rebound made it 45–24 with thirty-five seconds left. When they backed into a tight zone, B.D. told Smith to hold for one shot.

But Smith got an opening, drove and hit with twenty seconds left in the half and B.D. called time.

"Go for the steal," he said. "We have to get closer. Smith and Davis and Toner can afford to take one more foul each. But not Danny. I'm going to keep you in, but don't touch anyone. Let your man go by you if you have to. I want to give them something to think about in the locker room. Let's really come at them hard."

Toner fouled on the in-bounds pass, his first, and the Rutgers guard missed the first of his one-and-one free throws. Toner, alive, swung down the rebound and got it out to Smith. He drove to the key and hit again.

45–28.

Rutgers broke a man free from the press at mid-court; he passed to one of the forwards who drove at Collins and went past him for the lay-up. B.D. should have put one of the freshmen in for Collins right after Smith's basket and had him guard tightly. A coaching mistake. He couldn't afford any more.

It was 47–28 at the half.

After the initial silence, the locker pounding and the towel and orange throwing, they leaned back and he stood in front of them.

"We haven't lost anything yet," B.D. said. "They're not going to score forty-seven again, and we're not going to be held to twenty-eight."

Sizemore smacked his hands together.

"We played very well in the last three minutes. In fact we've come on to the point of playing our game the way we should be playing it. Let's open with a full-court press and drop quickly to the two-one-two as soon as they move over half court. Chet and Bobby harassing out front. If they go into any kind of stall we'll have to go back to tight man-to-man full-court pressure. And we might have to put them on the line early. Foul shooting's been their weakness all year. Let's just be patient."

"They've shown us every offensive and defensive pattern they've used this year," Phillips said then. "I doubt if they'll try anything new now with a nineteen point lead. They don't really have enough speed to surprise us. So hang in with what we've been doing. They've hit for an amazingly high percentage. They won't keep that up."

"Any questions?" B.D. asked.

There were none.

"Speeches?" He smiled.

No one smiled back.

"We're not going to lose," he said. "Not after coming this far. We're going to kick their fucking ass."

Cunningham got the opening tap to Collins. He flicked it to Smith who drove and hit a cool jumper from the right.

47–30.

Rutgers threw the ball out of bounds. The momentum change in the last few minutes of the first half was growing now.

Collins was free for a jumper from the left, took it and hit it.

47–32.

The Cushing band and cheering section was alive. One of the Rutgers forwards travelled.

Cushing swung the ball patiently to the right, to the left, dropped it into Cunningham, who faked right and hit Collins with a blind, over the shoulder pass as he slipped through the key. He slammed the ball home and got fouled. The Cushing cheerleaders leaped and reached out and touched his uniform. He hit the foul shot.

47–35.

Almost a game. Under seven, and it became one.

Rutgers hit a jumper.

Davis did the same from the right.

At the five minute mark, with fifteen minutes left to go in the game, Collins hit two free throws to cut the lead to 52–42.

They traded baskets and foul shots. Cunningham picked up his fourth foul and held his temper. Sizemore got his third and fourth quickly; he smiled at the referee after the third, bent over holding his head in both hands when he picked up his fourth for going over someone's back for a rebound.

With nine minutes left, and Cushing still behind, 60–52, Rutgers lost the ball out of bounds and B.D. called the first of his second-half time-outs.

"An important basket coming up," he said. "Obviously." He had to yell now to be heard. A television camera pressed in from the left end of the bench, moved behind him, zeroed in on the intense faces of his team watching him, listening, trying to catch the magic phrase that would keep them alive and send them on a plane to Kansas City.

"Lob dunk to Smith coming down the middle," B.D. said. "Luther will hang it up for you after Collins and Cunningham break together from the middle, the way we've practiced it."

"I'll dunk the fucker," Smith said, but Sizemore's pass was a touch too high and the ball clicked off Smith's fingertips and out of bounds as he sailed in untouched.

It would have brought them back to within six. Shit.

Smith stole the ball at half-court, moved, changed speed and drifted in for a lay-up, made it and got fouled. He hit the foul shot.

60–55.

Five points behind, and they stayed there, trading baskets and foul shots and turnovers, for three minutes.

And then it was 67–61 with five and a half minutes to go. Rutgers had the ball and they moved it to the left, held it and Davis fouled one of their guards. He missed the first shot but the rebound came out deep and he got it, drove and hit a short jumper. Collins missed a left-handed hook shot, one he seldom took, but the only thing open to him close to the basket. Rutgers broke fast and hit the lay-up.

71–61. It would take a lot to win now.

Smith lost his dribble and then fouled going for the ball. Rutgers hit the first foul shot, missed the second and Smith brought it up slowly after Cunningham's rebound and threw in a long, arcing jump shot from beyond the key.

72–63 with three-forty to go and the clock running.

Sizemore, exhausted now, fouled out at half-court going for the ball. The bench, the Cushing section, the crowd gave him a standing ovation as he came off the court. He sat, covered his eyes with his fingers and cried, hard. B.D. hugged him around the shoulders and he cried harder and said he was sorry he'd played so fucking badly.

"You've been great, Luther," he said. "And we haven't lost yet."

Collins took the rebound of a missed foul shot, fed to Davis who hit a long, off-balance jump shot from the left hand corner, then stole the ball in the back-court and hit Collins, who scored with a soft, banking hook shot to the right.

72–67.

Toner, subbing now for Sizemore, fouled with two-twenty left. But Rutgers missed the first shot again and Collins pulled in the rebound, fired his elbows and gave the ball to Smith, who moved to his left and passed to Davis at the top of the key. Davis faked a jump shot and hit Cunningham underneath. He scored.

72–69.

Rutgers called time. The crowd was standing now and its roar engulfed them.

"Hold back on the fouls," B.D. said. "Just full-court pressure, and then a tight two-three. You guys are amazing. You really are. Keep taking it to them."

Rutgers set up an in-bounds play to the left, got the ball over half-court, then slowed and swung it to the left, moved it around to the right and brought the clock down to one-twenty before B.D. yelled to Toner to foul. They made the two shots, but Collins, with just over a minute left, hit another twenty-foot jumper, making it 74–71, and Toner fouled on the inbounds pass. Fifty-two seconds left. Cushing had two time outs.

Dave Batten, the shooter, with fifteen points and ten rebounds, and blood on his jersey from cracking Collins across the nose on a move inside, missed the first and Collins, with the crowd erupting, pulled in the rebound. Smith hurried it down the middle, moved to the right and lost the ball out of bounds.

One of the Rutgers guards slipped away at half-court, drove into the corner, held the ball, then passed to Batten coming down the lane. He dunked it and Cunningham fouled him going in.

76–71 with twenty-eight seconds left.

Cunningham had fouled out, but his applause got drowned out in the Rutgers madness, the frantic pumping of their band and the thousands of voices from New Jersey. He slammed a towel on the floor and sat staring up at the clock and scoreboard. Batten sank the foul shot and Smith, left alone now in the back-court, hurried to the top of the key and hit a jumper. B.D. called time with nineteen seconds left.

77–73.

"Listen hard," he said. "We're not done yet."

Sweat poured off their faces.

"We're alive. I've still got one more time out. We've got to put them on the line and make them beat us there. Foul as soon as the ball comes in. Toner with pressure on the ball. Don't go for the steal. Just step in and grab."

They swallowed and stood up.

"All right," he said. "Get them."

Smith fouled. Rutgers made both shots.

79–73 with eighteen seconds left.

Collins drilled the ball to Smith near half-court and he hit Davis open in the corner for another clean jump shot.

79–75.

Toner fouled immediately, his fourth. There were nine seconds left.

Rutgers missed the first. Collins took the rebound again and got the ball to Smith near half-court, and he hit Toner under the basket. Toner dunked it.

79–77.

B.D. called time with four seconds left. The clock would begin again when the ball was touched inbounds.

He smiled, the camera on him. He hoped Stephanie Green was watching.

"There's time if we do it right," he said. "Collins hands up on the in-bounds pass. Once they get it in, foul immediately. Then Collins and Toner underneath for the rebound. Smith'll maneuver at the top of the key for the release. Davis and Young fake inside after basket hanging and come out for Smith's pass. You've got to throw it up as soon as you get it. Bobby, just throw it up if they're not open or time is running out on you. Do the same thing if they make the first or both. They might hit you on the way up. There isn't time to drive. If we steal the ball look for the open man and then take the shot."

Maybe he should have told them to go for the steal only, double-teaming the in-bounds pass.

Young fouled and the clock didn't move.

Darcy Menninger, one of the Rutgers guards, hit the first. 80–77, and B.D. felt his stomach fall away. He missed the second. Collins took the rebound, got it out to Smith who found Young underneath alone. He stuffed it as time ran out and they lost.

80–79.

He watched, they all watched Rutgers go insane for a moment. He put his arm around Collins' shoulder, then held Smith's forearm and patted him on the back. Smith was crying. The season was over.

They sat in the locker room. Everyone except Collins and

Chet Davis was crying, Smith harder than B.D. thought he would.

"You know how much I like and respect all of you," he said, finally, before letting reporters in. "I'm proud of what you've done and the season you've had." He waited. "I know it hurts. It hurts me. But there'll be other victories—I've got to let people in now. You don't have to talk to anyone if you don't want to. You were great. It was a great comeback."

Tom came in behind Boston television, reporters, a flood of noise and lights.

"Tough loss," he said.

B.D. nodded.

"I know what it must be doing to you now."

"I feel so bad for them," B.D. said.

"That's what happens when you come this far and are responsible for people. It's hard."

B.D. felt himself choking up. But he wasn't going to cry in front of anyone—and by the time he was alone, he thought, he wouldn't have to cry.

"I won't stay," Tom said. "We'll talk again soon. I'm just going to shake their hands and leave. It was a hell of a game."

"Yes it was," B.D. said.

"You going to be around Boston for a while?"

"I'm going back tomorrow."

They shook hands.

"I'm sorry about everything," Tom said.

"I am, too." He hesitated. "I can't apologize for some things, but I am sorry."

"I understand."

They hugged briefly.

"We'll talk," Tom said.

B.D. turned away.

Maury Golden had seen him on the court, told him it was a bitch and that he'd be in touch with him. The blonde who'd been sitting next to him in the stands was somewhere else, away from youth and the aftermath and combat, waiting.

Singleton's eyes were filled.

"Jesus," he said.

"I know, Billy," B.D. said.

The reporters left a deathly silence behind them. The plane left at seven. They were on the bus back to Cushing by ten o'clock. There was quiet talk on the bus and he shook their hands in the Cushing parking lot. He'd already promised to see them again at the winter sports banquet in two weeks.

"Thanks for saving our asses," Sizemore said, and Smith and Davis nodded and agreed, and then Smith choked up again and had to leave.

"You've been great, Danny," B.D. said to Collins. His girl friend, looking sad and distant, stood a few yards away, her breath dissolving into the tail end of winter beyond the campus lights. "You had a great year. Keep playing."

Collins took B.D.'s hand and his eyes filled. "I'm sorry I couldn't give you more today."

"You gave me much more than anyone could expect."

"Do you need a ride back to your apartment?" Singleton asked. He had followed the bus back to the campus in a private car.

B.D. shook his head. "It would have been fun to go to Kansas City."

Singleton nodded.

"But losing there would hurt just as much."

"More," Singleton said.

"Maybe—we did have an amazing winter, though, didn't we."

"We did."

They let several moments go.

"Coming by tomorrow?"

"I can't," he said. "I've got to get back."

"We'll have a long talk at the banquet," Singleton said.

"We will, Billy," B.D. said.

He waited until one o'clock to hear from Stephanie, then called the house and hung up when he got her answering service. He didn't expect to hear from Kate, or Janet. There'd be nothing to talk about now with either of them.

Steph called at three-thirty.

"I was at the Darts' anniversary party," she said. "I would have called you from there, but I didn't want to start crying. It was so close."

"We let them get too far ahead. I let them—"

He was going to ask her then who the Darts were, but remembered that Alan Dart was her agent, and he did have a wife.

"Were you asleep?" she asked.

"No—"

"Of course you were, B.D. How did your team take it?"

"They thought they were going to be national champs. It would have been better if I'd lost one with them. They're torn apart. But they're young, and they'll recover."

"Are you all right?"

"I'm fine," he said.

He waited for her to say that she loved him. She didn't. She asked if he were coming home tomorrow, as planned if they lost.

"Yes," he said. "I'll be home tomorrow."

"I'll see you then," she said.

8

HE LANDED IN LOS ANGELES JUST AFTER FIVE. IT was warm now and he rode toward Malibu with the rented car, windows down, and felt more empty, more tired than he had yesterday, even though his blood pumped with anticipation at seeing her. He should have spent a day at Cushing, to be around if the kids needed him to help ease the sprawling pain that arrives early on the morning after defeat. And even though he'd promised to be back for the banquet, it did look, in a way, as if he were abandoning them. He could have simply hung around Single-ton's office, taken whoever wanted to for a beer—maybe not. They had been together yesterday and last night. He had said goodbye. And it was, unfortunately, the kind of reality Collins and Smith and Young and maybe even Cunningham and Size-more, would face soon enough in pro ball.

He tried to swallow back all of the guilt of losing, and hide it in the dark places of his soul for the distant, lonely nights he knew would surely come, had to come if you were willing to take chances with your life. And he had to be careful now not to uncap the guilt he felt about Kate, about his mother's death, about having left in December, leaving her alone. He'd be all right in three or four days, he thought, especially if Stephanie was waiting for him and their evening moved into slow, perfect lovemaking.

He didn't know what he was going to do. Maury would begin pressing him in a few days about the television offers, the commercials, the book, the pro coaching possibilities for next year, especially since Stephanie had another two weeks of filming left and he would be around. Golden wouldn't want the memory of the winter to fade and diminish his market value. B.D. was in demand. But basketball, playing and coaching, was over. That was one of the two certainties in his life now.

He pushed the car faster. He hadn't been with Stephanie in two and a half months.

She was on the beach alone, drying herself against the darkening water. He watched her for a moment from the deck as she shook out her hair, folded the towel, stopped for a minute to stare down the beach, then move, with her head slightly down, toward the house. She had turned darker, lost a little weight.

He waved when she looked up and saw him. She smiled and waved back and took a few steps forward, then slowed again, her smile fading, he thought.

They hugged each other. Her hair and face were cool.

"Christ—" she said after kissing him.

"I know."

They looked at each other and breathed the ocean. She went into the house and brought out two chilled bottles of white wine and glasses and poured for each of them.

"We've been finishing earlier in the afternoon these days," she said as she sat and leaned forward and handed him the wine. "It makes everything a lot easier."

He sipped and took her in.

"How are you?" she said.

"I'm all right. It's good to be here."

She shifted, looked away, then back. "I'm awfully sorry about the loss."

"Thanks," he said. "We gave them a good run for it."

"And I'm truly sorry about your mother. Really, B.D., I liked her very much the two times we were together."

"She'd changed a lot," he said.

Her eyes filled, cleared.

"Want to go inside?" she asked a moment later.

"All right."

She rose up against him and he bit gently into her darkened shoulders and came quietly into her, too soon, much too soon. He held her, kissed her, but she was looking away and a moment later she smiled, kissed his forehead, searched his face and got up and dressed.

"I'll make us dinner," she said.

They ate steak and salad in the muted orange light of the kitchen and then went out and walked close to the calmed edge of the water.

"We have to talk," she said.

"All right."

She walked a few feet away.

"I quit the show. I'm just doing these last few episodes and then that's it. Maybe you heard."

"I didn't, but it's a good move."

"They were upset, but knew it was coming, and what I'd be offered."

He watched her.

"I signed today for one of the lead roles in *The Quiet Connection*. It's climbed to number five on the best seller list. It's going to make a terrific movie."

"I've heard," he said and thought briefly of Levine. Where

was he now, the old spy, the faker? How many other rides like that had he given? He smiled. She didn't see him smile. "And we talked about it in Chicago," he reminded her.

"That was fun, wasn't it."

"It was," he said. "How is everyone?"

"Great. Doing well all winter."

"I got a good luck telegram from your mother and father on Friday night, just before the semi-final game."

It was Monday night. If they had won yesterday they would have held a light practice today, studied films of Michigan's quarter-final win, some of their earlier games. He felt himself choking up. He had cried enough this winter.

"And I'm about to sign for the made-for-television movie. Alan has to work a few things out. It's going to be shown on six consecutive nights next January or February."

"Congratulations," he said, and knew it sounded right. "You're an excellent actress, and you're going to grow."

"Thanks, B.D."

"When would the filming start?" he said when she said nothing more.

"In June for the television movie. The first week in June. They hold to strict schedules, and it goes quickly."

"What about the movie?"

"October."

"Where?"

"Mostly here, I think. But parts of it in Europe. Rome and Paris."

"Nice," he said.

She walked a few steps.

"And then what?"

"There are other offers. Two promising scripts for a mini-series beginning in January. And another made-for-television movie that would be smaller. But I'm going to wait and see what grows from *The Quiet Connection*. I'm sure other things will. Alan's sure."

He almost asked if Gary Prince was sure, too.

"I want children," he said.

She shook her head. "We can't now, B.D."

"I want a son, and a daughter."

"I do, too—but it can wait a while longer."

"I'm thirty-five," he said. "We have to grow too. Our marriage has to. And that involves having children. I want to make you pregnant, now." He said it too loud.

"We can't." She looked at him. "What are you going to do? Have you made a decision about anything yet?"

"No, obviously. My season just ended yesterday."

"I know it just ended yesterday. But how can you have children if you don't know what you're going to do, or become. When I have children I'm going to give them stability. I'm not going to leave them for six months. I'm going to be established enough to be able to dictate where I'll be and what I'm going to do. And to do that I'm going to make this movie and television movie and do other things and do them very well. I can't get pregnant now. It's impossible. I've signed to do the movie. It's a beautiful book, and it's going to be a beautiful movie. I'd never be able to do it if I were six months pregnant. And it's unfair, after your going off to do what you wanted and had to do this winter, to impose that on me now. You got traded. God, I hated that when they traded you. But you wanted to play and you left. Then you hurt yourself, and I was going to Hawaii so you stayed in Boston and coached. You did what you wanted to do. Again. Now you come back and want to end my career just as it's beginning by making me pregnant. You can't. It was terrible here in December, B.D. And it would have been in February. I don't want to be "Dial California" the rest of my life, and I'm not going to be."

She gave him a defiant look.

"And that's it?"

"It has to be it," she said.

He put his hands in his pockets.

"You want it to be over now, don't you," he said.

"I guess it's going to have to be." She said it evenly.

He stepped back and waited for his heart and blood to stop, but they didn't.

310

"I didn't want this to happen today, tonight, after all you've been through," she said.

He thought she would be crying now, but she wasn't crying.

"There were nights when I called you and you weren't there," she said. "Very late at night. Just as there were nights when I'm sure you called and I wasn't here."

He hesitated, then walked past her and up to the house and made himself coffee while she came in and went into the bedroom. He walked out to the deck. He'd pull his blood and bones and skin through this night and tomorrow and the next day, and the next. Tomorrow he would call Maury and tell him to arrange things with CBS. He'd have to be on the go—

She came out and stood near him.

"I didn't want to lie to you, B.D."

"I appreciate that."

"What did you think you were going to come home to?"

"You sounded warm on the phone. And you did call on Friday night. I guess I wasn't listening closely enough."

"I'm sorry," she said.

"I just don't understand how you could have made love to him."

"I don't understand how you could have made love to your brother's former wife, no matter how beautiful and warm she was, or how lonely you were. Don't you think that hurt me as much as I've hurt you?"

"There's no point talking about anything else, anything more now." He rose and turned toward the ocean. "I'll leave you now if you want."

"No, you don't have to do that."

"What then?"

"It's your house. It's always been your house. I'll leave."

"Do you have a place to go?"

She nodded.

"Tonight?"

"Yes," she said.

"Go ahead then, but I'm not going to stay around and watch you pack. I've done what I wanted to do, and you've done exactly

311

what you've wanted to do. Your plans never changed for me this year, and they're not changing now, tonight."

She said nothing.

"What if I hadn't pressed you about children, would you have left anyway?"

"I knew you were going to press me. I don't blame you. I don't blame you at all. Just don't blame me too much, either."

He called Morgan's and asked for a private space at the bar and left without telling her while she was packing in the bedroom. He drank one beer and read a detailed account of his loss in the *Times*, then in the *Globe*, which he'd brought with him because it had been too painful to read in Boston. He talked to no one except Danny Morgan, thanking him for keeping everyone away, promising to be back soon.

When he got back to the house, an hour and a half later, she was already gone. Some of her clothes were still there. Shoes and dresses and coats. She wore little jewelry, but it too was gone, including his Christmas present. She had had her exit planned for some time.

He waited for the phone to ring, for her Porsche to swing into the driveway, but nothing happened. He didn't sleep, and in the morning called Maury Golden and told him what had happened.

"She really left?"

"Yes."

"Jesus, I'm sorry, B.D. Christ—does it have anything to do with the asshole she's doing the picture with?"

"I think so, I'm not sure—but don't feel too badly for me, Maury. I made love to two other women in Boston, and wanted to. I'm no hero. I'm a selfish bastard. All professional athletes are." He thought of Kate then, and Janet, and regretted nothing. Janet. He didn't even know her last name. "Is the CBS offer still open?"

"Of course it is. They just called again this morning. It involves some Friday nights and all Sunday telecasts from the coast until the season ends, and then from wherever the playoffs are. We can go over the details—who you'd be paired with, how much

312

assistance they'd give you—a little later. It's for a lot of money, Jordan, and it could grow, I'm sure it will grow, into something much bigger."

"Let's take it, starting this weekend."

"You're making a smart move. They're going to want to talk to you here, I think. Why not fly in for a few days tomorrow?"

"All right, Maury. But just basketball, and only on the coast, until the playoffs. Then I don't care."

"Great. Just one thing. L.A.'s doing badly, so I doubt if they'll be covered, but if they—"

"It won't be a problem."

"You're sure."

"I'm sure. Maury?"

"What?"

"There's the athletic banquet in two weeks at Cushing. I've promised to be there, and I'm going to be."

"Of course."

"Think of a few funny things to say in my speech. I want to try to make the kids laugh."

He walked out to the deck and watched the empty beach and water. Christ, he missed her now, and for a moment he toyed with the idea of driving to the studio and meeting her on her way out. But that, no matter how much he hurt, would be a foolish, self-defeating and degrading thing to do. She wasn't going to change her mind. It had been made up since the night he was traded. He knew that, and it would be one of the hardest things for him, finally, to accept.

He would go to New York, meet the right people, make interesting, sharp comments on national television, meet new women and make love to them. He was thirty-five, and there was a long way to go.

He leaned against the railing and gripped it hard. There was a long way to go, and he wasn't going to piss it all away. He wasn't a basketball player anymore and he wasn't a coach. He had played and coached well, but now it was all over.

He pushed himself away from the railing. He could never go

313

back to Cushing again, though they wanted him to and he deeply cared for the players and Singleton. But they'd never top the magic of this season, even though it had ended in defeat. It could never be as good as it was, and if they got eliminated early next year, or had a mediocre season, then all of the good memories with Collins and Sizemore and Smith and Davis and Cunningham and Toner and the others, yes, and Janet and Singleton—would turn more bitter than Sunday's loss, last night's goodbye.

He had left the east. Twice now. California was his home. He had struggled and earned his stripes here, had become an all-American, fallen in love, been an NBA all-star again and again—

He wasn't going to wind up drifting, following other athletes around until, finally, he'd have to kiss ass for an interview because the memory of what he had once been had long since faded. And he wasn't going to hang out once or twice a week with a blonde or two, his hair graying, his laughter growing hoarse, his eyes smearing at the thought of what he had once mourned, drinking at the end of Morgan's bar.

He walked back into the house, sat at the kitchen table and looked through a new issue of *Time*. His brother's face appeared in "The Nation" section, fixed across the microphones upon an aging black woman giving testimony to a senate subcommittee on the plight of the poor in America. Christ, Tom looked good, B.D. thought. Honest, alert, young, sympathetic. Though there were other senators on either side of him, the woman seemed to be talking directly to him, and he looked as if he really cared for her.

B.D. smiled and closed the magazine and took another turn on the deck. At the hospital in Lawrence, Tom had suggested he get involved in politics, run for office when he got back to the coast. Maybe, after meeting with Maury Golden, he'd fly to Washington and take Tom out to dinner, talk about his options for June, when the playoffs were over, when all of basketball was finally done.

A warm breeze played across his face. He thought of his father then, dead for fifteen years. In thirteen years B.D. would be the same age as his father when he died of a heart attack along the Merrimack River. But he didn't have to struggle with that now; he didn't have to make promises to his dead father. He wasn't going to waste the rest of his life.